THE SHIPBUILDERS

THE SHIPBUILDERS

GEORGE BLAKE

EDINBURGH
B & W PUBLISHING
1993

First published 1935
This edition published 1993
by B&W Publishing
Edinburgh
Copyright © 1935 George Blake
ISBN 1 873631 25 1

The publisher acknowledges subsidy
from the Scottish Arts Council towards
the publication of this volume.

British Library Cataloguing in Publication Data:
A catalogue record for this book is available from
the British Library

Cover design by Harry Palmer
Cover photographs: Business Records Centre,
Glasgow University Archives

To
MY SON MICHAEL

Printed by Werner Söderström

CHAPTER ONE

A SHIP IS LAUNCHED

IT WAS all over. The ship *Estramadura*, taking the water like a swan, was safely launched. And here was the party at cake and wine in the boardroom, garrulous in reaction from the strain.

Leslie Pagan knew that he ought to have been particularly pleased, but he felt empty and lost; and that worried and puzzled him. He was not, he reflected, a chap given to thinking much about his states of mind, and to be thus aware of detachment from the people about him was like feeling the first symptoms of an oncoming cold. Odd, indeed, to be standing thus before the big fireplace, ostensibly chatting to little Mrs. Moles, the Consul's wife, and yet to feel remote from it all, a mere spectator of the ceremony that succeeds the launching of a new vessel. Had the woman suddenly broken off her chatter and challenged him to repeat her last remark, he could not for the life of him have done it.

Perhaps it was natural that his mind should be on the ship. (A glance through the window across the tangled derricks and litter of the yard assured him that they were getting her safely to the fitting-out berth, the tugs nosing like little animals at her bow and flanks.) She was a beauty; to the making of her he had brought a passionate concern. Then, God knew, that last anxious business of her launching had been a trial for him, as it always is for every builder of ships. (Remember the *Daphne* that went over from the stocks at Linthouse and carried scores of good men to death in the Clyde.) For the man with the responsibility, the pretty ceremony of breaking wine on steel plates had been an irritating irrelevance.

But it had gone well. The *Estramadura* was safely launched. Little Mrs. Moles, after much giggling and a display of girlish ignorance, had raised the bottle in her gloved hand, cried the brave name aloud, and let the silken ribbons swing. A thin metallic sound of splintered glass, a small spirt of foam, a wet smear on the sheer bows of the ship—and then the awful moment when the hammers

1

thudded on the chocks and drag-chains rattled, and it seemed that she would never move; then moved ever so slowly, then seemed to stop, and at last slipped away, roaring and at a speed that brought the heart to the mouth, to take the water with a rush, plunge wildly once, shiver a little, then come to rest—safely launched and water-borne. Now they had her snug in the fitting-out basin, and Leslie Pagan saw with his mind's eye a flickering film of her progress towards completion, saw her steam out at length, all white paint and yellow funnels, for her trials over the measured mile at Skelmorlie.

And little Mrs. Moles, kittenish on this great day of her life, was still talking, while he said "Yes" and "No" and "Oh, indeed!" mechanically.

Distraction came at last.

"Excuse me a moment," he said hurriedly. "My father. . . ."

The old man had stood up and was rapping on the polished mahogany for attention.

"Ladies and gentlemen, will you see to it that your glasses are charged?"

A lovely figure of an old gentleman, Leslie reflected, the recognition coming on a wave of emotion. Seventy-eight, but tall and straight as a soldier; clean-shaven, with only a hint of the old-fashioned in his double-breasted buff waistcoat, his stock, and a suspicion of whisker, still ruddy like his thick strong hair, before his ears. A gentleman of the old school, indeed—though his grandfather had been a ploughman and his father had spoken nothing else but the broad Scots tongue.

Son watched father with the detachment that had so strangely come upon him. He saw him immobilize the hurrying waiters with a glance, marked the familiar grasp of the lean hand at the left lapel, heard the small preliminary cough. And he knew what the speech would be.

It was well delivered this day of the *Estramadura's* launching, but it had a new power to depress Leslie Pagan. Lord, how the old man lived in the warm security of the past, in the greatness of glories departed! Clyde-built . . . the grand old theme, but a bitter one in a year of doubtful grace.

Yes, they had built beautifully in Pagan's—clippers in the day of such beauties, swift steamers for coastal routes (for they left the bigger stuff to others), destroyers of grace and speed, yachts of moving loveliness. There were the half-models of them on the walls, as the old man's white hand indicated: a fine flotilla, created by men who had the art of the thing in their blood, mighty craftsmen before the Lord. It was a fine story to tell, and no one could tell it better or more lovingly than his father, who had lived through the most splendid chapters of it—but was it not near an end?

There was not a single order on the books.

That was what he could not get out of his mind. That accounted for his uneasiness and for the detachment of which he was so unusually aware. Not a single order on the books; the fine, long story of Pagan's come to an end after all these years. And the old man drivelling away—he used the word in his mind—drivelling away as if everything was as it used to be.

The devil of it was that he had tried more than once to get his father to understand, and failed. He had gone through all the obvious arguments—the fantastic shrinkage of world trade; the development of building abroad; state subsidies to foreign builders and owners; the ghastly mess of currencies. But the old man would just not see it, as if his wonted clarity of mind were befogged by the assumptions of age. A passing phase, my boy. Lived through half a dozen slumps in my day, and none the worse of it. It will all come right. No patience, you young fellows. Plenty of reserves. . . .

Yes, plenty of reserves. It was a thought that, to his vague surprise, frightened Leslie Pagan. If he were to chuck it all up tomorrow, he would still have plenty to live on, quite apart from the large sum of money he would get from his father in due course. Why, after all, carry on in face of those economic facts he could not elude? Why?

For relief from the problems that so instantly and awkwardly beset him he made his eyes focus on the scene about him. His father stood, tall and distinguished, beyond the mahogany table, talking. It was a fine fire that blazed behind him. (One at each end of the room! It was the first time he had thought of the wastefulness of it.) Faces of men and women round the table, smiling a little vacantly, nodding to the old man's periods, glasses in their hands.

The half-models glistened on the walls, taking the firelight as the October dusk closed in. A waiter, absurdly holding a bottle by its neck in a napkin, stood under the portrait (by Sir John Watson Gordon P.R.S.A.) of grandfather John Pagan. Through the window he could see the gantries against the evening sky that was darkling over the holms of Renfrewshire.

His eyes came to rest on the hat of little Mrs. Moles before him. In his aloofness from life he saw it as preposterous that a human being should cover her hair with such decorative absurdities. A shell of felt with a band of silk round it, and gee-gaws embroidered on the silk—good God! And he knew that it was a cheap hat. Poor little soul, acting the consul's wife and launching ships on her husband's six hundred a year!

The train of thought brought his eyes to rest at length on his own wife—Blanche, standing there near the old man and smiling encouragement and possession at once into his face. That was Blanche: not often to be discovered in public in an attitude quite perfectly natural. She was not an actress, not a fool in her poses, but inveterately it was a studied and composed façade she presented to the Scottish world about her. He hated the thought which invaded his mind in that moment of aloofness, but all his senses were too alert to permit of a conventional self-deceit. How could this Blanche, this Englishwoman he had taken for a wife, understand what the old man said of the traditions of the Clyde and the Scots artisan? And he knew that she cared little. He knew that the end of Pagan's, or the end of his connection with Pagan's, would naturally and inevitably delight her. Farewell to dirty Clydeside, to drab, unpolished Glasgow!

He was afraid, and more afraid of her power over him than exasperated by the intrusion of the feminine into his man's life. He loved her. He remembered the girl she had been. A thousand sweet intimacies could not be forgotten. She had taken his body to hers, craving to receive and nurture his seed. She was the mother of John.

Dear, difficult Blanche, for whom his love was at once a warmth and an uneasiness! Out of the windows of his detachment he was seeing her that day afresh. Middle-age, that comes early to her blonde type, was still at bay before her spirit and watchfulness. Her hair and complexion were as bright and fresh as ever, her eyes as

4

blue and quick. Was there a shade of heaviness showing under her jaws and about the throat? And for all the slimness of her ankles in their silk, for all the slender sauvity of her waist, was there not a tell-tale spreading of the hips? To admit these things to himself was to be all the prouder of her smartness. She was still eager in life, still gay in exile, with her neat and severe brown costume and her little hat snugged down over her left eye at that adorably girlish angle. Why, at this particular moment, must he see her as a sweet enemy?

He was checking himself for disloyalty in thought when a shuffling among the company told him that his father was nearing an end of his speech. There was a flutter of mild applause, then:

"And now that your glasses are charged, ladies and gentlemen, I ask you to drink good luck to the *Estramadura* and her owners."

Good luck! Good luck! Good luck! The phrase sounded round the table, polite and automatic for the most part. "The *Estramadura* and her owners!" Old, deaf Mr. Maciver of the Lighthouse Trust was a little late with his bellow of "Good luck to *Estramadura*— and to Pagan's!" and some ladies had to check their sniggers.

Leslie Pagan started to move through the press towards his wife, murmuring apologies. Señor Martinez, for the owners, was speaking, but he knew what the man would say. They had built ships for South Americans before and heard scores of flowery Latin insincerities. "The repootacion of the Clyde—we know it well in Araguay. . . . Tha name of Pagan, it is what you say 'ouse'old werd among ar peple. . . ." Damned little Dago, nosing for months past into other people's business, always exasperatingly polite and warily mean. The thing was to see that the ship was secure in the basin and to know how Blanche proposed to spend the evening.

He reached her side when the last toast was being drunk. "Pagan's. . . ." Well, his father had said all he wanted to say and would be brief in reply. "Pagan's. . . ." The people were stirring to get away even as the old man spoke. He whispered into her ear.

"Going home now, Bee? I've got the Riley outside, and I won't be a minute at the basin."

"Oh, good-evening, Mrs. Graham! So nice of you to come. . . ."

That was Blanche playing the hostess with perfect grace and complete insincerity. It had to be done, he supposed; and Mrs.

5

Graham and a dozen others deserved no more. What worried him was that the triviality should have so curiously affected him. She turned to him, the conventional smile fading from about her lips.

"My dear, I must go to the Club for an hour at least," she confided to him. "Whyte's waiting for me in the Daimler. I'll be back about seven. You'll remember that Sir Archie's coming in this evening."

"Oh, I see. Right you are, dear."

His answer sounded a little empty. He had so much wanted to be alone with her after the fuss and boredom of the ceremony. Vaguely he resented that pull of the Club—that passion for Contract that was to him almost incomprehensible; and he was quite definitely dismayed by the thought of an evening with Sir Archie, to him the empty and garrulous second holder of a Lord Provost's conventional baronetcy. It was a pity they could not have a cosy and intimate evening alone together.

Blanche stood up, smoothing her gloves over her shapely hands.

"About seven, then, darling?" she said.

"Yes, about seven. I've got some things to do here first," he answered.

2

He spent more time with the yard manager and the foreman rigger than he needed to do. Though he knew that they were anxious now, the ship safely moored, to get back to their Corporation bungalows up in Queenshill, something moved him to hang about where the tall vessel overshadowed the quay.

"Moorings all right now, Tosh?" he asked.

"Safe as houses, Mr. Leslie," answered the foreman rigger.

"It's not likely to blow tonight, is it?"

"I'm sure it's not, sir. Besides, I've got a squad standing by."

"Good!"

But still he could not go, and the other two waited while he walked the length of the ship and back again. He knew she was safe as she could be. But he did not want to go. Young John would be alone in his nursery at home. But would Blanche be gone in the

Daimler that he had seen standing behind the main gates?

He hailed the yard manager in a low voice.

"Any word from the boiler-shop, Mr. Crawford?"

"They're ready as soon as we are."

"Good!"

It was all very silly. There was nothing he could do. He was keeping two decent men from their tea. He felt their uneasiness rolling towards him out of the shadow in which they stood.

"Well, I suppose it's all right," he said at length, his voice echoing back from the high cliff that was the newly launched *Estramadura*. "She's a nice job, when you look at her."

"A topper!" said the foreman rigger gravely.

"As nice a job as we've ever done," added Mr. Crawford.

As nice a job as Pagan's had ever done. And there was not a single order on the books to follow her.

Leslie strove to order his mind.

"Well, there's nothing more, I suppose?" he asked a little emptily.

"Nothing, Mr. Leslie. She's fine now."

"Righto! I'll get along. Goodnight, boys."

"Goodnight, sir."

He walked up towards the gate, threading his way almost unconsciously through the piles of timber and angle-iron and over the rails and ropes that would have been the undoing of a stranger. Not a single order on the books—it was incredible. Yet he had to grasp and master it. "Pagan's Closing Down"—he saw the bills of the Glasgow evening papers. Or they would be more likely to make it "Clyde Shipyard Sensation"; and he would read it as he passed for the last time along the mean little main street of Dalpatrick, seeing it blaze from the boards before every grubby little newsagent's shop.

He came up to the Riley, standing by the timekeeper's office. Old Donald Macrae, superannuated from rigging these fifteen years, hirpled out to greet him.

"Hullo, Donald! My wife gone?"

"She's awa' in the big caur wi' the man."

"Right. I'll get along too. A nice launch today."

"It was that, sir," replied the old man, closing the door of the

7

car. "As clean a job as ever I seen. Goodnight, sir."

Goodnight! Goodnight! He was hearing too many goodnights with the note of finality in them, thought Leslie as he turned into the street. And now there was nothing to do but go home and await Blanche's return. She was off to her Club, to her inveterate bridge. (Again he had to try to resist the feeling of being deserted, and could not.) John would be at home in his nursery; dear, precious John, at the thought of whom his heart beat faster. But he could not spend two hours, three hours with John, waiting for Blanche to come home and complete the circle that seemed to have been so strangely and ominously broken.

He swung the car into the Dumbarton Road, with so much of the life of Glasgow pulsing along its sidewalks and in swaying, coloured trams and juggernaut buses, with the pavements aglow in reflections from lighted shop windows: all lively after the grey drabness of the streets by the riverside; and in the very act of turning he knew what he would do—stop at O'Glinchey's public house and find some of the old hands at the bar there and, as he loved to do now and again, stand them a drink. Danny Shields would be among them, and long Jock Macgrory out of the paint store, and Jimmy Affleck the cranesman. Tonight it seemed imperative he should see them, those rough innocents whose destinies were so strangely in his hands.

He was still seeing himself and his actions as from a distance. For the first time he fully realized the oddness, in the world's eyes, of master drinking with man. It would have troubled his father, who was just, but saw industry as a stern battlefield, with Capital and Labour as implacable and natural enemies. And it would have horrified Blanche, this rough drinking in such a place with such men.

Parking the Riley in the side-street, he pushed open a swing-door to be met by a gust of hot, exhausted air, heavy with the mingled smells of sawdust, strong tobacco, oily clothes and beer. The house was busy, burly men in working clothes and dirty cloth caps two deep along the counter. The ugly tongue of Clydeside assailed his ears, every sixth word a fierce and futile obscenity; they spat much as they seemed to breathe. He saw the scene as one of degradation, and yet, understanding, he neither recoiled nor condemned. They

8

were the men he knew—passionate, strong and true to the core.

His quick glance took in many a familiar face that smiled an uneasy greeting, but he saw the group of older hands he sought, deep in argument in a corner by the fire. They greeted him with respectful forthrightness.

"Evenin', boss!" said they all.

"Evening, boys! What about the usual drink to the ship? Yours, Jock?"

They all said the same "Hauf and hauf-pint, if you please"—that strange and powerful solace of the Scots working-man: a half-glass of whisky taken neat and washed down by a glass of the heavy Scotch ale. Leslie ordered glasses and pints for them, as he knew they expected, a whisky and soda for himself.

"Best respects, boss," the murmur went round the circle, and the whisky disappeared. They would linger over the beer to talk.

He was never uneasy with those old hands, who had taught him so much of their trades in his apprenticeship. Nor could talk flag long where Danny Shields was: Danny Shields, bow-legged, broad-shouldered riveter whom a hard life and four years of Gallipoli and Sinai and Palestine and Flanders had left with the heart and mind of a boy. Now, however, there was a gravity on that odd, birdlike face with the strong clean-shaven lips and jaw.

"Some of them are sayin' doon in the yard, boss," he began at once, "that there'll mebbe be a big pay-off."

Leslie's heart sank. How did these things get around? How could he tell them the cold truth?

"Things are not looking too good," he admitted gravely. Then he shook fear from him. "But there are enquiries—some enquiries coming in. We're not done yet."

"Aye, trade's gey bad all the same." This was long Jock Macgrory, a grave man with a thin, drooping moustache of grey and a nasal impediment in his speech. "Dalmuir closed for good. Fairfield empty. Caird's doon bye at Greenock closed for good. Thon wee place at Old Kilpatrick. . . . Christ! Govan looks like a bloody cemetery. It's hard times right enough for the Clyde."

"Well, we've been gey lucky at Pagan's," broke in Jimmy Affleck—desperately, as it seemed to Leslie.

And Danny Shields's strong spirit rose to meet the challenge of pessimism, to refuse it existence.

"Aye, and our luck's going to stay wi' us!" he cried. "Good health and respects again, boss!"

He plunged at his tankard and drained it vehemently.

"Yes," said Leslie, putting down his empty glass also, "we're not going to worry yet. And now I must get along. Can I give anybody a lift?"

"If you could drop me at Scotstoun, sir—" suggested Danny modestly.

"Come along, then. Goodnight, boys."

Goodnight! Goodnight! Always that sombre phrase. He hardly spoke to the man in the seat beside him as they sped up the busy road towards Glasgow. This new awareness of his responsibility would not leave him. The best part of a thousand men, with their women and children, depended on him. It was easy enough at most times to see them, in his father's way, as a mass, impersonally, but with eyes sharpened by the imminence of danger he saw them as individuals capable of suffering—decent able workmen like Danny Shields and long Jock Macgrory and Jimmy Affleck to be put out on the dole, to hang about street corners, to be denied their right to work, to know emptiness indescribable!

The voice of Danny roused him from his brooding.

"This'll do me, sir."

"Right you are, Danny."

He steered the car into the kerb and the little man clambered out on to the pavement.

"I'm very much obliged to you, sir—"

And must he, too, say that fatal goodnight—Danny Shields, who had been his batman from the beginning of the war to its end and was his friend, bound to him by ties innumerable and strong? They had shared danger, degradation, and folly. Above the relationships of master and man, officer and private, they had lived together every emergency of the masculine world; Danny Shields ever with the desperate humour of the western Scot on his lips, the grin of inexhaustible mischief on his face, and courage and steadfastness in his simple heart—a man.

Leslie had almost let him go, when something moved him to a confidence.

10

"Danny!" he said sharply.

"Sir."

"I say, Danny, if—if there have to be changes at the Yard, you're not to worry. I'll see that you have a job. That all right?"

The habit of the old soldier asserted itself in Danny Shields then. Squaring his body, he clicked his heels and swung his hand in a salute to the stained cap of cheap tweed.

"Yes, sir," he replied.

3

The car, as if it drove itself, turned northwards for Anniesland Cross, and Leslie Pagan, seeing now and again the myriad lights of Glasgow straddling in regular rows its innumerable hills or strung along these drumlins of clay, had a sudden vision of the city's unwieldy vastness, of a hopeless complex of lives and interests all resting on heavy industry in decay, with a canker at its heart; perhaps a city doomed. There was not a single order on the books. Seeking to disentangle and assess the factors in the economy of a world gone mad, he could not in the moment allow himself to hope.

His own house, when he drove up to its door along the drive through the dingy rhododendrons, seemed fatuously big. So many rooms for three of them to live in! (Had Blanche really been afraid of another child after the agony of the first?) It actually took four servants to minister to their wants—five counting Whyte, the chauffeur! Just waste—while Danny Shields went back to two small rooms in a Partick tenement: folly, self-indulgence and waste. Life was building ships and not this luxuriating among redundancies. He laughed at himself bitterly for leaving the car to be put away by Whyte—into the garage that was roomier and warmer than any house a riveter could ever hope to live in.

But there was John, and there was nothing he would not do to make John happy and secure. He whistled as he ran upstairs to the day nursery, away from this unwonted blackness of introspection, and shouted "Jocko! Jocko!" as he went.

"Hullo, daddy!"

The small voice was friendly but cool. John, at the age of eight, was liable to be absorbed in that to which he had momentarily set his hand. Now he was making an intricate model of Meccano parts so that his father had to stoop to kiss that soft, aloof cheek. It was Leslie's secret regret that he had to struggle always to rouse any sign of demonstration in his little son, so fair of hair, so dark and intelligent of eye.

"What are you making, old lad?" he asked.

"A stamp for crushing ore," the child replied. "What's ore, daddy?"

That was better. It gave him access to the sanctuary that was the boy's mind. Leslie squatted beside him, gravely explanatory.

"And I'd put that pulley in the middle of the spindle," he added, "right in the dead-centre. See, it's slowing up the whole affair by bearing on the flange."

"But it slipped along while I was screwing it in," the child explained.

"Yes, but a good engineer gets things right somehow. Look here. . . . Where's the screwdriver?"

He took up the absurdly small tool, John's eyes on his hands, and made the adjustment in a few dexterous, sure movements.

"There. Dead centre. Where's your driving belt? Too long— we'll shorten it a bit. Now then. Try that."

Gravely the boy turned the crank, and the model worked. They were happy; a job had been done. But as he watched the gravely rapt eyes of his son, Leslie took to thinking again of their relationship. It was perfect ostensibly; but why must he always have to grope to make contact with John? It was as if there was a technique of parenthood. It was hard for a man to have to admit to himself that even in dealing with his own child he was dealing with another individuality, a creature with his own separate rights and needs.

The passionate desire within him to have the boy's interest to himself drove him back to an old device. Knowing that John must listen, knowing that he could not help giving his attention, he started to tell a story out of his own experience.

"I say, Johnnie—" he began.

"Yes, daddy." The cool voice admitted no more than the fact that he had heard.

"That machine of yours reminds me of one we had to put into

12

a ship years and years ago, long before you were born."

"How old were you then?"

"Oh, about twenty-five, I suppose. It was a big ship, and she was built to carry frozen mutton from New Zealand."

"What was her name?"

"A funny name—the *Arakiki*."

"Oh!"

He knew then that he had all of John. When John said "Oh!" like that he had surrendered to a relation of absorbing fact. They were precious moments for Leslie when he had the boy in the power of his larger experience, and now he abandoned himself to narration, playing deliberately with the detail he knew should keep the child his slave for as long as the story might last. "Oh!" said John at intervals, and it was enough for the father. He wanted to hold the child in his arms, wanted to murmur the tale into his soft hair.

The door opened, and there stepped through it a girl dressed in an overall of austere and spotless white. She did not look at Leslie; she made him feel that he did not exist.

"Your bath is ready, John," she said.

The voice was English, and it was that of one inhumanly efficient.

"Oh!" said John impatiently, but he rose to his feet.

Leslie encouraged him. The rules laid down by Blanche had to be obeyed. Even a father dared not lead rebellion.

"Hop along, son," he said. "We'll finish the story tomorrow."

John took the girl's outstretched hand and passed through the door with her. It closed, and Leslie came to himself to realise that he was sitting, no doubt an absurd figure, among the discarded toys on the floor. The Norland nurse had beaten him. The boy belonged to the women-folk, and he, that father, could only borrow him. Rising and feeling for his cigarette-case, he remembered how Blanche had insisted on a girl of high efficiency, and an English girl. "Well, if he must be brought up in Glasgow," she had said a little peevishly, "at least he can be taught to speak decently."

It was all very queer. Now he seemed to be seeing his own life as from the outside—and it was all very queer. But he knew that he must not brood thus. It was just worry: worry about the Yard

13

and the state of trade. John would not starve. John would never lack for comforts. They ought all to be very happy together. They were very happy together. Blanche and John and himself. It was just a mood.

He passed into the lounge Blanche had furnished for herself. It was lighted by the reflection from painted ceiling and cream-papered wall of filaments within ornamental cases of frosted, tinted glass. Lalique stuff gleamed on the few low scattered tables whose legs rested on a thick-piled carpet of old gold. The squat, caressing chairs were framed in gleaming chromium. There was a Duncan Grant over the open fireplace, in which the logs burned bright. Among the books on the table a copy of *Ulysses* in its yellow paper covers was conspicuously exposed.

The evening papers lay on a stool by the fireside. The servants had laid out the materials for cocktails, but he ignored the alluring bottles and the shining instrument in which their contents could be mixed. Why trouble the tablemaid to bring ice when Blanche would come demanding fresh stuff? He opened the *News* at the commercial page.

Blanche had said that she would be home by seven, but he knew better than to expect her then, and it was twenty past before she did appear, bringing with her into the warm room the chill of autumn from out of doors. Her greeting was bright and off-hand.

"Hullo, old boy! Home long?"

She kissed him quickly, threw her hat into a chair on the other side of the room, and pressed a bell, saying: "Oh, my God! I must have a cocktail or die."

"What luck at the Club, dear?" he asked perfunctorily.

"Lousy! Perfectly lousy, my dear! Heaven preserve me from that woman Snodgrass as a partner. Her calls! My dear. . . ."

A maid appeared at the door.

"Ice, Cameron," Blanche ordered, and Leslie felt a spasm of annoyance. He hated to hear the girls ordered about by their second names in this English way. Cameron was always Lizzie to him; and a nice girl, too. But Blanche was rattling on.

"Seen John? How is he? Don't worry, old boy—I'll mix the drinks. We've got to hurry. These people are coming at nine. Sir Archie's bringing Antanari—you know, the Scottish Orchestra man. He looks divine, and he'll play, I expect. There you are, Lal. Loud cheers!"

He raised his glass to her silently, and they drank.

"Lord, but I needed that," sighed Blanche.

The door opened again, and there stood John, the girl in white behind him. He looked fragile, pathetic and lovable in his blue dressing-gown, with the pink legs of his pyjamas beneath it and his feet in red slippers. Leslie held out his arms to him, but the child went dutifully to his mother.

"Hullo, old lad!" cried Blanche cheerfully. "Been a good son today? That's fine. My yummy-yum-yum!" She kissed him on the lips and the neck. "Now go and sleep well—by-byes all night. Promise?"

"Yes, mummy," said John dutifully and made to turn for the door when Leslie's voice appealed to him.

"Goodnight, son."

"Goodnight, daddy."

It was a joy to get one's arms round that slim, small figure, to enfold its preciousness, to kiss the smooth cheek. Tonight the boy seemed dearer than ever.

"Sleep well, sonny," Leslie murmured, "and we'll make another model tomorrow."

"Yes, daddy. Goodnight. Goodnight, mummy."

"Goodnight! Goodnight!"

The boy turned to his nurse, and together they disappeared.

"You'll spoil that infant," observed Blanche casually. "But come and change. We're late."

"Damn these people, if you want to know my private feelings," groaned Leslie, rising.

"Hullo!" Blanche looked at him sharply. "The hump again?"

"Worry, I would call it."

"Why worry?"

It was a deliberate challenge, and he knew it. There was that of intolerance in her way of looking at him, and in her tone, that roused his defences. He spoke between tightening lips.

"For very good reasons," he answered. "There's no work coming to the Yard, for instance, and no sign of any."

Blanche's move towards the door was a comment on the nonimportance of the statement in her view.

"Give up the Yard seems to me the sensible thing," she said over her shoulder. Her tone was not pugnacious, but he knew that she was really fighting a case. At the door she paused and added, apparently in jest: "Your devotion to Glasgow, Lal, is delightfully pathetic."

"That's unfair, Blanche," he sought to arrest her, his voice harsh. "You know perfectly well that's not the point."

"All right, darling," she smiled coolly. "Come along and dress like a good man."

Always she seemed able to defeat him.

CHAPTER TWO

A RIVETER AT HOME

A TOFF and a gentleman, thought Danny Shields as he walked eastward along the Dumbarton Road that night of the *Estramadura's* launching; a toff and a gentleman.

His admiration of Leslie Pagan was flawless. To his decent working man's sense of respect for a good and efficient master there was added his memory of courage in battle, of steadfastness and kindness in the long trial of trench and camp. He never ceased to praise in his private mind and in the presence of whomsoever cared to listen the uniqueness of the younger man he adored and trusted with a faith almost religious. A toff and a gentleman!

Danny remembered much as he went along, drawing at his short pipe. He saw the fine, dark, clean-shaven face with the black hair silvered above the ears. He glowed in the recollection of brown eyes that could be stern and yet had kindness always in them. He remembered instances of the justice, the coolness, the generosity, the impatience with stupidity, the humour, and the authority of that man. He luxuriated in the pride of his knowledge that there existed between them a queer unbreakable link forged in the fire of grim experience shared. He was proud and happy.

Danny had worried in spite of his protestations. No worker on Clydeside could do anything but fear that this infection of unemployment would touch him yet. With the simple realism of his kind he knew that he was helpless under the great machine, and that even Pagan's might one day be as a score of yards up and down the river—empty, silent, while the men slouched about street corners outside and queued up automatically at the Buroo. That last offence to decency and pride might in busy moments seem unthinkable, but he knew very well in his heart that the threat was real and near.

And now Leslie Pagan had torn the black beast off his shoulders, and thrown it aside. Whatever happened, the boss would see him right and give him work to do and decent pay for that work. A fellow had nothing more to ask of life, and the Major (as he could not stop calling him, though Leslie had endlessly protested) was a toff and a gentleman.

Danny stepped it out cheerfully, making for the Horseshoe in Partick. He used this public house largely for the sake of the accumulator run among its regular customers by wee Hymie Harris, the bookie. Every Friday he hopefully subscribed his sixpence, praying that the teams he had drawn would score eleven goals in two matches and in two weeks win for him the prize of thirty shillings that usually depended on the issue of three Saturdays' play. Once Aston Villa, meeting small fry in the Cup Ties, had achieved this miracle for him, and though he had paid back into the pool a much greater sum than that since then, he remained unwearying in hope. Motherwell had already scored nine times in two weeks on his behalf; two goals against the Morton on Saturday and the money was his, but the beggars would probably pile up a victory, and that would tear it. Still, it was a chance.

The bar was empty when he went in. Tommy, the charge-hand, was bent over an evening paper on the counter, and Bill, the ginger cat, blinked peacefully at his elbow against the levers. They made an interesting picture, breaking up the stretch of polished mahogany against the gantry with its myriad alluring bottles.

"Evenin', Tom!" Dan greeted the barman. "Give's a half-pint."

Automatically the barman wiped a segment of counter with his napkin, took up a glass with a flourish, and filled it, the beer gushing to the touch of the heavy handle.

"Half-pint, Dan," he said. "There ye are. Three pence—right!"

"Wee Hymie been in?"

"Aye, about five. But he's gone now."

"Will ye give him ma tanner for the accumulator?"

"Sure. He'll be in afore nine."

The man picked the sixpence from the counter, placed it in a tumbler that stood by the cash-register on the gantry, and made an entry in a grubby book he took from a drawer.

"Doin' anything on the gees these days, Danny?" he asked.

"Naw," replied Danny stoutly. "I never touch that line. It's a mug's game, the horses, if you ask me."

"Oh, I'm not so sure about that," retorted the barman thoughtfully. "Big Jock Campbell had a three-cross double the day. Wee Hymie wasn't half mad."

"Aye, once in a lifetime!" Danny was scornful, conscious of rectitude.

"Oh, I dunno," Tommy persisted, keeping an open mind. "The boss, he was givin' me a tip the day—*Base Headland* for the three-thirty the morn. It's a good thing, mind ye."

"Mebbe it is. I'm stickin' to the footba'. Is Motherwell goin' to bate the Morton? That's the question."

"Sure. Nobs on." Tommy assured him.

"Aye, but they'll go and slap on four or five goals, and that's torn ma chance in the accumulator."

"I'm not so sure. The Morton's been playin' great these last weeks. See what they did to the Hearts, eh? And Aberdeen—"

"A flash in the pan," said Danny. He was an assiduous reader of the sporting pages of the newspapers. "Nae defence. Nae penetration in their attack. Thon big centre o' theirs is just a big cab-horse. See here. You take the Motherwell backs. . . . "

Now he was in his element, abandoned to the passion of a lifetime. It was a passion shared by all of his kind—this vivid, scientific devotion to football, this angry partisanship that is the industrial substitute for the satisfactions of clan warfare. For more than half an hour the two men argued to and fro, now differing fiercely on the merits of a player, then agreeing almost tearfully as to the unique, the splendid skill of the Rangers. It was such a debate as rages most anxiously on Thursday evening when the Clydesider is thinking how he will fill up the coupon, the betting forecast on the Saturday's results, that will go to the small bookmaker with his shilling or two.

"Have you filled your coupoon?" Tommy came to the crucial question at last.

"Naw," replied Danny, shaking a wary head. "That's the night's job for me."

"It's no' easy this week, right enough. It's no' easy this week, and that's a fact."

Only when he was out again in the fresh air of the Dumbarton Road did Danny realise that he had drunk more than was usual on that night of the week. Not too much; his legs were steady, but he was aware of a warmth, a recklessness, within him. It was that exhilarating talk about football that had done it. He had gone in to pay his tanner and have a half-pint; and he had talked and drunk a half of whisky and two half-pints. Jesus! No wonder the money went. But ach to hell! The accumulator was a dead snip, and—this he recollected with a sudden exultation—he was safe for a job at the Yard, whatever happened to the rest. He felt more than usually fit to meet Agnes, his wife.

His home was in a tenement block in a featureless street between the River and the main road. Kingarth Street, Number 33; two stairs up, one room and kitchen, at a rent of seventeen shillings a week. The close, as Danny called the entrance, was pallidly lit by an incandescent burner on the scratched, damp wall, and it smelt of cats and stuffiness. The stairs were worn and dirty, and the place had altogether the drab air of a barracks. Yet Danny whistled as he climbed the steps to the door that had his own name on a brass plate upon it and the home that could boast a bathroom, though that was dark and ventilated only through a barred window giving on the common landing.

The smell of kippers cooking met him as he stepped into the unlit lobby of the flat. He heard an infant cry. Nobody came to meet him, and he went into the bathroom to wash himself under the blue flame that licked through a broken mantle. When his noisy ablutions were complete, when his face was shining red and he was comfortable again in shirt sleeves, he passed through to the kitchen.

Agnes was bent over a frying-pan on a gas-ring. She wore a print overall, but her fair hair was in curlers. At his entrance she turned on him, but as if without interest, a big-nosed, big-mouthed face.

"On the booze again, I suppose," she said.

"Shut your face!" he retorted, but without passion. "Is ma tea ready?"

"Aye, when I'm ready. I take my own time for them that takes theirs."

Danny was not put out. He had never expected exchanges of any other kind as between spouses of eighteen years' standing. In fact, watching her at her domestic task he reflected genially that Agnes, at thirty-six, was still a smart one.

"Where's Wee Mirren?" he asked.

"Can ye no' use yer eyes?" she replied, still intent on the sizzling kippers.

The child, of course, was on the bed that, elaborately curtained, was but a shelf filling the recess behind the door. She lay there happy, a finger in her mouth, her brown eyes welcoming her father, her bare legs twisting ecstatically.

"Hullo, wee hen!" he greeted her adoringly. When he picked her up, her tiny, fat arms went round his neck. "She's her daddy's ain wee hen."

He found a chair before the fire, placed her on his knee, and made pretence to be a horse, jogging with his lady to the fair. Wee Mirren crowed. At nearly two she had little speech at her command. Then she began to whimper, and he knew that she had had enough of the cockhorse game. Automatically he produced the fat silver watch in its worn celluloid case from his waistcoat.

It was a stage of ritual. Wee Mirren seized the watch in two chubby hands and held it to her ear, then to his.

"Tick-tock!" she gurgled. "Tick-tock!"

"Tick-tock!" he echoed. "Tick-tock! Daddy's ain Wee Mirren!"

With that he enfolded her in his arms and held her close to him as one who guards a treasure. The child whimpered.

"That's right," came the voice from the gas-ring, "spoil her."

"Ach, shut yer face!" he retorted. "She's fine. Ye're fine, aren't ye, Mirren? You and yer daddy's fine, eh?"

Just then he became aware of a warm discomfort about the legs and cried out:

"Holy Jesus! She's wet ma breeks! Christ almighty, can ye no' put a hippen on the wean?"

The figure bent over the frying-pan was suddenly energized. It shot across the room and seized the child who screamed. Danny had a glimpse of the anger—or was it hatred?—in the blazing eyes of his wife.

"Ye dirty wee ticket!" she snarled at the infant. Then she turned on her husband. "That's you and yer bumping her about, you big fool!"

"Leave the bairn alone! Leave the bairn alone!" Danny warned her.

"Can I no' get cleanin' her?" she retorted fiercely.

That was Agnes all over—her bark worse than her bite. She was good to their children—a real good mother—he was proud to think. But always she had to make her domestic life an endless battle of hard words, as if she got satisfaction out of the wounds she made with her tongue.

Now she was vigorously wiping the limb of the child with a rag of flannel.

"Where are the other two?" Danny asked her.

"Billy's away a message for me," she replied, absorbed in her intimate task.

"And I suppose nobody knows where that Peter is," he grumbled. "Of all the useless loafers! God love a duck. . . ."

"Hold yer tongue, man!" Agnes interrupted him angrily. "Can ye not leave that boy alone for five minutes? Nag, nag, naggin' at him, and at me, too. It's no' his fault that he canna get work."

"No. But he can get the money to go to the Pictures, and dances, and buy these fags of his, and take his fancy molls into ice-cream shops."

"Ach, can it!" pleaded Agnes, placing Wee Mirren back in the bed. "Yer tea's ready, if these kippers are no' spoiled wi' you and yer nonsense."

They were sitting down when the boy, Billy, came in, a cheery infant of eight who whistled "The Sunshine of Your Smile" even as he handed his mother the parcel he had fetched. His roguish, sandy face grinned at his father. Then he threw his cap at Wee Mirren gurgling on the bed.

"Hullo, son!" Danny greeted him. "How's things?"

"Okay, big boy," answered Billy fetching himself a chair.

"And the school? How did ye get on at the school?"

"Swell, pop." Billy was a student of the Pictures. "Top o' the class."

"That doesn't mean ye can sit down at ma table wi' dirty hands. Away and wash them this minute," his mother chimed in.

"Ach, his hands are fine," Danny protected the boy. "Get on wi' yer tea, son."

"That's right," Agnes snapped. "Make a cod of me in front of him. Well, ye'll have the two of them to look after the night."

22

"Out, is it? Where d'ye think ye're going?"

"I'm not thinkin'; I'm goin'. Wi' Lizzie to the Pictures, if you want to know."

"Take me, maw," begged Billy cheekily.

"You'll just stay where you are and do yer lessons and get to yer bed quick."

"Pictures! Lizzie!" Danny snorted. "Ye're a couple of mugs, right enough."

"I suppose ye think ye're better wi' yer pubs and coupoons."

Danny did think so, as it happened, and he was vastly uneasy over Agnes's growing dependence on her sister, Lizzie. A high-stepper, that one, with her husband, Jim Dunsmuir, turning over big money in mysterious ways connected with the cinema, the motor, and the betting trades; with her semi-detached villa in Newlands and her Austin Twelve and her made-up face. She had started speaking Kelvinside too—her, out of a Partick fish-shop!—and God alone knew what ideas she was putting into Agnes's head! He was at heart miserably afraid of that flashy influence, which accounted for the curlers in Agnes's hair, for her ambition to have it permanently waved—at fifteen bob, if you please!—for the fancy, newly ironed frock hanging on the clothes-horse near the fire, and for her more and more frequent jibes at his working-man's ways, at what she regarded as the limitations of their condition.

But he had nothing to say to her in this respect. Give and take was all very well in the small rubs of their intimate life, but he could not face her, or risk her scorn and anger, in a matter so fundamental in his philosophy. If she was going to the Pictures with Lizzie, she would go to the Pictures with Lizzie.

"To hell wi' Lizzie and the Pictures!" he lamely countered her challenge.

2

With Agnes gone it was quiet in the kitchen. On a deal chair by the fire, his feet on the bar of it and his knees at his mouth, Billy pored over a schoolbook. Wee Mirren was sound asleep behind the curtains of the bed. At the table sat Danny, brooding over a sheet of pinkish paper.

The alarm clock ticked from the mantelpiece, and now and again from the fire ashes dropped softly. Down the street from the Dumbarton Road came the endless fabric of traffic-noises: the rush of the buses, the honk-honk of horns, the hum of tramway-motors, and the clangour of their wheels. But Danny heard none of these sounds. All his mental force was concentrated on the pinkish sheet. In an ecstasy of doubt, in an agony of reasoning, he was deciding on the bet he would make on Saturday's football.

The coupon was a document that might have bewildered even an intelligent layman, but to Danny it presented no difficulties save those of decision. Would he take Number 9 and play safe on six home wins at the frail price of 6 to 1, or play high on Pool Number 5 that had last week paid, he noted with appreciation and envy, 20 to 1 on four wins away? But Pool Number 2 had returned 54 to 1 on two home and three away results, and that, begod, was not a long shot for the man who knew his stuff. But the bookies were getting fly, cunningly limiting to those of doubtful issue the number of games a chap could choose among. It was only after much deliberation that Danny decided to put his money into Number 2, and even then the true agony of his study was only starting.

Rangers v. Hearts, Motherwell v. Celtic, Clyde v. Hamilton. . . There was the devil of it. Look at the League tables, look at the records of the teams, and Rangers and Motherwell were odds-on chances to win at home, but the Celts were fighters and might easily force a draw, and that would be another coupoon up the pole. Gees, it was difficult, an exquisite labour. Hibs to win against St. Mirren at home? Queen's Park to pull it off against Aberdeen away? The longer Danny pondered, the more confused did his mind seem to become, the more incapable of decision.

After an hour of it he pushed the paper away with a sigh. Thus it was every Thursday evening in the season. Tomorrow, he knew, most of his doubts would be resolved with the aid of the evening paper he bought on that day alone. But this Thursday agony was for him a necessary part of the ritual of the week, and he rose from it with the feeling of virtuous effort duly made.

He put out a hand, and pulled the absorbed Billy's hair. "Come on, son. Off to yer beddy-baw. Ye'll read yerself blind."

Unwillingly the child clambered from the chair, yawned, and shuffled moodily towards the door that led into the next room. As it closed behind him the thin girn of the baby sounded from behind the curtains. "Wheesht!" said Danny softly. "Wheesht, you!"

The cry was stilled for a moment, then it began again, unassertive but persistent. The father moved stealthily to the curtain, slipped behind them, and in the gloom of the cubicle started to croon to the infant, stroking at the same time the back of a silken-soft hand. But still she did not cease to whimper. Then the whimper became a cry. Then the small lump of humanity was transformed into a shrieking, kicking nexus of passion, and at that unmistakable sign Danny admitted to himself the nature of the crisis.

He was at the fire, the child on his knees, sponged and happy again, and he was in the act of wrapping a dry, warm napkin about the loins with sure, practised hand, when there shambled into the room a gawky lad of sixteen or thereabouts. His large tweed cap of aggressive pattern was still down over his suspicious eyes, and there was a half-smoked cigarette behind one ear. His shoulders were round, his feet dragged. But though he had an air of uneasy truculence, there was yet about him the pathetic, frustrated air of a boy.

That latter aspect of his son Danny could not see. The mere sight of the shuffling halflin had the power to infuriate him, since it symbolised all that he hated, that he could not understand: idleness, flashiness of mind and habit, stupidity. Only the baby on his knees prevented an outburst.

"So ye're home?" he said, roughly sarcastic.

"Looks like it," retorted Peter in his grumbling voice.

"My God!" stormed Danny, so violently that the child started in his arms. "I'll clatter ye one of these days, ye great, useless keelie."

"Ach, shut up, for crivvens sake!" the boy pleaded. "Give's half a chance. Did ma mother leave me ma tea?"

Danny laid the baby on the bed and drew the curtains.

"Leave ye yer tea!" he cried. "Come for yer tea when ye know it's ready and ye'll get it. Ye can dam' well make yer tea for yersel' if ye want it. And what's more, my lad, ye'll stay in here the rest of the night and look after the weans. I'm goin' out. D'ye hear?"

"Och, I hear ye all right, all right."

In a fume, Danny found his jacket and waistcoat and cap. While he dressed he glowered at the boy, now busy with the kettle at the sink. Always appalled by what he believed to be Peter's shiftlessness, now he was infuriated by the lad's apparent indifference to criticism. Fine men they were breeding nowadays! he reflected sardonically. Tarts and fags; dancing and betting—that was about their limit. A lot of work-shy young twisters. Another war, with conscription, would do them a sight of good.

"I'll be back about ten," Danny said finally. "And don't you stir a foot out this door or I'll lam the skin off yer backside."

Having made this last, somewhat desperate declaration of a father's authority, Danny went out into a street that was filling with an autumn fog. He packed and lit his pipe as he went and, having reached the Dumbarton Road, turned eastwards along it at a pace unusually brisk for him.

His wonted cheerfulness returned to answer the challenge of the busy streets; he delighted, though not consciously, in the life about him: the laughter of young people, the cosy respectability of married couples out for a stroll, the lighted shops, and the colours of the trams. About Partick Cross he paused to witness an interesting ejection from a public house. In a side-street near Byres Road a noisy speaker on behalf of the National Unemployed Workers' Movement was hoarsely proclaiming Communism to a quiet, if occasionally facetious, knot of people. There was a blaze of light from the facade of the Kelvin Hall, then housing, so Danny gathered with interest, a Radio Exhibition. He had always had a fancy to buy a set.

At the form of the roads he bore to the right up Argyle Street, and about three hundred yards along turned into the tunnel of an archway running under a lofty tenement. This led him into a dimly-lit yard that ramified in the most surprising ways—here to a stable where a baker kept his horses, that way to the premises of a firm astonishingly advertising itself as "Wood Turners and Bagpipe Makers," the other to the styes of "John Tolmie, Pigfeeder."

It was a veritable hamlet in the heart of Glasgow, a nook in which primitive and unexpected avocations were busily pursued. It smelt of the country, of base-feeding, coarse-mannered animals.

Its buildings were white-washed. It seemed to defy the city that had grown about it, a hardy relic, as indeed it was, of the days when the Anderston corks, as the merchant-weavers of the village were called, had their villas and gardens and coach-houses hereabouts in the brave days of Glasgow's first industrial expansion. The house that Danny approached through the pend and up a short lane was actually the stable and coachman's dwelling of a long-dead nabob, whose heirs had sold everything to the railway company so that a tunnel might be driven underneath.

A yelping of dogs answered his pull at the contraption of wires which opened the great gate of this establishment. That would be Cloonagh of Rathnahuna and Brackenburn Bailie, the greyhounds young Alston, the bookie's son, kept boarded here. (So they weren't racing at the White City tonight.) Danny silenced the nervous, cringing beasts with a word, and they slunk off into the darkness before him. Up an old wooden staircase he passed to the door of the antique house above their kennels.

A child answered his knock.

"Hello, Tommy! Is your father in?"

A woman, smiling, appeared behind the little boy.

"Oh, it's you, Danny! Come in," she greeted him. "He's in his bed, but he's feeling not too bad today." She turned to call indoors: "Here's Danny, Joe."

A weak voice answered from the back of the room.

"Bring him in. Come in, Dan."

The room was lit only by a paraffin-lamp on the mantel-piece and the flames of a goodly fire beneath it, but it had a bright cosiness that went to Danny's heart. Every ornament and utensil was polished to the nines, and all were arranged to produce an effect of easy orderliness. Deal tables and chairs were scrubbed white, the iron fender gleamed in the firelight, and if ever there had been a soiled or discarded object in the house it had been tidied out of sight.

"Ye're fine and perjink here, Jess," remarked Danny approvingly to his hostess, who smiled with pleasure. He marched up to the bed in the corner and held out his hand. "And how's things, Joe?"

He looked down on a pale and sunken face, that of the ghost of a man. A thin arm came from under the patch-work coverlet, a damp and feeble hand rested for a moment in his.

"Not so bad, Danny, not so bad," the weak voice replied. "The cough's been easier the day."

"That's fine, Joe. That's grand. I'll be up to take ye out a walk one of these days soon."

He always said that, but it had become an automatic and meaningless encouragement. He had long seen death in Joe Stirling's eyes, and he knew its inevitability to be accepted by Jess and Joe as well as by himself. They were three who shared a deadly secret and defied it in the sweet understanding of their friendship. Joe was one of the finest things in Danny's life since, like Leslie Pagan, he was of that period in which Danny had lived most richly. And Christ! it was hard to think that after passing quite unscathed through the battles and rigours of Gallipoli, Sinai and Palestine, Joe had been caught at last by the German gas in March, 1918, and was now this rotting invalid, dying on an Army pension.

He sat for an hour by the bedside and told Joe his news. He went through the story of the launch of the *Estramadura*; he told Joe how he thought of framing his coupon, gravely and elaborately justifying his probable choice of winning teams. Joe listened in silence, but his eyes were brightly attentive.

"I wish I could see a game again, Danny," he whispered once.

"You'll see a game again all right, Joe, ma son," asserted Danny stoutly. "Wait you till after the New Year. . . ."

Joe smiled patiently, and Danny hurried on to canvass the prospects for the great International at Hampden in the spring, that fantastic peak of the Scotsman's football year, when the army of spectators assembles more than a hundred thousand strong and roars to the fluctuations of the fight against the ancient enemy of England. Then Jess brought the tea she had made, and Danny drank four strong cups of it while they chatted of this and that.

"And how are a' yer folk, Danny?" Jess asked him conversationally. "Has Peter got a job yet?"

"They're a' right, thanks, Jess," returned Danny. "But Peter! Get a job! He wouldna' walk round the corner to get one."

"Ach, ye're too hard on him, Dan," she pleaded kindly. "A job's no' easy to come by these days. He's just like a' the rest—he canna

28

help himself."

"By God, he just won't!" insisted Danny vehemently. "Jazzin' and the Pictures and wenchin'—that's about the size of him. He's in wi' a lot of work-shy young twisters that should be put into the Army and have some guts knocked into them."

"It's no' so easy as a' that, I doubt," she insisted gently. "It's gey hard times we're living in."

"Aye, but that's no' an excuse."

He could not, however, press the argument with Jess beyond that point, for her generosity defeated him. When he had left the house, promising to be back on Monday to report on Saturday's football to Joe, he went homewards along Argyle Street with the influence of his friend's wife much upon him. The comforting kindness of her remained with him, a stimulant more potent than drink; and because it had come from a woman so good, and herself so much the victim of circumstance, he gave unaccustomed weight to what she had said about the bad times and the ill-luck of young men born into them.

Perhaps there was something to be said for Peter, after all; and for a space the father's love, that had been inverted, turned to flow outwards to his gawky, foolish son. And he remembered suddenly the Yard and the state of affairs in it and what Leslie Pagan had said to him when they parted near the road junction at Scotstoun. Bad, bad times—there was no getting away from that.

Danny felt then the need of company and, at the same moment, of time to think; and here was the Glenclober Vaults, which he knew well as a pub of the quieter sort. On the top of his supper and Jess's tea a wee one would do him no harm. Hard times, repeated something within him, and harder times coming; but his consciousness reacted desperately to that mean intimidation, and he turned into the bar.

3

It was quiet in there, only two small groups of men at the counter and an old, decayed woman sipping hot rum in the bogus privacy of a compartment. The barman nodded familiarly and talked about the weather while he served Danny with his half and half-pint. No fresh customers came in, and while Danny drank, they chatted emptily, the barman's elbows on the counter, discussing in the aimless fashion of such encounters this, that, and the other until they came, inevitably, to the subject of football.

It was then that the barman suddenly deserted his professional manner. He leaned forward over the counter, winked, nudged his head ever so slightly, and indicated three men who stood talking with intensity some three yards away—two large Jews in neat, waisted overcoats and a lad in shabby serge clothes with a kindly sheepish face.

"Know who that is?" the barman asked portentously and, at Danny's shake of the head, explained: "Packy Doonan, the featherweight. That's his manager, the big fella wi' the grey hat. The other's the manager of the Arena. He's a great wee fighter that."

Danny was impressed. He had the genuine feeling of being in the presence of greatness. Packy Doonan—that wee chap looking so gentle and simple; just a laddie not much older than Peter!

"Like to speak to him?" asked the barman, glorying in his triumph.

"Sure," said Danny, impressed and yet apprehensive.

"Wait till I get a chance," explained the barman.

He moved with an air of unconcern towards the group of three, halted near them, humming an air with laboured indifference, and at the first sign of a glass nearly empty darted forward with napkin poised to wipe the counter and a face expectant of another order. He got it—two large whiskies for the Jews, a baby soda, and a small tonic for Packy.

For Danny it was joyous agony to watch the play. As he served the drinks the barman called out to him, as if the pressure of business was heavy that night: "Just a minute, Danny, till I serve these gents. Won't be a sec."

Danny shivered with delight to see the larger of the Jews turn massively to survey him.

"Perhaps your friend would have one with us?" he suggested in a slow and heavy voice.

The transaction had been completed just before Danny knew where he was. He was overwhelmed, and yet something within him preserved a detachment, in which he saw himself shaking hands respectfully with the ponderous and equable Jews, vigorously with the grinning pugilist.

"And yours, sir?" boomed the larger Jew; then to the barman: "The usual for our friend, Tom."

It was a situation in which all his cheerfulness and independence of spirit deserted Danny. He was reassured by the simplicity, the childishness, of Packy Doonan, but the big men were too much for him. Ike Harris, one of the biggest men in the game, and Joe Silver of the Arena! Life was wonderful, but overpowering. This would be something to tell the boys in the Yard tomorrow. This would impress Peter with a real sense of his father's importance. He scratched in his mind for something to contribute to the talk and could find little that did not sound empty when expressed. But the marvel of it was that the big men seemed to expect nothing of him but that he should drink at their expense and listen.

He had three drinks with them and heard many marvellous stories, tales of famous fights of the past that he had only read about and these wonderful men had actually seen, exposures of the erratic private lives of great men he had worshipped from afar, and revelations of huge sums of money made and lost in this business of entertaining a public devoted to sport. And in this magnificent sublimation of a profound instinct Danny found forgetfulness of problems that were beginning, subtly but uncomfortably, to beset him.

When they parted outside the public-house just before closing time there began to dawn on him uncomfortably the feeling that he had not, after all, counted for much in the gathering. Packy's grin and firm shake of the hand were flattering, but the Jews waved only casual farewells, gestures that patently ignored his individuality, and hurried towards an approaching tram with their valuable charge. Still, it had been a great experience, something that had lifted the day far out of the ruck of days. His heart was high as he walked homewards; and "Ach, to hell!" he valiantly said to himself when a lurch into a passer-by let him know that he had drunk a little more than was good for him.

The tides of people flowing backwards and forwards along the Dumbarton Road delighted him. It was fine to see folks out and about, he thought: lads and their lassies, decent middle-aged and elderly couples making home from the Pictures, and bold files of girls abreast, many a bonny piece among them.

The warmth of the human bond was astonishing. What was it Rabbie had said, speaking for the people? That bit about honest poverty and the guinea-stamp—a man's a man for a' that. And Rab, by God, was right! Folks were decent if you looked at them the right way: all plain bodies like himself, a wee bit misunderstood, but cheerfully going home along the Dumbarton Road to their decent beds. Danny began to think of Agnes. He was humming, almost singing, "The Lea Rig"as he turned off towards Kingarth Street.

Even down there towards the River there were people about on this quite remarkable night, people getting home, people coming away from the firesides of friends. Many a window glowed with the light of hospitality behind it. Every close held its silent, locked couple or its crooning group of boys and girls. From one came the unmistakable voice of his own son, Peter. The lad was nasally intoning one of those mournful songs of negroid love in which he delighted; and as he passed the lighted mouth of the close Danny saw his first-born, shoulders hunched, hands in pockets, shuffling a dance for the entertainment of his friends.

A spasm of the old anger seized him. His kindly feeling towards the world at large changed suddenly to a black contempt for that one young man—messing about with his fancy molls. And he had left the house against explicit orders. Gees! It was Danny's impulse to step into the close, seize his son by the scruff of the neck, and drag him home. Then there came, like a wave of warm comfort, the thought that Agnes must have returned early, and he passed on to his own doorway.

He halted at the entrance to the kitchen, amazed. The gas was burning bright, the fire still glowed, but Agnes was not there. Instead, he saw only Billy, in his shirt-tails, holding aside the curtains of the bed and staring in horror at something that lay there, screaming.

Danny leapt forward. The infant on the bed had twisted its body into a fantastic shape; its face was a livid purple. He snatched her up.

"How long has she been crying?" he snapped at Billy.

"She wakened me," the boy replied, afraid.

"When did Peter go out?"

"I don't know, pa."

"My Christ!" hissed Danny, tearing at the baby's clothes. "Away to yer bed, son. Away and sleep. She's all right now."

He worked rapidly on the child. She had quietened now. He had come just in time. Needing attention, she had cried for it; and getting none, had taken to screaming and throwing herself about, so that the neckband of her nightgown had tightened about her throat. A near thing it had been, but babies were like that. For the second time that evening he patiently performed the rites of cleaning.

He was about at an end when Agnes returned. There was colour in her face, her eyes were bright, and it struck him even then that she was pretty and desirable in her tight-fitting blue hat, her coat with deep fur collar, and her trig shoes.

"What's wrong, Dan?" she asked, as if the cries of the child still echoed somehow about the room.

He told her, and she snatched up the infant, held its face to hers, and crooned to it.

"It's that useless lump, Peter," growled Danny. "Leavin' the bairn alone like that! When I told him, too! My God, I'll skin the backside off him when I get him."

But Agnes did not seem to be listening. She was laying the baby back in the bed, crowing foolish things to it. Then she drew the curtains, threw her hat and coat upon the table, and sat down on a chair before the fire.

"My, I've had a grand night!" she sighed.

He saw that she was excited, a good deal above herself. The nagging woman of the house had disappeared, and the girl had come to life again. Patiently he listened to her story. It had been a lovely picture, then she had gone in with Lizzie on the way home and had three wee ports.

"I'm just about tight, Dan," she giggled. "I bet you are too."

With that she drew her skirts above her knee and stretched her toes towards the fire.

"How's that for a leg?" she asked.

His heated senses responded to the challenge, and soon they

were in bed together beside Wee Mirren, the queer hazards of the life about them all forgotten.

CHAPTER THREE

A SHIPYARD CLOSES

THE portfolio lay open on one of the low tables of Blanche's chromium-plated lounge. Before it, in an attitude that the detached observer would have recognised as dutiful, sat Leslie Pagan. His father paced the old gold carpet, backwards and forwards before the fire, a Turkish cigarette between his gesticulating fingers.

"Beautiful stuff, my dear boy, beautiful!" the old man expatiated. "Old Jack had devilish fine taste. I'll say that for him, but he never thought in 1920 I'd be buying his stuff at auction in 1930. Ha! Ha! He never thought that. No, by Gad! A big pile in Army contracts he made. Too much. There was that committee of enquiry. But he got away with it. And now, broke to smithereens, the dam' fool, monkeying about with currencies. And I get that portfolio of his there for, for—what was it?—a couple of hundred! And look at it, boy! Look at that Bone. No, not the Zorn. Nasty man, Zorn, and a cheap-jack. Yes, that one. And the Cameron. Superb, eh? Superb. Now if you turn over, there's an engraving by a fellow, name of Gooden. Don't know the name, but he's good, devilish good, eh? Thought I'd like to give Blanche her pick."

"Nonsense, father. You keep the whole shooting-match and enjoy them."

"Thinking you'll get them later on?" the old man twinkled.

"Thinking nothing," Leslie laughed. "Have a drink. Where are the drinks? Touch the bell, father, would you. . . . As for later on, there'll be none if trade doesn't hurry up and improve," he concluded glumly.

"Trade!" The old man waved an ugly interruption aside. "I thought we were talking about prints—and drinks."

"The drinks are coming, and I've seen the prints, and I'll see them again," said Leslie lightly enough. He knew that nowadays he must humour his father in any discussion that was really grave. "But if you want to know the truth, I brought you here to talk business, and you're going to do it. Now, look here, dad. . . ."

"My dear boy—" the old man began to protest.

A knock and the entrance of a maid checked him, and Leslie was quick to rise and move to the tray the girl put down on a table near the door. He held up a decanter invitingly.

"Sherry—the Tio Pepe? Or is it too dry?" he asked.

"Nothing could be too dry if you insist on talking business." Old John Pagan would have his little joke.

"I don't insist, dad—good luck to you!—it forces itself upon me. We've got to pay off a lot of men or go on losing a lot of money. That's what it comes to, and you've got to decide."

The old man sipped his sherry.

"Charming! Not everybody's taste, but charming!" he murmured approvingly. "But this is surely nonsense, Leslie. A big pay-off?"

"A very big pay-off," answered his son remorselessly. "A fortnight since we launched the *Estramadura* and not a blessed sign of anything—not even an old tramp for repair. The riggers and the carpenters and that lot are all right on the fitting-out job, but we just can't go on letting gangs of constructional men kick their heels about the place—platers and riveters and so on. Much as I'd like to."

The old man paused in his striding, then lowered himself into a deep chair by the fire.

"Pagan's have always tried to be decent about that sort of thing," he said, grave for the moment. "And work will come along soon, you'll see."

"Will it? I wish I could think so."

He was full of the awareness of a bitter paradox inherent in this situation of the two men responsible for Pagan's unwilling to make the gesture of defeat, but for reasons totally different. He knew that an ancient pride in the Yard, a faith in the holy destiny of the Clyde was alone what kept his father from making the melancholy admission that the brave days were gone. He had himself passed that point already, and his tenderness was all for the men—and quite irrational in the grey philosophy of commerce.

"Leave it for a day or two," the old man said, rather helplessly for him.

"And we can't. This is Wednesday. Friday's another pay-day."

36

It was to their relief that the door swung open then to admit Blanche, her fairness glowing against a foundation of black velvet, milky pearls gleaming at her neck.

"Hullo! Hullo! Hullo!" she greeted them. "All very grave and reverend. What's wrong?"

The old man stood up beside her at the fire and put his arm round her waist.

"Your husband has lost his nerve," he whispered playfully. "He's going to hand Pagan's to the broker's men."

The pleasantry was like a knife running into Leslie, though he exonerated father and wife from every charge of malice aforethought. A fine, friendly pair they made: she so handsome and so frank with her elderly beau, and he in his turn so courteous and so distinguished in his dinner jacket of dark purple and his deep stock. Yet their amiable juxtaposition had for the man who watched them an implication of fearful irony. He knew absolutely of both what these two could only dimly guess about each other—that the passing of Pagan's would be death for the old man, that it would be for her, weary at heart of this drab Scotland that could not give her the life she craved, a release unspeakable.

Did Blanche apprehend the strain that was upon him? Certainly her tone seemed to him harsh with nervousness.

"And am I not to have a cocktail?"

The thread of tension snapped. A family joke came to their rescue. Blanche was smiling mischievously even before the old man broke out vehemently.

"A cocktail! Great Heavens, girl, *must* you ruin your palate and your constitution with these poisonous things? Gall and wormwood—a nasty mess of beastly raw spirit and Italian syrups! Nasty—"

She grinned over the frosted glass she had raised to him.

"Dear daddy!" she cooed. "I love that piece of yours. And here's to your blue eyes."

"I'd prefer to have it in decent clean sherry, my girl, but I know you're incorrigible, and that Leslie can't manage you properly. And who is coming tonight to share the poisons with you? Anybody interesting?"

"Oh, just a fragment of the Family."

"The Family—yes, the Family. I begin to see just how much use I am to you, my dear girl—handy old fellow to have about at your duty dinners." He sat down with a sigh. "And what particular type of infliction am I to endure tonight?"

"Cheer up, daddy!" she laughed at him. "Only Aunt Margaret and Alasdair. And there will be some nice people coming in later."

"Dear me! Oh, dear me!" sighed the old man.

"I like young Alasdair," she challenged him.

"The trouble is, dear," Leslie interrupted, "that it's impossible to separate him from Aunt Margaret."

"A dreadful woman," observed old John Pagan. "She killed poor Tom."

"Daddy!"

Even as they spoke they heard the tyres of a heavy car crisp over the gravel as the visitors rolled up to the front door; and a minute later they were receiving with every sign of cordiality the wife of Leslie's uncle and her son.

She was a woman in her sixties, elaborately bejewelled, the powder thick and grey on her broad and heavy face—"uncomfortably like a bulldog," old John Pagan once had described her. The son was in the nature of an item of her luggage. Rather short and slight, with uninteresting hair and a moustache that might as well have not existed, he did not even get from his dinner jacket the spurious distinction that garment confers on most men.

Mrs. Thomas Pagan's greetings were decisive. It was as if she had come knowing precisely what she meant to say. She refused a glass of sherry and was palpably interested in a faintly disapproving way when Alasdair accepted a cocktail. She was ready with her answer to Blanche's formal question.

"We have been wonderfully well, my dear," she intimated, "wonderfully well. Alasdair has been golfing regularly, and I have been taking a very helpful course of massage. Very helpful. But of course I can't winter in this place—simply can't. So I'm off to London next week. Then I go to Spezia in January."

"Alasdair too?" Leslie could not help asking.

Her formidable eyes swung to take his as if she had scented an impertinent challenge.

"Certainly," she said, closing every avenue to a possible discussion. From Leslie, as if contemptuously, she turned to her brother-in-law. "And how is the business, John?"

The old man made a faintly protesting gesture with a thin hand.

"So, so," he answered. "It is like every other business just now, Margaret; it could be a good deal better. In fact, we've got to face the possibility of closing down. Temporarily, of course, temporarily."

"That would be nonsense," pronounced Aunt Margaret.

Leslie watched his father's face at that moment. Then he glanced at Blanche. The irony, the perfect irony of it! Then, as a maid appeared at the door with a word for Blanche, came the old man's astringent response.

"It is likewise nonsense, my dear Margaret, to keep on paying wages to scores of workmen when there is nothing for them to do."

"Come on, good people!" Blanche cut in. "Dinner. No shop tonight, please."

And, after a laborious gathering of bag and handkerchief, Aunt Margaret took old John Pagan's arm and swept before them across the hall.

It was such a dinner as Blanche invariably provided especially for her father-in-law—cup of consommé, *sole au vin blanc*, pheasant, and a soufflé of cheese as light as air. A glass of Montrachet with the perfume of violets in it, the Corton of '21, and black coffee—everything chosen to fit the taste of an exigent old gentleman, and no concessions to such as Aunt Margaret.

Food was indeed not an interest with that forceful lady. She had many decisive things to say in her spirit of command over the section of life she had chosen for her own, and she said them; so that though she was at his elbow and he had a hospitable duty to her, Leslie could retire into that hinterland of detachment he had come to know so well of late and from it regard the small drama played by the company round the table that returned reflections from mahogany and silver of the shaded lamp above.

It was a fantastic group as he studied it, its constituents so strangely interdependent. There sat his own father, the long tradition of Pagan's embodied, but ready now in age to forget responsibility; the elegant veteran. There was Aunt Margaret, limited and endlessly assertive, a parasite on Pagan's, living on money made out of Pagan's, still drawing money its men laboured to earn. Alasdair? A Scotsman spoiled—Uppingham and Oriel, with a small book of undergraduate essays to his credit; and a parasite at second-hand, overlain by his mother, living on her, and through her, on Pagan's—so useless in Leslie's stern conception of a man's job that he almost disliked the harmless boy. And at the head of the table Blanche—radiant, agreeable, but making no more, he knew, than the best of a bad job among his relations and far from her own people. She could not care for Pagan's; she could not know what it meant, and must long in her heart to take him and John away from its power. For all of them, whether they knew it or not, destiny was in the fate of Pagan's; and he—Leslie Patullo Pagan—he must, apparently, decide what that fate should be.

"What were you saying about the Yard, John," he started out of his reverie to hear Aunt Margaret pronounce, "is most disturbing. Most disturbing."

"A mere matter of business, my dear Margaret," the old man muttered, and glanced an appeal at Blanche, who, rising, answered it promptly.

"Shall I send in more coffee, Lal?" she asked with a superb assumption of casualness. "I think, Aunt Margaret . . . "

So they were spared, and with young Alasdair between father and son, there was little of reality in their talk until, with the outer door opening to arriving guests, they moved to join the growing company in the lounge.

There came Blanche's stand-by, Sir Archie, relic of one of Glasgow's merchant families, a bachelor and rich, infinitely decorated with the orders of the smaller nations, a repository of the West End's gossip, and endlessly indiscreet. There came the gossip-writer of an evening paper, a little dirty as to his linen, short-sighted, and elaborately cynical. The dark girl in the yellow dress was, Leslie knew, that daughter of a county family of Argyll who had achieved a reputation for courage in adversity by starting as hairdresser in Buchanan Street. He smiled to see old Sir Peter Cunningham, small, frail, porcelain-pallid, and tottering, but incalculably rich on oil. A young minister who had successfully dramatised his welfare work in the East End sparkled within a ring of pretty girls by the fire. Over Aunt Margaret there bent massively a Rugby Internationalist in kilt, red waistcoat, and lace cravat.

In their superficial aspects Leslie liked these gatherings that Blanche had the genius to convene. It pleased something elemental in him to hear such a crackle of lively talk under his own roof, to ply the guests with drinks. Blanche had created a colourful novelty in this grey city of the north. Others could gather folk to play Bridge or to endure the formalities of a musical evening, but to few other houses in all the great town would people come, as they came at Blanche's bidding, just to meet and talk. Even over Glasgow her superb Englishness had triumphed. He was proud of her.

Yet on this evening of his personal anxiety, and though he was pleased to know that the party went well, he could not lose himself in it altogether. These chattering people—some thirty of them—were not the recipients of a hospitality altogether disinterested. He hated himself for thinking so, but he could not get away from the profound knowledge that thus and thus did Blanche, by buying Glasgow with her wealth, seek to escape, however naturally, the dour reality of it. At one moment, while he was supposed to be in talk with Sir Peter's Miss Meiklejohn, the sour reflection occurred to him that the cost of this bright evening in hard cash would keep for a week five of such families as must suffer at once through the closing down of Pagan's. Even as he passed on to chat with the fashionable missionary of the East End there came over him a petulant wish to challenge the creature on the fantastic disproportion of human life.

He was still with the parson when a tug at his sleeve brought him round to face his father.

"I must go now, Leslie," the old man murmured.

"So soon, father?"

"Yes. Blanche is a wonderful hostess, but she doesn't budget for age."

"I'll see you out."

They were alone in the cloakroom, suddenly and surprisingly isolated from the rabble in the lounge. Father and son were together. The directors of Pagan's had met. And between them lay a problem unsolved.

"Are you to be at the office tomorrow?" Leslie asked.

He asked it innocently, but the question's implication dawned

41

on him at once, and he was glad then that he had put it. The old man carefully arranged the white silk scarf about his neck.

"I don't think so," he said. "No, I don't think so. Is my car at the door?"

He led the way into the hall; then paused there as if in abstraction, his eyes downcast, his black felt hat in his hand.

"This is Wednesday," he mused. "Two days till Friday. Dear me! Dear me!"

He raised his eyes to take Leslie's. They were gentle, faintly quizzical, yet grave in their challenge.

"It's your decision, son," he said. "I'm too old now. Goodnight."

As the front door opened to let him out, so did the door of the lounge, and the chatter of the people in there came to Leslie's ears like the first blast of a rising and ominous gale.

2

As he moved from the boardroom back into the small office he preferred to call his own, he was conscious of the eyes of clerks and typists upon him. This sense of uneasiness seemed to have pervaded the counting house of Pagan's since, at twenty minutes after nine, he had hauled Jimmy, the office boy, over the coals for forgetting to alter the date on the calendar. Had he so openly displayed the fretfulness that possessed him? Certainly he might have been less irritable with Miss Macgregor because she had more than once asked him to repeat a hurried sentence in dictation. They had good reason to wonder at the tantrums of a boss usually quiet and tolerant.

But there was more than that. They knew. They could not help knowing. All the yard and shop managers and sub-managers were not called at once to meet the managing director in the boardroom for nothing. They must have noticed how grave were the faces of the men as they passed out from the interview. Pagan's closing down—it was in the air; it would be all over the yard and well into Glasgow by five o'clock.

It had been damnable. His irritation and his unwonted ferocity were the measure of the effort he had had to make to bring himself to do it. To sit alone in the big boardroom, waiting for them, had been a misery. He had sat there for five minutes, staring at the half-models in their cases on the walls, thinking of the good and beautiful ships that Pagan's had sent down the River to the sea in ninety years of sail and steam, wondering—as if the thought came fresh to him—that this northern River, of all the rivers in the world, had cradled such a superb and mighty flotilla. Then the men had come, quietly, their dusty bowler hats in their hands. Decent, competent men, they faced patiently the fate they knew to be ineluctable.

He had taken their views, as he could do without presumption or suspicion of arrogance; and one by one each of these born builders of ships said that he saw nothing else for it. They were Scots, taught by birth and training to weigh facts justly, and neither sentiment nor regret nor self-pity could affect their judgment. There must be a closing down. Perhaps things would get better. But the Yard could not stay open with only one ship fitting-out and nothing to fill the berths that lay empty to the sky, the gantries like blackened skeletons above them.

It had been easy, too easy. They were too damnably reasonable, these quiet men in blue serge suits. Leslie almost wanted from them a demonstration to justify his own unhappiness. But they subscribed in few words to a plain proposition, made no speeches, and trooped out to their jobs. Only old Alec Flett, fifty-three years, man and boy, with Pagan's, lingered behind to shake hands. He said not a word, however; only his wet eyes betrayed the fact that tragedy had come to him in his old age.

Well, it was done, the decision made. The people in the office knew by now. Already it would be running through the drawing-office. Some sub-manager could be counted on to tell it in the Yard, and so they would all know. It was almost with relief that Leslie sighed. Then he rang for Miss Macgregor and told her to send Mr. Dakers to him.

The secretary-accountant of the firm came eagerly, as it seemed. A scraggy man with a small mean face and rimless eyeglasses, he patently rejoiced in his contacts with authority and struggled always to display an easy acceptance of heavy responsibility shared. Leslie revolted from the first sight of that smug, alert countenance.

"We're closing down, Dakers," he said abruptly.

"Yes, I thought we would have to," the man replied. "In fact, I was going to speak to you about it."

"Oh, were you?" Leslie was in no mood to humour nonentities subtly assuming familiarity. "Well, it's done now. Better get the notices out. Tell the cashier's department. All the arrangements—you'll know what to do."

"I know," said Dakers, a faint note of pride in efficiency and foresight creeping into his tone. "In fact, I've prepared—"

"Well, go and get it done," Leslie was ruthless now. But I want to see the lists of the men affected. There are a few I may keep on."

"Is that quite wise, Mr. Leslie?"

"Oh, go to hell, Dakers, and do what you're told!"

And no sooner had the door closed than he was sorry and ashamed. It was absurd and humiliating to give way thus to temper. This was no way to face a crisis. Yet was it not the strain of the crisis that caused the irritability? And yet again. . . . He wondered for a little if he was ill. It was all strange and puzzling. Staring at the green blotting-pad before him, he felt like something in a trap.

He was roused from his uneasy reverie by a knock and the entrance of Miss Macgregor with a sheaf of letters to sign. Ah! Something to do. Not that the letters seemed to matter much now. But life did have to go on. It was the break in the continuity of things that he was really resenting. The letters were welcome.

"I'll sign these at once, Miss Macgregor. Don't expect I'll be in this afternoon."

He read the sheets with quite unusual care, clinging to the illusion of normality. He had no faith within him in such of the letters as answered enquiries, forwarded estimates, or otherwise related to future business. To a surrender of all that he had contrived to brace himself; it has done with, and he did not wish to think about it. But it was something to have on hand this little job of reading, altering a punctuation mark here and there, and putting down his signature on behalf of the firm. He was very conscious of the small manicured hand of Miss Macgregor resting on the edge of the desk before him, the diamonds glistening from a ring on the third finger.

"Is the marriage fixed yet, Miss Macgregor?" he asked lightly, though still apparently absorbed.

"Oh, yes, thanks, Mr. Leslie!" Miss Macgregor was surprised. "In the Spring some time—April, I expect."

"That's fine. We mustn't forget that."

"Thanks very much, Mr. Leslie."

She gathered the letters and went out, neat and quiet. No hope of confidences from that quarter. Miss Macgregor knew her place. Miss Macgregor had her own little life all nicely arranged and had no time for light conversation with a superior at a loose end. And why should she? But his little failure to touch her humanity made him feel dreadfully alone.

Slowly, doubting just what he would do next, he put on his hat and coat. It was his custom to lunch with the others in the canteen, but now, not out of fear but from a haunting sense of futility, he thought of the daily ritual as unbearable. The Club? A horde of old gentlemen grumbling about the state of trade over Cockburn '08 in the dining-room. Then it occurred to him with the force of an inspiration that he might go home, surprising Blanche and John, and his mind leapt to accept a distracting decision.

The big house seemed empty when he reached it. Ringing for a maid, he found that Blanche was out and would not be back until the evening—gone to golf at Turnberry, the girl understood. But yes, Master John was back from school and at play in the day nursery; this was the early day at Miss Taggart's establishment.

"He'll lunch with me, then, Lizzie," said Leslie. "I suppose it can be ready by one."

John was on his stomach on the carpet before the nursery fire, his elbows propping his head, his whole self lost in a book. In a deep chair near at hand his nurse sat sewing. Neither made any marked acknowledgment of Leslie's entrance. It was John's way to be completely absorbed by whatever took his fancy to do, but Leslie's prejudice rose against the distant insolence of the girl, her immobility confessing faith in her own divine right of control within this room.

"John is lunching with me today, Nannie," he said. "Hullo, John! Not going to say how-do, you old sausage? There you are. What about an adventure this afternoon?"

"Where to, daddy?"

It was fine to get that eager response.

"Mrs. Pagan's instructions were that John was to go to the Botanic Gardens this afternoon."

"I'll take the responsibility. Please bring him down to the lounge when his hands are washed."

Lunch with John was an adventure for both of them. Only at midday dinner on Sundays did Blanche suffer him to appear at the family table, and then in austere conditions, and it was grand to have this stolen chance of being with the child in intimacy, of seeing how he was growing out, of searching for his confidence. How little one can ever know about a child! Leslie reflected. And what queer corners there are in the mind of any one of them! Gravity and rough fun; curiosity and strange indifferences—ravishing compounds!

This day the mood of fun prevailed between them. John was not very good with knife and fork, and Leslie laughed to see how he sawed fecklessly with the one at his cutlet and used the other as a species of spoon. Himself, he pretended extreme discomfort in eating, making large rude noises and strange faces, while John laughed and laughed almost to the point of choking. It was a great and delicious secret between them when Leslie let the child have two chocolates out of a special box kept by Blanche on the sideboard.

"And where shall we go today, old son?" Leslie asked at length.

"Edinburgh Zoo," answered John promptly.

"Too far, and it'll be dark too soon. Would you like a surprise?"

"Yes, a surprise! Where?"

"But it's a surprise, so you've got to wait and see. Run upstairs and tell Nannie to get you ready—plenty of clothes on, too. It's a big surprise, and you mustn't get cold."

In due course John took his seat in the waiting Riley but there were many things he had to have explained before they started off. The red tell-tale light on the dashboard attracted him first of all. Then it occurred to him to speculate on the operation of four-wheel brakes and very seriously to doubt the capacity of a single pedal to motivate front and rear brakes simultaneously. The working of the speedometer had to be explained to him, and as they turned down the drive they were deep in a discussion of the steering-gear's peculiar activities.

Leslie found himself absurdly happy, explaining. It was simply a joy to hear the toneless "Oh!" of John in the act of imbibing knowledge. With a pang he realised that the child had never before sat by the driver of a car, but had always been tucked away, something at once precious and negligible, in the back seat of the big Daimler. And he was an engineer born, a proper Pagan, not merely wanting to know why in the way of any child, but to know exactly why. The "Oh!" was the reward only of an explanation completely detailed. It was a complete satisfaction to give that young mind the food it hungered for, and there was a delicious flavour in the consciousness of the fact that their outing was an escapade stolen from life as by custom ordained.

Speeding down the Dumbarton Road, he pointed out each shipyard as they passed its closed gates and told the boy of the great ships built here and there. It was his own first real discovery of the splendour of the story his family had lived for generations, and he wondered moodily if John would help to carry it on, or ever be allowed to do so. Again he told how, in the great days, there was not one of these yards but had two or three big ships a-building, so that up and down the River the bows of vessels unlaunched towered over the tenement buildings of the workers and people passing could hardly hear themselves speak for the clangour of metal upon metal that filled the valley from Old Kilpatrick up to Govan. The silence that reigned now made him afraid, and he reflected that Pagan's, after all, could count itself lucky in having carried on so long. For some of these yards were never to reopen again. It was written. The supreme glory had departed.

But it was all a raree-show for John, ecstatic beside him and surprisingly observant, noting how closely the Kilpatrick Hills pressed on the River; wanting to know how, if somebody wished to build a very, very big ship, it could be done without cutting a tunnel into these hills, and brooding with a toneless "Oh!" over the explanation that there were limits to the size of ships, let alone the fact that the canalized Clyde was narrow enough for the vessels its eident sons had built already. The question of tides held him till a turn off the main road took them down to Renfrew Ferry and he was distracted by the monstrous pylons carrying the wires of the Grid across the River and by the antique vessel that took their car and hauled itself by chains across the stream, bumping in the wash of a City liner outward bound: a ship gigantic in the narrow channel, overtopping the houses along the banks.

"But where *are* we going, daddy?"

"Not long now, son," Leslie assured him and dropped into the homely idiom: "Just you wait."

It was with a boyish pride in the grandeur of his surprise that, five minutes later, he turned the car through the gates of the Aerodrome and ran her straight into the vast hangar of the aviation company, opening the door so that John might step out under the enormous wing of an Avro Ten.

Keenly he watched the boy's face and found there his reward. This was veritably wonderland. White aeroplanes of all sizes rested under the high span of the roof. Some stood, like birds resting, with their wings folded back. Others were being washed down, as it were lovingly, by women in white jackets and trousers. Two young mechanics, on ladders, were bent studiously over the engine of a small machine that had been wheeled into the light from one of the great doors. By the door at the other end of the hangar a squad was busy about a shining Dragon.

John had to see everything and was endlessly and surprisingly anxious about details: and Leslie was mildly astonished to realise how much of the new technique the child of the age could take for granted. He could himself remember the first of the motor cars, and here was an infant recognising easily, from his books, recondite types of plane—a Fox here, a Puss there, and some private person's ancient Spad in a corner.

They were very happy together, and Leslie's happiness was twofold. It was not only that John's absorption was complete and a reward for many of life's pains; he loved himself these white birds of the air, the shapeliness of them, their pertness, their efficiency. Something fundamental in him was satisfied by the knowledge that not one of them could take the air unless its condition was perfect. He gloried in the thought—it was almost a feeling—of engines beautifully tuned, wires taut and controls adjusted to a hairbreadth. It was the stuff of his personal poetry.

The ground engineer superintending the squad by the Dragon hailed him cheerfully in bright Cockney.

"Afternoon, Mr. Pagan."

"Afternoon, Bill. What's wrong with the Dragon?"

"Overhaul. Tuning up now. This your boy? Here, Joe,"—he called to a lad working in the cabin of the machine, "lift up the kid 'ere and show him the works."

So John was cheerfully hoisted into the plane, and Leslie smiled to think of the boyishness of all who have to do with the air.

"Is she going out on test by any chance?" he asked Bill on a sudden impulse.

"Soon's we're ready. Jimmy Herring's taking her."

"I'll pay for two passages. John,"—he called through the door to the boy, proud in the pilot's seat—"like to go up for a spin?"

"O-o-oh, daddy!" came a strained voice.

"That's all right, Bill," said Leslie. "I'll see the people in the office."

Recklessness had him in charge. Something at the back of his mind said that he should not do this thing, that it was somehow unfair to Blanche, but he could not stop now. He ached to give pleasure to John, his own son, for the afternoon; he wanted to liberate himself in this fantastic way. The late autumn sun was shining bright. There would be escape up there above the earth. There was nothing in it. . . .

The inevitable wait for the machine to be ready was galling. At once he completely approved and despised the long tests of the roaring engines. The mechanics seemed fools as they hopped about, doing odd finicking jobs at the last moment. "Get up! Get up!" he wanted to cry. "Put her nose in the air!"

They got off at last. A slow, bumping run to the far end of the long field and a turn into the wind; a pause there to spin the motors once again; then the power went on, and she began to race over the ground. The turf streaked past. More power, more noise. Jimmy was giving her the gun. She rose. The streaking turf was below now. There came the queer feeling of being suspended at the end of an unbreakable rope of elastic. Up and up and up. Sometimes she shuddered, sagged, seemed to stumble. Now the earth was absurdly tilted towards the sky, and in momentary confusion Leslie

49

looked to plot his universe by the block of buildings at the end of the 'drome. He saw Jimmy Herring wave a reassuring hand to John, and saw John wave back like any brother in arms.

John was all right, not a trace of apprehension about him. Leslie saw his intelligent young eyes now on the revolving petrol-gauges, then on the air-speed indicator. Nothing wrong with John: to this he had been born.

The plane steadied at last on her course some two thousand feet above Clydeside, and all that crowded realm lay below for all the world as if a child had laid it out on the nursery floor. Insects crawled along narrow ribbons, cars on the innumerable, quaintly intersecting roads. Houses were mere comic blocks set in silly rows; the bunkers of a golf-course were rosy pock-marks on diseased skin. The great River itself had narrowed to a strip of lead and in Leslie's brooding eyes the gantries over the empty berths of the shipyards lining the banks from Dumbarton up to Glasgow seemed at once frivolous, pretentious, and pathetic.

The scene opened up as the machine sped westwards towards the Tail of the Bank. He could see in the enclosures of the Gareloch and the Holy Loch, small black marks on their silver surfaces, scores of ships laid-up, out of commission, paralysed. He saw with interest that two tramp steamers were a-building in Port Glasgow, but they stood out like monuments in the long range of silent yards. There was a C.P.R. liner at anchor off Greenock; over all the wide expanse of the Firth he could see otherwise only a lighter puffing its pigmy way past the Cloch and a river-steamer crossing from Rothesay to Wemyss Bay.

But though it seemed as if the stagnation of the Clyde were being paraded by arrangement before his eyes, Leslie no longer felt the oppression of that consciousness upon him. The splendid frieze of the Cowal hills, the winter sunshine on them, held him with delight. There ahead were all the islands, green, water-studded Bute, the red and emerald of the Greater and the black of the Lesser Cumbrae, with Arran's peaks majestic in purple beyond. His eyes delighted in the silver filagree of lochs and kyles, and he exulted, a man escaping from an ominous shadow behind, in the easy rush of the plane through the sunshot air, in the creaming line of seawater round the horns of a remote and sandy bay, and in the rapture of John in the seat before him, his grave eyes on the swinging petrol gauges.

They were above the steeples and red sandstone of Largs when he became aware that Jimmy Herring was seeking to attract his attention. Contriving to get head and shoulders into the pilot's tiny cockpit he heard the shout:

"Had enough? She's going like a clock."

"Right, Jimmy!" he cried above the roar of the engines. "Home now."

And they headed inland then, the wings banking in the sweet poetry of a turn, passed over empty, brown moors, and in a few minutes were above the sprawl of Paisley again and circling down upon the landing-field.

As the machine bumped to rest before the hangar, Leslie got up and swung his son to earth with a happy flourish.

"And how was that, Johnny boy?" he asked eagerly.

"Oh, daddy?" he got his reward. "It was lovely, lovely!"

Then he coughed, a series of little dry barks, and Leslie, regarding him with sudden intensity, seemed to see him shiver.

"Are you cold, son?" he asked sharply.

"No. Only just a teeny little," the child confessed.

"Come along. Run for the car. You've got to get home, quick."

Twice on the road home John coughed, two brief spasms of that hard, small barking, and Leslie's heart was in his mouth. He ought to have seen to the boy's complete comfort. He ought to have remembered his disposition towards these sudden attacks on the chest. The shadow of a reckoning with Blanche closed down upon him.

"I've got to go back to the office, dear," he explained as they came over on the ferry, "but Burns will drive you straight home. Promise me to tell Nannie to give you a hot bath at once and a great big tea afterwards. Promise."

"Yes, daddy," said John obediently. Then: "Daddy!"

"Yes, John?"

"Does Jimmy Herring's aeroplane carry water to keep the engine cool?"

It was seven o'clock before Leslie followed his son home. Blanche was alone in the lounge, apparently absorbed in the evening paper. She did not rise to greet him. She took his kiss almost mechanically, and guiltily he knew that the Thing had obtruded between them. She began coolly.

"You did not tell me that you were taking John up in a plane?"

"I didn't know myself until it occurred to me," he answered, laughing uneasily. "Sort of sudden inspiration. He liked it."

"And as a result," she continued relentlessly, "he's got another cold. He's got a temperature. He's coughing. I do think you might consult me about that sort of thing."

He thought of her at Turnberry, of John left alone with that hard English girl, and he wanted to fling the thought back, like a missile, in her withdrawn face. But the power of one unspoken word, the dreadful word pneumonia that they never exchanged but was always in their thoughts when John went down with one of his colds, thrust that meanness from his mind.

"I'm sorry, Blanche," he said, "ever so sorry. Can I see him?"

3

Leslie wakened on the Friday morning to see the fog down over Kelvinside. Shivering at the bedroom window, he could see only the tree-tops on the other side of the drive, ghostly scrolls of guarded boughs floating in the dank sea of mist. There was evidently little moving along the Great Western Road, for only once did he hear the clangour of a tramway bell; then a muffled rumble and silence. Far down the River a big ship's siren boomed dolefully. The clatter of a milkboy's cans seemed to come from another world.

It was oppressive. Even at that early hour of the morning he felt that something evil portended, and he stood long at the window, held there by the paralysis of realising that indeed it was for him perhaps the worst day of all his life—John lying ill in the nursery along the passage—Pagan's closing down. John ill especially—he ached to know what sort of night the child had passed. Was Blanche still asleep?

"Getting up soon, dear?" he whispered hopefully through the twilight of the room.

"Just coming," her voice came clear. "And don't stand there

shivering. Go and have your bath."

He went willingly, strangely relieved to feel that the house was alive once more, that the slow, negative interregnum of the night was over, and that they could not keep him long now from news of John. He was quick to get through with the business of shaving and bathing, listening all the time for the sound of the nursery door opening to Blanche. When she came out again, he was quick to follow her back to their room.

"How is he?"

"A little better, I think." His heart leapt. "Nannie says he's not been coughing nearly so much. And I think he's not so fevered as he was. But we'll see when the doctor comes."

"Oh, good! I hope he comes early."

He could not bring himself to go to the Yard after breakfast, and to placate his conscience he fell back on all sorts of pretexts—the fog, the imminence of stagnation at Pagan's, the illusion of making by phone an appointment with his solicitor. He was uneasy enough to know that Blanche's eye was upon him, but he was grateful to her for making no comment as he mooned from room to room, took up the morning paper and dropped it again, or changed the roll on the barograph. And would that old devil of a doctor never come? He allowed himself a passionate grievance against the members of that profession, choosing their own time, keeping heart-broken people in suspense.

It was after midday before the doctor did come, and then to pass an exasperatingly cheerful word and disappear into the forbidden territory of the nursery. Leslie, however, forgot and forgave everything when he came out again, beaming, and sat down to a cigarette and a glass of sherry in the lounge.

"Yes, Mr. Pagan, John should be all right now," as if the recovery were a product of his own unique wisdom. "The temperature's down. He's easier all over. Another week, and he'll be up again. Your good health! A very pleasant sherry, if I may say so. Poor John and that chest of his! Do take care of him in this beastly climate, Mrs. Pagan. It's sunlight and warmth he needs, that boy."

There it was again—that stab of the sharp, secret issue between him and Blanche. He was careful not to look at her. But John was well again. The spectre of the great fear had receded into the shadows. The burden of guilt had been lifted off his shoulders. Dear, dear John was well again. He would see him soon. And did every parent have to know this agony of love?

The fog had lifted somewhat after lunch. The absurd Victorian turrets of the large villa across the road began to loom through the haze, and there was a hint of iridescence from the sun on the woolly peaks of the mist-layer towards Anniesland. Fog or no fog, however, Leslie knew that he could not longer delay his approach to the day's last dreadful emergency and could not, whatever the circumstances, hesitate before the sombre duty. John was well again, out of the dark glen of danger, but the personal relief could not lighten the load of responsibility. He must hurry down the road to see it through. And how, he wondered moodily as he drove cautiously through the fog at Anniesland Cross, would the world seem with the gates of Pagan's closed?

It was queer to be back in the office when already in his mind he had said farewell to it. It gave a man the feeling of being an actor in a play. There was all that unreality about the fashion in which Miss Macgregor drew his attention to some items in the morning's correspondence. The letters, and all the responsibility bound up with them, seemed irrelevant now. Dakers could deal with them. Dakers would love dealing with them. Leslie told Miss Macgregor to take them to the secretary, but he did not fail to notice her glance, compound of curiosity, surprise, and pity. Deliberately he set himself to study a set of blue-prints that came in for the drawing-office, and, in the technical problems they raised, was lucky enough to lose himself.

His father came about four o'clock, and he took tea with the old man in the boardroom. They had little to say to each other. Behind the assumption of cheerful cynicism Leslie could discern uneasiness. Perhaps it was a discomfort greater than his own. A longer bond than his, after all, was about to be broken. Pagan's closing down. Lord, but it made a man think far beyond the bounds of the personal!

The dusk came down, and yet they did not switch on the lights. It seemed necessary to remain in the tactful gleam of the coal in the great fireplace. Standing by the window, Leslie glanced backwards once to see a figure strangely dramatised, his father in a deep armchair, his head on one hand, his fine, brooding face lit by the glow. From that he turned quickly to gaze sombrely across the misted yard towards the River and to think how queerly the large, inscrutable forces of economics dealt with the lives of men.

His train of thought was interrupted by the voice from the fireside.

"So this is what it comes to?"

"I don't see a way out," answered Leslie emptily.

"Well, it's not the first time in my experience," sighed the voice.

So they remained until it came near five o'clock and Leslie saw, streaming noiselessly towards the gate, the crowds of men who were to lift their last pay as they went out. It was like seeing the passage of a phantom army, and there was a lump in his throat as he watched them: so helpless and patient did they seem, streaming out on to the unfriendly streets that foggy winter night. He was gripped then by the sentiment of the old days of war and remembered the endless files of Scottish men he had seen come and go, rough, cheerful, fatalistic, endlessly and blindly suffering. He remembered how, once in Gallipoli, up by Backhouse Post and momentarily blinded and shocked by a shell-burst, he had groped his way about the trenches, crying: "Boys! Oh, my boys!" since he believed himself to have betrayed and lost his company. And was that suffering worse than this?

He dragged himself from the window at length.

"I must go and see Dakers," he said abruptly.

"Dakers? Ah, yes!" the old man sighed, then rose. "I'll get along myself. We must have a talk one of these days, Leslie. Perhaps Blanche will give me tea. I must see John."

John—yes, Leslie himself wanted to get back to John, whom nothing save the act of God could take from him. For an hour or so he made himself busy about his own room, but at length he had to force himself to go out on to the streets in the wake of the men who had gone out perhaps for ever.

The fog was thickening again, and it was bitter cold. The thought of warmth and company allured him, and he wondered if he might not once again look in to see the boys in O'Glinchey's. The notion was barely in his mind when he dismissed it, as if it were impertinent. No more O'Glinchey's for him. From that innocent condescension he was debarred for ever. The boys were no longer Pagan's boys, his own boys, but individuals now, defensive and possibly hostile. He did not in his mind deny them the right to be so. All he knew was regret and pity as, automatically, he steered the car eastwards through a shrouded world.

There was nobody in the lounge at home. A maid told him that his father was gone, and that Blanche had run into town to do some shopping for Master John, who was asleep. He found that the evening paper did not interest him, not even a column of rumours about the giant Cunarder, symbol of the Clyde's stagnation, an unfinished shell on the stocks at Clydebank. He let the paper drop to the floor and closed his eyes to think. There was such a lot to think about.

He stirred to the touch of lips on his cheek and the feel of soft fingers running through his hair. There was a perfume about him. Blanche. He must have been asleep.

"Hullo, old man!" her voice, now very tender, greeted him. "Very weary?"

She was on her knees before him, smiling bewitchingly into his face.

"Sweetheart!" And he drew her face to his and kissed her. "So sorry!"

"My dearest!" she murmured. "There's just no need to be sorry. You're tired out. I'm tired, poor old John's tired. And it's a miserable world tonight with the fog and the cold. Oh, can't we all go away for a holiday!"

He smiled at her, his awareness of her small strategem blending not unhappily with his affection.

"Rascal!" he twitted her, tapping her cheek with his finger.

"But you mustn't misunderstand me, old boy!" she protested. "There's John—we must give him a chance to get well. You heard what the doctor said. And you're just wearied out yourself, my own dear. Oh, do let's go for a month—down to Cuckton, the Riviera, Italy, anywhere! I know daddy will love to have us for Christmas. And I do so want to buy some pretties in London."

He laughed then.

"I wish I could think why not!" he answered her. "God knows I could do with a rest for a bit."

CHAPTER FOUR

SATURDAY IN GLASGOW

IT took him a long time to make up his mind. Habit and impulse fought endlessly against caution and sympathy. But Danny Shields did not in the end go to O'Glinchey's that night of the big pay-off at Pagan's.

He had stood enough chaff and seen and heard plenty of sneers that afternoon. There was more chaff than sneers: he would say that for the boys. Many of his old mates, jesting in the face of calamity, had found it possible to invent rough artisans' pleasantries.

"Hear ye're being kept on to finish the Cunarder at Clydebank, Danny."

"Hey, Danny! Will ye be good for a sub next Friday?"

Or, "Another bar to your medal—eh, Dan?"

There were others, however, especially among the younger men, who took the trouble to make him feel ashamed and angry.

"Here's the boss's fancy man!" they would cry at his approach, and laugh sardonically.

"G'on, ye lousy wee sucker!" one man said angrily as they collided in a dark alleyway of the *Estramadura*.

He was actually squaring up to fight Cocky Magee when the gaffer came along and sent them about their work.

No: he was a marked man one way or another, and he would give O'Glinchey's the go-by, much as it hurt him to miss the usual yarn and drinks of good fellowship with Jimmy Affleck and long Jock Macgrory. This was something to tell Agnes, anyhow—kept on while scores of others were put on the street. It was only a damned good man that was kept on nowadays. That was something there was no denying. He began to feel there was a virtue in cutting out O'Glinchey's as the red tram bore him eastwards. Wasting money: that's what it came to when you looked at it the right way. These were hard times, and after what had happened that afternoon at Pagan's a chap had to think twice about things.

Somehow it did not clash with this philosophy to get off the tram at Partick Cross and make direct for the Horseshoe. There was the sixpence to be paid up for the accumulator, and a wee half and a half-pint wouldn't go far wrong; then home to a quiet evening with the coupon for tomorrow's games.

The bar was busy on that evening of pay-day, but Tommy the charge-hand was quickly forward to take his order.

"Hear there's been a big pay-off doon bye, Danny?" he eagerly enquired.

"That's right," Danny was proud to reply. "Coupla hundred men, mebbe."

"Jesus!" said the barman. "That's a ruddy knockout, eh? Is it a' right wi' you?"

"Sure!" replied Danny gallantly, then lowered his voice to a confidential mutter. "Me and the boss gets on fine, see." And he winked.

"Is that so?" queried Tommy, handing over a creaming glass.

"I was his batman, see. Gallipoli, Egypt, Palestine, France. Four sucking years of it. The boss is standin' by me, see."

"You've clicked right enough," said the barman, impressed.

"Sure," observed Danny again, "and knobs on."

At that point, in the glow of his pride, he saw that another half and half-pint would be within the bounds of moderation, and as he ordered it, a friendly voice spoke over his shoulders.

"Heard ye saying ye was in Egypt and Palestine, Mac?"

"By God and I was!" cried Danny defiantly.

"Same here," said the voice.

It belonged to a tallish man with a sandy, thin, humorous face. He had the look of the out-of-work upon him; his clothes neat but worn, his tweed cap stained, his mouth pinched.

"What was your mob, son?" asked Danny.

"Sappers. 'Member the pipe line?"

"Pipe line!" Danny addressed the Gods. "Holy crivvens, I nearly broke my flakin' back on yer pipe line! Workin' parties—Jesus!"

"I remember," the stranger chuckled. "Sweating in thon heat!"

"And thon camels!" Danny capped him. "*Imshi! Ee-e-ch!* Remember the bastards? Gave ye a dose if they bit ye."

"Remember!"

"Were ye there the night the Ak-an'-Esses-Aitch, the Greenock mob, pinched the rum at El Maadan?"

"Aye—the dirty sooners." The stranger drained his glass of beer.

"Here, mate, what are you having?" Danny insisted. "Half-pint, my foot! Tommy—hey, Tommy! Two halfs and two half-pints. Crivvens, boy, it's great to see one of the old crush! Remember the train from Alex. *Toot-toot! Sidi Gabr?*"

The old comrades laughed uproariously at that sweet, redolent memory of the brave days; so loudly that the barman looked at Danny and shook a warning head. But Danny was beyond such a meanness of discipline now. He was living again, a soldier, a man, one of the right sort beside him to understand the loveliness of their monstrous liberation.

"Ach, they don't know what it was, these young toots!" cried Danny, contemptuous of a softer generation.

"Holy God!" said the stranger. "I'd like to see them up to their backsides in cold mud somewhere outside Eeeper thonder."

"Aye, Eeeper," Danny agreed. "Somewhere near thon pill-boxes about Steenbeck. But here's a funny thing—" he went off at a tangent sentimentally. "D'ye know this? D'ye know that the birth of my nephew—Willie, that's the oldest—was posted up in Eeeper? Right in the main square thonder, in battalion orders. 'To the wife of No. 59341 Lance-Corporal Shields'—that's my brother—'a son.' Right in the bloody main square! Eh?"

"Is that a fact?" His friend was properly impressed, but was not prepared to allow Danny to luxuriate in the reminiscence. "Reminds me of a mate of mines," he said, "Alf Barrett, a Cockney block in our mob. His wife was away the trip when he sailed for Alex., and when we got to Malta—"

"A great place Malta," Danny interjected.

"Aye, but listen to this. This block, Alf Barrett—a right Cockney he was. . . ."

They were off, afloat on the wide and turbulent stream of reminiscence that flows when two old soldiers are gathered together. On its breast they drifted back through time to the land of youth, back out of isolation and the misunderstanding of the laity to the places that were scarred and outraged by war but ever dear

59

for their redolence of youth and danger and comradeship, back from the slavery of the commonplace to the freedom of the prime. They ranged large areas of the world's surface, these two—much of the Scotland and England of the training camps, the licentious London of leave, the Mediterranean littoral, the Holy Land, France and Flanders. They brought in relations and friends to widen their scope, the stranger a brother in Mesopotamia, and Danny a friend with the Navy. They were elaborate in creating the atmosphere of every anecdote. They lost each other often while a tale domestic to the narrator's unit followed a tortuous trail. Latterly they were not listening to each other at all, but merely dipping the bucket into the well of memory in a glory of competition.

From this jumble of cross-currents they returned at length to mutual awareness over an issue concerning the conduct and progress of the Second Battle of Gaza.

It was Danny who held the field at the moment. In spilt beer on the counter he had drawn with his forefinger a plan of the operations as he conceived them to have shaped and was demonstrating his own unit's unique part in them with the eager exactness of a pedagogue.

"See here now," he begged his companion's concentrated attention. "We were lying there—" and he laid a finger in a canal of beer athwart the counter. "The Ack-an'-Esses-Aitch was *there*. An' the 6th H.L.I. was *there* in reserve. See?"

"They was not," said his friend with surprising decision. "The 6th was in the line on the right. It was the 7th was in reserve."

"It was not," said Danny firmly. "It was the 6th. Christ, I was there myself, wasn't I?"

"Christ, and so was I! I'm tellin' ye, mate, it was the Seventh in reserve. See? The *Seventh*."

"And I'm tellin' ye it was the *Sixth*."

Their voices started to rise, and the barman cautioned them with a quiet word. They quite ignored him.

"It was *nut*," the stranger asserted.

"But it was *sut*," cried Danny angrily.

"I suppose you were the only bloody soldier in the battle," the other sneered.

"Aye, a soldier," Danny snorted, "not a bloody sapper."

The bond between them snapped. The warm ties of blood-brotherhood were split asunder. Now each saw the other as an enemy predestined, as an intolerable claimant to a share of his own unique distinction. Ancient and ineradicable loyalties flamed in their hearts. Neither could bear that the other should think to have made such a contribution of courage and sacrifice as his own to the Cause that was their original bond.

"By God, ye bowly-legged runt," cried the sapper, "I'll knock yer block off!"

"I'll plug ye, ye . . ."

Danny's hands were on the man's lapels to tear off his jacket when he was suddenly and firmly seized from behind. Shouting his anger and defiance, he was rapidly frog-marched to the swing-doors of the shop, pushed rudely through them, and sent staggering across the pavement. Recovering, bent on the destruction of his enemy, he found himself face to face with the barman who stood in the doorway, his hands on his hips, ready.

"Let me get at that twister," shrieked Danny, seeking roughly to push past the white apron.

He got a blow on the chest that sent him staggering again.

"Beat it, now," said the barman firmly, "or I'll call the cop. D'ye hear? Beat it."

There was that in his tone which momentarily snuffed the flame of Danny's anger. The firm mention of the police permitted the detonation within his heated mind of a number of sobering ideas—the fundamental insecurity of his job at the Yard, his obligation to Leslie Pagan, his subscriptions to the accumulator, Wee Mirren, and the absolute necessity that he should see the Rangers-Celtic match at Ibrox next day. His eye caught the white coat of a traffic policeman at the corner. He hesitated.

"Beat it, now," said the barman.

"I'll get that ruddy twister yet," grumbled Danny truculently and turned away.

He had drunk too much, and was aware of the fact, but the knowledge had no power to subdue him. There was a fire in his belly that could only be quenched in combat of some sort: he needed the satisfaction of triumph over the enemies by whom he was beset. Now and again he laughed out loud as he went along, then his mood would turn black at the thought of the unspeakable stupidity, the complete hatefulness, of the man in the Horseshoe. That swine wanted his block knocked off and would get it one of these days. Then he remembered those who had sneered at him in the Yard and again burned to fight.

This mood of independence and pugnacity was not soothed by the sharpness of the greeting Agnes gave him when he entered the kitchen of their home.

"Oh, ye're back, are ye?" she snapped at him. "Boozing, I suppose."

His hands clenched. Too often she tempted him to strike her.

"Ye'd drive any man to it with your nag, nag, nagging."

She evaded his anger. To him it seemed that she did not recognise it or any justification for it.

"Well, remember we're going to the Pictures with Lizzie and Jim. Away and get yourself washed and dressed."

Danny sat down to unlace his boots.

"I'm goin' to no Pictures with Lizzie and Jim," he said. "Lizzie and Jim can go to hell for all I care."

"Aye, I've heard ye at that before," she retorted coolly.

"Lizzie and Jim! I'm fed up hearin' about Lizzie and Jim! He's only a dirty wee bookie."

"But ye'll waste yer night on the coupoons all the same," she said with a justifiable irony that passed, however, over his head.

"I'm damned if I'm going out with Lizzie and Jim, if that's what you want to know," he repeated vehemently.

"Well, you can just stick," she retorted.

2

These asperities were quite forgotten by the morning. They were too much the common currency of their domestic exchange to be remarkable in any event, and it so happened that the Friday evening passed very pleasantly for each of them.

A large tea inside him, including a black pudding of considerable size, Danny achieved peace of mind. The alcoholic anger melted from his consciousness and left him the friendly glow of repletion.

Agnes did not return once to the obsession about Lizzie and Jim and the Pictures. Before the meal was over he was boasting to her of his unique immunity in the matter of the pay-off at Pagan's and she, after her fashion, was complementing him on the distinction and exclaiming at her own luck. Then, when she had gone, Peter stayed behind and assisted in the filling up of the coupon, revealing a particularly helpful knowledge of the form in the South sub-section of the Third Division of the English League; and he stayed in while Danny went out for a final drink at half-past nine. Billy sat like a mouse by the fire, reading, and went to bed when he was told. Wee Mirren slept the evening through and stirred only when her mother returned at the back of eleven, her face flushed.

Agnes, too, had passed an agreeable time. She had seen Ronald Colman on the screen of one of the swell picture houses in Sauchiehall Street, and Jim had risen to balcony seats and ices. He had had his car parked in Holland Street, and after the show, had run them down to the lounge of the Adelphi for a round or two of drinks, in which Agnes's favourite wee ports figured pleasantly, and then had run her home as far as Partick Cross.

"Oh, and Dan!" she blurted out finally. "They're awful keen for us to go out the morn's night. Not to the Pictures, but a wee supper. Jim's got a friend from England coming up, and they want to give him a night out. Could you not come after the match?"

A sudden shadow of resentment clouded Danny's mind. He could not like Lizzie and her husband, and he vaguely distrusted their influence on Agnes. But there was something in her eagerness that melted him, something that his Friday evening complaisance could not resist—and she had by an implication more cunning than he quite appreciated indicated that she would not nag him if he wished to go to the match.

"Ach to hell! I suppose we might as well," said Danny.

If he regretted that desperate affability by breakfast time on Saturday, he did not confess the fact. There was never time for argument in the rush of getting to the Yard by eight o'clock, nor did Agnes ever quite emerge from sleep while he made his own breakfast, gulped it down, and hurried out. And on this great day of the Rangers-Celtic match at Ibrox, Danny was almost incapable of thinking beyond the thrills of the afternoon.

Anticipation of the game was indeed an obsession. An honest, keen workman, he found his labour in the Yard that morning an irritating irrelevance. If he worked hard, it was so that the hour of release might seem to come more quickly. Unhappily for him, his position as one who was there by favour, as a riveter for whom no task of riveting remained, was uneasy.

"I suppose I'll have to make work for you," the foreman sneered. "A riveter's no damned use to me. Och, go and give old Tom a hand in the Store there. We'll see on Monday. . . ."

The man went off grumbling, and Danny was left with a double burden. He knew there was nothing for him to do in the Store that would keep him decently occupied; and the weakness of his supernumerary position had been emphasised. He greatly feared that particular foreman and his prejudices. What if the Major should forget the promise? A blue lookout indeed, and a nice come-down from the triumphs of yesterday!

These anxieties he quickly forgot in friendly chat with brosy old Tom, who had himself not sufficient work to keep him going, and his heart leaped when the foreman popped his head over the half-door of the store about eleven and called on Danny to run across to the engine-shop with a message to the foreman there. For this meant a licensed escape from the yard at a vital hour, and Danny had just remembered his need of something necessary to his enjoyment of the afternoon.

In their wisdom, the Magistrates of that part of the world in which Pagan's was situated had long ordained that public-houses should open at ten and close at noon on Saturdays. The ordinance was based on the theory that the working-man should not be tempted to squander his wages on strong drink on his way home, and had no doubt a bearing on public behaviour at the afternoon football games; but as the artisan had for many a day past been paid on Fridays it was only an interesting anachronism of local administration and bore hardly on such as Danny who desired refreshment in anticipation of other enjoyments. So the foreman's gruff order rejoiced him. It was easy to slip into Mackenzie's, between Yard and engine-shop, swallow a quick half and half-pint, buy a flat half-mutchkin of whisky for the pocket and the cold vigil on the terraces, and time his return to the Store almost as the whistle boomed the signal for the weekend release.

Thereafter there was nothing in the world for him but the Game. He hurried home, hurried through his washing and changing and eating, and, as if all the claims of family and hearth were nothing now, was out on the streets again half an hour before two o'clock, a unit of one of the streams of men converging from all parts of the city and from all its outliers on the drab embankments round an oblong of turf in Ibrox.

The surge of the stream was already apparent in the Dumbarton Road. Even though only a few wore favours of the Rangers blue, there was that of purpose in the air of hurrying groups of men which infallibly indicated their intention. It was almost as if they had put on uniform for the occasion, for most were attired as Danny was in decent dark suits under rainproofs or overcoats, with great flat caps of light tweed on their heads. Most of them smoked cigarettes that shivered in the corners of their mouths as they fiercely debated the prospects of the day. Hardly one of them but had his hands deep in his pockets.

The scattered procession, as it were of an order almost religious, poured itself through the mean entrance to the Subway station at Partick Cross. The decrepit turnstiles clattered endlessly, and there was much rough, good-humoured jostling as the devotees bounded down the wooden stairs to struggle for advantageous positions on the crowded platform. Glasgow's subway system is of high anti-quarian interest and smells very strangely of age. Its endless cables, whirling innocently over the pulleys, are at once absurd and fascinating, its signalling system a matter for the laughter of a later generation. But to Danny and the hundreds milling about him there was no strange spectacle here: only a means of approach to a shrine; and strongly they pushed and wrestled when at length a short train of toylike dimensions rattled out of the tunnel into the station.

It seemed full to suffocation already, but Danny, being alone and ruthless in his use of elbow and shoulder, contrived somehow to squeeze through a narrow doorway on to a crowded platform. Others pressed in behind him while official whistles skirled hope-lessly without, and before the urgent crowd was forced back at last and the doors laboriously closed, he was packed tight among taller

65

men of his kind, his arms pinned to his sides, his lungs so compressed that he gasped.

"For the love o' Mike. . . ." he pleaded.

"Have ye no' heard there's a fitba' match the day, wee man?" asked a tall humorist beside him.

Everybody laughed at that. For them there was nothing odd or notably objectionable in their dangerous discomfort. It was, at the worst, a purgatorial episode on the passage to Elysium.

So they passed under the River to be emptied in their hundreds among the red sandstone tenements of the South Side. Under the high banks of the Park a score of streams met and mingled, the streams that had come by train or tram or motor car or on foot to see the Game of Games.

Danny ran for it as soon as his feet were on earth's surface again, selecting in an experienced glance the turnstile with the shortest queue before it, ignoring quite the mournful column that waited without hope at the Unemployed Gate. His belly pushed the bar precisely as his shilling smacked on the iron counter. A moment later he was tearing as if for dear life up the long flight of cindered steps leading to the top of the embankment.

He achieved his favourite position without difficulty: high on one of the topmost terraces and behind the eastern goal. Already the huge amphitheatre seemed well filled. Except where the monstrous stands broke the skyline there were cliffs of human faces, for all the world like banks of gravel, with thin clouds of tobacco smoke drifting across them. But Danny knew that thousands were still to come to pack the terraces to the point of suffocation, and, with no eyes for the sombre strangeness of the spectacle, he proceeded to establish himself by setting his arms firmly along the iron bar before him and making friendly, or at least argumentative, contact with his neighbours.

He was among enthusiasts of his own persuasion. In consonance with ancient custom the police had shepherded supporters of the Rangers to one end of the ground and supporters of the Celtic to the other: so far as segregation was possible with such a great mob of human beings. For this game between Glasgow's two leading teams had more in it than the simple test of relative skill. Their colours, blue and green, were symbolic. Behind the rivalry of players, behind even the commercial rivalry of limited companies, was the dark significance of sectarian and racial passions. Blue for the Protestants of Scotland and Ulster, green for the Roman Catholics of the Free State; and it was a bitter war that was to be waged on that strip of white-barred turf. All the social problems of a hybrid city were to be sublimated in the imminent clash of mercenaries.

Danny was as ready as the next man to fight a supporter of the other team, but he had no opportunity of doing so. They were solid for Rangers within a radius of twenty yards from where he stood, and time until the kick-off was pleasantly taken up with discussion of the miracles their favourites could perform. They needed no introductions to one another. Expertise was assumed. The anxiety was that the Rangers team, as announced and on form, could be relied on to beat the men from the East. It was taken for granted that the Rangers were in normal circumstances the superiors of the Celts; but here, it seemed, were special circumstances to render the issue of the afternoon's match peculiarly obscure.

Danny had some heartening exchanges with a man, smaller and older and grimmer than himself, who at his elbow smoked a clay pipe with a very short stem. The small man was not prepared to be unduly optimistic. Rangers were a fine bunch of boys, but the Celtic had been playing up great these last few Saturdays.

"It's a' in the melting-pot," declared the small man, who had been reading the newspapers. "I'm tellin' ye—it's a' in the bloody melting-pot."

"Melting-pot, my foot!" Danny insisted gallantly. "It's all in Alan Morton's left toe, out on the wing there. Wait till ye see the wee dandy."

"Alan's fine," the small man allowed gravely. "Alan's a dandy. Alan's the best bloody outside left in fitba' the day. But I've been studying form, see?" He paused to let an attenuated dribble of saliva fall between his feet, and it took him a long time to wipe clean the stem of his short pipe. "I've been studying form. Aye, I've been studying form—reading a' the papers, looking back a' the records, and it's like this. When ye've the Rangers here and the Celtic there and there's no much between them in the League—"

His discourse was interrupted by the irreverent voice of a youth behind. "Does the wife know ye're out, old man?" it asked.

Laughter, half-friendly, half-derisive, rose about them.

"I'll knock your block off, young fella," said the old fellow, turning gravely on the youth and slowly removing the pipe from his wet mouth.

"Please, teacher, I'm sorry I spoke," his tormentor assured him, mock-afraid.

They all laughed again; and so it went on—rough give-and-take, simple wisdom and facetious nonsense, passion and sentiment, hate and friendly laughter—while a brass band pumped out a melody in the lee of the grand-stand and press photographers hovered restlessly in anticipation of the appearance of the teams.

The Celtic came first, strangely attractive in their white and green, and there was a roar from the western end of the ground. ("Hefty-looking lot o' bastards," admitted the small, old man at Danny's side.) They were followed by a party of young men in light blue jerseys; and then it seemed that the low-hanging clouds must split at the impact of the yell that rose to greet them from forty-thousand throats. The referee appeared, jaunty in his shorts and khaki jacket; the linesmen, similarly attired, ran to their positions. In a strange hush, broken only by the thud of footballs kicked by the teams uneasily practising, the captains tossed for ends. Ah! Rangers had won and would play with the sou'westerly wind, straight towards the goal behind which Danny stood in his eagerness.

This was enough to send a man off his head. Good old Rangers—and to hell with the Pope! Danny gripped the iron bar before him. The players trotted limberly to their positions. For a moment there was dead silence over Ibrox Park. Then the whistle blew, a thin, curt, almost feeble announcement of glory.

For nearly two hours thereafter Danny Shields lived far beyond himself in a whirling world of passion. All sorts of racial emotions were released by this clash of athletic young men; the old clans of Scotland lived again their ancient hatreds in this struggle for goals. Not a man on the terraces paused to reflect that it was a spectacle cunningly arranged to draw their shillings, or to remember that the twenty-two players were so many slaves of a commercial system, liable to be bought and sold like fallen women, without any regard for their feelings as men. Rangers had drawn their warriors from all corners of Scotland, lads from mining villages, boys from Ayrshire farms, and even an undergraduate from the University of Glasgow. Celtic likewise had ranged the industrial belt and even crossed to Ulster and the Free State for men fit to win matches so that dividends might accrue. But for such as Danny they remained peerless and fearless warriors, saints of the Blue or the Green as it might be; and in delight in the cunning moves of them, in their tricks and asperities, the men on the terraces found release from the drabness of their own industrial degradation.

That release they expressed in ways extremely violent. They exhorted their favourites to dreadful enterprises of assault and battery. They loudly questioned every decision of the referee. In moments of high tension they raved obscenely, using a language ugly and violent in its wealth of explosive consonants—f's and k's and b's expressing the vehemence of their passions. The young man behind Danny, he who had chaffed his scientific neighbour, was notable in foulness of speech. His commentary on the game was unceasing, and not an observation could he make but one primitive Anglo-Saxon epithet must qualify every noun—and serve, frequently, as a verb. It was as if a fever of hate had seized that multitude, neutralising for the time everything gracious and kindly.

Yet that passionate horde had its wild and liberating humours. Now and again a flash of rough jocularity would release a gust of laughter, so hearty that it was as if they rejoiced to escape from the bondage of their own intensity of partisanship. Once in a while a clever movement by one of the opposition team would evoke a mutter of unwilling but sincere admiration. They were abundantly capable of calling upon their favourites to use their brawn, but they were punctilious in the observation of the unwritten laws that are called those of sportsmanship. They constituted, in fact, a stern but ultimate reliable jury, demanding of their entertainers the very best they could give, insisting that the spectacle be staged with all the vigour that could be brought to it.

The Old Firm—thus the evening papers conventionally described the meeting of Rangers and Celtic. It was a game fought hard and fearless and merciless, and it was but the rub of the business that the wearers of the Blue scored seven minutes from half-time.

The goal was the outcome of a movement so swift that even a critic of Danny's perspicacity could hardly tell just how it happened. What is it to say that a back cleared from near the Rangers' goal; that the ball went on the wind to the nimble feet of Alan Morton on the left wing; that that small but intense performer carried it at lightning speed down the line past this man in green-and-white and then that; that he crossed before the menace of a charging back, the ball soaring in a lovely curve to the waiting centre; and that it went then like a rocket into a corner of the Celtic net, the goalkeeper sprawling in a futile endeavour to stop it?

It was a movement completed almost as soon as it was begun and Danny did not really understand it until he read his evening paper on the way home. But it was a goal, a goal for Rangers, and he went mad for a space.

With those about him he screamed his triumph, waving his cap wildly above his head, taunting most foully those who might be in favour of a team so thoroughly humiliated as the Celtic.

From this orgasm he recovered at length.

"Christ!" he panted. "That was a bobbydazzler."

"Good old Alan!" screeched the young man behind. "Ye've got the suckers bitched!"

"A piece of perfect bloody positioning," gravely observed the scientist on Danny's left.

"Positioning, ma foot!" snorted Danny. "It was just bloomin' good fitba! Will ye have a snifter, old fella?"

So they shared the half-mutchkin of raw whisky, the small man politely wiping the neck of the bottle with his sleeve before handing it back to Danny.

"That's a good dram, son," he observed judicially.

Half-time permitted of discussion that was not, however, without its heat, the young man behind exploiting a critical theory of half-back play that kept some thirty men about him in violent controversy until the whistle blew again. Then the fever came back on them with redoubled fury. One—nothing for Rangers at half-time made an almost agonising situation; and as the Celtic battled to equalise, breaking themselves again and again on a defence grimly determined to hold its advantage, the waves of green hurling themselves on rocks of blue, there was frenzy on the terraces.

When, five minutes before time, the men from the East were awarded a penalty kick, Danny's heart stopped beating for a space, and when the fouled forward sent the ball flying foolishly over the net, it nearly burst. The Rangers would win. "Stick it, lads!" he yelled again and again. "Kick the tripes out the dirty Papists!" The Rangers would win. They must win. . . . A spirt of whistle; and, by God, they had won!

In immediate, swift reaction, Danny turned then and, without a word to his neighbours, started to fight his way to the top of the terracing and along the fence that crowned it to the stairs and the open gate. To the feelings of those he jostled and pushed he gave not the slightest thought. Now the battle was for a place in the Subway, and he ran as soon as he could, hurtling down the road, into the odorous maw of Copland Road station and through the closing door of a train that had already started on its journey northwards.

He even got a seat and was glad of it. Now he felt tired and flat after that long stand on a step of beaten cinders and nearly two hours of extreme emotional strain. It had been a hell of an afternoon, right enough! At Partick Cross he paused only to buy an evening paper before darting into the public-house nearest at hand. It was disappointing that the barman already knew the result, thanks to the daily miracle of the Press, and he saw in a glance at the stop-press that his coupon was burst again—Queen's Park down to St. Mirren at home, the bunch of stiffs! But the accumulator looked good, his team having nine goals to their credit in two matches and a 2—1 victory as like as possible next Saturday. And there was the glory of telling with authority how Rangers, those shining heroes, had won at Ibrox that very afternoon.

Danny was happy and in his contentment thought kindly of Agnes at home. There remained in his mind the substance of his promise to her, and he did not linger unduly over his glass and pint. She too would welcome his news of victory, and he hurried home to tell her.

"My, that's fine, Dan!" she triumphed with him. "It must have

71

been great. But I've left your good clothes ben in the room, and ye'd best go and change now. We're to be at the Commodore at six."

3

He realised soon enough that his enthusiasm for the outing was very much a product of self-deception.

To begin with, the donning of his good clothes did not square with his conception of an evening's enjoyment, for he hated both their stiffness and their associations. That blue serge suit, that cold, white shirt with stiff cuffs and collar—they were fine for a funeral or a marriage when a degree of formality was to be allowed and life a penance for the time being. It was for Danny, however, a strange and vaguely inimical world that Agnes was drawing him into with its notions that you had to be rigged up like a toff and haltered like an animal before you could begin having a bit of fun.

A grievance worked within him as he dressed. He cursed the linen collar and would gladly have torn its buttonhole if he could. It was the only one he had, and his longing concentrated on the soft one he knew to be in the drawer.

And of course Agnes was not nearly ready when he re-entered the kitchen, hot from the struggle. She was still in her petticoat and was very intent before the mirror at the sink with powder and a pencil for her eyebrows.

"For God's sake!" he upbraided her meekly enough. "I suppose ye're going to keep me late?"

"What's yer hurry?" she retorted coolly. "There's plenty of time."

Was that not a woman all over? Chivvying him in to change and now herself indulging in a selfish deliberation. Well, there was always the paper to read; but he got no great joy that evening from it. It was not a Sports Final, and the reports were sketchy surveys of first-halves only. With some interest he read a news story of an order booked by Scott's of Greenock for a tanker—but the point was: when would Agnes get a move on? There was a fuss with the dress after she had slipped it over her head. Then it seemed that her hair called for extremely solicitous attention. Then, to his dismay, she put on an apron and started to attend to Wee Mirren.

"For the love o' Mike . . ." he appealed to her.

"Ach, shut yer face and let me get on," she snapped at him.

She was late, of course. It was five to six before she stood ready, her bag under the arm of a brown coat with fur collar and cuffs. And then she said: "Are ye never coming?"

"Ready," he answered. "On you go."

Moving warily behind her, he lifted from the peg on the door the cloth cap he had worn at the football match and pulled it down over his forehead, but she was waiting for him on the landing.

"Aye, I just thought it," she said, snatching the thing from his head. "Ye'll go back and hang that where ye got it, and ye'll put on yer hard hat, see?"

Grumbling, but meekly, he obeyed. There was no escape. The bowler of formality lay where she had left it out for him on Billy's bed, and he had to put it on.

"Come on, then," she said purposefully when he rejoined her.

Anybody who saw them pass up the street towards the tram stop in the Dumbarton Road must have recognised in them a couple bent on an unusual adventure. Poor Danny marched self-consciously, for all the world like a seaman ashore for the first time in a year, extremely uncomfortable in his hard hat and stiff collar. About Agnes there was an air of bustling, fussing eagerness, and she hurried along somewhat awkwardly in the high-heeled shoes of patent leather she had bought for the occasion. Little passed between them, for they could not comfortably discuss the evening's prospects and they were aware in their hearts that their fellow-travellers in a crowded tram would stare should any chance remark establish an association between their good clothes and an unusual sort of night out. It was necessary to appear composed and at ease. Producing his black pipe with its metal cover on the top-deck of the tram, Danny was reminded by a sharp dig of Agnes's elbow that he must again forget the habits of a lifetime. So he smoked a cigarette out of a packet he had bought to grace the occasion, handling it clumsily, almost as if it were distasteful.

The sobbing of violin-strings welcomed them into the Commodore. His sensibilities defensively acute, Danny noticed also an acrid charge of perfumed disinfectant in the air and what seemed to him an excessive number of men in uniform or evening-dress under the dome of the reception hall. At once he felt an alien in this atmosphere of elegance, which was much more artificial than he knew, and was immediately conscious of his dress, of his gawkiness, and of the sharp, excited pleasure that Agnes took in being in it. As he followed her past the shining desks and lighted kiosks and among the pillars of bogus marble, a deep resentment, compound of the senses of betrayal and presumption, and an attitude of defiance shaped themselves in his mind.

The great lounge of the place was packed, each table held by a cohort of lower middle-class Glasgow folk rejoicing in the release into metropolitanism provided by the Jewish management of the Commodore through the medium of cocktails and music at moderate rates. Danny was bemused by the spectacle and the shimmer of festival sound, but to Agnes it all seemed delightfully familiar.

"There's Lizzie and Jim!" she belled suddenly, catching him in the ribs with her elbow. "Come on."

Rapidly she threaded her way among the tables, Danny at her heels, his heavy boots clattering on the spaces of parquet floor between the rugs. He saw the robustly welcoming figure of his brother-in-law rise from behind a table near the orchestra.

"Come away! Come away, the two of you!" cried Jim heartily. "We thought you had got lost. Agnes, Danny—meet my friend, Mr. Leake, from London."

"And call me Alf," said Mr. Leake agreeably.

"And ye'll have a drink," Jim went on rapidly. "Waiter! Waiter!" His fat, arrogant hand pounded the knob of the bell on the table. "Where's that bloody man got to?"

Danny was silent in the face of this tornado of hospitality and of the febrile garrulity of the women folk. Something told him that this was an atmosphere unfavourable to the ordering of a half-pint with the whisky he craved, so he contented himself with a modest request for "a wee one," only to hear his modesty derided by Jim and to be assured violently that he could either have a big one or go to hell.

That was the new Jim: the Jim he did not understand and uneasily suspected. The old Jim of five years before had been a decent, quiet-living chap, foreman vanman in the Govan Dairies, but he had strangely changed. That fortunate little investment in the Dogs had recouped him at the rate of three hundred per cent per annum, and now there was a new Jim, who, as Agnes enviously and proudly phrased it, had done so well for himself, with his queer, ambiguous interests in bookmaking, the films, boxing and, indeed, all those activities that, catering for an uneasy generation, shelter and sustain in affluence so many latter-day pimps.

This Mr. Leake, this Alf, was also of the breed, as Danny realised very quickly. He wore a very natty suit in dark grey and pointed shoes of patent leather, and a heavy perfume of pomade hung about him. He was tall and dark, and his manner to the ladies was an exquisite blend of deference and patronage. Agnes positively flowered in the easy warmth of his addresses and, jealously aware of her silliness, Danny unconsciously erected another barrier of dislike against the man, who, if he was not a Yid, was at all events an Englishman and, as such, suspect in the eyes of any decent man. It was dirty, he thought, the way he kept pressing Agnes to have still another wee port.

Three rounds of drinks—two on Jim and one on Alf—had cheered them before they went to eat. Danny was well aware that he had a little more than enough, but he was secure in his conscious aloofness from his companions. Rooted in suspicion and disapproval, he saw himself taking part in a silly game. The clatter of the lounge was distracting, the task of picking his way among the tables confusing, but he was determined not to surrender his integrity to this cabal of two fancy men with more money than they knew what to do with and two women reduced to giggling nonentity by port wine and the allure of easy money. He would stick it. Jim was generous, and Agnes was happy. But that this was his idea of a night out, or that he approved this way of carrying on, he would never admit.

The silence imposed by this frame of mind made him a dull figure at the dinner table, and what seemed a bevy of stiff-shirted waiters and a menu in French were only coals for the fires of his resentment. Jim, however, was in command, and Danny was morosely content that he should be so.

"I'll order yer dinner," cried Jim. Dinner at seven o'clock at night! "I'll keep ye right. Here, Francie!" he beckoned the chief waiter. "Francie and me's old pals. Eh, Francie! Aye, well, look here. We're havin' horse doover. Five, that's right. Then we're havin' chicken—done in thon pot affair wi' bets of veg: ye know the stuff. I forget its bloody name. Then we'll have. . . . Well, I'll tell ye later what we'll have. Run you away an' get the horse doover. And send me that guy wi' the wine list."

Jim's intromissions with that document were extremely direct.

"Where's yer champagnes?" he demanded to know. "A drop of bubbly, girls, eh? How's that with you, Alf? Good! Here Antonio," he addressed the wine waiter. "What's yer best? This. . . . Well, go and get a magnum of it and look slippy. We're mebbe from Greenock, but we're dry."

It seemed that Agnes and Lizzie could do nothing but laugh—laugh and admire the large knowingness of Jim and the wit of him. The tradition of their sort dictated a pretence of horror of his extravagance, but it was a delighted, admiring horror. They had surrendered. Individuality departed from them. The sisters became two pulpy, blonde masses of exclusively biological interest.

It was not merely his prejudice that made Danny dislike the meal. The *hors d'œuvres* seemed to him but arbitrary pickings from among a collection of left-overs. In the lottery of the waiter's dives into the casserole he was unlucky enough to get but a wing of chicken and an ambiguous cross-section of its rump, and a generous helping of small vegetables and gravy did not conceal the inadequacy of the portion from a man accustomed to have something like a pound of solid meat, five or six slices of bread and butter, about a quarter of a pound of cheese, and at least five cups of good strong tea for his evening meal. The champagne tingled feebly on his palate. That it was a high-class drink he knew, and the knowledge gave him a certain satisfaction, but in his heart he knew it to be a poor wersh beverage, wholly lacking in the thick and odorous satisfactions of honest whisky.

Towards the end of the meal, highly decorative ices having followed the chicken though Danny had hoped for a lump of decent Cheddar, Jim was insistent that they should drink more.

"A wee likewer, Aggie? That's right. You, Lizzie? Ach, I know about you, Alf. Where's Antonio? Hey, boy! See here, four Starboard Lights. Cream de mong, understand? No speakee English? Away and—Four cream de mong, and put a snap into it. Oh, but you, Dan? Cream de mong? Good for the guts. . . . "

"I'll have a wee whisky," said Danny sombrely.

"That's right, Antonio," repeated Jim blithely. "Four cream de mong and a big Scotch. And put your back into it.

It was at this stage that Danny, for all the sobering influence of his preoccupation, began to lose his grip on the situation. It was as if the transparent walls of a sphere closed in upon him. Through these walls he could hear gusts and peals of laughter and could catch glimpses of his companions, of waiters, and of people at other tables, and through them occasionally he could shout a remark. Now they seemed to press very close upon him so that he felt sick and near suffocation, and then they would miraculously withdraw to allow him full contact with the world outside. Thus he heard Jim and Alf vehemently discuss where they would go next.

Jim was for the Dogs at the Winter Gardens, Alf for what he called a Hall. Jim boasted of having the right of entry to every music-hall in Glasgow and mentioned the managers by their first names, but he felt strongly that it would be fun to have a flutter.

"The girls want a flutter. Eh, girls?" Danny heard him cry. "You go to hell, Alf. The girls want a flutter."

He had his way, of course. Danny decided that he was drunk. Safe within his own crystalline walls, he felt indifferent to the antics of these flash people. Dogs or halls—it didn't matter now.

They removed themselves from the Commodore somehow, Danny aware only of an extremely palatial lavatory and of a long wait in the lounge for the ladies. When they came at length, he had some trouble with his hat, confusing it with the cloth cap of custom. Then, following a hiatus, he was sitting in the front seat of a motor car beside Jim and being driven at a great pace down the Paisley Road towards Ibrox.

Suddenly the walls split and disintegrated, suddenly he was sober and aware of Jim, drunk, taking the most lunatic risks over the busy crossings of a Glasgow Saturday night and among the mammoth trams. He was afraid and, shortly, disgusted. Sounds from behind told him that Alf was making himself very agreeable to the womenfolk, and a blackness of jealousy invaded his mind. But nearly all his powers were absorbed by the devilment of Jim as a driver. The man would go smashing past a tram drawing up to discharge and take on passengers. In a spirit of mad fun he would guide the car almost to brush the skirts of an old lady crossing the street. Once, after a dash past the control at Morrison Street, Danny thought to hear the blast of a police whistle and reported it to his companion.

"Hell them and their whistles!" cried Jim gallantly. "I never heed them. The Super and me's old pals."

And so on through the twisting streets of old Govan, past the docks and the shipyards of the South Side, till the car drew up at length, and as by a miracle, at a floodlit gateway in stucco.

The sharp yelping of kennelled animals rose above the roar of the crowd within, and behind these recognisable sounds was a mysterious diapason of click-click-click, click-click-click, as of a machine working dispassionately. There were dark touting figures about, seeking to sell tips and discarded programmes, and a few grey and desperate figures begged the price of admission. But Jim dealt lordily with the situation in all its aspects, wafted them past the turnstiles through special gates and even past the Grand Stand into a separate and privileged building with the aspect of a villa and the atmosphere of a lounge under the control of the Public House Trust.

"This is the Club," he explained proudly. "Something like, eh?"

"Oh, this is posh!" cried Agnes.

"Well, nab that table at the window till I get the girl," ordered Jim. "Ye'll see the Tote and the racing from there. But what are you having first of all?"

Again it was a case of wee ports for the women; and Danny glanced anxiously at the flushed face of Agnes. Her response was to grimace at him mockingly. Alf declared for Scotch, and Jim was with him.

"Beer for me," said Danny grimly.

"For God's sake!" Jim appealed to him. "Beer!"

"Aye, beer. A wee dump o' Bass."

"Holy Mike!" sighed Jim. He hailed the waitress. "Here ma lassie. . . ."

There was no getting away from the drinks. Sobered by the vicissitudes of the drive and conscious of virtue with only a small

Bass before him, Danny saw the others as people abandoned. Jim was simply drunk. Lizzie and Agnes were in precisely the same condition of giggling helplessness, and that was horrifying. Something out of generations of Presbyterianism told Danny that decent married women should not behave thus, and when he thought of what such habits meant to the wife of a working-man, when he thought of Wee Mirren innocently asleep in the big bed on the other side of the River, he knew an angry disgust. It only added to his exasperation that Alf seemed reasonably sober and, with that advantage, looked to be paying rather excessive attention to Agnes.

He could not quite detach himself from the group, and it annoyed him that they would pay no attention to the Dogs. For himself, he got only vague impressions of what was happening under the arc-lights of the vast arena outside. He heard continually the click-click-click of machines registering bets, and was fascinated by the flicker-flicker-flicker of numbers on the great board at the far end of the ground. When the greyhounds came out to be paraded round the track in the centre of the ring he roused himself to an intense interest in the actuality of living things and was oddly touched when a bitch among them squatted to relieve nature. He pitied the beasts as they were boxed for the start, then awakened to eagerness when the bogus hare came searing along the electrified rail and the flag fell and the eager dogs went tearing after their quarry. Ecstatically he marked how an old hand among them could cut a corner and from the fourth place take the lead, and how a powerful one among them could, by the mighty drive of its hind-legs, gain ground on the straight.

But it was the ecstasy of half a minute. The mechanical hare went miserably to ground under wooden boards, leaving the eager hounds to yelp in frustration and snap at each other. They were seized and chained and led away. The winning numbers flashed from a pillar. On the great board the totals for the next race went flicker-flicker-flicker. It would be half an hour before another batch of dogs came out to live their thirty seconds of madness.

A mug's game, Danny decided, especially since Jim showed no sign of indulging them in that little flutter he had promised. He finished his dump of Bass and sat staring through the window, a figure detached from the cackling group beside him. In that aggrieved isolation he remained until Jim's glass was empty and the call came to order for another round.

"Nothing for me," said Danny shortly. "I've had enough."

"Hell to that!" shouted Jim. He called the waitress.

"Here, ma lassie—"

"We've had enough, Jim," Danny said sharply. "It's time me and Agnes were getting home."

"Speak for yourself," snapped Agnes, and the Englishman laughed.

"Home!" protested Jim. "Ye'll be damned lucky if ye're home for yer breakfast." He hiccupped. Then he made a solemn suggestion, as if it were the product of a lengthy process of thought. "I vote we shoot up the road to the Trocadero."

"Oh, aye!" cried Lizzie, and added with pride: "The Trocadero's lovely."

"Oh, I'd love to see the Trocadero!" sighed Agnes.

"Come on, then."

Danny could not protest. Another drink, and he could have made a scene. As it was, he was lost between discomfort and a sense of being in the grip of major forces.

They went out into the dark behind the stand, and Danny was momentarily moved by the sharp sounds of a greyhound yelping to the stars. There was much facetiousness and coy giggling as they packed themselves into the car. Danny found himself again beside Jim and was uneasily aware that a hand groping for the gear-lever was not too capable of discriminating between it and his right knee.

Yet the journey into town was not so hair-raising as the outward dash had seemed. Perhaps an awareness of his condition had imposed some slight sense of responsibility upon Jim. The streets were certainly emptier now. The lamp-edged stretch of the Paisley Road was impressively straight and easy, with the peach-coloured lamps, swinging in the wind, heaving great shadows across it. As they crossed the new bridge, the steely surface of the River was aglow with the reflections of whirling sky-signs. Hope Street rose like a racing-track before them. The traffic lights at the Sauchiehall Street junction shone green to allow the car to sweep westwards and, in a moment, draw up at a narrow but brilliantly-lit doorway that looked to Danny to be the side entrance to a great drapery warehouse with a stern, modernistic facade in concrete.

A huge commissionaire in a purple uniform turned the handle for them and pushed back swing-doors for them to enter. At the end of a narrow passage a boy in a buttoned suit of sky-blue accepted them into the bronze casket of a lift. This vehicle in its turn took them to a floor higher up in the building, to a desk where entries were mysteriously made in a large book and Jim handed over a note, to a lavatory of greater magnificence than Danny had ever imagined to adhere to such conveniences—with a machine for drying your hands in a jet of hot air!—and, ultimately, into a long, low room ebulliently furnished and decorated in crimson and gold.

The splendour of the setting, as he thought it, had all Danny's attention in the first place. Then he saw that even in this gorgeous environment Jim still appeared to be completely at home, addressing magnificent waiters in tail-coats as "Alec" and "Peter". Finally, another glass of whisky before him but his eyes wandering, he was awed and his mind immobilised by the realisation that most of the people at the tables about them were in fine clothes: the men in evening-dress, with fancy white ties and waist-coats and red or white flowers on their lapels, the women like creatures out of a play in fine, diaphanous frocks. With alarm he observed that the backs of most of the women shone bare and alluring almost down to their rumps.

Extreme discomfort seized him. Those naked backs communicated a perfectly sincere sensation of horrified disapproval. Something in him revolted at the display of wealth and at the affectation of accent and deportment he heard and saw about him. He despised what he would have called the softness of it all. Above everything, he had the feeling of being an interloper on this territory proper to the toffs.

In this state of self-consciousness he was rawly aware of the folly of Agnes in her cups. Now she was talking wildly and loudly and he knew of the woman who shared his bed that both defiance and pretentiousness, over and above the drink, were moving her to make this sorry exhibition of herself. Her face had gone red, her eyes were hazed. She had torn off her hat, and her fair hair was miserably disordered. Now and again she laughed, so loudly and incalculably, that people all over the room turned to look at her.

It was as the result of one of these explosions that Danny suddenly caught sight of Blanche Pagan. She was at a table in a far corner of the room, but it seemed as if she were not interested in her companions and was absorbed by the spectacle of this tipsy woman. Though her appearance was respectfully familiar to him, Danny knew that she could not know who he was, but the apparition had the effect of sending him into a panic. There was the sudden stab of the fuller realisation that he was intruding. There was the swift horror at the thought that Leslie Pagan, the boss, must be in the building somewhere.

Just then, Agnes hiccupped loudly. Scores of eyes swung to look at her. She rose, her face drawn and grey, and it was plain that she was going to be sick. Dreamily and tottering as one blinded, she made for the exit, Lizzie, apprehensive, on her heels.

Danny got to his feet.

"I'm going to hell out of this," he said angrily to Jim.

"For the love of Christ!" Jim protested drunkenly and laid a hand on his arm; and Alf also eased himself out of his chair.

"Let me go, I tell you!" cried Danny, knocking their hands down. Through an avenue of blankly staring faces, he made for the lift.

CHAPTER FIVE

DEATH OF AN OLD SOLDIER

TO THE thin but piercing wail of Wee Mirren demanding food and attention Danny wakened about six on the Sunday morning. The cry got from him an automatic response, but before he reached the curtained bed a quite lengthy series of dismal thoughts passed in flashes through his brain.

He was stiff, having fallen asleep on a deal chair before the fire. His head ached, and his heart pounded. In his mouth was a foul taste, as if a deposit of sticky filth were upon his tongue. He belched, and a gust of stale whisky fumes passed through his nostrils. The gas-mantle above the mantelpiece was brightly alight and hissing in a businesslike way as he had left it. He swayed as he rose.

It was all explicable in the simplest terms. He remembered with extraordinary clarity how it had happened. In anger he had left the party at the Trocadero, but not so very drunk that he did not know what he was doing. He could almost feel the fresh wind that had blown down Sauchiehall Street to cool his heated face, could see still the blue light of the Scotstoun tram coming along past the Empire to take him home. Did he sit inside or on top? Have the exact fare ready for the conductor?

No, all that was lost. He did, however, remember coming up the stairs, having no difficulty with the key, and sitting down to wait for Agnes. In his anger he had meant to give her a leathering with his belt. Had he, or had he not, got a bit of cheese for himself from the cupboard? His notion was that he had. The sour taste in his mouth suggested as much. And here was Wee Mirren crying to be looked after.

He tended her deftly though his stomach threatened to turn on him and his head seemed like to burst. When he was done with her she lay happy, crowing at him past a finger in her mouth. That appeal he recognised, but he could not answer it. Now, fully awake, he realised that Agnes had not come home, and it was an awful thought.

His first impulse was just to dash out into the street, calling her name. A panic desire to waken the neighbours seized him. Then he thought of the police, and then of an ambulance wagon drawing up at the door. He put out a hand to the mantelpiece to steady himself.

A straight line of reason cut through the whorls of his mad alarms. Agnes had been too drunk to come home. Lizzie would have taken her with her, especially after the row. There had been a big row; that had to be admitted. The next step was not going to be easy, whichever way you looked at it. But that Agnes should have stayed the night with Lizzie was the essence of the business in the meantime.

Danny then became aware of an unendurable thirst. He moved to the sink, let the good cold water run at pressure through the tap for sheer delight in its cool briskness, and started to fill and drink cup after cup. In the sixth of these, through the lens of the liquid, clear against the china, he suddenly saw the complacent, dark face of Alf. He put down the cup, staring straight in front of him but seeing nothing save a tall and flashy man's lecherous, leering stoop over a foolish, drunken woman. But he did not brood long on that ugliness. It was so deadly as to be decisive. To hell with Agnes!

He was unspeakably weary. He could not grapple with the enormity that haunted him. Nothing for it now but bed and sleep, sleep. He stripped quickly, letting his garments lie where they fell, turned out the gas, and groped his way to a place in the bed beside Wee Mirren.

When he wakened again all sense of time was gone from him. The curtains had been drawn, and the grey light of a winter's day filled the room. He turned his head to see the boy, Billy, on the chair before the fire that roared now; he was reading. The gurglings of Wee Mirren rose from the floor where she crawled.

"What's the time, son?" asked Danny.

"A quarter of twelve," answered the child, glancing at the clock on the mantelpiece. "Where's my mother?"

"Staying with your Auntie Lizzie," replied Danny. "Has Wee Mirren had her breakfast?"

"Aye."

"Where's Peter?"

"Out. Would you like a cup of tea?"

"Aye. Make me one, son."

He wanted that cup of tea, but it could not cure unhappiness. The sheer decency of this young son of his, and the pathos of his position, cut him to the heart. Dear wee Billy, always quiet and orderly and practical, a standing reproach to the silliness of his mother and the folly of his father! But while remorse gnawed at him, something in Danny rose in his own defence. At least he had come home, and if Agnes had come with him they could have made some sort of shape at carrying on the family life in the morning. But Agnes had not come home, and it looked as if the whole foundation of their community had been cut away.

His mind darting down ugly channels of speculation as to the reason why, Danny could yet not escape that obsessing sense of calamity impending. Something big and black had happened, never mind why. Lying there on the kitchen bed, he could make allowances for his own depression after drink, even for his wife's behaviour, and yet there brooded over him the realisation that the old, safe life was falling to pieces about him. It was a grey, cold world he looked on. Agnes had gone over to the swank and silliness of new-rich Jim and Lizzie. Her head was turned. She had come to fancy herself too good for a working-man. She had left her children. The completeness of her conquest by the passion for pleasure was declared in this last, fatal act of staying away all night. If she had slept with Alf, that was only an incident of her essential infidelity.

He brooded for a time on his mental picture of Alf, and a bitter hate of that suavity made him want to inflict physical hurt on the man. But Alf—just an English nyaf! Agnes was the trouble, Agnes and her selfish folly. It truly amazed him that she should take this turn at such a time; for there came upon him as he lay miserable the awful knowledge that he and his kind were living in hopeless insecurity.

It was all very well that the boss, for old times' sake, had kept him in a job, but now he saw that the position was false and dark. There was no real work going on Clydeside. Up and down the River the yards lay empty, and he could remember the day when there was hardly a berth to spare for the orders that poured in: liners, battleships, oil-tankers, and everything down to tugs. It was no use a man trying to kid himself that all was well. It was bad, hundreds, thousands of his mates on the Dole or the Parish. That he had known and sought to hide from himself; but now he knew. The boss was a toff and a gentleman, but even the boss could not nowadays give real work and wages honestly earned to a man who had all his life wrought on that understanding.

The cloud hung over Danny till long after two o'clock had pealed from the tower of the University. He had had nothing but the tea Billy had made for him. The boy had cooked a rough meal for himself and Wee Mirren—two rashers of bacon, tea, and bread and jam. Then in his queer, businesslike way Billy had dressed the baby for the open air, got the go-cart down the stairs, seen his sister out to it, and wheeled her off for an airing in the park at Whiteinch. Danny could not face food. Peter had not returned. Sunday afternoon began to trail its drab languors over him.

His body would have resigned itself to sleep, but there was something at the core of his brain that urged him to do something. What that might be he could not determine, but the urge was active enough to keep him restless, and he was moved at length to rise by the sheer need for a positive grasp on existence.

His head spun as he stepped out of bed, and his stomach rose within him. A hand on the chair, he stooped for his socks and nearly fell into the fireplace. It was a weariness to dress, dismally complicated by the fact that they were his best clothes, smelling of stale smoke, that Billy had piled up ready for him. To get the old suit down from the hangers behind the door was an undertaking. But he could automatically fill the kettle at the sink and put it on to boil for more of that strong tea, which was all he craved.

He was at his third cup when familiar steps and familiar voices sounded on the outside stairs. A movement of the hand was checked so that the saucer out of which he had been drinking remained poised near his chin. He listened intently. Somebody laughed. There was a shuffling of feet, and a key rattled in the lock. His hand trembling a little, he placed the saucer on the table. People were crowding the tiny lobby.

"Hullo, Dan!"

That was Agnes home again.

"Hullo," he answered.

The moment was pregnant. Anything might have been said and done then. But there followed Agnes into the kitchen Jim and Lizzie. No sign of Alf. Jim was as cheerful as ever.

"Hullo, hullo, hullo," he cried. "Havin' a drop of tea for your dirty mouth, you drunken ol' b? By God, ye need it! Nice cargo you had last night, Dan. Feel like a bit of chewed string myself, if you want to know. Gees, what a night!"

It was not blarney, Dan saw at once. According to Jim, they had had a good night and must pay for it. The man saw it all as having been very funny.

"As for Agnes," Jim resumed cheerfully, "Christ, ye'd have laughed! Talk about a jag—she had one on, and then some. Couldn't get sense out of her this morning till she had a pint of champagne in her tank. Ye'd miss her when you wakened, Dan?"

Lizzie cackled at that.

"Oh, I felt like death warmed up, right enough," she sighed. "That's me finished with port wine. I'm telling you. It was a rare tare all the same. Ye enjoyed yourself, didn't ye, Danny?"

Danny glanced at his wife, and her eyes avoided his.

"And what about your fancy friend, Alf?" he grimly asked Jim.

"Alf? God knows!" Jim turned gravely to Agnes. "Did you see Alf after we left the Trocadero? Damned if I can remember."

"I don't remember," said Agnes emptily.

"Ach, we can remember sweet dam' all, the lot of us," observed Jim fatalistically. "It's some fresh air we're needing. Come on, the lot of you, and we'll run down to Luss. Are ye game, Dan?"

"Not me," said Danny. "There's some bairns to look after in this house."

He glanced his challenge to Agnes, and she answered it, her eyes hard.

"Billy can look after everything fine," she said.

"Och, come on, Dan," Lizzie urged.

"On ye go, the lot of you, if you want," said Danny, stubborn. "I'm staying where I am."

It was just like Jim not to perceive the signs of tension in the air.

"Ye're still drunk, ye old b. That's yer trouble. Away back to yer bed and sweat it out of ye. We're away. See ye when we come back."

They left him alone, and once again he heard their laughter on the stairs. It angered him, but behind his passion there weighed on him more onerously the dead burden of bafflement. The downrightness of his wonted philosophy had been robbed of its power, and for the first time in his simple life he had lost his way in a maze of conflicting relationships and responsibilities. That awareness seemed to have its physical effects. Habit urged him to do something—to set to the washing of the dishes, to go for a walk—but he could neither do anything nor believe that anything was worth doing.

For a long time he pottered aimlessly about the little house. Now he would look into the boys' room and helplessly contemplate its untidiness. Then he would pick up the Sunday paper and read the bludgeoning headlines on the front page, forgetting at the same time the rich interest of the football section at the back. One of Billy's coloured comics held him for a time. At another moment he found himself staring into the press where Agnes's clothes drooped, deflated and tawdry, from their hangers.

Nothing but impatience with these dissatisfactions drove him out of the house at last. At least he could walk up the road to meet Billy and Wee Mirren. It was all that Sunday in Glasgow could offer him.

Walking along, he savoured with distaste the sour flavour of the day. It depressed him to pass doorsteps off which the morning milk and the newspapers had not yet been lifted. For the first time he realised that people of his sort lived amidst untidiness—the gutters littered with discarded papers and cigarette cartons, groups of aimless girls and boys leaning against the windows of Italian ice-cream shops, and a horde of halflins, Peter among them, playing football on a patch of bare ground, their shouting coarse and offensive against the depressed peace of the Sabbath afternoon.

It was more cheerful on the Dumbarton Road, and he was touched to a wistful envy by the quiet neatness of the streets of little villas to the north of it. He saw how the rows of limes and chestnuts set by the kerb made for grace and decency, and he wondered if he should not have done better with his life, and studied and saved to be a foreman with a wee house of his own. Other fellows had done it. And why should the desire have come to him so late, too late?

The sight of Billy approaching with the go-cart drove those sombre considerations from his mind. The vision of his innocent children touched him, but he had great joy in being with them again, as if after a long absence. Eagerly he listened to the tale of their outing and, as he wheeled the go-cart down the hill again, gaily promised them sweets from the first shop they could find open. Then they were to go home and have tea and a game together.

"Is my mother home yet?" asked anxious Billy.

"Aye, she's been home, but she's away out a motor run with your Uncle Jim and your Auntie Lizzie."

"I wish she was home," said Billy doubtfully.

But they had great fun over their tea and a grand play afterwards, Danny growling first as a bear under the table for the benefit of Wee Mirren and then spending a thoughtful half-hour over Billy's favourite game of Ludo. They kept it up far beyond Wee Mirren's bedtime, and even then Danny promised Billy that he might stay up to read and himself took over the job of putting the baby to bed. He gave her a bath. He made and fed her with saps of bread and milk and sugar. For quite a time he played with her while she lay gurgling in the big bed, delighting in her small, happy laughter until her yawn told him it was time to stop.

When it was all over and the kitchen was quiet that the infant might sleep, but only then, his worries returned to plague Danny. There was no sign of Agnes returning, no sign of Peter, and the sense of irrevocable disruption gnawed at him. It came to him sadly now, and he could have wept at the sight of Billy, the good wee boy, bent over his book on the chair and at the thought of the baby's trustful helplessness. He did not doubt that Agnes would come home again, but she had already committed her sin of defiance and neglect. Defiance—well, that did not matter; it was between the two of them. But to work out her revenge through the children seemed to him an awful thing. And could she stick to her oath against a succession of wee ports?

It was about nine when he spoke quietly to Billy, looking up from those football reports he had neglected in the agony of his afternoon thoughts.

"Ye'd best get ready for yer bed, son," he said.

"I'm just finishing a story," the boy replied.

"Well, finish it quick and away with you."

In a minute or two Billy closed his book, yawned largely, and rose.

"I wonder where my mother is?" he said.

"I told you she was out motoring," Danny spoke sharply. "She'll be back soon enough. Away and get ready and mind your own business."

Just then the door-bell rang. Danny hesitated, listening for sounds of talk outside, and, subconsciously, to hear if Wee Mirren had stirred to the peal. There was not a sound to be heard.

"Away and see who that is," he commanded the boy.

In a trice the child was back, his eyes wide.

"It's wee Tommy Stirling," he gasped. "His father's ill, and they want you along."

"Come in, Tommy!" cried Danny, and as the small boy entered shyly: "What's the trouble, son?"

The red eyes and smeared face of the child told that he had been crying. Out of breath and palpably scared, he told his story through a storm of sobbing.

"It's my father. He took a turn at his tea. He's coughing blood and I'm feared he's going to die. My mother sent me for ye. She wants you there quick. Oh, I'm feared, I'm feared!"

"That's all right, Tommy," Dan comforted him briskly. It was as if he leaped to embrace the distraction. "He'll no' be so bad as all that. I know these turns of his. They give you a start, but your father's good for a while yet. Wait till I get to him."

Already he had grasped his coat and was slipping into it.

"See here, son, you stay here with Billy and don't worry yer wee head. I'll run along and see what's what. Billy give him a piece and put him in beside Wee Mirren. He'd best stay the night. Tell your mother. I'll away. . . ."

He was out and down the stairs before the children knew it. Up the street he ran for the tram along the Dumbarton Road. All the spirit of him, all his racial capacity to face a crisis dourly, rose almost happily to the occasion.

That Jess Stirling had been waiting for him anxiously he knew when the door of the little house above the kennels opened even before his foot was on the lowest rung of the wooden ladder that led to it. She came out on the landing to caution him. They spoke in whispers.

"He's terrible bad, Dan," she confided tearfully. "It came on him last night. I was up till seven this morning with him, and then he took another fit of bleeding at his tea the day. I've never seen him so bad, and I'm feared, oh, I'm feared!"

He grasped her plump arm and squeezed it firmly.

"It's just that you're tired out, Jess. Ye'll have had no sleep?"

"No," she responded emptily. "What with the bairns and the house—"

"I've left Tommy with Billy," he explained quickly. "He can sleep the night there. Is there a neighbour can take in Nance and Peggy?"

"Mrs. Macpherson might. But, Dan—"

"Away and get them ready and take them across," he said. He felt the mood to command upon him, and he was vaguely confident that the weary woman responded gladly. "I'll stand by here, and when you come back we'll see what's to be done. Has the doctor been?"

"Half an hour ago. He said there was nothing he could do. There's a bottle."

Patting her back, Danny urged her into the kitchen.

"You keep yer mind easy, Jess," he insisted. "Get the weans away first and then we'll see. It'll just be one of his turns."

The big kitchen was warm but shadowed. The paraffin-lamp had been turned low and shone towards the door and away from the bed on which Joe Stirling lay. The light of the fire played on the frightened, eager faces of two little girls. Danny touched their heads in passing, whispered a word of greeting, and moved on to peer down at the wasted face of his friend. There was a brownish smear on the pillow.

It was like looking on one dead, and Danny floated off for a moment on a cloud of sad and tender thought, only to be surprised out of that abstraction by the sudden realisation that two eyes had opened wide and were fixed on his.

"Dan!"

It was a whisper only, but there was gratitude in it.

"Joe, old pal," he whispered back. "But not a word. Ye're not to speak. I'll be here with ye, Joe, if ye want me."

He would have grasped a hand if one had lain on the coverlet to hold. Instead, impulsively, he put one out of his own and ran the fingers of it gently across his friend's curly, greying hair.

He sat down on the deal chair by the bedside and waited for Jess to get the children ready. When they appeared from the shadows behind, dressed for out of doors and carrying pathetic bundles wrapped in newspaper, he rose to go to the door with them and gave Jess his counsel.

"Stay you out for a bit if you can," he confided. "See the lassies into their beds and have a cup of tea with Mrs. Macpherson. It'll do ye good. And when ye come back, it's straight to bed with you. No, no!"—when she would protest—"ye've got to get yer sleep, and I'm as fresh as paint and game for a night of it. Go on, lass, and don't worry yerself one wee bit."

He found a curious contentment in being alone with Joe, perhaps because—though this he could not know—it restored to him the sense of purpose. While he sat there before the fire, passing now and again to the bed to peer into the drawn face, his mind was strangely at ease. The sordid vicissitudes of the day and of the night before lost all their urgency and receded into distant memory to lose reality and meaning. He did not brood at all on the crisis that seemed to have arisen between himself and Agnes. Indeed, in the sweetness of fireside reflection his mind went back to the days of the war and to pictures of camp and trench in three continents and to the good comradeship of Joe, now apparently asleep at his elbow.

It was blissfully quiet in the kitchen. He could hear the zoom of the trams along Argyle Street, the occasional rushing of cars, and the impatient hooting of their horns. Once in a while a train, passing through the tunnel below, shook the antique building. But the real sounds were the loud ticking of the clock on the mantelpiece, the fall of coals from the fire, and, when he listened, the long-drawn, troubled breathing of Joe. These things were of a little world in which he was content. It would have satisfied him to know that he could spend all the long hours of the night alone with his friend.

Before the full hour had passed, however, he heard the footsteps of Jess on the wooden stair. She brought the fresh chill of the night with her.

"How has he been?" she whispered anxiously.

"Champion," Danny replied. "Not a cough, and he's slept like a bairn."

"Ye're good to us, Dan," she said thoughtfully.

"Enough of that," he remonstrated, embarrassment coarsening his phrases. "Away you and lie down. That's all that matters the now."

"Dear knows I'm weary," she sighed. "Ye'll call me, though, if he stirs. If I could just have an hour's lie-down. That'll do me fine."

"Ye'll lie till midnight anyway," Danny declared firmly.

"Promise, then?"

"Away with you!" he protested, giving her a playful push.

He watched her bend over her husband, flick a sheet into order with a deft hand, and disappear behind a curtain at the darkened end of the room. He heard the creak as she laid her tired body on another bed in there. The silence was his own again; and his unconscious prayer was that she might sleep long, that Joe might be spared the rack through the small hours, and that he himself might be left to the satisfaction of keeping watch for them both.

The world grew smaller and smaller about him as the external noises of the Sabbath night grew rarer and fainter. He heard the last of the trams moan into the distance. Only once in a while did a rushing roar signify the passing of a belated motor. Now and again the footsteps of a late pedestrian reverberated along the cliffs of the tenements a hundred yards away. Deeper and deeper grew the silence until, from beyond the narrow circle of clock and hissing coal and a leaking tap tinkling in the courtyard outside, there came only the monstrous peals of the University bell announcing the hours: so loud, so arrogant, that he wondered how anybody could sleep within a mile of its clangour.

But Joe Stirling seemed easily at rest every time he tiptoed to the bed to look at him. He lay so still in his back that sometimes Danny, a lump of apprehension in his throat, had to watch with narrowed eyes for the rise and fall of his chest and strain his ears to catch the weak, strained rhythm of his breathing. Nor was there a sound from where Jess lay behind the curtain. Beyond the tending of the fire there was nothing to distract him from the thoughts that revolved, slowly and without urgency, in his mind.

Thus seeing his life and all life in the mirror of the fire's hot heart, he had dozed over when a horrible sigh of breath painfully intaken brought him with a jerk to his feet. That terrible sound was followed by the uglier, more urgent burbling noises of choking. Joe. . . .

He leapt to the man and with strong, tender arms raised his friend to the sitting position, and against that posture the tortured body protested jerkily. The man's head hung forward. Danny could feel with his arm the labouring of his torso as he gasped and groaned and coughed in the battle for breath. There came a spasm of almost ecstatic violence, to be followed by a strange calm as a dribble of blood and sputum fell from the quivering lips to the counterpane.

Suddenly Dan became aware of a spoon held out before his eyes.

"The medicine," whispered Jess's voice urgently.

He grasped the spoon with his left hand, and lowering his right arm to get Joe's head back, slipped it between the parted lips. They closed on it as if unwillingly, but automatically the tongue sucked at what lay in it, and Danny watched the motions of swallowing on the skinny throat. Then, as Joe sighed like a child that has drunk deep, he gently lowered the head and shoulders of his friend to the pillow.

"He's fine now," he said to Jess. She was wiping the mess from the counterpane.

"Aye, they're terrible these turns," she whispered back.

"I'll bet you he sleeps till the morning," Danny insisted with conviction. "Away back to yer bed." He lied, "It's just turned eleven.

"No, I'll sit with him now. You have your work in the morning."

"I'm tellin' ye, there's plenty of time. Ye've another hour yet. I'll

94

give ye the knock at twelve."

"Ye're a good soul, Dan," she whispered across the body of her husband.

"Away with you, and don't blether!"

Thus, more adroitly than he knew, he recovered his agreeable isolation. The sense of crisis encountered and survived lent to his meditation before the fire a fresh quality of satisfaction. Now he was re-established as the man of action he had to be in order to be happy. To handle the job in hand—that was his fate and his delight. Only thus could he be content. After his wanderings in that world of drinks and fancy food and swank that Agnes loved he was happy to be concerned entirely with looking after Joe and keeping the fire going and letting Jess have a sleep.

The bell of the University proclaimed the hour of one to the city, and he hoped that Jess had not heard that witness to his lie. Then the lamp on the mantelpiece burned low, and he must search for the can of paraffin and, in the light of the fire, fill the container and trim the wicks. Once, hearing from Argyle Street the raw laughter of young men, he began to think of Peter and the problem he represented; but he deliberately wrenched himself free from that intrusion by the world outside the warm kitchen and went over to see how Joe fared. His friend slept in his weakness.

He heard two strike, and three, and four and then he had to admit to himself that he would gladly fall asleep. A faint nausea of hunger troubled him, and the pounding of blood in his head told him that he was not yet free of the poison of the night before. Something stubborn in him would have kept him awake and watchful. He remembered long nights in the trenches with Joe and the timelessness of warfare. But though the thought of the increasing years did not occur to him he could not forget that he was due at that gate of Pagan's at eight, and that a man must not be lax in duty in hard times.

It was nearer five than four when, reckoning carefully that she had had the best of seven hours' sleep, he wakened Jess.

"Is it twelve, Danny?" she asked anxiously.

"It's all that," he replied, putting a laugh into his whisper.

When she saw the clock on the mantelpiece she was horrified.

"Oh, Danny Shields! Of all the things to do! Leaving me there, and you with yer work to go to!"

"That's all right," he comforted her. "I'll just walk along the road and have a bit wash and a cup of tea and get along to the Yard."

"Ye'll do nothing of the sort!" Her woman's sense of order was aroused. "Ye'll just go and lie down on the bed there, and I'll have your breakfast ready for you at seven. Walking home at this time o' day! It's nonsense."

The innocent simplicity of the suggestion appealed to him at once. His admiration of Jess's good sense bounded higher than ever. Her idea would save precious time, and he would always be beside his friend in case of need. He wished her goodnight, made her promise that she would waken him at once in case of alarm and, pausing only to loosen his tie and collar, went to lie down on the bed behind the curtain.

When he opened his eyes again, to see Jess standing by the bed with a cup of tea in her hand, it seemed only a moment since they had parted. It was still dark. The kitchen remained in the soft grip of the silence. The acquired habit of the old soldier remained with him, and that he wakened fresh indicated nothing. If she had told him that he had slept only ten minutes he would have believed her.

"It's a quarter to seven, Dan," she whispered.

"How is he?"

"Sleeping like a bairn. He hasn't stirred since that turn."

"That's great!" declared Danny. "My, but that is a fine hot cup o' tea."

"Oh, but Dan! I'm fair ashamed. I've hardly a thing in the house for your breakfast."

"Never mind ma breakfast. Ye've more to think of."

But as he lay drinking the tea with delight he heard her back at the fire, heard the sizzle of a frying-pan at work, and smelt an odour that caressed the nostrils. Emerging from behind the curtain, he found that she had prepared for him a great plate of bread fried in dripping, a bulbous egg—her last, he was sure, but could not say so in protest—and as much crisp toast as he could eat.

He went over for a last look at Joe before departing. Now an emaciated arm lay along the coverlet, and he picked up in one of his the wasted hand with the long, fine fingers of the bedridden; but there was not a flicker of response on the gaunt face.

"I'll be back after twelve to see how ye're getting on," said Danny, turning to Jess. "If I've time I'll look in and see if Agnes has got Tommy off to school all right. Then I'll be back about six again."

"But, Danny!" she protested. "Ye canna spend all your time—"

"Can I no'?" he retorted jocularly, and went away to his work.

3

There was much to worry him in the Yard that day. Ever since the night of the big pay-off he had known himself a marked man about the place. A riveter kept on with not a hull under construction. Danny himself knew that it was a preposterous favour he had received. He knew, too, that the foreman to whom he had been allotted had to make work for him, using him perforce as an orra man for odd jobs outwith the main effort to get the *Estramadura* ready for the sea. Nor did the foreman, coarse Peter Menzies, spare his taunts at the boss's fancy man.

But a job was a job, and Danny clung to a strong and almost mystic faith that he was only marking time until, shortly, he would be back with the squad at the hammer, holder-on and mate and rivet-boy in a happy sodality of work. When Peter Menzies started picking on him more bitterly than usual, he wondered at first if the dissipation of Saturday night and the vigil of Joe's bedside had not in fact combined to make him slow and handless. But he seemed to see as the day wore on that the attack was deliberate in its consistency. There was more than one telling-off that infuriated him by its unfairness. And so, remembering that Leslie Pagan was far away, a dull apprehension accompanied him through every task.

At the noonday break he hastily swallowed a pie and drank a glass of beer, then dashed off in a tram to see how Joe fared. His friend was awake again, but so weak that he could only smile his recognition. The doctor had called and had had little to say. Another prescription had been written, and that Danny hurried to have made up. To save waiting at the druggist's counter he went out and bought what he thought Jess might need—a loaf, butter, eggs and a gill of public house brandy for Joe. By the time he had returned with these and given them into the tearfully grateful custody of Jess, there was no possibility of looking in on Agnes, and he had to hasten back to the Yard.

He saw Agnes for about twenty minutes in the evening and that at the end of an afternoon even more troublesome in the Yard than the morning had been. Her manner was hard and distant; only her own sense of guilt, he knew, stood between him and the lash of an angry tongue.

"Have ye shifted yer lodgings?" she began with a challenge as he entered the kitchen, and that despite the fact that Billy and little Tommy Stirling were asprawl at their play on the mat before the fire.

"For the love o' God, Agnes!" he pleaded wearily. "You know fine what's wrong."

"Oh, I suppose I don't matter," she retorted.

Only with an effort did Danny restrain himself. He spoke sharply to the two children.

"Billy! Tommy! Run you into the next room and play like good wee boys. We've something to talk about here."

When the children had obeyed, he turned angrily on his wife.

"You cut that stuff out, my girl, or I'll have something to say to you. It's past the day when you could try that innocent business on with me. Joe Stirling's dying, and he's my pal, and I'm going to look after him. See?"

"I suppose his wife's ill too. Or mebbe that's the attraction."

"Shut yer face!" he roared at her. His hands itched to hit her. But a lurking sense of the security of his position as against hers lent him enough restraint. "If you had any right to talk I'd listen to you."

Plainly, his indignation impressed her.

"Aye, but I've got to look after the boy," she argued weakly.

"That'll kill you, won't it?" he retorted bitterly. "You'll keep him and you'll be decent to him till this is all over. God knows it can't be long!"

"Is he that bad?"

Her Scots passion for the detail of sickness and death got the better of her petulance then. She plied Danny with questions and listened, mouth agape, to his recital of ugly detail—the smear on the pillow, the froth of blood and mucus, the paroxysms of the fight for breath, the laboured breathing of the man at rest. "Oh, dear me!" she said, and "The poor soul!" She wanted to know exactly how Jess managed, what had happened to the two girls, what food there was in the house, and why no relatives had gathered round the death-bed. At one moment she even hinted at her willingness to take her place in these interesting proceedings.

The grim catalogue had at least the effect of distracting them from their mutual suspicion, and Danny felt awkward, like a boy, when the time came for him to say that he must get back to his post. He made certain that Agnes was not short of cash, that Peter was behaving himself reasonably well, and that the stability of the household in general had been re-established. Then he picked Wee Mirren from the bed and hugged her close. On Billy and Tommy, the latter pathetic in his indifference to the upheaval in his life, he bestowed a penny each. But it was not so easy to take farewell of Agnes.

"Well, I'd better away now," he began.

"I suppose ye'd better," she answered coolly. "Mebbe you'll look in tomorrow?"

"Sure!" And he added grimly. "If I'm not back before then."

It was a relief to get out of that house. It was like returning home to enter the big kitchen of the house in the pend off Argyle Street and to find Jess having a cup of tea by the fire.

"He hasn't had a turn all day," she reported gratefully. "I do believe he's getting better. And, O Dan! The Legion was down the day, and they're sending me a bag of coal and the money for the rent. Isn't that great?"

They had tea together—and only when she was preparing it did he realise that Agnes had not offered, nor had he asked her, to do as much for him. It was frightening that he should feel more at home in the stricken house than in his own, but there it was. He glowed in the ease and comfort of Jess's simplicity. It was fine to give her a hand with the dishes afterwards, and fine to have her trust reposed in him when she ran across the road to Mrs. Macpherson's for an hour with the girls.

She came back about nine. He did not tell her that in her absence Joe had had another turn. It did not last long, but it was fierce and dry while the paroxysm raged, and the dead way in which his friend fell back to the pillow at the end of it put fear into Danny's heart. It was as if a done man had made a gesture of hopelessness; in a fashion beyond analysis or description it seemed to signify surrender. Joe, relapsed, seemed to have passed already into a world of his own. And lest she should notice with a wife's subtlety of perception the change in her man, Danny lied to Jess and engaged her at once in a debate as to which of them should take the first watch of the night.

On the ground that he must be fresh for the morning it was easy to persuade her that she should rest until he wakened her. She made him promise that he would not let her lie so late as he had done the night before, and, unconsciously eager to be alone in the quietness before the fire, he gave her the undertaking. The University bell was banging out ten as the bed behind the curtain creaked under the weight of her body.

Jess had two hours sleep that night, and Dan had none. At first a thought depressed by what had passed in the Yard that day, and heavy with worry as to what would happen to their children if he and Agnes were in a bitter and ineluctable issue to part, he nevertheless dozed off about midnight, to be wakened, as the clock on the mantel-piece told him, at a quarter to one.

Somebody was choking. The chair in which he had slumbered overturned with a clatter in the violence of his leap to the bedside of his friend.

They were up with him all night. That first attack was the herald of a dozen. Danny's right arm was stiff and sore supporting the helpless body; he could have wept to see a man, and his friend at that, shaken so sorely, helpless in the grip of disease, degraded in his helplessness. They hardly dared let him rest on the pillow between the bouts. It seemed that to let him fall back would be to suffer his beaten spirit to resign the battle. With hands and bottle and towel they kept him face to face with the enemy, saw the man's face turn grey and then nearly black, and still laboured to prop him up so that he might fight. In their concentration they could not realise that the effort was hopeless.

He wilted and died under their hands about seven in the morning. One paroxysm started with a horrible whoop. Danny held the quivering torso tight. The whoop trailed off into a gasp, and the head collapsed over the rotten chest, as if the neck were the stem of a fragile flower suddenly broken. Danny raised the chin, but it weighed heavy in his hand. He saw that the eyes stared sightlessly. He laid the body back.

"I doubt he's done for," he said.

"Joe! Joe! Oh, Joe!" cried Jess, and collapsed beside the bed.

Danny paused for a moment, looking down in a queer detachment on that demonstration of grief. Timidly, hopelessly, he laid a hand on the woman's heaving and heedless shoulders. Then he went out to look for an undertaker.

4

He did not reach the Yard until after ten that day, and by the time he had punched the clock he had braced himself defiantly for the trouble that was surely coming from the foreman.

Peter Menzies greeted him sardonically. "Was yer chaffoor late wi' the motor this morning?" and went on to abuse scrimshankers, fancy men, and workshys in general. Danny knew that it was hopeless and dangerous to retort and sought to lose himself in the job the squad was at. Menzies knew very well why he was late, and it was hard to keep silent in the face of that monstrous injustice. But the harder he steeled himself to silence, the louder and coarser the taunts and abuse of his foreman.

"Shut yer ugly big mouth!" he was forced to protest at length.

Then he had to face Peter Menzies, who, his big fists clenched and raised, his face red with passion, stood over him roaring.

"I'll sort ye, ye bowly legged wee bastard! I'll put ye in yer place! That's the ruddy limit of your run, ma lad, and I'll ruddy well see it's the plank for you on Friday."

There was more than that, but it was enough for Danny. At the back of his mind there lingered a vague, wild hope that Menzies had not the power to do as he threatened, that Leslie Pagan had left him a certificate of perpetual protection. In his heart, however, he knew the hope to be faint and feckless, and as a man of his own harsh world he knew that life in the emptying Yard would be henceforth intolerable. That sheer pride fed his desperation. If it was coming to him, it would come, and he was cringing to no lousy brute of a foreman and Agnes would now begin to learn on which side her bread was buttered.

He made no formal application for leave to go to Joe's funeral on the Friday. Defiantly he believed that it would be refused; so that the procession up the long and hilly route to Lambhill and the ceremonies there symbolised his own burning of the boats. The British Legion did well by Joe in death as in life. They buried him as a soldier, with a band to head the cortege, its drums draped in black, and buglers to blow over the grave on the heights; and a queer mixture of pride and sorrow and anxiety so possessed the mind and soul of Danny Shields, chief mourner, that he ended the day in a state of exaltation.

Strange male relatives of the dead man had assembled for this last gorgeous manifestation of Joe Stirling's individuality, and Danny inevitably got involved with them.

They were austere, sandy cousins from somewhere about Kirk o' Shotts; all very sombre in frock-coats and tile-hats of great age. Neither their awkwardness of manner nor their formality of dress, however, affected their willingness to accompany Danny into a public-house at Saracen Cross in reaction from the strain of the obsequies. There they remained for over an hour, drinking nips of whisky neat, praising Joe and the decency and patience of him, speculating gloomily on the future of Jess and the children, wondering at the splendours of the funeral, and emitting at intervals that curious gasp, neither an affirmation nor a whole-hearted sigh, through which the Scots express their sense of the pain and pity of death.

Indeed they were in the public-house until the barman called "Time" at half-past two. Then nothing would do but that Danny should see the cousins off by bus from Cathedral Street. He enthusiastically accepted an invitation to visit them in their Lanarkshire fastnesses and, only when he was left alone, realised that his state was one of utter helplessness.

He was wearing his best suit, his dark overcoat, and his hard hat. He had broken all the rules of the Yard and would assuredly get his lying-time that night if he did go back. He was separated by an ocean of misunderstanding and suspicion from his wife. At one moment a bus inspector moved forward to ask if he could direct this odd, bemused figure that stood like a lost soul on the kerb.

The whisky working in him, Danny decided at last to go as he was to the Yard and get it over one way or another. Peter Menzies could say what he liked and would get something back. Peter Menzies could go to hell. There would be something to say when the Major returned. So, fired by this crazy determination, he got a local train from Queen Street westwards and, at the gatehouse of Pagan's, sent a defiant message to the foreman to come and see him.

Coarse Peter Menzies stormed across the yard to deal with him. The man was so angry, so loud in his passion, that Danny could only listen. He realised then that the worst, the incredible, was upon him. He was abused, jeered at, despised. A great red face with small ferrety eyes mocked his helplessness.

"Ye can lift yer walking-ticket now and get to hell out of here," the foreman snarled, turning on his heel.

Then Danny was on the street, staring along its emptiness, angry and hurt and haunted by a bleak surmise.

CHAPTER SIX

TRIAL TRIP

LESLIE PAGAN, pacing the terrace that runs the length of the Elizabethan frontage of Cuckton Lodge, looked across the Weald and was once again vaguely annoyed that the suave barrier of the South Downs cut off the view of the sea he should have had from these heights under Crowborough.

It was a superlative morning, too, this first of the New Year, the sun just making its heat felt through the frosty air, a lighted peace on the gentle English landscape, and the spires of Lewes dreaming in a fine haze. Country sounds were carrying far in the stillness. The barking of dogs came from farms away by Halland. He heard once the clamour of the Hunt, and thought of Blanche, her face glowing, happy in the wake of the hounds. The foolish toot of a locomotive whistle somehow borrowed a quality of fitness from the environment and accentuated the sweetness of the soft, safe English scene.

An awareness of this settled gentleness of England was very much in Leslie's mind. It challenged him, roused him to comparisons. It was grand to be walking the terrace in the crisp air, easy in tweeds and his pipe radiating incense, but his consciousness of physical contentment mocked a fundamental uneasiness within him. He had not yet acquired the cool balance of the country gentleman. The habit of work and a growing sense of responsibility rose continually to distress him. It had been all very well during the first weeks of exile. A man needed a rest now and again. There was nothing for him to do in Scotland. Blanche was living afresh among her own people. John exuberantly healthy and happy in the life of the open air. There were means to keep them going here forever, and to spare. Why worry?

But that worry persisted, as a dull ache of the body indicates the lurking disease. He had no doubt at all that it was Sidney's silly mockery of the Hogmanay rites that had caused the eruption of his long-suppressed concern.

Blanche's youngest brother, down from Cambridge, had insisted the night before on a celebration of Hogmanay according to the Scots custom. Facetiously, at midnight, the boy had called for glasses of neat whisky, jesting in a mocking version of the dialect and the Gaelic, his tags drawn from Harry Lauder. He had called in fun for haggis and the bagpipe. "What do we do next? Sing Old Long Syne?"

It was all very harmless, but Leslie had been hurt. He could control his merely passionate objections to the familiar assumption of superiority to lesser breeds without the English law, but his mood was such that young Sidney's parody offended a fierce, deep-seated pride and set up a positive sickness of longing for the familiar North and his own people.

He thought of his boyhood and of his mother's house on New Year's Day, the cake and wine set out for the sincere ritual of friendship. He thought of plain people, without any bookish culture, without any metropolitan confidence, with only their high traditions of craftsmanship in wood and metals, moving from house to house for the warmth of the Ne'erday dram and the greater comfort of the confession of common humanity it symbolised. He thought of Danny Shields and his kind, and suddenly felt himself a stranger among his wife's people, positive hostility against them in his mind.

It was mainly the sense of having deserted a post that afflicted him as he walked the terrace. It would have been beyond him to say exactly what irked him, but behind mere habit, behind his instinctive belief that Pagan's must and would go on, was this feeling that he had suffered himself to be doped by the ease and grace of the English life, and that he was betraying the decent men who stood, idle, about the street-corners of Glasgow in the rain. And for the first time in weeks there afflicted him a really sharp awareness of time wasted, a really certain knowledge that, blind himself as he might try, the battle was still before him, and that he must return to where his responsibility lay.

He had John to himself at lunch, for Blanche, her father, the Colonel, and Sidney were out riding to hounds. The theory had been that he would amuse himself among the rabbits in the spinneys; and that he had idled the morning, thinking, only intensified his awareness of detachment from the life of the upper classes of England. It was his concern to talk to John about ships and the Clyde, the ships Pagan's had built and the ships Pagan's would build, and he got some sort of satisfaction out of the child's emphatic declaration that he would love to go home again even though he knew that any child will leap to the prospect of change.

For an hour after lunch he dozed in the library, a yellow-wrapped novel fresh from London in his lap. Every time he wakened it was to realise that he had not escaped his problem. It seemed to stick to him like a terrier, and when he was fully awake at length he knew that he must talk to Blanche, if only to see if she realised what was in his heart of hearts and would support his faltering will.

He went out on to the terrace again, and from that commanding point saw a remnant of the hunt approaching the house across the fields below. The horses walked, their heads down, and the humans on their backs let them go easily. The day's work was done, Leslie reflected a little sourly; the calm English day had ended with the gory kill in some distant covert. He picked out Blanche on her bay. There was the Colonel in his pink coat on Shaitan, the black gelding.

Decent, intelligent, courageous, honourable English men and women coming home as if they had performed a duty! They would do no more that day. Drinks, bath, tea, billiards, bath again, cocktails, dinner, and Bridge—then they would go to bed to be fit for the same round tomorrow. Contemplating that magnificent façade, Leslie Pagan felt baffled and subdued.

When he heard the clatter of hooves in the courtyard behind the house, he went indoors to greet his people. They were flushed, happy and healthy; something of the day's clean crispness came with them into the warm lounge. The butler appeared with whisky, soda, and shining glasses on a tray, and they all laughed when Leslie excused himself.

"You should have been out with us, old boy," the Colonel cried, very hearty. "Nothing more glorious in the world than the fag after a good run."

But Leslie remained outside their compact world and was restless until Blanche rose, stretched herself with a happy sigh, and gurgled her pleasure in the prospect of a hot bath.

He followed her upstairs. Once in their room, the door shut, he suddenly took her in his arms, pulled her close to him, and kissed her face over and over again.

"My dear!" she protested, emerging from the embrace pleased but yet surprised.

"Oh, I'm just glad to have you back all to myself," he laughed.

"Darling!" She kissed him very tenderly. "Was my old man lonely?"

"Yes, and I want to speak to you."

"Come and help me to undress then. These beastly boots to begin with."

As he tugged at the tight cylinders of shining leather and, with gentle hands, helped her soft and still girlish body to emerge from its pseudo-masculine husk, the sense of their mutual trust and utter intimacy returned to warm his heart. He felt suddenly and completely at home again, safe in an exquisite confidence, and as he went about his little services for her he appealed shyly to her understanding.

"By the way, darling," he began, tugging at the sole of a recalcitrant boot. "I'll have to clear out to London in a day or two. (Oh, damn this thing!) There are one or two bits of business I've got to see to, and (now the other one) and I thought you might care to come along. Put up in some nice hotel and do a bit of shopping and a theatre or two. What do you think?"

It was a slow and circuitous route to Glasgow, and he knew it, but there was no conscious guile in his method. Just instinctively he knew that to get Blanche away from Cuckton for a space was a necessary first step, and one that she could not be persuaded to take if it was to lead directly to Scotland.

"My dear!" she delighted him with her answering cry. "That would be lovely! There's lots of shopping I've got to do, and I do want to smell the Berkeley Grill again, and I'm pining to see a decent show, and—oh, and it will be lovely, just the two of us! She paused. "We'll leave John here with daddy, of course."

"Yes, of course. Certainly. . . ."

But he had not thought of that, and it complicated his innocent plan.

Sir Gordon Rowse removed his white-spatted boots from the glass top of his desk, placed them firmly on the floor, and leaned forward.

"I wish to God, Pagan," he said, "that I could give you an order for twenty ships. Your old dad built the first I ever owned, and she's afloat to this day. But man, man, man—tell me what I could do with them. I've got six laid up as it is, and I'll sell you the rest for a few thousands, cash down. Ships! There are too many damned ships in the world just now, and too damned little to put into them. And mark this, my boy: it's going to get worse. It's going to be just hell for you and for me and for all the other poor fools in the business. Not a hope for us for years, if then, with all this tommyrot of tariffs and subsidies and general suicide. Build ships! You might as well ask the man who looks after Hyde Park to buy a square foot of turf. No, my son. The only sensible thing you and I can do is put on our hats and go out and split a pint of champagne. Come along."

Leslie smiled. He knew the inwardness of the situation just as well as the head of Rowse and Rodgers. He had been hearing it from various authorities up and down Leadenhall Street for days on end. As they stepped into a taxi, he wondered whimsically why he went on inviting the conventional lecturette.

Yet the force of habit and (infinitely more powerful) a hunger to give himself at least the illusion of activity kept him for days on end on the trail that might lead to orders, if orders for new ships, even a small repairing job, were to be had. He sought for anything that would take him back to Glasgow, anything that would reasonably break an intolerable monotony, anything that would help to keep a tradition alive. And the tale everywhere was that told by Sir Gordon Rowse. A strange, mocking fatalism had settled on the world of shipping. No trade, and the Government talking either economy or disarmament, and hence no ships of war. The vast machine seemed to be kept going, and that slowly, only on the strength of its original volition.

The behaviour of Blanche through what was for him a period of crisis gave Leslie matter for wondering but tolerant contemplation. It was as if she had recovered ten years of her youth. Her relief at leaving Scotland had been manifest, but in London she positively blossomed afresh in gaiety and charm and fondness. Her second honeymoon, she called it frankly. She bought clothes and wrote fat cheques for them with a girl's insouciance, cheerfully trailing her husband from the expensively dignified to the not inexpensive *chic* between Piccadilly and Oxford Street. She must see all the shows of the town. Hospitality she returned with a cocktail party of great exuberance and glitter in Claridge's. Any night they had alone together meant a dinner—she rejoiced in Jermyn Street and its momentarily fashionable haunts—and dancing into the small hours.

Leslie did not miss the fantastic paradox, this riot of meaningless spending in a world slowly starving, but he certainly did not grudge her her happiness. It was worth everything to have her back securely in love, and indeed it irked him more to think that the turn of industrial fortune had given him more than she could ever spend on fripperies and frivolity. He worried only to see a woman apparently wedded to the metropolitan life.

One day he caught her suddenly in an attempt to seduce him from his loyalty to the North. They had taken tea with a friend of hers in Mayfair, tea in a flat so exquisitely proportioned, so sweetly decorated and lighted, that even Leslie knew envy and covetousness. And as they came away through Shepherd's Market to Piccadilly, Blanche must rave about its charm.

"My dear, what a dream of a flat! And Gerturde, poor darling, has got to give it up and live in a beastly bungalow in Kenya!"

"It certainly is a lovely house," he agreed heartily; then jested: "How would it suit you and me, old girl?"

"Well, why not?" she said swiftly.

"Oh, I say—"

He had voiced his chaffing protest before he realised that she had spoken seriously, but she fell suddenly and stubbornly silent, and he knew with relief that they had been on the edge of the ultimate issue between them and, with concern, that the facing of it could not be easy.

The week in London became a fortnight, and they were well into the third week before the signs of surfeit showed themselves in Blanche and those of irritated boredom in her husband. It was she who saw his uneasiness before he realised that, short of their settlement there, the West End had given her all it could give. The happy ardours of the second honeymoon cooled, so that the discovery of a new restaurant simply meant for him just another variant of the same old dinner, and the choice of a new place to dance signified no more than hearing played in a different way the tunes that raged at the moment. She knew exactly what his trouble was and, checked in that matter of the Mayfair flat, was watchful to be the first to suggest a change.

The day came when they found themselves with nothing to do, as if the cornucopia of London's entertainment had suddenly emptied for them. A blank afternoon stretched its mockery before them. It was all very well for Blanche to say that she had her hair to wash and mending to see to. It was not her habit to do such things for herself. The endless resources of their hotel were at her service, and he knew that she was bluffing. Yet they pretended that nothing was amiss and settled down to two of those hours that hang so heavily over hotels between lunch and tea.

In their sitting-room he read and dozed, and awakened to read again while Blanche, ostensibly busy, flitted in and out of the bedroom. It was in the course of one of her preoccupied incursions that she deftly threw her challenge to him.

"Well, I suppose we should soon be getting back to young John, old man," she said.

"Yes," he returned promptly, "we've had our fling. Nearly three weeks."

"Jolly it's been, all the same."

"Rather! I've loved it."

Then he quite suddenly realised the futility of that sort of talk. All his subconscious resentment of the web she could weave about him, all his directness of drive, rose to brush aside the velleities and half-meanings and get to the root of their trouble.

"We're going back to Scotland very soon, of course," he said.

"What on earth for?" she pretended to take it lightly.

"Don't be silly, Blanche," he reproved her sharply. "You know perfectly well why. It happens that the trial trip of the *Estramadura* is due next week, and I suppose I could make that an excuse. But I'm making no excuses. My job happens to be up there, and I'm going back to it. I've been a damned sight too long away."

With brilliant swiftness she adapted herself to his mood.

"My dear! Of course, I understand. You've been a darling, being so patient, and I know the Yard matters everything. All the same, Lal"—and she became suddenly the soul of reason—"I do think it would be a ghastly mistake to take John up there just now. You know what it is in February and March with those east winds. And then to go interrupting his lessons. You'll admit that."

"Yes . . ." he hesitated.

"We'll come up in the spring, about Easter—that's the thing," she announced blithely. "When do you think you'll go North?"

"Tomorrow night," he said.

3

The greyness of Glasgow frightened him a little when he saw it again. Glasgow he had heard called ugly, undistinguished, crude, but he knew it to be neither worse nor better than any other urban creation of the industrial age. It was the absence of colour that depressed him, so that even where the Great Western Road had its own air of handsome dignity he could not away with the feeling that he was back in a stern land, a land where laughter was a waste and the battle grim and folks like Blanche were interlopers.

The fact that he was homeless added weight to the burden on his spirit. He could not bear to think of re-opening the big house in Kelvinside that would be all the emptier for its echoes of Blanche's laughter and John at his play. The notion of going to the Club and hearing the endless talk of bad times and shrunken turnovers and the southward drift of industry was positively repellent. A room in the station hotel? He would be driven back to Cuckton in a week.

He made naturally for the Yard in the first place. There, at least, was a base. But even as he walked up the familiar stair and through the counting-house to his room he marked with the clarity that absence had conferred on him how quiet were the passages now, how few men and women were at the familiar places in the general office.

He was early, and no heads of departments were available. Having opened the few letters that lay on his desk and read without understanding what they had to say, he wandered moodily into the great boardroom, cold on this morning of January, and bleak to his senses. From one of the windows he gazed down on the yard and its long series of berths, all empty. The deserted ways and static gantries seemed positively to assert stagnation. Over in the basin lay the *Estramadura* in her grace. Men moved about her decks, and she was being painted fresh from the sea. But she was the last. A week, and she would have run her trials; a day or two later, and she would be off to her distant port of registry. And then?

He turned to the half-models on the walls, conning for the hundredth time the long, fine story they told. There was Pagan's first one of the ocean's innumerable Kestrels—a full-rigged ship of iron, still afloat in the service of the Finns. There was his own first complete responsibility—B173, the destroyer for Chile. The passion of skill he had brought to her design and building: the rapture when he gave the signal, and the propellers hit the water under the drive of the turbines, and her stern settled, and she went scudding like an arrow past the red villas of Skelmorlie to do her thirty knots over the measured mile! He smiled at a photograph of the *Winnepesauke*, the elephantine yacht they had had to build for old Dwight Runton of New York, who had had his own notions of comfort and stability and, being rich, could indulge them. For a long time he stood staring at the shapely lines of the *Arnbora*, that sweet job of an intermediate liner, sunk off Rathlin in early '18, taking four hundred men with her to doom.

History. Too much history of skill and beauty and enterprise and craftsmanship for one who must now contemplate its end. He was almost glad to hear the door open and see Dakers advance towards him, a self-consciously hearty hand outstretched.

They chatted of this and that for a minute or two, then moved back into Leslie's room. There they sat looking at each other across the empty desk.

"So there's nothing doing, Dakers?" said Leslie at length.

"Nothing," the man replied. "Not an enquiry. Not even a tuppence-ha'penny repair job. How was it in London, sir?"

"Dead."

"That's about the size of it," said Dakers.

There was no use talking. Each man had wearied himself in the search and hope of work for Pagan's. It had been so much shouting in a desert cavern.

"I'll take a stroll down to the ship and see how they're getting on there," said Leslie.

The few men working about the place looked up from their tasks as he passed, some smiling, some touching their caps, but all with that in their expression that seemed to ask a question. "Hullo, Jimmy!" or "Hullo, Mac!" he greeted them as cheerfully as might be, but he felt like an actor in a play near the end of its run.

There was plenty to interest him about the decks of the *Estramadura*. With a technician's contempt he looked at what the furnishers and decorators were doing to the saloons and cabins—dolling them up like boudoirs, and making, as an old foreman had once bitterly remarked, a whore's bedroom of a good ship. The South American taste was imposing on this one decorative ideas of unusual effulgence, and Leslie was glad to pass from these landlubberly excesses down to the engine-room where the real men in their dungarees were happy in their battle with the fretful complications of a huge power unit—a fractious beast in early youth but destined to lovely efficiency before it would pass out of their hands.

It was a joy for him to walk along the lighted alleyways, to smell the fresh paint, to see this squad and that at their appointed tasks, all labouring according to a beautifully coherent plan to get the ship ready for the sea. Here were electricians, infallibly expert, testing circuits. On the promenade deck the caulkers were busy, so quick with chisel and mallet and tarred fibre that it was at once a delight and an education to watch them. There were more electricians on the navigating bridge; a fractional error in their trials of the vessels' nerves might cost a thousand lives. At one point he came on a solitary man lost in the task of adjusting to a nicety the control-panel in the wireless cabin. It was on the poop that he ran across the squad headed by Peter Menzies. His eye ran rapidly over the figures of the men who composed it.

"I thought Danny Shields was in your squad, Peter?" he said.

"That's right, sir," answered Menzies, uneasily scratching his

113

head with the hand that also held his hat, "but I just couldna' keep him on. Late every day, playing the old soldier, and too many drams. It wasna' fair to the rest o' the boys, sir."

"I see," said Leslie grimly.

There was nothing he could do. He was hurt and saddened. Danny remained with him as a symbol. But judgment has to be suspended for the time being. The excitement of his interest in the new ship passed suddenly off, and he returned moodily to the office.

"Do you know where my father happens to be just now?" he asked, thrusting his head round the door of Dakers's room. The man jumped nervously to his feet.

"At Edingray, Mr. Leslie, I quite forgot to tell you. Phoned yesterday to say that he felt the need of a rest and was going into the country, and would I let you know. Very stupid of me to forget. Shall I tell the girl to get Edingray on the phone, sir?"

"Please, Dakers."

When the call came through it was the voice of his father's housekeeper that answered.

"That you, Miss Cassells?" he said. "Leslie Pagan speaking. Is my father there?"

"Hullo! Hullo!" came the faint, flustered voice in the accent of Fife. "Oh, it's you, Mr. Leslie? You're back again. Your father will be awful pleased."

"Yes, but is he there?"

"He's here. He came yesterday. And he should have been here a week ago. Running about Glasgow with that heavy cold on him!"

"But is he in bed? Can't I speak to him?"

"He's not in his bed. But he's not coming out into this cold lobby to speak on the phone to anybody. He'll just stay cosy in the library in front of the fire. Have you a message for him?"

Leslie laughed. There was no arguing with Miss Cassells when her mind was made up in the maternal direction. He and his father had long acquired the habit of amused submission to that autocracy.

"Tell him I'll be out right away. I want to see him."

"Will you be staying for your dinner?" The voice was cautious.

"For my dinner and for the night, if you'll have me, Miss

Cassells."

"I'll away and air your bed then."

But if it amused him at the moment, the conversation left Leslie anxious. It was not at all like his father to submit to a fancy. He was of the sort that, out of sheer vitality, had to come fussing whenever a telephone bell rang. As the car raced out through Bearsden and over the Stockiemuir Road, there was upon him a queer, dumb feeling that fate was setting the scene for his trial and decision with an almost artistic care. Leslie Pagan alone against circumstance—quite a pretty piece. When the car slipped over the crest and he saw before him, beyond the valley of the Forth, the majestic blue frieze of the Grampians against the winter sky, the sense of large issues ahead was queerly intensified by the suggestion of the cosmic in the scene.

A lump came to his throat when at length he saw his father, a ramshackle old figure in a dressing-gown before the library fire. How difficult it was to believe that this was the lively, dressy, orderly John Pagan of his accustomed image. Something had happened. His face had changed. The spirit was out of him. And most painful to Leslie was the unconcealed eagerness of the greeting he offered his only son.

"Dear boy!" Two thin hands gathered and pressed the one Leslie held out. The facade of detachment had crumbled away. "This is splendid! I'm so glad you're back. Sit down, son. Tea—or a drink?"

"But you've surely had a bad chill, Father?"

"Well? Seventy-eight, my lad. What can you expect? I have had a bad chill, a damned bad chill, and I feel very ill indeed. You can't fight it at my age. The fact is, Leslie, and we may as well face up to it, if you hadn't come up by yourself I'd have wired for you."

"But you simply can't take it like this. A chill—well, think how cold it has been."

"My dear boy, we're not going to sit here swapping conventionalities. I feel most damnably ill, and I don't worry a single curse for myself, but I did feel pretty lonely till your call came through—that woman, Cassells, should get her neck wrung—and I wanted to feel . . . well, that everything was shipshape. Blanche didn't come up with you?"

"No."

"John still at Cuckton?"

"Yes."

They left it at that. They could not dare to exchange even a glance. Both knew what lay unresolved between them.

"I'd like to see little Johnnie," the old man murmured.

A girl came then with tea, and in the eddies of interruption the urgency of the thing between them was eased. They talked of this and that: of the development of John, of Sir Gordon Rowse and folk like him, of hunting in the South, of the old man's autumn trip to the Mediterranean—of anything save the likelihood of the Pagan partnership being broken up. Even when they sat down to an intimate dinner, set and served by Miss Cassells herself on a small table before the library fire, the old man must make an occasion of it, fussing cheerfully about the wine and proposing all sorts of preposterous toasts, as if he deliberately sought to avoid those extremely personal issues that lay between them.

The were spared the long hours of the evening when anything might have cropped up in talk to embarrass them. It was just after nine had struck that the housekeeper appeared, formidable, in the doorway, and fixed her employer with a relentless eye.

"It's time you were in your bed," she said.

"Right you are, Miss Cassells. If you say so."

"And don't you be keeping him up, talking," she warned Leslie.

They exchanged a smile behind her retreating back.

"That's what it has come to," the old man smiled wryly. "Just a damned old crock. But the woman's right. I do get tired."

He sighed as he rose, and Leslie moved forward to help him. The proffered arm was brushed aside irritably.

"Good God, boy, I'm not quite dead yet! I can walk perfectly well. Just got to take it easy."

Leslie watched him move uncertainly towards the door. Then his father paused, turned round, and smiled whimsically.

"The epilogue will follow," he said—and there seemed a quality of raptness in the voice. "Just a damned old crock, Leslie. The *Estramadura's* will be the first trial trip I've missed in sixty years. Odd. Very odd."

"I'm sorry, father." It was all he could say.

"Yes, a pity. Changes. All sorts of changes. I wonder. Have you ever worked it out, son? What you will do?"

"Carry on," said Leslie curtly.

"Thank God for that!"

The voice of Miss Cassells along the passage intervened between them again.

"Are ye no' away to your bed yet?" it demanded indignantly.

"Coming, Miss Cassells. Coming. Goodnight, Leslie. Make yourself comfortable. I'd be glad to see you in the morning before you go. You've relieved my mind. . . . Yes, dammit, woman, I'm coming! Don't stand bawling there."

4

The *Estramadura* went down the river on the Wednesday afternoon, and Leslie Pagan travelled with her. He was busy and preoccupied while the tugs moved her from the basin in their fussily efficient way. She was still his own, and the more precious for being the last he had in that kind. His heart was in his mouth when her cruiser-stern cleared the pierhead with only a foot to spare. He was haunted by daft fears that this winch would not function and that bollard fail to hold the pull of the tow-ropes. The extinction of a series of lights on the promenade deck at one moment gave him the panic notion that the dynamos had broken down. Knowing well that the apprehension was excessive, he was haunted by a sense of the fallibility of the intricate and interdependent mechanism of the ship; her security, the thousands of pounds of value she represented, resting perhaps on an abraded inch of insulation on a mile or so of electric cable.

As soon, however, as she was fair in mid-channel, her head downstream and her beautiful light hull towering over the riverside buildings, he suddenly resigned his creation to chance and the skill of the pilot. At another time he would have been fretfully active until her anchor-chain rattled over the Tail of the Bank, dodging now into the engine-room, now up steel ladders to where the steering-gear churned forward and back again with its own queer air of independence, and then hurrying to the bridge and the battery of telltale lights up there. But now he did nothing, keeping

117

in a mood of uneasy detachment out of the way of busy men in overalls. He found a corner for himself on A deck, well forward below the navigating bridge, and in that retired position stood for a long time—watching, as it were, the last creation of his own hands pass forever beyond him.

It was in a sense a procession that he witnessed, the high, tragic pageant of the Clyde. Yard after yard passed by, the berths empty, the grass growing about the sinking keel-blocks. He remembered how, in the brave days, there would be scores of ships ready for the launching along this reach, their sterns hanging over the tide, and how the men at work on them on high stagings would turn from the job and tug off their caps and cheer the new ship setting out to sea. And now only the gaunt, dumb poles and groups of men, workless, watching in silence the mocking passage of the vessel. It was bitter to know that they knew—that almost every man among them was an artist in one of the arts that go to the building of a ship; that every feature of the *Estramadura* would come under an expert and loving scrutiny, that her passing would remind them of the joy of work and tell them how many among them would never work again. It appalled Leslie Pagan that not a cheer came from those watching groups.

It was a tragedy beyond economics. It was not that so many thousands of homes lacked bread and butter. It was that a tradition, a skill, a glory, a passion, was visibly in decay and all the acquired and inherited loveliness of artistry rotting along the banks of the stream.

Into himself he counted and named the yards they passed. The number and variety stirred him to wonder, now that he had ceased to take them for granted. His mental eye moving backwards up the river, he saw the historic place at Govan, Henderson's of Meadowside at the mouth of the Kelvin, and the long stretch of Fairfield on the southern bank opposite. There came Stephens' of Linthouse next, and Clydeholm facing it across the narrow, yellow ditch of the ship-channel. From thence down river the range along the northern bank was almost continuous for miles—Connell, Inglis, Blythswood, and the rest: so many that he could hardly remember their order. He was distracted for a moment to professionalism by the lean grey forms of destroyers building for a foreign

Power in the sheds of a yard that had dramatically deserted Thames for Clyde. Then he lost himself again in the grim majesty of the parade. There came John Brown's, stretching along half a mile of waterfront at Clydebank, the monstrous red hull of Number 534 looming in its abandonment like a monument to the glory departed; as if shipbuilding man had tried to do too much and had been defeated by the mightiness of his own conception. Then came, seeming to point the moral, the vast desolation of Beardmore's at Dalmuir, cradle of the mightiest battleships and now a scrapheap, empty and silent forever, the great gantry over the basin proclaiming stagnation and an end.

Even where the Clyde opened out above Erskine, with the Kilpatricks green and sweet above the river on the one hand and the wooded, fat lands of Renfrewshire stretching to the escarpment of Misty Law on the other, the sight of a legend—FOR SALE—painted large on the walls of an empty shed reminded him with the effect of a blow that Napier and Miller's were gone, shut down, finished, the name never to appear again on a brass plate below the bridge of a good ship. And he suddenly remembered that there lay on his desk at the office a notice of sale of the plant at Bow, Maclachlan's on the Cart by Paisley. His world seemed visibly to be crumbling. Already he had been appalled by the emptiness of Lobnitz's and Simons's at Renfrew, and the sense of desolation, of present catastrophe, closed the more oppressively upon him.

As they rounded the bend by Bowling, passing close under the wooded crags of Auchentorlie on the one hand and, as on a Dutch canal, past the flats of Erskine on the other, his eye was taken by the scene ahead. The jagged, noble range of the Cowal hills made a purple barrier against the glow of the westering winter sun. Now he was lost for a space in wonder that this cradle and home of ships enjoyed a setting so lovely. Through the gap of the Vale of Leven he could see the high peak of Ben Lomond, and his fancy ranged up those desolate, distant slopes. But then the dome of Dumbarton Rock, the westernmost of the chain strung across the neck of Scotland, brought him to think of the mean town at its base, and of Denny's yard in the crook of the Leven behind it, and of the lovely, fast, small ships they could build, and of the coming of the turbine. And another yard, there, Macmillan's, derelict.

Past Dumbarton, the river opening to the Firth, the scene took on an even more immediate grandeur. The sands of the Pillar Bank were showing in golden streaks through the falling tide. The peninsula of Ardmore was a pretty tuft of greenery thrust out towards the channel. Dead ahead lay the mouth of the Gareloch, backed by the jagged peaks on the western side of Loch Long. A man could almost feel the freshness of the open sea coming to meet him over the miles of island, hill and loch; and Leslie Pagan marked how the fresher and larger waves slapped against the sides of the *Estramadura* and could almost imagine that the ship responded with quiver and curtsey to their invitation.

That openness of the river below the derelict timber ponds of Langbank, however, is deceptive; for still the channel must run round the end of the bank and close into the Renfrewshire shore. There are miles of waste space there over the shallows, and Glasgow is more than twenty miles away before a ship of size has more than a few feet of water between her keel and the bottom. Port Glasgow and Greenock look across miles of sand and sea to the Highland hills, but the yards there must launch their ships into narrow waters; so that the man who had built the *Estramadura*, scanning the shores, saw thereabouts an even thicker crowding of berths than he had marked on the upper reaches.

It was another roster of great names, older, more redolent even than those that had become namely about Glasgow with the deepening of the Clyde. Ferguson's, Duncan's, Murdoch's, Russell's, Hamilton's. . . . Even he could not be sure that he had them right; there had been so many changes. Out on Garvel Point, under the old marooned Scots mansion-house, stood Brown's—the "Siberia" of the artisan's lingo. There came Scott's East Yard—was it not once Steele's, where the clippers were built? There came the Greenock and Grangemouth, once the artisan's "Klondike." Then Scott's Mid Yard; then Caird's, the last of the lot—closed down. It was queer to see how Newark Castle survived in its pink grace and antiquity among the stocks and gantries.

Here history went mad—the history of the countryside and the history of shipbuilding in fantastic confusion. Here they had moved a sixteenth century church stone by stone that a yard might be extended, and with it carted away the poor bones of a poet's love. This town of Greenock, sprawling over the foothills of Renfrewshire, had had its heart torn out to make room for ships. It was as if a race had worshipped grim gods of the sea. And now the tide had turned back. Greenock's heart lay bare and bleeding—for the sake of a yard that had never cradled a ship since strangers, afire with the fever of wartime, took it and played with it and dropped it. Never again, in any calculation of which the human mind was capable, would the Clyde be what it had been.

That was incredible, surely. The fall of Rome was a trifle in comparison. It was a catastrophe unthinkable, beside which the collapse of a dynasty or the defeat of a great nation in battle was a transient disturbance. How in God's name could such a great thing, such a splendid thing, be destroyed?

As they swung the *Estramadura* to anchor at the Tail of the Bank, Leslie Pagan wrestled with this enormity. He saw the million ships of the Clyde as a navy immortal and invincible. Launches, yachts, tugs, hoppers, dredgers, tramps in every conceivable shape and size, tankers, destroyers, cruisers, battleships, liners, and now the largest and last of them all, the Cunarder on the stocks at Clydebank—there was nothing the Clyde could not do in this business of ships. Out of this narrow river they had poured, an endless pageant, to fill the ports of the world.

Why had he forgotten, passing Port Glasgow, that John Wood had built there the *Comet*, the first effective thing using steam of all? Or, sailing by Denny's, that there were shaped the perfect historic lines of the *Cutty Sark*? The last, mightiest Cunarder of all up at Clydebank; and here in Greenock Robert Duncan had built the first—the *Britannia*, all of wood, a mere two hundred odd feet long, only fit to cross the Atlantic in fourteen days under the drive of her two primitive engines. (She could have been housed handily on the boat-deck of the *Estramadura*.) He remembered—for the great stories came crowding—how the name and tradition were immortalised by that *River Clyde*, built in Port Glasgow, which carried the soldiers to the bloody and splendid assault on the heights above V Beach.

But the story was to end. So the fates indicated in terms unmistakable. Tomorrow, the day after, the dagoes would take away the *Estramadura*. Then there would be nothing left to him and little left to the Clyde, with its few poor hulls building here and there and its indentations packed with idle vessels. Perhaps it was just another phase, an ill turn of the wheel. But the flashing thought left him uncomforted.

He had to resist the eagerness of Señor Martinez and a bevy of olive-skinned officers to have him accompany them on the search for pleasure in the improbable region of Greenock, and that night he dined quietly in the ship with his own technical staff, and was happy enough hearing them discuss their problems. He took a turn on deck before going below. The sou'-westerly wind blew fresh from the open sea, and there was something in the tang of it that touched him to a sweet melancholy. He could see across the dark levels of the anchorage the ceaseless winking of buoys and beacons and over a distant, black hillside the unresting beam of the lighthouse at the Cloch. A phrase, a tag, something subconsciously remembered, glowed in letters of sombre fire before his mind's eye: "Goodbye to all that," ran the legend. And was it a final message?

Through the proceedings of the next two days he went automatically. There was everything to interest him and nothing to touch him. They swung compasses off the Powder Buoy. On a morning of winter sunshine the ship bore down on the Cloch and, at a signal from him, went racing past the white poles that mark the measured mile. Up and down and up again she went past the shores of red rock set in green fields, and between the Cumbraes and Bute they swung the ship about like a car to see how she steered. These were hours of high and eager concentration, but they suddenly became bleak when he learned from hard-faced men in overalls that she had topped her scheduled speed by a good knot, and that all her intricate mechanism functioned as perfectly as man could make it. He realised then that he had not expected anything else.

He had to drink a glass of wine in the upper lounge. He had to make a facetious speech. He had to listen to flowery ones from Señor Martinez and the new captain. The *Estramadura* was theirs at last, and he drove back to Glasgow empty-handed.

Dakers was waiting for him in the office, full of questions. He answered him impatiently and asked some on his own behalf.

"So it's a pretty clean sweep," he concluded grimly. "Only a maintenance squad in the yard and a skeleton in here. We'll keep two or three draughtsmen going, of course, but I suppose it's just a waste of money. It's these clerks and girls that worry me, Dakers. God Almighty, it's awful! But what can we do?"

"Nothing, sir. But there's nothing new in unemployment."

"I know that. But, good God, man, don't you see that you and I are unemployed, too? I dare say we can live, but there's no work. I'm telling you, Dakers, there's no *work!*"

CHAPTER SEVEN

HIGH COURT

OVER A pint of heavy ale in a little pub he had deliberately sought out for its remoteness from his usual haunts, Danny Shields faced up to the facts that he was at last a man out of work and must, within an hour or so, go through with the job of telling his wife what had happened.

His choice of refreshment oddly symbolised the indecision that had him in its grip. His first reaction to the shock of the actual discharge, so much more disturbing than all his imaginings could suggest, was a glorious desire to go out and drink a lot of neat whisky. Then he realised, as in the light of a flash of bleak white flame, that a workless man, even with his lying time in his pocket, has no right in decency to be drinking strong and costly waters. But a fellow in such a position needed and deserved a drink: there was no doubt about that; and a glass of beer was not going to do him any good. So he arrived at the happy conclusion, the carefully balanced result, that his circumstances justified a pint, and a pint of the heavy ale at that.

This quiet and logical resolution, satisfying at once his private passion and his sense of responsibility, served indeed to keep him calm. Regarding the beer with almost affectionate care, marking how each gulp left its tell tale ring of froth on the glass mug, he was helped to face his personal problem temperately. A fellow, in short, did no good to himself or anybody else by flying off the handle, and did best to look at the thing from all sides.

In the false security of this assumption Danny certainly took some strange views of his situation as he made his way cautiously through the pint. At one moment he saw himself the victim of misfortune complicated by spite. At another he was wrestling with the immediate problem of how to phrase his first words to Agnes. Then he would be plunged into sheer gloom at the thought of the long and empty days ahead. Then he was sure that Leslie Pagan, the boss, would never let him down. Then he remembered that it was not the simple, loving Agnes of old he had to deal with, but a woman already discontented with her lot. Then he writhed with pain at the thought that even upon him, Danny Shields, journeyman riveter and old servant of Pagan's, had come the fate common to all the work-shy labourers and lazy halflins on Clydeside. He brooded for a space on the lot of Billy, his younger son.

As he walked home in a downpour of cold winter rain his mind was quiet, because he knew that he must keep it so, but it was the battleground of a dozen conflicting plans and impulses. There was just no tidying up and putting away the fact of unemployment and all it meant. Nearing home, indeed, he returned again to the problem of those first words he must say to Agnes. Tell her plump and plain that he was going on the dole, and let her put that in her pipe and smoke it? Or go to her with an appeal and ask her to share his bitter anxiety? If only he knew how she would take it!

Then suddenly he ran into her on the Dumbarton Road where she stood under her umbrella before the window of a shop full of attractive foodstuffs, haggis, puddings black and white, brawn, sausage rolls and pies. She swung to the touch of his hand on her arm.

"Oh, it's you!" she said.

He saw her eyes focus on his face, and he tried to smile.

"What's wrong that you're so early?" she asked.

Still grinning, he said nothing, only shrugged his shoulders. The bleak signs of alarm spread over her features.

"Ye've no' been sacked, have ye, Dan?"

"That's it," he said. "Out on the bloody street at last."

Her right hand moved impulsively. It had moved to grasp his in sympathy, but she retracted the gesture swiftly, and the hand went back to grasp the straps of her bag.

"That's a nice lookout, isn't it?" she said darkly.

"There's no use talking about it here, anyway," Danny replied.

"I've got to get something for yer tea. I'll see ye later," she dismissed him.

It was sad to enter the small house and, seeing and feeling the cosiness of its kitchen, know that it was threatened. He found his rough cheek pressing against the soft one of Billy, reading as ever by the fire, his feet up in the so characteristic way on the spar of the high deal chair. Over Wee Mirren, kicking in aimless happiness on the bed, he bent in a long ecstasy of love and pity. With the two of them he spent so much time that when Agnes came back and crossed to the sink with her dripping umbrella she had an opening for a crisp: "Have ye no' even washed yer face yet?"

Shortly they settled down to tea, and Danny knew some minutes of happiness. He loved this hour of family intimacy, Agnes and Billy and Wee Mirren and himself in a warm sodality about the small table. He had long ceased to be irked by the absences of Peter. The two little ones were life enough for him. And even if now there hung over wife and husband the dark knowledge of disaster, all the sweeter were the small talk of the infants, their comic actions, and the daft curiosities. This was liberation. The greyness of discussion and arrangement was there about them, but it was held at bay, like a prowling animal of the night, by the brightness of the domestic fire. At the back of his mind Danny was almost looking forward to a kind and sensible talk about their position with Agnes.

Wee Mirren had been given a portion of bread and jam, however, and her handling of it tried her mother sorely. Glorious smears appeared upon her cheeks. A large blob of the jam fell to the table. She spat out a mouthful that contained a foreign body in the shape of a stone or a seed. And with every breach of the code Agnes's irritation increased. First, she cautioned her baby kindly enough. She made a tart jest of the next infringement. With the next she lost patience and scolded the infant to tears, Danny protesting mildly. But when Wee Mirren reached the black crust of her piece and, finding it unpalatable, let it fall to the floor, Agnes cuffed her.

"Ye dirty wee brat!" she cried above the clamour of the child's howling. "Wasting good food like that! Do ye no' ken yer father's out of work? Well, ye'll learn. And so will you, Billy. Scrape that butter off the edge of your plate."

Billy's voice cut through the silence that followed.

"Oh, is my father out of a job?" It was a cry of fear.

"Ye heard what I was saying," Agnes snapped. "Get on with yer tea."

Her eye caught Danny's, and he saw a challenge in it.

"That was a damned silly thing to say," he blazed.

"It's the God's truth, isn't it?" she viciously returned.

But he was not going to quarrel with her across the table and before the children, and a sense of the enormity of her breach of faith helped him to keep quiet. They finished the meal in silence.

Putting down his last cup of tea with a conventional sigh, Danny looked straightly, hopefully, at his wife, but her eyes, a frown over them, evaded his.

He did not blame her for that. The presence of Billy, let alone Wee Mirren, ruled out the possibility of a fair discussion of their plight. If he could count on her taking it calmly, good and well, but there was no such confidence in him. Perhaps he could send Billy out somewhere, and the baby would go to sleep. Or they could pack Billy off to bed early. But when he realised that a device was necessary, Danny also realised, and with a stricken heart, that no sort of quiet talk informed by love could he ever have with Agnes now, and that they had been hopelessly alienated even before this crisis that might have drawn them together in sweet defensive union.

Still his lingering faith in the ultimate validity of comradeship kept his eyes anxiously on her movements. He watched her rise in her silence of self-absorption to clear away the dishes. He saw the steam rising from the sink she filled, and remarked how boldly, and yet deftly and safely, she plunged the soiled earthenware into the scalding water. It seemed to be an assurance of domestic stability, and through a pause in the clatter, while she vigorously dried an ashet, he threw a conversational question to her.

"I wonder where that boy Peter is?" he said.

"You may ask," she replied tartly. "He's got in with a right bad lot, that one."

"I'll sort him," threatened Danny vaguely.

"Aye!" she retorted. "You might ha' thought of that before this."

He was held at arm's length. She would not enter into any communion with him. He who must henceforward live in the home was overtly denied a part in its affairs.

He heard her address herself almost exclusively to Billy, as if only through the child could she speak to him. He was to move his chair from in front of the fire and make room for his father. He was to keep his eye on Wee Mirren, back in the bed. He would see that

127

the fire did not go out. Sickening with fear and bitterness, Danny watched her powdering before the small mirror above the sink, then saw her move to take her coat and hat from the peg behind the door.

"Are you going out?" he asked, incredulous.

Agnes was careful not to lose her temper. She answered him as a polite stranger would, using the distinguished West End accent she had acquired since Jim and his wife had introduced her to exalted circles.

"I've a date with Lizzie and Jim, if you want to know," she said icily. "We're going to the pictures. And you'll see me when I come back."

The words seared him, dropping into his heart like molten lead on a tender skin. Blind anger could not meet the agony. He felt as if suspended over an abyss of complicated horrors. He saw the importance of Billy, huddled up on the high chair, his knees nearly at his nose, of Wee Mirren, innocent on the bed. Her betrayal was more than a declaration as between one man and one woman. It was a treachery to a system.

"My God, ye're a right twister!" was all he could find to fling after her as she passed like a Hollywood heroine through the door.

But his immediate concern was to seek to convince Billy that the episode had anything but its ostensible importance. He had caught the child's quick, alarmed look from parent to parent, and his heart was torn to see the beloved son exposed to knowledge of the cruelty of life. The chuckling innocence of Wee Mirren was irony enough; the thought of Billy, frightened and hurt, was unbearable. Quickly he assumed a kindly jocular manner and pressed the boy, away from his alarm, as to what he was reading, what he had read, and how he did at school. Then he suggested a game of dominoes and knew, as they played, that the boy wondered, while he delighted in the fact, that he should have so much of his father's attention.

When Billy had gone to bed at length and Wee Mirren slept behind the print curtains, Danny sat before the fire and wondered. He was a man adjusting himself to the effects of two earthquakes: that which had hurled him out of work and on to the dole, and that which had shaken the family life to its foundations. He reflected (and smiled wistfully as he did so) that his normal reaction to the latter calamity would have been to go out and get drunk. The temptation to take that way of escape gnawed persistently at his subconscience. But the plain consequences of unemployment kept him where he was, a dole-drawer in front of a dying fire.

Quite clearly he saw all the bleak readjustments that must be his lot. Bad enough they would be with Agnes at his side; without her they appeared monstrous and intolerable as he sat there, staring at the polished knob of the gas-oven and thinking at the back of his mind how easy it would be to escape altogether. A sleep and a forgetting; but Wee Mirren could not be betrayed, and Billy needed him. He began, swinging in horror away from the dreadful possibility, to flush at the thought of passing before the eyes of the neighbours to queue up with the workshies and the halflins at the Buroo, that last humiliation of his artisan pride.

Weary and lost among his small, hopeless problems, he took up the evening paper at length, and the paragraphs of the football experts gave him a brief release from worry. Then there was nothing for it but bed, there to lie with the griefs and anxieties spinning in his brain. When Agnes returned about eleven he pretended to be asleep.

She moved quickly about the kitchen, and through the bleared slit of his slightly opened eyes he could not see that she was anything but the decent housewife undressing swiftly for the night. In her nightgown and carrying a candle, however, she passed into the other room and, emerging again, spoke as if she had from the first disbelieved his pretence of unconsciousness.

"Is that Peter not in yet?" she asked.

"I haven't seen him," Danny muttered.

"But you went to your bed," she jibed sharply. "I wonder where he is?"

"There's no use wondering," Danny spoke as if out of the torpor of sleep. "He'll be all right. Come into your bed and don't worry."

2

The clangour of the door-bell wakened the household out of sleep. Danny came to full consciousness in a flash. Nearly all his life he had jumped to the summons of an alarm clock, and for a moment he almost believed himself called as usual to another day of labour. But there was no alarm clock for him now, and that resonance of sprung metal was more peremptory than the familiar whirr of American mechanism.

"Who's that?" he whispered to Agnes.

"Go and see," she replied, her voice unsteady.

Wee Mirren was crying out for attention and the door of Billy's room opened tentatively. "Get back to your bed!" Danny was roaring as he pulled on his trousers. The bell spoke once-more.

It was a woman who faced him from under the wan gleam of the incandescent burner on the landing. She was half-dressed, and her hair hung in grey streaks about her wild-eyed face.

"For God's sake, what is it, Mrs. Mailer?" Danny cried, recognising the wife of a drunken neighbour.

"It's no' me!" she cried, triumphantly. "It's you! Yer Peter's in the nick. There's been a murder."

"Murder!" Danny gasped. "What—"

"It was overby in Govan," the woman rattled on. "In yin o' thae dance-halls. I just couldna' rest till I telt ye. The Rafferty boy, Vincent, is in it too. The polis has been at his mother. Have they no' been at you yet? It's a bookie's runner that's kilt—slashed owre the neck wi' a razor. He died in the ambulance to the Victoria. There's six o' them in it—a gang, like. Ca'd themsel's the Sing-Sing boys. Yer Peter was lifted right aff. He's in the Central. I couldna rest till I telt ye. It's an awfu' business for you and Mrs. Shields. The man dying and a'. They say the blood was something awfu'. I thought ye'd like to know. . . ."

It seemed that she could go on for ever. Before her flow Danny stood stupefied, though he recognised with a bitter and angry contempt that she luxuriated in the horror, making out of his tragedy a heroism of her own. He saw her run to every neighbour to be first with the news, the leading actress of a day.

"Get to hell out of here, Mary Mailer, and mind your own business!"

The voice cracked across Danny's shoulder. Agnes had heard everything, and less troubled than he by implications, brought the useless, ludicrous interview to an end.

He followed his wife into the kitchen.

"Agnes!" he appealed to her. "This is bad—"

"Ach! Hold your tongue!" she snarled back at him.

Then he saw her eyes close and her face go white. Her right hand shot out to grasp the table. The weak fingers failed to engage on its edge. A shuddering sigh, and she was a heap on the floor.

"Agnes!" he cried again; and as Billy's frightened face was thrust round the door of his room: "Get back to yer bed, damn ye!"

Something out of the past came to help him. The ancient discipline of an ambulance squad prompted him to vigorous action. He did not lament over Agnes but very briskly lifted her into the sitting position and forced her head as far down towards the feet as he could. In a minute or two she was lying back in his arms, her face very white but her eyes open. Propped against a leg of the table, she sipped the cup of water he quickly filled for her.

"It's all right," she gasped. "It was just the fright. I'll be fine now. Away you along to the Central and get the truth. I don't believe a word that bitch says."

The grey light of morning had crept into the kitchen and in its glimmer Danny saw the hands of the alarm clock pointing to half-past seven. The notion of breakfast did not occur to him, nor did he think to shave. The thing was to get into his clothes and away as if the saving of Peter from the police was a matter of minutes. With a quick "I'll be back" to his wife, he hurried out, still busy with the buttons of his waistcoat.

There was a small crowd at the mouth of the close, but he was ready to batter them aside, and they parted in a sudden hush of silence at his urgent appearance. Mrs. Mailer was among them, and she sought to go with him up the road, running at his back with lunatic protestations of sympathy, but he dismissed her with a vicious "Get to hell out of this, you dirty old bag!"

He was lucky with the trams, a red, one, moving leisurely eastwards, waiting on his desperate whistle. The morning was grey and chill and the city only half awake and the bleakness conspired with the faint nausea of emptiness in him to accentuate the feelings of isolation, fear, and unreality that the first shock had put upon him. He felt himself voyaging in unreality. Beyond Partick Cross he was, like almost all suburbans of great communities, geographically out of his depth, the long dreary length of the street only a tunnel through which he had passed to the occasional excitements of a night in town. Then his mission was to the police, those aloof authoritarians his class at once feared and disliked and respected. And at the end of the journey there was Peter in the hands of the police, raising himself and his people to the status of public figures—pitied, admired, abhorred, envied and despised all at once.

The warmth and calm of the big office in St. Andrew's Square comforted him a little. From the unsentimental friendliness of the officer at the desk he got a grateful impression of the orderly dispassion of authority. It genuinely surprised him that the sergeant who dealt with him seemed not to be angry with Peter but particularly anxious to think the best of the boy. (In an odd flash of insight Danny beheld the difference between a helmeted police officer and the same man bareheaded.) Almost paternal, the sergeant cleared much of the muddle out of Danny's mind.

It was a bad enough case—a man killed by the stab of a dagger at the root of the neck. That dead man was no loss to the community, but it looked like a murder charge and a grim day or two in the High Court. (And Danny's heart seemed to stop beating for a space at that.) The discretion was with the Procurator-Fiscal. It was all in the day's work for the police. The wonder was that it did not happen oftener. Gangs of idle, unemployable boys, fed on American films and bad Sunday newspapers, seizing on so-called religious or sporting prejudices, arming themselves as they could, going about in bands, looking and hoping for trouble.

The sergeant frowned sternly at Danny.

"I'm surprised at a decent man like you letting your lad get in with a crowd like the Sing-Sing gang."

"That's right enough," Danny admitted meekly, "but it's not so easy these days. I'm just out of a job myself. . . . D'ye think I could see the boy?"

"He didn't ask for you. That's why we didn't send."

"He's frightened," said Danny promptly. "I'd better see him if you can manage it."

The sergeant permitted himself a moment of extremely official deliberation. Then he left Danny and conferred with a colleague. He returned portentiously.

"You can have five minutes. Calder—!"

A young officer beckoned on Danny to follow him, and out of the warm office they passed into an unfriendly region of iron bars and sallow tiles. A turnkey with a cheerful face received them into his highly sanitary realm and at a word from the uniformed clerk led them along the passage to the door of a cell. The movement of a long key, selected from a bundle hanging from the turnkey's waist on a large ring, revealed to Danny the sight of his firstborn in custody.

The boy lay on a pallet that reminded the father of hutments on the moors of Yorkshire. He had been asleep but, clearly, not for long. His hair fell untidily over his forehead in thick, dark wisps. His eyelids were swollen and fiery, and Danny knew that he had been crying. The young, loutish, stupid, pathetic face betrayed weariness and fear.

"Get up, you!" barked the turnkey. "Here's your father."

Peter rolled sullenly out of his blankets and stood up, a sheepish criminal if ever there was one. He had taken off collar and tie. His cheap suit, shaped and flashy, looked crumpled and shabby in the thin light of the cell. But where other eyes would have seen but a Glasgow keelie, a hooligan debased and hopeless, Danny saw his son and loved him.

He saw the lad who had never had a chance. He remembered the night of his birth in the single room in Cramb Street. It had fallen on a sweating night of July. There flashed before his eyes the pictures of the neighbour woman braced between the wall and the struggling mother, now and again holding a sweating limb at the bidding of the district nurse; of himself ordered about to fetch hot water and towels; of a brick-red face emerging from white woollens; of fond nights before the fire with the infant gorging at Agnes's white breast, all their hope and affection playing about it.

And now a bad, sullen boy stood before him. Danny made his voice sound stern.

"This is a fine mess you're in," he said.

"It wasn't me," mouthed Peter. "Joe Cassidy had the knife."

"Shut your face!" rapped Danny angrily. He glanced hastily over his shoulder to see if an officer was listening. "That's for the lawyer. We'll have to get you a lawyer. But oh, son, ye've nearly

133

killed your mother!"

Peter hung his stupid head.

"It wasn't me," he insisted. "I was with the crowd."

"That's just it," commented Danny bitterly, and did not know what to say after that.

He posed some automatic questions about the boy's health, his clothes, his needs, and to every question Peter returned an infuriating: "I'm not right sure."

That was the whole trouble, Danny reflected sorrowfully. Peter and his kind were never exactly sure. They were at eighteen in mind exactly as they had been left by elementary education at fourteen. Nature had covered parts of their bodies with hair and given them urges, but the world of men had denied them every decent means of expression. A boy like Peter used to go automatically to his trade, but now there were no trades to go to—only the pictures, the dance-halls, and the wireless to occupy a growing man. That murder in Govan, that silly gesture with a knife, would never have been done or made by a boy who had worn himself out in a fitting-shop or on the rusty deck of a ship in the making. Waste was only proliferating out of waste.

Some dim sense of the economic crime that had been committed against his son fortified the pitiful passion of the father in Danny, and he would have been happy if only the boy had rushed into his arms and cried; but that was not the way of their Scottish kind, mistrustful always of emotion. Well, it was something that he had been ashamed to send home word of his plight. And for Danny it was just Peter, his son, in difficulty. Call him what you like, he was still his son, bound to father by a bond as strong as it was intangible.

"That's about your time," said a voice from the door of the cell.

"Right," replied Danny. He sought his son's reluctant eyes. "I'll be going, Peter," he said. "I'll have to see about a lawyer for you. Anything you want. . . . Your mother'll want to know. We . . . we'll not let ye down."

"Okay," said Peter.

The Law of Scotland proceeds with grave and reticent strength towards its grim decisions. If it has serious affairs on hand, it wastes no time on the Coroners' Inquests and commitments for trial that give an air of pantomime to criminal proceedings in regions where the Roman code does not so austerely prevail. Past Magistrate and Sheriff the substantial malefactor moves rapidly to stand his trial, and one trial only, before the dispassionate tribunal of the High Court of Justiciary—a judge aloof in his robes of red and ermine and a jury of fifteen sober citizens.

Thus the Scots Law dealt with Peter Shields and the miserable gang to which he had in folly attached himself. If, after his talk with the officer at the bar of the Central, Danny had dreamed that, somehow, through the sheer improbability of it, his son would be recognised as a mere foolish unfortunate, the dream was to be shattered. Glasgow had endured too long the senseless brutalities of its unhappy children. Fear and sadism shrieked in the correspondence columns of the newspapers—and were echoed by ponderous sounding-boards of what they called public opinion. The jungle-law was to prevail; an eye for an eye, a tooth for a tooth—and a hooligan was to swing for a parasite.

In that strangely easy way of theirs the police made it all quite clear to Danny. Already they had surprised him by announcing that the Crown, prosecuting, would nevertheless bear the costs of the defence: a fact which he received with wonder and admiration at first, only to think in the long run that the Law was playing a cat's game with his flesh and blood, with the helpless baby who had squalled so pitifully in the warm kitchen in Cramb Street on that distant night in the summer of 1913. He had to realise then that his boy was beyond his aid, that Peter, this helpless, foolish son of his, was utterly in the hands of a power that would deal with him justly but inexorably. They were certainly taking him to the High Court, that dread place whose very name had the power to appal Danny, there to answer the awful charge of murder.

Authority was casual and kindly.

"The Stipendiary would give the lot of them a birching and call it a day," said the officer, "but the Fiscal just canna let it go at that. One of the five of them knifed Scanlan, and that's certain. I don't say it was your boy: I don't believe it was. But he was in it, the bloody young fool, and the thing's going on. Aye, it's damned hard on a decent man like you, Shields, but there it is." He shut a big official book with a slam. "If you want to know my private opinion, it'll be 'Not proven' of the knifing for the lot of them and six months for rioting and assault. And they'll be damned lucky at that if old Shotts is on the bench."

There was no comfort for Danny. There was no escape. It was much to be able to believe that there would be no hanging, no cold walk to the scaffold in the grey of the morning for a frightened boy, no indelible brand for Agnes and himself. But shame and degradation remained. Peter's mere fall into the hands of the police terrified him and outraged every article of his creed of decency. Most unbearable of all was the knowledge that he had fathered a waster, a work-shy, a keelie. A bit of a booze and a fight—good enough and all in the day's work; but never to have done a hand's turn, and to have fallen among hooligans, and to be a sissy about dance-halls, and to be capable of coming up behind a man's back with a knife . . . that was shame. Danny could pity, and he could vaguely comprehend what had made his son a criminal-fool, but that his seed could fall so low his pride would not allow him to understand.

The notoriety vaguely comforted him at first. It was a recompense to be stared at by the children in the street and to be halted by some curious man or woman, and there was balm for bruised vanity in holding forth about the ways of the law as one who knew them all and in passing on wisdom and technicalities from above. It was not long, however, before he saw through the veil of sympathy that screened mere morbid curiosity. Soon his own sense of degradation was exacerbated by the pointing fingers and the smooth enquiries of neighbours. Only the sharp intervention of Agnes kept his fists from the face of a young reporter hot on the trail of a story for his Sunday paper. It became an infliction when women came knocking at the door of an evening—"I thought I'd juist look in for a bit crack," they all said. Then he admired Agnes, who snapped at them and sent them off either completely cowed or fertile in retorts that betrayed the real motive of the visit. Could it have been contrived, he would have gathered their small possessions and moved to the other end of the city where their name and shame would have been unknown.

But that was just what could not be contrived. Danny was a man unemployed, dependent on the dole. While he was obsessed with the fate of Peter the fact did not weigh on him painfully. It was but a dull background of pain to the sharp agonies of immediate fear and humiliation.

He registered at the Buroo. He stood in queues with others like him. He hung about street corners, hands in pockets, staring emptily at passing trams, hearing the others exclaim profanely over the results of horse-races run four hundred miles away. But in all that he had the sense of companionship. There were hundreds of thousands in the sinking ship with him, and his immediate pain was actually a distraction from the personal calamity.

Sometimes he would come out of a trance to find himself one of a crowd about a cobbler's window—men drawn by envy and wonder to see others work. Then he would remember Peter blubbering in the cell at Duke Street and be almost happy that there was that agonising obsession above and beyond his own anxiety. It was when he realised that he was helpless to do anything big and fine for Peter, when he saw his married life as a waste and a frustration—it was only then that the bleak helplessness of his condition appalled him.

The horror of his split with Agnes was that it left him friendless. The war had taken away all his true companions, and to no one had he formed any substantial attachment since. Poor Joe Stirling—he had been a helpless ghost these last years and was deservedly at rest. Jess had her own fill of troubles, and he could not have brought himself to ask her even for sympathy in his trial. In the first shock of Peter's arrest he had thought wildly of an appeal to Leslie Pagan and had dismissed it promptly, so much would it have looked like a bid for another job. If Pagan's were finished with him officially it was the whole basis of his pride that he could not go near them again. Somehow he could stick it out. It was a lonely business; but he would stick it out.

This dourness in him made him, perhaps, as guilty as his wife of the sins of suspicion and hostility that kept them apart. Under an armed neutrality the affairs of the household went on, but as soon as Peter's bed was free they ceased even to sleep together. She did not nag him; worse than that was her aloofness that implied contempt. And to that he in his turn had to react, so that the temptation to violence, to beat her into sense with his fists, often irked him while they sat silent at meals or while, before the fire of an evening, he saw her swiftly prepare to go out to the pictures with that distant menace, Lizzie. If ever she discussed their plight it was to gibe with cold venom at the police on the one hand or at employers of labour on the other. More than once she lashed out at Leslie Pagan and his pretensions of friendship, and then he had to silence her with angry threats.

It was not long after one of these venomous outbursts of hers that, one evening just before tea, Billy came rushing up the stairs from his play on the street to gasp out the news that a great car had drawn up at the door.

"There's Mr. Pagan's motor!" the boy gasped. "He's just coming up behind me!"

And a moment later the tall figure of the Boss seemed to fill the kitchen. It bowed a little stiffly to Agnes. His eyes filling, Danny grasped an outstretched hand.

"Good evening, Mrs. Shields. Evening, Danny. I'm not in the way, am I? And this is your younger boy . . . what is it? Billy? Here, Billy, run out and buy yourself some sweets."

The Boss was nervous, Danny could see. A fine gentleman, by God! This would show Agnes. . . .

"I say, Danny," Pagan resumed. "I'm terribly worried about all this. It was only this morning I heard. My old father, he's been pretty ill, you know. But is there anything I can do? We've got to do something, you know."

Agnes, who had politely drawn out and dusted with her apron a deal chair for him, took it upon herself to reply. Nippily she countered his eagerness to help.

"Oh, we're managing not so badly, thank you," she said. "The Poor's Agent is good enough for the likes of us."

"Oh, I know all about that," Pagan waved aside the disclaimer in his irritation, "but this is a serious business, Mrs. Shields. I can't believe that boy had anything to do with it. We've just got to get the best man we can. And if you'll only allow me. . . . It's an impertinence, I know. . . . But I'd like to do something. . . . Danny and I are pretty old friends. . . ."

His heart near bursting with pride, Danny watched that duel of wills as it were something displayed on a stage. He saw with perfect clarity the charm, most it of sincere, some of it deliberate, with which Leslie Pagan appealed to Agnes. He saw her struggle as between the bitter need to resist and her anxiety and gratification.

"It's for him to say," she said at length, sullenly indicating her husband with a toss of her head.

"It'll be a terrible expense," wailed Danny.

Pagan laughed then and stood up.

"What's expense in these days, Danny?" he asked cryptically. Then he bowed over Agnes's hand. "That's all right, Mrs. Shields. We'll get it fixed, and it's nice of you to let me help. It's just a question of doing all that can be done. And don't let me keep you from your tea."

He kept up the flow of apparently easy talk while Danny showed him to the door, stuttering hopelessly in his gratitude.

"I'll get my own lawyer on to it tonight. He'll want to brief a really good man. If we could only get Mervy-Sandeman. . . . Not at all, Danny. For God's sake don't talk about it! Old soldiers, you know."

They paused, both of them uneasy, at the stairhead.

"And I must see about a job for you," Pagan seemed to muse. "It's no use at the Yard, of course. That's a wash-out for the time being, I'm afraid. But there are some things to do up about the house. I'll let you know as soon as I can. So long, Dan."

He hurried away downstairs, and not before he had heard the whirr of the car's starter did Danny turn indoors. He went boldly and proudly to face Agnes.

"There's a right gentleman for ye," he declared.

"Aye, it's easy enough for the likes of him," said Agnes.

139

The sunshine of early spring gleamed through haze to light up the flat vistas of Glasgow Green and to pick out the metal points on the uniforms of tall policemen ranged before the sandstone mass of the High court building in Jail Square. The charm of the morning touched even the heavy heart of Danny Shields as he made his way down the Stockwell to see and hear the trial of his son on the charge of murder. It was a day for escape out of the busy, indifferent city and away from its pressing burden of the sordid and the unhappy into green fields. A sense of the beauty of liberation burdened him, who was himself so heavily enchained by fear of what might happen in that crowded room of all the thousands of rooms in Glasgow. He looked with contempt on the loafers who, hands in pockets, had gathered about the gates of the Green and would wait there for days on end, vultures over the battlefields of the law and only vaguely hopeful of the sight of carrion.

The lawyers had told him to go straight for the main entrance and boldly explain to the constable on duty who he was, but his passage up the flight of steps was diffident in the extreme. He had absolutely no sense of privilege as the father of a prisoner: much the reverse, indeed. The policemen at the big door, however, were strangely tolerant. (He was learning to admire the police.) They bent patiently to hear his explanation of his unusual appearance at that privileged portal; and while one called an officer from inside, the other gave him a friendly pat on the shoulder.

"See this gentleman gets a seat," said the senior to the young constable who came to fetch him.

Danny found himself in a rubber-floored lobby he thought magnificent. Clerks and journalists bustled about, and it seemed strange to him that they could laugh so lightly. He saw a tall figure in wig and gown hurry from door to door, and was vastly impressed. Then his guide nodded to a policeman standing in a doorway marked "North Court," counselled silence with a gesture, ushered him through swing-doors and into an empty place at the end of a pew, and whispered: "I'll see they keep that place for ye every day. Don't you worry now."

So he was at last in the High Court of Justiciary on circuit in Glasgow. And he was at once awed, fascinated and reassured. He saw the Judge under the mace, stern and aloof in scarlet robes, and he saw on the Judge's left hand the Minister of the Cathedral in lace and silk and doctor's hood. Below the bench, at a large round table, sat the advocates, young-looking and whispering like boys for all that they wore wigs and gowns. The two large vessels of glass on that table, holding the blue and white papers of the jury ballot, puzzled Danny and took on in his mind a sombre significance. He marked the Lord Provost and the bechained magistrates in their appropriate pews and understood something of the communal significance of the occasion. Then the whispering and furtive jesting and fluttering of the reporters in their pew opposite the jury restored to the scene the quality of the commonplace.

Looking about him at the rows of mere spectators, their faces seeming strained and pale in the cold light that came through the frosted skylights, he saw priests, one officer from the barracks at Maryhill in the kilt of the Black Watch, two or three ministers, a postman, and many plain women of the type his mind associated with the ownership of small confectionery or tobacco shops—and it was precisely like the audience at the first house of any of Glasgow's music-halls. As for the jury it might have been picked at random from the body of the Court. In Danny's eyes it lacked authority. Nine men and six women: and most of the men looked too young for the job, all the women, save one comfortable matron, too spinsterish and foolish. Even so, the mere obvious weakness of their humanity comforted him. They had not that dreadful remoteness of the Judge.

All this he saw in a flash. It was his first glimpse of the High Court that held in its hands the keys of life and death. The scene was bewildering in its strange amalgam of the formal and the casual, the curious and the solemn. What there was in it of the commonplace reassured Danny, but the undertone of fatality was always there to oppress him. He could not take his eyes off five youngsters in the box. They sat side by side, two helmeted policemen, with white gloves holding drawn batons rigid across their knees, on either flank. Five foolish boys—Peter and three others like him, untidy and hangdog, and only one, a little older, with a fine Italianate face so poised on a slender neck that it seemed to sneer at the Law. (At the first sight of him Danny marked him guilty.) Merely five foolish boys, if with an obviously intelligent, subtle ringleader. The Jury could not send to their deaths those other four, so flashily clad, so uneasy in their demeanour, so young and foolish. But there were always those two policemen, statuesque, their boots highly polished, their batons across their knees held in large, white-gloved hands. . . . It was so easy to imagine a way of escape, so difficult to believe in the possibility.

And as Danny was absorbing these confused and contradictory impressions a policeman with a bundle of rolled plans in his hand stood down from the witness-box, the Advocate-Depute almost casually called a name, and a meek, poor specimen of a woman in black unrelieved was assisted on to the rostrum.

A rustle of interest passed through the Court like a little wind of autumn. It was the dead man's wife. Illimitably pathetic she looked, thought Danny, and all his sympathy rushed over the bowed head of his own son towards her: poor, harmless soul. Then he was suddenly afraid to see the Judge rise from his seat and to the witness sternly say: "Hold up your right hand."

The great oath of the Law of Scotland rang in his ears and frightened him.

"Repeat after me," said the Judge. "*I swear by Almighty God.*"

"I swear by Almighty God."

You could hardly hear the voice.

"*As I shall answer to God—*"

"As I shall answer to God."

"*At the great Day of Judgment—*"

"At the great Day of Judgment."

The woman boggled over the words.

"*That I will tell the truth—*"

"That I will tell the truth."

"*The whole truth—*"

"The whole truth."

"*And nothing but the truth—*"

"And nothing but the truth."

And then there was immediate anti-climax. Rising to examine in chief, the young Advocate-Depute seemed casual. It was as if some transaction, accomplished years ago in distant parts, were under discussion by arbiters completely detached.

Yes, the woman's deceased husband had been thirty-two years of age. Yes, he was a bookmaker's clerk. Yes, he went out often at night. Yes, it might be said that he was out every night. Was he associated with any gang?

Another, older advocate jumped to his feet to protest against the question before it could be answered, but it was not a violent protest. It was an appeal to reason. The Judge chimed in temperately. The three men seemed to confer remotely, reasonably, dispassionately. They were, thought Danny, like technicians discussing a problem of ship-construction as often he had heard them. The Judge motioned the Advocate-Depute to proceed. The friendly, cool voice went on asking questions of the woman in black.

Even in the matter of the identification of a bundle of filthy clothes the lawyers were seemingly casual. An officer held up a dirty pair of flannel trousers, their braces still dangling foolishly. They were stiff and dark with congealed blood, and Danny, who had seen so much death in battle, was nearly sick at the sight of that ensanguined filth. He saw the woman in black tremble, saw her fingers clasp the rail before the stand, saw her sway.

"And these," said the Advocate-Depute, "were the trousers your husband was wearing when you saw him last?"

Danny was horrified; and yet as the day wore on there grew on him a calloused familiarity with the dispassionate technique of the law. He became as keen as any advocate or journalist on dredging the shifting sands of human evidence for the authentic gold of fact. It seemed to him that the Crown worked clumsily. Often he itched to shout a question that would call the bluff of this or that witness. Then he would be glad that he had not shouted and saw how the lawyers were getting at damning truth in their own slow, but terribly effective way. Then it would all seem very tedious, but for the fear gnawing at him.

He did not go far from the Courthouse at the luncheon interval. A decent woman in a small shop gave him a heaped plate of boiled beef and potatoes for sixpence. He fought down desire and habit before the doors of a public house—a hectic fight with the longing to lose himself in a pint of good beer. The consciousness of virtue gave a wistful charm to his walk along the macadamised paths of the Green and by the banks of the Clyde, sluggish and sullen above the Weir, shadowed by the dull buildings of the Adelphi. He was in his seat in the Court twenty minutes before every man and woman in it rose to acknowledge authority in the red-robed person of the Judge.

The Advocate-Depute rose at once.

"John Donnely," he called.

At once there rustled through the court, like that passing of a wind over brown leaves in October, a crepitation of shuffled feet, legs uncrossed and crossed again, throats cleared, and papers folded. By some queer telepathy passing from the few who knew to the most obtuse of onlookers it became clear to everybody in that crowded Chamber that the Crown was producing its most deadly witness.

He came shuffling towards the box, a small man in the late twenties, bow-legged, hen-toed, round-shouldered, a dirty tweed cap in his hand. His face was of a gnomish ugliness, his eyes were small and wary. The cheap serge suit he wore was glossy and patched. He had neither collar nor tie, but a white scarf of artificial silk was crossed below his chin, its ends tucked under his waistcoat. When he spoke, it was with such a clotted, throaty enunciation of the slums that many of his phrases had to be translated to Bench and Bar by an officer.

Danny knew the type and loathed it, since he at once feared and despised it. It was the worst even Glasgow could produce—stupid and cunning, treacherous and ingratiating, dirty and smart in its own ugly way, useless for man's work and restless in self-seeking. It was absurd that the oath should be administered to one who knew not even the name of honour, who was a worm even beside the prisoners at the bar. But yet the story he told impressed and frightened Danny.

He, John Donnely, was a cousin of the dead man. They were in the habit of frequenting the Corona Dance Studio together. They were not members of a gang, but the Corona had its regular frequenters, sometimes known, the witness hesitated, as the Fourpenny Fancies: that being the price of admission to the hall. Dancing went on each night till two or even three in the morning.

144

Yes: he remembered the night in question. It was a night of slashing rain. He had been dancing with a girl called Lizzie Dougan ("I'll produce her later, my lord," interpolated the Advocate-Depute casually) when his cousin had come up to him and said: "The Sing-Sing mob's coming along and there's going to be dirt. Run for the police." He was in the act of doing so and was in the corridor ("AB on the plan, my lord") when he saw the Sing-Sing boys stride past the pay-box without taking tickets.

There were perhaps nine or ten of them. They did not take off either coats or caps though these were soaking. The witness dodged into the attendant's room ("D on the plan, my lord") and was about to run again for the door when he heard a crash from the direction of the hall and women shrieking. The crash might have been made by a bottle breaking. He ran back to the door of the hall ("A on the plan, my lord") and saw the strangers hustling his cousin. He recognised them clearly, knowing them all by name. He had seen Cosh Tanelli—Thomson—McGarva—Rafferty—Quinn—Sullivan—Lally—Shields . . . all known to him as members of the Sing-Sing gang from Anderston across the river. Yes, he could recognise some of them in Court. There they were in the dock.

Peter recognised as a regular member of the Sing-Sing mob! It would go hard with him. A spasm of sickness afflicted Danny.

"What did you see then, Donnely?" the Advocate-Depute asked.

The man mumbled virtuously. He had seen a knife raised in a man's hand. It was plunged into the root of his cousin's neck, and Scanlan fell. Then he rushed forward. There was fighting in every corner of the room, women shrieking, whistles blowing. He was struck on the head with a bottle. He remembered slipping in a pool of blood. He wakened up in the Victoria Infirmary.

"Now tell us, Donnely," suggested the Lord-Advocate mildly, "in whose hand you saw that knife."

Danny held his breath.

"Cosh Tanelli's," said the witness. "Him in the middle there."

A gasp seemed to come simultaneously from two hundred throats. Forgetting his own despair, Danny leaned forward to gaze along the row of faces in the dock. He saw Peter's head hanging, his mouth working. On the face of Vincent Rafferty was an insolent smile. But the fine Italianate head remained poised, immobile, inscrutable.

"Danny! Move along."

It was a whisper in his ear, and he made room for Leslie Pagan edging into the pew.

"It's all right," the Boss was whispering urgently. "I've just been speaking to Mervy-Sandeman. He's bet me a fiver he'll get Peter off. The Crown has no corroboration. And wait till you hear this swine cross-examined."

Danny could believe that. He knew well enough the terrorism that could be exercised in the dark province of gangdom. He knew that blackmail had been levied on small shopkeepers and innocent householders to pay for the defence of all save Peter, for the Law was not backing the briefs of the two formidable K.C.s who sat with the great Mervy-Sandeman. This rat, Donnely, was being paid and protected to squeal. There would be no conviction for murder. But Peter had assuredly been with the Sing-Sing boys in a riotous assembly.

Though the technique of the procedure became more and more comprehensible to him, and less and less formidable, that burden weighed on him for two long days and a half. What oppressed him most heavily was the casual fashion in which Mervy-Sandeman, K.C., seemed to go about his defence of Peter. Of few witnesses did he ask questions, and when he did put one it was so casually, with such a smiling confidence, that Danny bitterly believed him to be just a big man taking a fee and caring nothing for his client. Though he was plagued by a sense of gratitude to Leslie Pagan, he was still more deeply hurt by a feeling of injustice. He believed that Peter's advocate should be a fighter, sailing flamboyantly into the fray and demonstrating in two minutes the sheer impossibility of the conception of Peter as a murderer, even of Peter as a willing associate of murderers. Then, suddenly, a sickness of depression and weariness would succeed the furious grievance, and he would see Peter again as a waster and a disgrace.

It was on the third day that Danny's spirits sank to the nadir. There was fog over the city. The lamps were lit in the Court and gleamed against slow-moving whorls of vapour. Men and women coughed, their barks sounding hollow and unfriendly. The Minister of the Cathedral was gone from his seat and, as it seemed, had taken some grace of civilisation with him. Testy with witness and advocate, the Judge was plainly hurrying to be done. Policeman after policeman in the box spoke of gangs and their known habits. The case for the Crown was closed at noon.

A silk gown rose from beside the round table.

"My lord, I am calling no witnesses."

Another said the same.

"I am calling no witnesses, my lord," said Mervy-Sandeman in his easy, charming way.

So it was hopeless. They had nothing to say. Danny's fingers were interlocked in tension. He could have jumped up to protest. Then he became aware of a hand grasping him firmly above the left elbow.

"Do you see the game?" whispered Leslie Pagan. "The case for the Crown is so hopeless they're going to riddle it on its merits. Come on out for a drink."

The kindness flowed over Danny like a rich and warm wine. The tears started from his eyes and rolled down his cheeks. Oh, the loveliness, the sweet, sad beauty of one man's kindness to another! He suffered himself to be raised from the bench and led out of the courtroom like an invalid.

"Come on, old man," he heard the voice of the Boss. "Old soldiers never die. It's a good big drink we want. There's a nice pub up in the Stockwell."

He felt so helpless, lost between two loves. He nodded agreement with everything he was told. Yes, he would take a good long walk after a square meal. He promised not to go back to Court until about five. He would try not to worry. Good old soldier.... When the Boss shook hands with him, hurrying away to an appointment, ancient habit made him click his heels and stand rigid before an influence far beyond his resistance now.

The glazed wen of the People's Palace, the turgid Clyde, great buses, blue and red, passing over the bridge into the Gorbals—queer Jewish signs over doorways there—meaningless interminable streets of tenement houses, a horde of idle men at Bridgeton Cross, the evening papers with the racing results close to their eyes—two women fighting in a side street, one of them with a smear of blood through her thin white hair—the Green again, empty and menacing in the fog that was gathering once more for the dark. A fierce, hopeless, ugly, endlessly interesting city, he thought in his detachment from it.

The constable on duty at the entrance to the North Court halted him.

"You're laughing, son," he whispered fraternally. "Old Hamfat's told the Jury to let your boy off. They'll be back in a minute. In you go."

The members of the jury were filing into their box even as he sidled into his familiar place. Through a humming in his ears he heard the formal challenge. Through misty eyes he saw the Foreman, a thin, anxious person, rise to voice the will of the people. The man blundered through what he had written on a sheet of foolscap—so many prisoners, so many charges. Not one of them guilty of murder—not even a Not Proven against one of these boys. (A reporter rose and hurried out.) Of rioting and assault at least three of them were guilty. Of forming part of a riotous assembly. . . . It seemed to Danny interminably stupid. Then the dull voice said: "Peter Shields—not guilty on all counts."

Danny's elbow was seized by the large hand of a policeman.

"Away round to the wee door in Jocelyn Square and tell them who you are. Come on quick! Beat it before the crowd."

He obeyed the whisper. Uniformed men in the lobby stopped him to shake hands, but they were only barriers on his way back to Peter. He ran round the building. To the constable on duty at a small door he explained himself in a gabble.

"Wait you there, then," said the officer sternly. "I'll see what's what."

As he stood in the foggy street, burning to see his son, Danny saw that men had followed his hasty footsteps and were gathering in the gloom about the doorway. He hated them for a moment; then realised that they were merely men without work, with nothing better to do, and that he was just as they, now that his son had been restored to him.

CHAPTER EIGHT

OUT OF WORK

ALONG THE length of Glasgow's Union Street stretches an array of foodshops. They are neat, spacious places with wide, alluring windows piled high with rich and savoury things to eat. Here a nation of great bakers exhibits its expertise in cereal goodness. Cakes and biscuits and shortbread, colourfully packed, attract the most casual eye; from many of the doorways stream the intolerable odours of good food cooking.

Through plate-glass you may see girls in white mixing batter and tossing pancakes and scones, with honeyed smells, on spotless hot-plates. The neighbouring shop will display a wealth of *delicatessen*; lean and melting hams from Yorkshire, quaint and savoury sausages from France and Italy, curious dried fruits from the Levant, mysterious comestibles in tins, and the whole range of native succulence—haggis, puddings black and white, potted head, pork ribs, mutton pies and Forfar bridies. Another vaunts the skill of the confectioner, delicately expert in variations of sugar, almond, chocolate, fruits, coconut, marzipan and cream.

The street suggests a world overflowing with goodness, a city with a healthy appetite and money to indulge it; and when Danny Shields found himself definitely, ineluctably idle, the intervening excitements of Peter's trial all dissolved, he could hardly keep away from it.

It was a part of his discovery of the Glasgow he had never known before, the Glasgow in which wealth and poverty rub shoulders, tweed caps bobbing among the models from North Hanover Street. These central thoroughfares had been legendary before, and now it was daft to wander, and to be able to wander, through them.

He trod the long length of Sauchiehall Street, marking shrewdly the burden of cosmetics in the air, the richness of shops catering for the rich, the flaunting of whores and of rich women, not much better, clambering insolently from glistening cars. He got on the slope of Renfield Street the impression of a careless, busy city in which, after all, not everybody was obliged to hang about the drabness of Anderston Cross, waiting for the results of the three-thirty at Lingfield. He saw in the transverse gully of Gordon Street the press of comfortable bourgeois in bowler hats, making towards the evening trains for the dormitory towns. The windows of silversmiths in Buchanan Street held him wondering.

Yet not a single twinge of envy plagued him. In his simple, acquiescent mind the concentrated wealth of the city inspired only interest. It was a wonderful place after all, this Glasgow. It was a place to be proud of. To think that a chap could live all his life along the Dumbarton Road and never realise the variety and fascination on free display only a mile away! Had a Communist, taking advantage of his condition, pointed the sharpness of the contrast, Danny would not have listened. Times were hard for some, but Glasgow lived still. In those walks through the crowded, wealthy streets he positively acquired faith in the permanence of life as he had always known it.

There was always Leslie Pagan, the Boss, belonging by right to this secure and shining world. Had not the Boss virtually promised him a wee job? This unemployment was not a fatal blight. It was hard to be idling, pausing like a boy to watch cobblers at work or to see the great printing presses humming in the basement of a Hope Street newspaper office, but a fellow had to see it as an interregnum, a sort of holiday.

Yet he could not get away from Union Street and its crowded windows. Before a baker's shop there he would stand for minutes on end, counting with the loving care of a child the things he would buy and eat (sharing them always with Billy in imagination) some day. He did not realise that he spent so much of his time gazing at covetable foodstuffs. He did not know that hunger was getting at him, and that his man's body needed more than the tea and bread and jam, with an occasional sausage, that had become his lot. He had not really noticed the decline of Agnes, according to the fate of her kind, from the state of an urgent, eager, natty housewife to that of a drab who, rid of the necessity to get a well-fed man out to his work in the morning, lay abed late and emptied things out of tins and let the kitchen grate retain its stains from the sparking sausages that were all she would bother to cook. He was content with the knowledge that they had little money to spend.

It was not as a slacker he saw Agnes in those empty days that followed the escape of Peter from the Law. All he could comprehend was the changed, sullen Agnes to whom the release seemed to mean nothing, the woman who would not come back out of pride and petulance to meet him in their joint difficulty. She gloomed about the house, snapping now and again at them all. She would discuss nothing. In the slightest danger of being left alone with her husband in the evening, there were always her hat and coat behind the door and a mutter of some promise to go with Lizzie to the pictures. And that scowling wraith he could not capture.

It saddened him. On his most unwilling mind a grievance against Agnes was impressing itself. She was not playing the game, as he understood it; let alone not pulling her weight, she was positively pulling it in another direction and splitting the whole fabric of their joint existence. When he thought of the hold that Lizzie and her husband had upon his wife he was almost sick with anger and resentment. A good drink one of those days, and he would knock the face off somebody. Lucky for them, he thought, that he was off the drink and indulged himself only in a Threepenny Roll-Up on dole days—a packet of Woodbines, a glass of Empire wine, and a quarter-pint of beer: that little moment of warmth in the decent workless man's week.

Lizzie and Jim had kept quiet when Peter was in trouble, taking dashed good care to be out of the road. Not a word of help or even sympathy had Danny heard from his brother-in-law in all these weeks of trial. Free and easy enough with his money in indulging himself was Jim, but it took a gentleman like the Boss and the urge of real feeling to do something worthwhile and stand the racket. And now that Peter was free, now that Danny had taken all the worry and Leslie Pagan all the expense, Lizzie and Jim started coming about the house again, full of proprietorial interest and helpfulness. Lord, but it was sickening to hear them make a hero of Peter! A hero! Danny knew all about that.

"Aye," Jim had said sententiously, arriving on the very night of Peter's release, "It's been a bad business. Lizzie and me could hardly sleep when it was going on. Many's the night we sat up worrying our heads off, the two of us. I wish we could have given you a hand."

"You could easy have given us a hand if you felt like it," growled Danny.

"Well—" said Jim judiciously.

"Oh, Danny!" protested Lizzie.

"What are you shooting out yer neck about?" Agnes rasped at him.

"Oh, nothing much," retorted Danny dryly. "But there's some that's grand helpers when it's no' going to cost them anything."

"Are you referring to us?" asked Lizzie grandly after a horrified pause.

"I'm referring to anybody that likes to take it to themselves," Danny was fierce. "All I know is that I was blooming well left on my backside to do what I could. We didn't hear so much then of folk that couldn't sleep for worrying."

Jim held up an experienced and reasonable hand.

"That's all very fine, Dan," he said generously. "I know how you're feeling and all that. That's all very fine. But if you—" and here he insinuated a subtle argument, waggling a knowing fore-finger—"if you go and bring in your boss, this Mr. Pagan, ye're not expecting me to butt in, are you? Now, are you?"

Danny laughed harshly.

"For Christ's sake, Jim, get off it! You give me a pain in the guts, so help me God, ye do! Look here, son. Peter was in the nick three days before I heard a word from Mr. Pagan. But *you* knew—you had plenty of time to come along and give me hand if you wanted to. God Almighty, man, I'm not saying you should ha' done it. I wasn't asking you. But when you come girning here about the worry ye've had and losin' sleep, Holy Christ,"—and he spat viciously into the grate—"you make me want to spew!"

His outburst was followed by seconds of glacial silence.

"Well, of all—" protested Lizzie piously.

"Ach, don't heed him. He's drunk or daft—or both." That was what Agnes said.

"Well, I can understand how you're feeling, Dan," said Jim justly. "I'm a man that can make allowances. It's been a tough time for you, right enough. But—"

"Ach! Go to hell the lot of you!" Danny swept them aside and, seizing his cap, rushed away from that intolerable company.

And that was only the beginning of it, the beginning of a whole series of fresh complications.

Every other evening Jim and Lizzie came to the house to sit in the kitchen. If he stayed with them, it was to be sullen and silent on his own part, and, consequently, to be ostracised by them. If he fled, it was to give them the victory and to have to walk the streets or stand at corners, penniless, lonely, hungry, thirsty—for still he could resist the lure of the pub. He knew that he was at war with his wife's people, and that in his absence their prejudice against him was hardening in the fires of reminiscence and discussion. Agnes was assuming the stature of a heroine, misunderstood and maltreated by a boor. The case of Peter was becoming for them a romance in which they figured as the tutelary gods of a hero.

On one of the nights he chose to stay about the fire with them Danny listened in sardonic silence to Jim's approach to this attitude. It appeared that Jim that day had been among a number of what he called "big men, you know. The real Mackay. Bailie Maconie and that lot, and thon brother of his from London, the big chewing-gum man." It was indicated that the talk among these cronies had been of the trial, Bailie Maconie—"a big man, right in the know, you know,"—holding that the police were more to blame than anybody.

"It's the polis that make the gangsters, see?" expounded Jim. "They see a lot of young fellows goin' about havin' a bit of fun, and they call them a gang. They get to know the young fellows that goes about together, and they wait for them, and a decent boy like Peter, out of a decent home, he goes with his mates to a dance hall, and some mug starts a bit o' rough house, and the polis is just waitin', and the likes o' Peter gets landed. And for what? For sweet dam' all but havin' a bit o' fun."

"I suppose they gave Cosh Tanelli eighteen months for having a bit o' fun?" suggested Danny dryly.

Jim laughed tolerantly. "That's just where you don't know what goes on behind the scenes, Dan," he said slyly. "Did it ever occur to you that Cosh Tanelli's a Pape and the old man on the bench is a Billy Boy, blue and orange as they make them? Think that one out."

Danny encountered Jim's superior wink.

"Baloney!" he exploded.

"Aye, ye can say baloney if you like, but that's what I'm tellin' ye."

"Oh, it's dreadful!" Lizzie chimed in. "Of all the dirty big twisters, I think the Glasgow polis is about the limit. The things Jim's told me!"

Danny counted himself lucky in that that was one of the last of these unwelcome visitations. Shortly thereafter, as if they had observed a due period of mourning, the three of them took to the old ritual of picture houses and small ports and other distractions that Danny could not trust himself to think about. He was happy enough to be left with Billy and with Wee Mirren, as good as gold on the big bed. He and Billy took to halma, keeping the score of games won and lost over a week at a time. It was a grand game, thought Danny, though he was apt to lose his rag over it while Billy went from victory to victory with the detachment of boyhood. And they started to save up pennies for a box of dominoes.

Strangely, it hardly ever occurred to him to worry about Peter. Peter had suddenly come out of the shadows of life, postured pathetically in the light for a space, and then receded into silence and mystery. His father could see some change in the boy; there was a little less truculence, perhaps, a little more willingness to talk at the table in the simple family way. But of the movements of Peter he had no more knowledge and control than ever he had had.

Now and again he preached to Peter the necessity of a proper young man looking for a job, but he did so without much fervour. The lad, wherever he got the money to keep himself going—perhaps from his mother, perhaps from Jim—seemed at least never to be mooning about the house, his sluggardly habits in the morning apart: and what did these matter in the home of an idle man? Often he was not in for the midday meal. Danny had the suspicion that he played billiards in the afternoons. He was punctual enough for tea, but he remained the mystery of the night, seldom returning home until the rest of the household was abed. And the father could not agitate himself about the son. It was as if he had given the lad up as a sacrifice to the obscure gods of the strange new world.

How Agnes thought about Peter he could never determine. Sometimes, when Jim and Lizzie were there, she seemed to share their pride in his notoriety and their faith in his essential goodness, but then Agnes was bound to be on the other side from her husband. Within the family life she took no more notice of Peter than she had ever done—as if the boy were just a part of the unit with which she was so dissatisfied. Only Wee Mirren could draw tenderness from her these days, and Danny, perceiving a subtlety in a rare flash of insight, believed it was because she needed the still undeveloped baby in her own camp. Somehow, Billy stood in his self-containment in a neutral zone and got the lash of her tongue only when he had ostensibly preferred the interests of his father.

It was over such a humiliating triviality they quarrelled one evening. Over a nothing the banked fires of resentment flared to the point of explosion. They had finished tea, and while Billy ran out on an errand and Agnes was busy with the baby, Danny started to make an innocent beginning with the clearing of the table for the customary game of halma. A slip of his hand, and he had tipped over a pot of jam to smear the American cloth on the table.

"Ach, you clumsy big lout!" she barked at him over the infant's bare buttocks. "Can you not leave things alone?"

The attack was vicious. Hatred was in her tone, unmistakable. Danny was stung to fury. But he made one effort to keep the peace.

"It was an accident. I was only helping to clear away."

"Aye, and ye're not even fit for that."

It was as if she had, in a flash, grown fangs and as if the accumulated grievances of months had turned in a second to venom that must be discharged. No man, except that he saw her a person diseased, could take what she flung at him, and Danny had no sense of neurosis and no fine awareness of what may be allowed to women approaching the middle years of life. Through flames of anger he saw her only as the enemy, plain and implacable. Two strides took him to stand over her where she sat. She half-rose, the baby in her arms, her face defiant. He swung his right fist back to hit her. Then the baby in her arms came between him and her hatefulness. His arm dropped.

"You're just a poor, silly fool!" was all he said, but there was in the words a final considered renunciation of the bond that held them.

She did not answer. He saw fear, and the momentary surrender filled him at once with contempt. Ostentatiously indifferent to her fate, thenceforward he turned away from her, found his jacket and cap, and slammed his way from the house.

He knew as soon as he was in the street that the gesture was meaningless and inconclusive. He had done something that was intended to be effective and only made him feel foolish. Another man would have given her the hiding she deserved: brutal but just. So he realised that his marriage had finally and completely failed, and the knowledge left him hopeless, baffled and sad.

He walked a long way that night, right up as far as Kelvingrove and into the West End Park. Moments of violent anger against Agnes alternated with moments of longing for the old cosy understanding with her. Now and again he was tempted by a passion to seek out Lizzie and Jim and tell them what he thought of them. Then he would wistfully see it all as an outcome of this strange process that had left him workless, a man on the dole. But Agnes should have stood beside him in that emergency. At ten to ten he slipped into a public house at Overnewton and wildly spent the best part of two very precious shillings on a glass of whisky and a pint of beer.

The unaccustomed drink went to his head quickly. In a few minutes, walking westwards along Argyle Street, he regained his full stature as a man. He seemed to see it clearly as his duty to hurry home and give Agnes the hiding of her life. Then a subtle and deadlier way of hurting her occurred to him. He would go and see Jess, the widow of his dead friend, and contrive it so that he might sleep with her.

In that volition there was more than the spirit of revenge. Jess was kind, and for kindness Danny was as hungry as a starved baby for the breast. It would be glory to let himself sink into that softness and start afresh in the sort of partnership life ordained for a man's needs. They could take Billy into the family. The mere need to care for Jess and the rest of them would get him work.

Not very confidently, even with the drink he had taken, he made for the pend off Argyle Street. The entry was unfriendly, with the night wind blowing the gas in the single lamp to send swinging shadows up and down the whitewashed tunnel. In the yard he came upon a waiting taxicab, its driver asleep in his seat under the feeble glow of a bulb in the roof. There was a confusion of parked coal-carts and ice-cream barrows before the heavy gate that led to Jess's cottage; and, groping his way among them, his eye was caught and held by the glow of the oil-lamp gleaming through her window.

He stopped at the sight of it. It suddenly had for him, even in his ravishing mood, a serene and holy quality. It whispered into the night good tidings of comfort and modesty and peace. His passion oozed out of him. He glowed virtuously in the imagined serenity of the fireside clime. Jess ceased to be a morsel of warm, desirable flesh and became a creature remotely sweet and sacred. Like a boy whipped into a sense of decency, Danny turned away and tiptoed his passage through the assortment of vehicles. To the chauffeur, awake now and lighting a cigarette, he cried a cheery and virtuous "Goodnight!"

Agnes was sitting before the fire when he got home. That she had been out he saw from her coat and hat, lumped on the table. She seemed to him now a stranger with whom one could have business-like relations.

"Peter in yet?" he asked casually, hanging up his cap.

"You can see for yourself he's not," she replied.

"Starting his nonsense again, I suppose."

"Fat lot you need to care," she answered levelly. "He's got a job anyway."

2

It was hard to bear, this knowledge that Peter had a job while he, journeyman riveter and hard grafter all his life, was on the street.

All the circumstances were bitter. Peter had qualified for nothing, but Peter could, and did, come the big man in the house on the strength of a job.

The nature of the job itself was disgusting enough—doorkeeper of a small cinema in the East End beyond Bridgeton Cross. The boy was never out of his bed till ten or eleven in the morning. He quickly fell into the habit of ordering his mother about, demanding that the midday meal should be served at such and such an hour, so that he might do whatsoever he wanted to do and yet be at the picture house in good time for the afternoon session. It seemed that he had always something to do on his own—see a chap about a dog running at Carntyne in the evening, or place a bet on a sure thing for the three-thirty at Wolverhampton.

He grew in a brash, easy confidence that infuriated Danny. It became one of the father's secret grievances that Peter never came home in his uniform but went about in a flash suit, changing into braided, plum-coloured tunic and trousers in the remote obscurity of the picture palace. It was infuriating to see him yawn about the house and stretch his arms and ask again and again if the dinner was not ready yet. The bastard seemed to think he owned the place: all because he now paid his mother a lodger's rental of seven and six a week. Then he would come slamming into the house long after midnight, wakening them all up and grumbling that there was no food handy in the cupboard.

The emergence of his son as a man might have delighted Danny in other circumstances, but now it was all wrong. The boy's job he despised—one of these flash, cheap, unskilled billets that lads were tumbling into nowadays: no apprenticeship, no early hours, but just a game for any mug at a labourer's wage, and all very fancy with their jazz and chit-chat of film stars and dancing. Very soon he was to discover that Agnes was not standing for any criticism of Peter, that Agnes would even use the example of Peter to sneer at him. (Although, a strange thing, she would take no nonsense from the boy!) And the bitterest thing of all was that Peter's job was all Jim's doing. Jim had some remote interest in that seedy picture house, or some vague influence with its owner; and Jim could pose as both the powerful man of affairs and the influential and generous helper of lame dogs. While Danny knew very well that Peter, his useless son, had as the martyr of a notorious trial a commercial value shrewdly assessed by his brother-in-law.

It was enough to drive a man daft, at least to drink, but he kept himself to the strict letter of his new code. He drew the dole, handed the most of it over to Agnes, and rarely indulged himself in more than the Threepenny Roll-Up of his need. In the house he kept as quiet as he could; silent if Agnes was stirred out of her resentment to lash at him, grimly tolerant of Peter's new largeness of manner, taking only a decent pleasure in the petting of Wee Mirren or in a game on a quiet evening with Billy. Jim and Lizzie had ceased to come about the house; Agnes was often out with them, and how they amused themselves he never knew.

All he could do was walk the streets, and soon a large area of the city of Glasgow had nothing to interest him. Even the foodshops of Union Street became merely maddening in their allure. Again and again he would awaken out of a coma and find himself staring at the deft, rapid hands of a cobbler working in his window, hypnotised by the sight of a man actually at work. Or he would walk the docksides, vaguely curious as to the lives and work of the coolies from Clan and City liners, wistfully watching a vessel warped out of the Queen's Dock and setting down river for the Mediterranean ports.

He came to know all the parks within his range—Whiteinch with its bleak fossil grove, the charm of Kelvingrove, the reeking hothouses of the Botanic Gardens. On many a night he could not sleep, and sometimes he would slip out of bed and into his clothes and out of the house in the summer dawn to have the empty world of streets for his own. It was one of the big pleasures of the period to form an acquaintance and pass the time of day with an old man who led a pug into Kelvingrove every morning at six. And he also learned to nod to lamplighters and railwaymen hurrying early at regular hours to the day's work.

Life lost definition and colour and order. It came to mean nothing certain and colourful save the precious game of dominoes or halma with Billy in the evening. He knew himself to be going soft in mind and body. In Royal Terrace one evening a doctor was in trouble with his car and called him to help. He contrived to turn the engine two or three times and then gave up, his arm numb, his chest aching. The doctor glanced at him shrewdly, gave him half-a-crown, and told him to go and buy a square meal. The failure rankled.

Yet in all these weeks of idleness he made next to no attempt to find work for himself. To be sure, the sense that the search would be nearly hopeless was always at the back of his mind, but his incuriosity had deeper roots than that. There persisted in him a

159

wholly blind faith in shipbuilding, in himself, and in Leslie Pagan. Battered by circumstance, he still could not believe that this stoppage, that dismal array of empty berths along the banks of the river, might last for ever. It was incredible that Pagan's would not reopen within a month or two. And since, in his ingenuous philosophy, an early resumption of work was a certainty, it was just quite impossible for him to understand that he might not be among the first to be called back to the gates and the time-clock and the old familiar darg.

The faith reposed ultimately in the Boss. The Boss would never let the Yard down. The possible defeat of his hero never haunted even his worst moments. And had not Leslie Pagan said that there was a wee job or two to be done about the house, pending the moment, the inevitable moment, the Yard would be busy again?

There were moments when Danny wondered miserably if he had been forgotten. For a long time after the trial of Peter he heard nothing from or of the man in whom rested all his beliefs. It was impossible to believe in such a terrible abandonment, but God knew the days were slow and empty.

There came one day when he could stand it no longer. In his conscious mind he was determined that he would not be a sponger. All he wanted to know was just where the Boss had got to—to England with that toff wife of his, to London to look for orders, or to some remote and elegant holiday place. So he made up his mind to go down to the Yard and see old Macewan, the commissionaire, and find out a thing or two. There was always the chance that he might be seen. . . . Indignantly he suppressed the selfish thought.

Sergeant Macewan, late of the King's Own Scottish Borderers, a row and a half of bright ribbons on his left breast, showed himself to Danny a milder official than he had been a year before. There was a time when not a soul, save an employee, not even the Chairman of the owners himself or his Marine Superintendent, could pass into the Yard without a sojourn in the Sergeant's office, a wait while that slow and suspicious dignitary made enquiries over the house telephone, and a ritual signing of a large book.

Now the old man seemed to glow at the sight of even a visitor so humble as Danny. His tunic was open at the neck, there was a newspaper in his hand, and he pulled at a pipe. There was dust on the desks of his little room. Easy-osy, he came strolling to the door who once would have barked in his fiercest parade-ground voice at a tradesman bold enough to come that way.

"What's brought you here, Shields, my lad?" he boomed. "Want to buy the place? It's going cheap."

Danny laughed obligingly. "No, Sergeant," he retorted with the sardonic twist proper to Clydeside. "I've just bought the big Cunarder at Clydebank, and that's enough for the day. What I want to know is where Mr. Leslie is."

"He'll not see you."

The teachings of decades still worked spasmodically within the sergeant.

"I'm not asking you to let me see him. But you see, Sergeant, he was good to me about that silly boy of mines, and there's one or two things to be settled, and I know he's not in his own house."

"That's right enough. He's not." The sergeant then surprised Danny by moving quickly to the door and bawling down the passage: "Quigg! Quigg!"

A lad came slouching to obey the command.

"Here, boy!" ordered Macewan briskly. "You look after the office till I come back. You can tell anybody but the First Lord of the Admiralty to go to hell. We've given up building ships and are selling striped paint for barbers' poles." He took his cap from its peg.

"Come on, Shields. They'll just be open."

Danny hesitated. "I don't think I can manage, Sergeant. . . ."

"Come on, man. It's on me the day. You just don't know how bloody glad I am to have a good excuse."

Days were strangely changed, thought Danny as they crossed the road to the varnished doors of the Turbine Vaults. The sergeant idle, bored, glad to have any sort of caller, and—he, most loyal and austere of the old servants of the Yard!—to be jesting about stagnation and striped paint for barbers' poles and suchlike bitterness. He was glad to have the assurance of the large pint put down before him.

"Yes," said the sergeant, "you were wondering where Mr. Leslie is?" It was clear he was about to make an announcement. "I'll soon tell you where he is. He's at the bedside of one of the finest

161

old gentlemen that ever stepped God's earth—good luck to him!"

Sergeant Macewan raised his mug and drank deep.

"The old man?" Danny asked sharply.

"Dying—and has been this month past. Cancer of the liver, the poor old bastard. A toff and a gentleman, if ever there was one, a toff and a gentleman."

"He was all that," agreed Danny fervently.

"And that's where your Mr. Leslie is. Out at Edingray with his old father that's dying. God knows he's just as well there as here. We're all bloody well dying in the Yard and shipbuilding and the Clyde and all."

The sergeant spat violently into the sawdust. But Danny was paying no attention to the outburst. There was light in his mind again. Leslie had not forgotten him but had his own troubles to bear. The fact of comradeship, renewed in their several sorrows, glowed vital and rewarding once more. He astonished the sergeant by shaking hands with him at the door of the public house.

"You're a right toff, Sergeant," he protested. "I'm obliged to you, very much obliged to you. Some day I'll be able to return your hospitality."

"Better get into the banana trade, then," retorted Sergeant Macewan with grim relish and returned to his box and his paper before the empty fireplace.

And it was all in the papers before the week was out. Danny had been wandering far from home along the Canal and Port Dundas one afternoon when, coming down out of that lost region of silent warehouses and stagnant water to the flurry of the Maryhill Road, he saw it on the bills of evening newspapers before a tiny shop.

"Death of Famous Clyde Shipbuilder," said one in crowded type. "Loss to Clyde Shipbuilding," another. Footsore, he had promised himself a halfpenny ride in the tram along the bleak stretch of Sauchiehall Street westwards from Charing Cross and could not face spending another penny on a paper, but he had the luck to see a man, dropping off at Kelvingrove Street, leave a *News* on his seat. He pounced for it; and there was the whole story on the front page under deep headlines. He read eagerly—the old man's origins, age, career, political and charitable activities, and achievements as shipbuilder. "One of the old school," ran a reportorial phrase that gave Danny a power of pleasure.

The affair elated him. It gave him a feeling of significance, of belonging to something big and fine and sempiternal; it raised him right above the pretty typists and bowler-hatted clerks going home to the bungalows of the housing schemes. When he decided that he must attend the funeral, it was completely a declaration of faith and not at all a claim to recognition. He saw the parade as part of a man's duty.

The thought, however, sent his mind questing along lugubrious channels. Suddenly he saw in the state of his clothes the measure of his own decline. The old brown suit was shabby all over and greasy down the waistcoat. His boots were nobbly and dull for lack of the polish Agnes never troubled to give them now. In place of collar and tie he wore a cravat of artificial silk crossed under his chin. His cap was weatherstained and broken about the peak. All the same (he reflected, unconsciously bracing his shoulders) he could make a show. His best blue suit lay neat and clean under tissue-paper in a drawer. He could still compass a white collar and black tie and clean shirt as well as the next man. The bowler hat of his formality was safe in its box in the wardrobe in the boys' bedroom. Danny Shields would still be a decent figure in the column of fours behind the coffin of old man Pagan.

Next morning he was out early to look up the death notices in the *Herald* at the Free Library at Partick Cross. Even at ten in the forenoon the Reading Room was crowded with tweed-capped men bending over periodicals so esoteric as the *Aryan Path* and the *Hibbert Journal*—anything for idle men to read. Before the newspapers on their stands the press of younger men was heavy. There was always the chance of a job advertised, and hope still lingered in men's hearts. Because he wanted to look at a front page Danny could not share the *Herald* with another fellow, but by dint of holding his place in the queue with the main force of his elbows and of explaining to a neighbour that all he required was a glance at the Deaths column, he had not above twenty minutes to wait. He had brought paper and a stub of one of Billy's pencils to note it down.

"On the 12th inst., at Edingray, Stirlingshire, John Semple Pagan, shipbuilder, in his 79th year. Funeral private."

Funeral private! The intimation astounded Danny. He had vaguely dreamed of an endless cortège, of shuttered shops, of brass bands wailing Chopin to respectful crowds on pavements and, in general, of a city in mourning for one of its great men. This notice was altogether too stark and modest. Severely it seemed to exclude the likes of him; and he had sincerely believed that the Major should have his old batman at his elbow on such a day.

Still purposeful, however, Danny trudged from the Library the long westward way to the Yard. He had no sense of pushing himself forward. It was honestly in his mind that grief and preoccupation had led the Boss into this curt negation of all that was right and proper. The sergeant would know if this affair was really to go on as indicated. He could not believe it.

Sergeant Macewan was more subdued than at their previous meeting. Himself ageing, the fact of death was beyond even bitterness.

"I told you, Shields," he said heavily. "There was no hope for the old gentleman. It comes to us all in the long run. Aye, aye, it comes to us all, and there's just no getting away from it. Ye'll be at the funeral?"

Danny's heart bounded at that.

"But there's this 'private' business. That's what was biting me."

"Ah, but you see, it's to be a cremation, son," the sergeant proudly explained. "Seems the old man wanted it that way—decent, quiet old gentleman that he was—and what could Mr. Leslie do? But it's all right for the old hands that wants to pay their respects. He was on the phone this morning—Mr. Leslie was—said he'd be glad to see a squad of us up-bye on Thursday afternoon. You come along, my lad. The two of you soldiered together. He'll be glad to see you."

The sergeant's manner was portentous but assured, and Danny was happy again. It was a bitter business that he could not go as a decent worker from the Yard—but how many would go in that capacity? The sergeant, one or two out of the Counting House, an odd draughtsman, and old Dan in the Store. Even Peter Menzies, the foreman who had done the dirty job of sacking on him, was out of work and would have no status as a veteran at the funeral. That was only for the old, the authentic guard.

They assembled before the big house in Kelvinside, sheepish in their unaccustomed clothes, on a close, dull afternoon of May, and Leslie Pagan himself came out in his sombre garments of ceremonial to greet them where they stood uneasy before the porch.

"Come in, boys," he invited. "There's a little service going to start." He had a word for each as he passed, bowler hat awkwardly in hand.

"You, John! This is kind of you. . . . Hullo, Alec! My father would be pleased. . . . For the sake of old times, William." His face glowed at the sight of Danny: "This is grand of you, Dan."

Sincere fingers pressed his arm and, his face red and his eyes wet, Danny passed into the great house. Well used he was to funerals in tenement kitchens with the coffin, its lid propped open, on the table, so that old friends might look on the face of the dead and sigh over it, but this was the simple and ordered ritual of another world. He sat with his mates in the back rows of chairs set against the walls of a high and dignified chamber, the dining-room he guessed it to be. He saw in the places before him men old or handsome or distinguished, and recognised the great in the land, peers and baronets and leaders in the world of affairs. He saw the Minister of the Cathedral, whom last he had seen in the High Court, rise to speak the lovely words of Ecclesiastes xii. No coffin was there, but Danny was content. Old John Pagan was passing as a great man should, mourned by his peers and his true servants; even better, sweeter, truer was this mourning than the pomp of processions.

Again, as he passed out with the others, his elbow was gripped by the Boss.

"There are cabs for everybody, Dan," came the whisper. "See that the boys get their places."

Danny stood behind the parapet of the steps and watched the roll of history unfold. Men bore a plain coffin through the door and placed it in the hearse (why not the dipping of colours, the bugle's challenging note, the fatal throb of drums?). Into great cars, stooping like common men, disappeared the rich and titled. Officials, lawyers, servants, and mere friends swarmed round the hired Austins. The men from the Yard were taken by the last four cars of all and, in the banality of low gear, the cavalcade moved northwards.

It was quiet and a little chill in the chapel amid the gravestones. Already the coffin was under a purple pall on the catafalque. The Minister of the Cathedral waited for them all to assemble. The rows of people, rich and poor, seemed fused in a common decency of respect. Only the figure of the Englishwoman, Leslie Pagan's wife, struck an odd note of disharmony. But she was on her knees, her face buried in her hands, her femininity suppressed.

"Let us pray," said the Minister of the Cathedral.

The poetry of the service rolled over bowed heads. As he listened to every word lovingly enunciated even Danny knew the sweet awe of the Promise.

"I am the resurrection and the life, saith the Lord."

In the presence of death the validity of life was assured beyond all question. All men stood together in that. All men went the same road home.

"Earth to earth, ashes to ashes, dust to dust."

He saw the coffin begin to sink through its bier. And did he really hear a roaring and the clang of metal? The Benediction stirred him out of deep, searching thought, and he shuffled after the others into the close, dull air of the early summer afternoon.

Leslie Pagan emerged with his wife on his arm and, as he passed to their car, made a sign to Danny to wait. In a moment or two he came over to the lingering group of his working men.

"It was good of you to come, boys. I'm very grateful. The cars will take you back. Danny—" He drew the little man aside and dropped his voice. "I want you up at the house at nine on Monday. There's a job for you."

3

He had known that it would come all right, and his trust was rewarded. Peter could be the fancy man about an East End picture house, and Agnes could sniff as she pleased, but he, Danny Shields, had a job and that would show them what he was good for. Good men had stood for years in the dole queues, but native worth had got him out of that degradation in the space of months. It was neither riveter's work nor pay, but it was bigger money than came out of the Buroo, and it gave a man his charter, a new insurance card. Regular hours, plenty to do about the place, and prompt pay every Friday afternoon made Danny perfectly happy once again.

It was not exactly his trade: there was always that at the back of his mind. Being the odd man about the big house in Kelvinside was not to brace powerful muscles against the thrust of hydraulic power and see plate after plate build up the forms of fine ships. It was not a world of rough heartiness and coarse free speech. But it was work, a job, an engagement with life, and he took with eagerness every challenge it had to offer him.

There was always something to be done about the place. The Boss had sold the big car, and the chauffeur with it, to a hiring company in the city, and Danny had the Riley to look after. Every morning it had to be cleaned—a great hosing with Glasgow's abundant water, an anxious dusting of leatherwork, and a fierce polishing of plated parts. He was mechanic enough to have complete responsibility for the machine's supplies of petrol, oil, and tyres; and he was never happier than when a small defect had to be remedied and he could experiment with the grave assurance of his breed amid the complexities of broken valve-springs or a disabled ignition system. That small aggregation of moving parts became his pride and his delight. Its fitness ministered to a fundamental aesthetic within him, and the care of it was a satisfaction. He learned to drive, and sometimes, if he were wearing a neat suit, he would take the Boss's wife about the town. It was a great day when he was sent to fetch the Boss himself from a conference in Edinburgh.

Then there was the garden. It had never been much of an interest with either of his employers, and the jobbing man who came about the place had enough to do to keep the lawns and paths and borders in trim. So in his spare time Danny dug and manured and weeded a large and neglected vegetable plot behind the house and planted what would still grow usefully while the summer lasted.

For this he earned the amused praise of Leslie Pagan, who came upon him working there one evening long after his due time to go home.

"My hat, Danny!" he cried. "You would think you were on piecework. This is a real job you've made of the place. It's grand."

"That's nothing, sir," Danny explained with large gravity.

"We're just getting it into shape for next year. It'll be a grand garden, this." He waved a possessive arm. "A fine patch of potatoes down there by the hedge. Lettuces up and down this side—the mistress'll want a salad now and again. There'll be parsley here and mebbe celery there. And rhubarb—I was thinking of a stick or two in the corner yonder. D'ye think, sir, Maister John would like a bit o' rhubarb whiles?"

"I'm sure he would, Dan," Pagan replied gravely. "But where did you learn all these tricks?

"Oh, just moochin' about the allotments down at Clydebank yonder. There's many a workless lad has learned to be a fine gardener this year or two past. I'll show some of them next year!"

That was the feeling he had—of belonging, of being part of the living organism of the big house. Perhaps his starved instinct for the domestic and the comfortable was appeased by the calls of the place upon him. He was almost proprietorial when Mrs. Scroggie, the cook, called him indoors to replace a washer in a kitchen tap or the vagaries of the patent boiler forced him to assume the mantle of plumber. It was his particular pride to fit up shelves in a spare room in which Master John proposed to establish a museum. Anxiously he would point out to the Boss where a rhone leaked or a tiny window could do with a lick of paint.

It was his own achievement in becoming a personality about the place that gave him most satisfaction, if he had only known it. Somewhere at the back of his mind was the feeling that he stood out, solid, rugged and reliable, in that smooth and elegant world. For that type of service which is at its best a partnership in responsibility (as it had been with Leslie Pagan in Gallipoli and Palestine and France) he had a natural instinct. If it had been proposed that he should become permanently of the staff and live in the house, he would have slipped into the post with perfect naturalness.

As it was, the going home to Agnes and her grudges and tempers every night kept happiness and contentment out of his reach. When she chose to speak she had him understand that she despised his employment. That hurt him bitterly, for he did not see that she was simply jealous of his innocent approach to the substance of her dream. One night, infuriated by her sneers and half-hints, he

168

thundered at her.

"By God, Agnes, you can count yourself dashed lucky, if you ask me! I've got a job—mebbe not much of a job to your way of thinking, but it's more than most men can say these days. And Peter's in a job. Holy Mike, what do you keep grousing and girning about?"

"Fat lot I get out of Peter," she retorted.

"He pays you his board."

"Aye, when it comes up his back. If you'd take an interest in the house you'd know a damned sight more. You didn't know he's thinking of getting married, I suppose."

"Married!" Danny was appalled.

"Aye, married! Perhaps you didn't hear me the first time. He's got to. Seems she's three months gone."

"Who is she?"

"That wee Curran bitch—Rita, or whatever it is they cry her. Fine lot I've got in this house, isn't it?"

"Peter! Rita Curran!" Danny could not comprehend it. "I'll see them."

"Oh, you'll see them all right. Glad you're interested, I'm sure."

It did not particularly shock Danny that Peter and his girl had anticipated the marriage ceremony. So much was almost common form in the world he knew best. It was his pride of family and possession that was offended. A lad like Peter, just a bit of a boy and not long out of trouble, to be challenging the authority of his father! Never done a stroke of real man's work in his life, tumbled into a soft job, making a cod of himself outside a picture house, and now talking about taking a wife! The boy just hadn't the sense for it, didn't know what he was in for. Danny reckoned that Rita Curran, whom he could not quite distinguish in memory, would be one of these fancy molls they were breeding nowadays.

He met her a few days later. Seemingly Peter had staged it so that Rita would be in the house one Saturday morning when Danny came home from his work. She turned out to be small and slightly bow-legged, though she was draped to the ankles in a cotton dress that, under a loose red coat, looked to Danny the sort of thing a lassie might go to a dance in. She had a cheeky small face under a severe fringe of black hair. She chewed what was either gum or an extremely durable caramel. Her shoes were white and fancy and dirty and over at the side, and within them her bare legs were protected only by sockettes. She seemed completely the cheery mistress of her brittle self.

"Here's Rita," was Peter's sheepish introduction of her to Danny while Agnes pretended to be lost in noisy affairs at the sink.

"Oh!" said Danny weakly. But it was beyond him to be severe with a woman so young and helpless. He went on, roughly facetious: "So you're thinking of getting married, Rita?"

"Sez you," Rita agreed.

He laughed. Her pert confidence amused him. Only he wished she would stop chewing for a minute and twitching and lifting her feet in the monotonous rhythm of the modern dance. It was as if she was a slightly unwilling and completely detached visitor from another world.

Danny found conversation with Rita extremely difficult. At no point could he make real contact with her, and he did not understand the phrases that, culled from the lips of Hollywood beauties, were all the language she seemed to know. He was very much relieved, and distinctly exhausted, when at length she whirled away with Peter, the only human being in the house with whom she apparently shared some vague understanding.

Then Danny spoke to Agnes's ostentatious back.

"She seems a bright wee thing," he said tentatively.

"Aye," came the dry response, "ye'll think that when she comes to live with you. At least, that's Peter's big idea. He'll have to think again if I'm staying."

It was an ultimatum. The war was still on, and breaking out in a fresh place. It was a sad and puzzled Danny who walked along to see the cricket at Hamilton Crescent that afternoon.

CHAPTER NINE

WOMEN AT HOME

THE SHOWER caught Blanche as she paused to pass behind a tram across Great Western Road. It came raging up the gully of the Clyde, swift and harsh and chill, and mocked the inadequacy of her small and pretty umbrella. A motor car, overtaking the tram on the near side, splashed its libation on her skirt and stockings. The rain filled the gutters with miniature torrents and, leaping that which scurried muddily down the line of the northern pavement, she brought one inadequate shoe down in a puddle that had formed behind the kerb.

The discomfort of cold and wet worked on an irritation that had been fermenting all afternoon. Louise Marshall's party had been a bore, and then a torment. Louise was sweet enough in her flabby way, but to go and land her with that Mrs. Macniven who had once been to Monte Carlo and could talk of nothing else—in an atrocious Glasgow accent! Mrs. Macniven, whose little finger, perked out genteelly from her teacup, was an affront to Blanche's sense of suavity. Then to be paired with the feeble, fluttering Miss Denholm at Contract—"Oh, dear! I've played the wrong thing again"—and to lose eight and sixpence in consequence had completed the ravage of her afternoon.

From the rise of Cleveden Road she saw the rain, always menacing this Glasgow. It scudded along the Kilpatrick Hills, damping out their colours; it blotted out the noble background of rock and mountain, a grey ceiling low above chimneys and gantries. Her mind resisted the nobility of the orange glow of wild sunlight behind the curtain, accepted only its menace of falling leaf and winter storm over a city that had few compensations of light and laughter and frivolity to offer. It frightened her, and she hated it, this inveterate grimness of the North. The fear of its winter closed upon her. She thought of Bond Street in the crisp October dusk, of puppies in a window, of dainty teas served out of old silver and eggshell china before warm fires.

At home at last, her skirt and stockings and shoes wet through, she was short with the maid who anxiously offered tea before she could have a bath. It was a vicious appeasement to trouble the girl by lingering in the blessed warmth of the water and over the task of dressing again. It angered her to find the tea already waiting for her in the lounge, and the girl, answering her ring, had to hear sharp criticism of the toasted teabread and be sent for another jug of hot water—"really hot this time," added Blanche. And when Lizzie came back with that, she sent the girl away again for aspirin.

John was gravely engaged with the top of a boiled egg when Blanche went at length to the day nursery. He would vouchsafe no more than a cheek for her kiss; eggs are such interesting things to deal with; and he merely murmured a polite "All right, thank you," to her "And how are you, darling?" The egg, deliciously curved, so smooth when you cut through the white, was the thing.

"I think John has started a cold," said the Norland girl severely, speaking as if John were far away in bed.

"Another!" Blanche cried. Deliberately she challenged Nannie. "Really, it's too bad. Is the boy properly clad?"

"If he's allowed to play with that Shields boy in the garden," the girl demurred with bland insolence. "And I can't help the weather, madam."

"John is not allowed to play with that child. See that it doesn't happen again."

Back in the lounge, she found herself infuriated by the weakness of the retort. The Norland girl had won the round. A mother ought to have known that the Shields boy was coming about the place with the father, whom Leslie had rescued in his incomprehensible way. But Leslie really ought to have known that John would make friends with him. And what did that fool of a girl think she was doing to allow it?

The irritations of the day worked on her, one fusing into the other, till she knew herself that they were beyond reason. She tried the woman's page of the *Scotsman*, but it could not hold her. The switching-over of a knob flooded the room with the emollient strains of a cinema organ from some southern suburb of London, and she turned it back again. There was to be no distraction for her till her husband came home.

All her petulance came back to him in the long run. It was he and his queer, unreasonable ways that kept her in this impossible city and its impossible life—the rain, the futile Bridge parties, and the rest. If Leslie had work to do in Glasgow, she reasoned plausibly, if it was really necessary for him to stay near the Yard, she would have no grievance at all. Loyally, through every year since the war, she had stood by him in a place wherein, he knew well enough, she could not learn to be really happy. But now, on his own admission, shipbuilding was nearly done for, and though they had all the money they needed, and more since the old man was dead, he would not leave Clydeside. They could be perfectly happy in Surrey. John would be free from this eternal risk of chill that terrorised her. Yet Leslie Pagan lingered under the menace of another winter. It seemed to her a stupid denial of happiness.

That she could not honestly understand how his mind worked was a grievance in itself. . . . She wandered to the window and looked out disconsolately at the wet, rigid rows of the city's lamps, lit so early since Summer Time had ended the day before: drear intimation of the gloom ahead. She began to think how Fate and her husband had conspired to trap her. She knew that she could have got him back to her feet in Surrey in the long run, but the old man had died to put upon her a duty of respect and sympathy that she quickly and gladly obeyed. Did that gladness not spring out of a feeling that the death was the breaking of Leslie's last link with the North?

Her obsessed mind shied away from the awkward thought. She had done her duty, and gladly; on that her conscience was clear. She had been prepared to face life at Edingray, rebuilding a quiet life away from the squalor of Glasgow—if it was understood that they would go abroad in winter. But Leslie, without a word to her, had sold Edingray to the Corporation to be used as a convalescent home or something and had coolly brought her back, her will strangely numb for the time being, to the big house in Kelvinside and the respectable fatuities of Glasgow's social round.

The immediate irritations of the afternoon died down. She was left with a feeling of emptiness and frustration, lavishly shot with the sense of martyrdom. Leslie Pagan, coming in with the chill fresh air of the night about him, found her in an unwonted pose of tragic

173

idleness.

"Hello, old girl!" he greeted her, stooping to kiss her hair. "What a ghastly night!"

"Awful!" Blanche agreed emptily.

"How have things been?"

"Oh, just the usual. John's got another cold."

"Good Lord! Does that girl look after him properly?"

"Certainly she does." Blanche's tone was sharp. "But she can't go chasing after him every time he runs into the garden to play with that Shields boy—messing about in the wet and picking up by the way the most appalling Glasgow accent."

Leslie glanced at her quickly. He was careful to be patient in his answer.

"Perhaps you had better tell Nannie that John is not to play in the garden on wet days or with Billy Shields."

"So John isn't to get into the garden because you allow this boy to come about the place?"

Leslie gripped himself. They were on slippery ground, Blanche and he. But he could not altogether compromise with his sense of justice. Danny had punctiliously asked if he might bring the boy about the place now and again, and he had agreed at once. He understood the man's pleasure in the child. He spoke to Billy one day and liked him. It gave him pleasure to think of a boy from the mean streets happy in the rambling garden, learning perhaps the hang of a decent trade.

"There's plenty of room for everybody," he told Blanche patiently.

Her response astounded him. It was as if he had struck her on the face with his hand.

She sprang to her feet with the electric angularity of an automaton.

"Oh, my God! I'm *sick* of this place!" she hissed, as if to a large and spellbound audience.

The next he knew she had slammed the door behind her.

In September Rita Curran came as Peter's wife to join the Shields household. She came cheerfully, quite unashamed of the very obvious burden she bore in her womb and not at all apologetic about the rearrangement that meant for little Billy a shakedown in the kitchen with his father and mother and Wee Mirren.

Billy privately approved the scheme; allowed to sit up longer, since the kitchen was the living-room for all, he had more time to read, and between him and the newcomer there quickly formed itself a curious bond of understanding. As Danny himself put it in his private thoughts, it was not Rita's way to shoot out her neck. She made no claims on others. It was her habit to slop about, crooning aimlessly, her heels twitching in an imaginary dance. A lazy lump, if ever there was one, but easygoing and placidly detached; and most of them liked her for that.

She was interesting because she was puzzling; a phenomenon they had never encountered before. Rita thought nothing of walking out of the room she shared with Peter in her knickers—and Billy there to see everything. She was always smoking, letting the ash drop from her cigarette where it might. (But Danny could help himself from her packet as he pleased, and she took it for granted.) If somebody else cared to prepare a meal or do a bit of scrubbing, Rita would let them do it, but she would do it quite calmly, though not very efficiently, if she must. She never rose before ten: and why should she, since there was nothing to do but get Billy out to school, which was Agnes's job?

Most of the time she spent before the fire, a novelette, folded small and held close to her eyes, in her hands. (A sure bond between her and Billy.) With her sweets she was as free as with her cigarettes, and often she would consume both together. She seemed to live for the pictures, but they could not always lure her from the animal ease she enjoyed, her skirts tucked up and her legs apart and her stockinged feet on the fender. She took it for granted that the coming of her child meant an end to her dancing, but she voiced no bitterness as to that. Rita Curran was nearly pure animal and, as such, at once strange and frightening and attractive to the men about her.

Danny took to boasting of her uniqueness to neighbours and acquaintances.

"My, she's a right tear thon!" he would cry proudly to other men of his generation. "Into the kitchen wi' just her drawers on and asks me for a light for her fag, as cool as ye like. Just her drawers! Christ! . . ."

Then he would raise a leg and slap his thigh in high delight.

Much of that pride, however, was in unconscious defiance of Agnes; for Agnes despised Rita and bitterly resented her capture of Peter, her invasion of the house, and her easy conquest of the others. The girl's habits honestly offended her sense of the proprieties, both in the relations of the sexes and the business of keeping house. A short cylinder of cigarette on the waxcloth was an offence. Rita's indifference to the condition of her room even to the exposure of the most intimate symbols of marital life, shocked her to the core. She could not understand, and therefore disliked, the temperament that had no consciousness of sin or waste in doing nothing.

But if the heart of Agnes could have been turned out, all its secrets exposed, it would have been seen that the sheer hatred of jealousy battened within her on the disapproval she could honestly maintain. She resented the intrusion of this other woman in her lair. It was humiliation to know that the girl had captured Peter and taken him quite away from his mother. With all his faults, Danny was her own property on which it was agonising that Rita Curran should dare to make any claim. Her queer understanding of Billy and his tolerance of her amounted to a seduction. And her own sense of isolation feeding her self-satisfaction, Agnes felt ready for war the moment Peter brought his wife to the house. She was not of those cut out for martyrdom.

Her devotion to Wee Mirren during these uneasy days was extreme and ostentatious. Danny, passionately attached to the child, noticed at once and dimly understood, even if he resented it. Once Rita in a rare mood of happy activity picked the infant from the bed and began, dreamily, to waltz with it round the kitchen.

Agnes, busy over the sink, wheeled round as if a knife had been run into her shoulder.

176

"Put that wean down, you clumsy great bitch!" she barked.

Rita jazzed complacently back to the bed and laid Wee Mirren in her place.

"Sorry," she retorted lightly. "I didn't know she was made of glass."

"No, you know nothing," Agnes went on wildly. "You know nothing and you do nothing and you never will."

"You should be on the movies, so help me God," observed Rita.

"I'll movie you—" Agnes took a step forward, her fingers flexing to scratch.

"Shut up, the two of ye!"

The roar came peremptorily from Danny. He had watched them with horror, seeing hatred naked before his eyes, almost smelling the rawness of their natural enmity—as if wild beasts had hissed venom at each other. This was Agnes at her very worst. The girl had meant and would have done no harm. But having commanded silence he made haste to secure peace.

"Ye'd best not touch the bairn at all," he said to Rita.

"Okay by me, big boy," she agreed equably, reaching to the mantelpiece for her cigarettes. Agnes turned in black silence to her washing up.

That was within a fortnight of Rita's coming among them, and there was never anything but a lowering armistice between the women thereafter. A man felt helpless between them, whose enmity might crackle and explode at any moment. It would be no row of Rita's seeking. She was one for peace, if they would leave her alone to enjoy it in her own way. The trouble would come, and at any moment might come, from Agnes who had got beyond all reason these last few months. Not, Danny admitted, that she hadn't her rights. It was her house, whichever way you looked at it. But if it came to rights, what about himself?

He was irked in every way by the changes that had come over his life since the fine ship *Estramadura* was launched. A couple of cats filling the kitchen at home with the electricity of their dislike so that a man was simply driven on to the streets. Agnes in declared rebellion against her lot. Agnes sharing his bed again but with as much allure and response as a lump of granite. Rights! A chap had his rights and his needs, had he not?

177

Perhaps it was just sympathy that Danny needed, the confidential sympathy of a woman that Agnes denied him and Billy could not give. Perhaps it was a blind biological impulse that hungered for expression and satisfaction. It was deliberately and defiantly, however, that he set out one night to look up Jess Stirling in her home in the pend off Argyle Street.

His knock was not immediately answered, and when she did come to the door, Jess peered round its edge with apprehension.

"Oh, it's you, Dan?" she greeted him nervously. She hesitated. "Will you not come in?"

The welcome was not enthusiastic but Danny did not allow that to stay him. He was in his heartiest mood, shaking Jess warmly by the hand and bearing her back into the big room where the stilled children, recognising a friend, broke into clamour again and swarmed round him. As if on a sudden rediscovery of the kindliness of life he regained his stature as a man, strong and authoritative.

"Man, Jess!" he cried, taking a seat by her fire. "It's great to see ye again. Ye're fine and cosy here, the lot of ye."

And while the children played in the dim background of the big room, the man and the woman told each other how they had fared during the weeks since last they had met. There was little story for Jess to tell, just a recital of the small domesticities, the endless tale of struggle to live in decency and keep the bairns in food and clothes. Danny's tale was long and sorry, and very earnestly and simply he told her everything, shaping nothing to point a moral, but drawing from her the easy sighs and protestations of her sympathy.

"Aw, Danny! It's a fair heartbreak! You with all that trouble about ye and times that hard! What's come over Agnes in all the world?"

There was an interlude of happiness and laughter while they put the children to bed, but when all was quiet again and they sat before the fire, the bond of suffering pulling them towards each other, the tone of their talk deepened into intimacy. The glow of the coals seemed warm enough to melt sorrow and hardship into sweetness wonderfully shared. Their voices sank low, and they spoke wistfully of happiness long past. As the fire died, their chairs grew closer and closer together until their bodies almost touched.

178

Desire thrilled tenatively through Danny's body. It came not out of the flesh but from his sense of her kindness and sweetness, and from his hunger for understanding, and from his will to protect another whom life had used hardly. There was need to begin again, and perfection could come even at a late hour. Her tired, gentle face drew love from his eyes. There was an untidy lock of hair hanging down her cheek that seemed a confidence between them. He put an arm round her shoulder.

"No, Dan! Not that! Stop it!"

She spoke sharply, fear driving understanding from her. Vigorously she shook the arm from her body.

"That's not a way to behave," she upbraided him, the decent widow again. "Don't you forget Agnes and the children."

She was just; she was illogical—he could see it both ways, but his kindliness guided them easily out of the hot jungle in which they had so nearly involved themselves.

"It's all right, Jess," he whispered assurance. "I'll not worry you. But—but it's a pity."

His hand closed over the one that rested on her knee, and she let it stay there, the great rough fingers enveloping and warming hers. Through her garments the man could feel the softness of woman's flesh. The dark tide flowed through his veins again, and he squeezed the hand in his.

"I'd like fine to stay with you, Jess," he whispered.

"But you can't do that, Dan," she returned softly, wistfully.

Suddenly she rose to her feet.

"You'll have to be going, Dan," she spoke firmly. "This is just nonsense. Come on. We're just a couple of old sillies."

She started pushing him towards the door, as if she would drive temptation from her life. And he laughed at her, for her haste was an admission that she too had known the significance and temptations of their hour together.

"Away with you!" he chaffed her roughly. He was happy. "Frightened of a wee bit cuddle! Think I was going to eat you? Here, Jess, what about the pictures one of these nights? I'd like fine if you'd come."

"Oh, I'd like to go with you to the pictures, Dan. It's an awful while since I've been."

The draught through the open door whirled her skirts round her legs and made of the stray lock of her hair a pennant, so that she looked a girl again.

"There'd be no harm in that," she said hopefully.

3

It became a habit with them. They slipped without awkwardness into the custom of going every Thursday night to a mean house with the splendid name of Corona where, from the fourpenny seats, they saw Hollywood unroll its marvels before them.

The were quite uncritical of their entertainment, Jess in particular having the capacity to marvel at and be deliciously shocked by the ways of women and men in that vague, grandiose passionate world of the cinema; and if Danny might not naturally have chosen to amuse himself in this way, he took a huge, simple pleasure in the company of his friend.

The desire of his flesh was fixed upon her, and well she knew it. But there was sweetness in the mere companionship; and though they first set out on these expeditions with a slight but disturbing sense of shame, the innocence of the occasions and the luck of meeting none they knew quickly brought them to believe that they were secure and, in due course, completely and almost defiantly innocent—as innocent as the threepenny poke of sweeties that became Danny's conventional offering on that one happy night of the week.

Jess remained rigorously virtuous. Sometimes, when he called as usual at the back of seven to take her out, he would insinuate that the night was wet and that they could be happy enough before the fire, but every notion of the kind so plainly alarmed her that he abandoned the technique.

It was more difficult in the hour of parting when they said goodnight in the pend, and she was warmly grateful for his kindness, and the shadow of the inevitable bleakness of his return home seeped into his understanding. Then he would be insistent, whispering urgently to her bowed head, and she would listen for a time, nearly toppling into the whirlpool of passion. Often he clasped her in strong, lustful arms and always she fought free, beating him back with either indignation or an appeal to his decency. And neither method ever failed with Danny.

Never once, however, did she allow him into the house at the end of such a night together, plead as he might in the drear lamplight and the rain.

So they went on until one week, the Corona closed for redecoration, they elected after grave discussion to go to a place in Clydebank called the Express. It was a cheap and backward house in a side street, but Jess had seen somewhere that her favourite Richard Dix was playing there in a belated run of "The Wheel of Life," and the remoteness of the place gave their enterprise the allure of adventure and security at once.

They were very happy and jocose going down the road together in the tram, and they laughed to discover that fourpenny seats in the Express were of a higher order than those at the same price in the Corona. The big picture delighted them. Champing at her caramels and lost in fairyland, Jess lay back in her seat towards Danny; and when he put his arm round her shoulder she let it rest there, snuggling indeed behind that barrier against a cruel world.

And when they came out at half-past nine they ran straight into Jim. He was talking to the manager, but his eyes were on the people emerging from the first house, and Danny, making his own dreadful recognition, knew that he, too, had been recognised with surprise, and that fantastic circumstance had trapped him once more. It was all so simple, so abominably ineluctable. Jim had his own queer interests in betting, the pictures, the dogs, and what not. That he should be there on the night, of all nights, Danny had chosen to patronise the Express, was at once absurd and inevitable.

The thing was to get out and away with it. The accident had happened, and that was all about it; Jess kept on talking about the marvels she had seen. As they passed Jim, Danny raised two fingers to the visor of his cap.

"Hullo, Jim!" he said brightly.

"Hullo, Dan!"

Nothing and everything. Jim's greeting was ostensibly casual, but Danny perceived the nuances of surprise and suspicion in it. It would all come back to Agnes, and very soon. There could be no dodging the consequences now. Jess squeezed his arm as they walked eastwards home along the Dumbarton Road.

"You're terrible donsy tonight, Dan," she said, secretly anxious to understand what had come over him so suddenly.

"Am I?" he was roused to jest. "It's these caramels of yours."

But he could not keep it up, and after they had walked on for a time in silence she tried him again.

"Was that a friend of yours you spoke to coming out?"

"Oh, a chap I used to know," he prevaricated.

A minute or two later Jess suggested that they should take a tram after all, and when they were back at last in the pend off Argyle Street they did not linger together, though a full moon shone blandly upon them from a mild sky.

"You'd best get back and have a good sleep, Dan," said Jess kindly. "I doubt ye're tired."

"Aye," he agreed sententiously. "I'm not just feeling too good the night."

They parted, and he hurried home, preparing himself for anything.

But it was very quiet in the house. Wee Mirren slept in the kitchen bed, and only Billy was on guard, perched as usual on the chair before the fire, his knees high and a book resting upon them.

"Bed, son," said Danny at once. "Come along with you."

They turned in together. The University clock boomed half-past ten. Soon Billy was asleep, but Danny lay awake, listening for Agnes. She came about eleven.

"Hullo!" he greeted and challenged her.

"Hullo!" she answered coolly.

Swiftly she undressed and joined him and the baby in the great bed, curling herself up on the edge in deliberate isolation.

"I suppose those two'll come in when they like," she observed sourly of Peter and his wife. "Waking folks up."

And that was all she had to say. Danny, wakeful and worried, heard her pass to the long quiet breathing of sleep. But he lay with his eyes open long after Peter and Rita came noisily home, knowing that the crisis was not over and had yet to reach its height.

Young John Pagan's cold became a fever, and from a fever developed into a desolating influenza that made of him a thirsty, silent, pathetic morsel of hot flesh. They had nurses in for him, and the doctor came twice a day, and though the latter was professionally brisk and sanguine, Leslie saw the anxiety in his eyes and could hardly sleep at nights for the agony of wondering if life would be worth living were John to die. Nobody in the hushed house ever dared to utter the dreadful word, but the spectre of pneumonia haunted them all.

It had a strange effect on Blanche, this reduction of her only child to a bundle of inflamed tissue, in which armies of germs struggled remotely for domination of the little heart. Now she retreated behind the defences of the sick-room, everything of her in a silent passion of concern for the child, her habitual contacts with her husband and society forsworn. Pathetically Leslie believed that grief should bring them together again, but hers she would not share. She was all mother through the crisis, living exclusively in her own small world of concern. With her husband she was gentle enough and confidential enough when they must be alone together, but the secrets of her heart she could not give nor he achieve. They lived in worlds apart. The kind, whispered words, the soothing caresses he would have offered her, were uttered and given in his mind only.

Day after day the chart on the chest of drawers in the night nursery showed its line of jagged peaks above the level horizon of the normal. The room became a small world in which only women ministered, the starched efficiency wilting only when the Olympian doctor appeared. There was no room in it for Leslie, and he came to see that his tiptoe approach to the bed and his whispered "Hullo, old boy!" were futilities. One night he was not allowed even that small satisfaction. The doctor came when they were due to sit down for dinner, and he ate alone, mechanically. It was after nine before the medical man came to him where he paced the lounge.

"It's all right now, I think," said the doctor, "and a dashed queer case. A sort of false pneumonia, if you get the idea—no real congestion, but the curve and the crisis and the symptoms all right. It's often like that with kids."

The fatal word was out, and the better for being so. "He's through, then?" asked Leslie eagerly.

"So far as one can tell. Weak, of course, but the nurses are there. Good nurse, that Burnett woman: knows her job. He'll be all right."

"Thank God for that!" Pagan cried. "Have a whisky and soda."

"Don't mind if I do," said the doctor. "It's been one hell of a day."

Blanche joined them just as the doctor rose to go. There were all the signs of strain on her face, and the way she flopped into a chair was an appeal to a man's pity. Unconsciously Leslie hurried his guest to the door and hardly waited to hear the engine of his car start. He hastened back to the lounge.

There she sat in her chair, weary and remote. He paused at the door, smiling, but she hardly looked at him, and before he could go to her, her voice, cold and faintly hostile, reached him.

"And that's the last of that," she said decisively.

For a moment that seemed like an hour, a moment painful yet exquisite, Leslie swayed on the razor-edge of a decision, pulled one way by the joy of release and desire to take her to his heart, and the other by a swift, instinctive resentment of the challenge, the plain reproach in her tone. He hesitated, and hesitated the merest shade of a second too long.

"Yes, thank God it's over," he said lamely enough. "A ghastly time you've had, darling. I felt simply useless.... But you'll get him away now for a bit," he resumed eagerly, "away to Torquay or Jersey. Or do you think the Mediterranean?"

He stood above her chair, and his hand dropped to her cheek. It was soft and warm against his fingers, but she kept her head steady so that there was neither a withdrawal from his caress nor the pressure of a response.

"Leslie, my dear," she began to speak—as if it were a rehearsed piece delivered from a distance. "I'm afraid we're misunderstanding each other about this. I must certainly take John away, but I simply don't see why he should ever be brought back to run the same risk again."

She raised a finger to check his protest.

"No, listen, dear! I mean what I'm saying, and I mean it very seriously, and I think you know exactly what I do mean. There's no reason in the world why we need to stay in Scotland at all. I know why you do stay, and I've tried my best to understand, and I think I've been very patient—"

"Of course you have, dear," he blurted unhappily.

"But I do think your attitude has really become unreasonable. Oh, what's the good of trying to believe that the business is ever coming back, and that it's worth while wasting money, waiting for something to turn up? You know it's hopeless. And I certainly don't see why we should all be unhappy when we can quite well afford to be happy somewhere else."

The sweet unreason of the speech appalled him. How could she assume that to live in Scotland was necessarily purgatory? How could she be blind to the validity of a man's love for his own place and his own people? Was a woman quite incapable of realising that responsibility implies a duty?

"It sounds rather like an ultimatum, Blanche," he temporised.

"It's as you care to take it," she said, rising to her feet and raising her shoulders ever so slightly.

"Anyhow, the point is that John's getting better," he blundered. "We'll have to think about the other business."

And he knew as soon as he had said it that he could think as he pleased, but that the mind of his wife was made up. No friendly suggestions, no appeals, no sketches of a compromise could affect her now. She had given him his choice, and he must make it.

While John improved from day to day they continued to live at a distance from each other. He went to the Yard in the mornings, only to find that there was nothing to do save look hopelessly into the hopeless face of Dakers, pretend before his skeleton staff of draughtsmen that there was really a chance of an order from the Hogarth people, and delude himself that an occasional ship in for repair could keep Pagan's going till things got better. There was many a long hour in which he seemed to realise that things could never be much better for every yard on the Clyde, and that it was the cold sense of his own case to close down completely. In another mood he would dream of spending reserves on new docks and basins and equipment, believing that those who could hold out against the depression would reap the benefit in a year's time, in two years—sooner or later anyhow.

But what did it all come to when a man went home at night to find his wife inexorably preparing to leave him if he would not forget his work and come with her? In all sorts of queer little ways he saw what a big and purposeful work was in progress in the house in Kelvinside—trunks dragged out of lumber rooms into the hall, piles of garments heaped on beds, the maids and the Norland nurse wearing that air of happy preoccupation which comes on women when a great domestic event is toward. Blanche was assuredly going, and taking John with her. Leslie had to endure the humiliation of hearing from Danny Shields (as if the thing were common property among the servants!) how proud the little man was to be making a box "for Maister John's toys and things."

The damnable divagation of their courses, so coldly plotted on Blanche's side, made it all the more difficult for him to say anything at all. She had reduced him to helplessness. Neither tears nor the severe exercise of authority could meet the problem she was forcing upon him. Things just slipped along with a cold inevitability. He let them go so far that she was able, one evening, after an uneasy dinner together, to present him with the assumption of an accomplished fact.

"The doctor says John should be able to travel next week," she began.

"Good!" he answered mechanically.

"I've arranged for rooms at Ventnor," she went on, "but I suppose we'll go on to Cuckton—about the middle of next month, I suppose."

"I could run down there, of course."

"Yes, but where are you going to stay?"

"Here, I suppose," he retorted resentfully.

"That means keeping Cook and Minnie, at least." She seemed to lose herself in difficult but businesslike calculations. "Let me see. . . . Yes, that ought to be quite enough if you insist on keeping Shields in the garden. He can help them with the heavy work. Minnie should be quite all right with the laundry and your clothes.

I've told her."

"Oh, I suppose I'll contrive to exist. There's always the Club."

The bitterness was wrung from him. She looked at him steadily down the length of the table.

"Martyrdom comes easy to you, Lal," she said.

So there came the evening when he took them down in a hired Daimler to catch the Night Scot. His heart broke to see John, so small in his blue pyjamas in his berth in the sleeping car—John all flushed and excited to be travelling in a big train through the night, but, his father's own son, very thoughtful about the fan and the light that burned blue and the working of the shutter over the window. It was like having something torn out of his heart.

He bent to kiss the freckled cheek.

"Good-bye, old son!" he whispered. "I wish I were coming with you."

The two small arms went round his neck, tight and dependent.

"Come soon, Daddy. I want you to come."

Leslie's eyes were full as he stumbled along the corridor, past porters with luggage and excited old ladies, to where Blanche awaited him on the chilly platform. He saw that she was handsome and decisive, and he admired her.

"Said good-bye to John?" she greeted him.

"All over," he answered, and knew that he mocked himself with that light reply. "You'll have to be getting in soon."

Feeble, bitter words—and in the hour of a separation almost legally complete!

"Yes, I suppose so," she said; but of what her tone meant he could make nothing. She put out her hand to take his. "Well, Lal, old man—"

They kissed, ever so gently, ever so sweetly.

"You'll write," he stammered.

"Oh, my dear, I'll write!" she cried. And her eyes were wet. "And you'll write to me. And soon you'll stop being an old juggins. Kiss me again."

A warning whistle blew. The dignity of their parting collapsed. She scrambled into the coach, and they stood looking fecklessly at each other. Ever so slowly and gently the train began to move, but its movement was relentless and final.

The train had been there with Blanche and John in it; then there was no train, only red lights dwindling to points as it crossed the bridge over the Clyde. To walk back towards the barrier was like walking into emptiness. She loved him; he had seen tears in her eyes. But she had left him, inexorable in purpose to the bitter end. There was nothing to do but go and get drunk or pick up some dirty, lusty bag of a woman in Sauchiehall Street.

Still pondering how the situation ought to be met, he made his way back to Kelvinside and let himself into the silent house.

5

Danny and Jess had been to the Corona which, a thought late in the day, was offering its patrons the spectacle of Charlie Chaplin in "City Lights."

It was not the picture Jess would have chosen for herself, but as the simple appreciator of what one manager cared to provide for his patrons she sat it out patiently. She "tchk-tchk'd" with her tongue at the vinous extravagance of the millionaire and at the sight of so much money carelessly exchanged. She was horrified by the rudeness of the small boys to the pathetic hero. But if subsequently she admitted the little man to be "a right wee comic," she was touched only by the episode of the blind girl and her mother and, to great indignation, by the same girl's failure or refusal, her sight restored, to recognise in the tramp her benefactor. "It's a downright shame, that's what it is," said Jess.

On Danny, on the other hand, the picture had a curiously disturbing effect. At riotous doings with bottles and motor cars, at the sublime absurdities of the suicidal scene on the embankment, he roared like any happy boy, slapping his knee, nudging Jess with vigour, and crying repeatedly: "Christ! I'll bust my boiler if he doesna' stop." But the exquisitely handled pathos behind the farce got under his skin. All its significance came upon him with the force of a personal appeal from one man who had known idleness to another, and it made Danny think. Suddenly he realised that such as he might be as helpless and pathetic and ludicrous in the eyes of the busy well-fed world; and it sort of took the pins away from a chap and made him feel uncomfortable.

It was on this topic that he discoursed to Jess as they walked homewards along Argyle Street. Her very moderate enthusiasm mildly provoked him, and he spoke as one who had just emerged from a rich spiritual experience.

"No, no, Jess!" he declared. "Thon block knows what's what— you take it from me. He's a sight more than a coamic, I'm telling ye. He didn't learn thon look—you know: wi' the silly wee smile and the big eyes—out of books. Thon's a man that's had it in the neck, and—" He was visited by a flash of critical insight—"he wouldn't be such a coamic if he hadn't. By God, it makes you think?"

Jess was very anxious to understand him, and since she could not do so, her every effort at appreciation made him all the more eager to press upon her the unique subtlety of the point he had to make. He got rather excited about it all and talked loudly, and they were so wrapped up in their innocent discussion that, as they passed the Kelvin Hall with its hot neon lights announcing a Housing and Health Exhibition within, they quite failed to see that there stood in a group on the pavement, and beside a large car with an open door, Agnes and Lizzie and Jim and a tall and elegant man of the youngish sort.

Agnes's voice, amused and ironical, cut into their rapt isolation.

"Hullo! Having a nice night together?" it said.

Danny stared open-mouthed at that quartette of enigmatic faces.

"Oh, hullo!" he returned lamely.

He hesitated, but a pull at his arm carried him on. The menace passed behind. He was bewildered.

"Good God!" he said hoarsely. "That was Agnes."

"Well, we've only been at the pictures," retorted Jess defiantly.

"That's right enough, but—"

"And who was she with?" Jess asked pointedly.

Yes, that tall chap with the superior air. . . . Danny's memory went back to a wild night long ago with Jim and Liz and Agnes and a cheap sport who insisted on being called Alf. His dislike and suspicion of Alf had persisted in his subconscious mind all these months, and now it burned up in flame.

So that was her game, was it: dirty stuff with that English

nancy—if he wasn't just a lousy yid? He and Jess had at least kept strictly on the near side of decency. No harm in the pictures once a week, surely! It would just be what Agnes deserved if he were to stay the night with Jess, and sleep with her, and let the curtain be rung down on the farce at home for ever. Home!

But he was abstracted when the time came to say goodnight to Jess in the pend and, knowing what irked him, and having a vast respect for the sanctity of marriage, she did not try to keep him with her, fiercely as the woman in her rose to meet the claim of the other woman upon this decent, kindly man.

"I'll be seeing you," she said hopefully.

"Sure, Jess," he assured her gallantly. "I'll let you know."

The assurance sounded mechanical, however, and a chill feeling of desertion came over her as she climbed the wooden steps and let herself into the room where her fatherless children were sleeping. Danny, on the other hand, went westwards on a tram, hurrying home to face what must come now and in a fight, if fight there must be, to have it out with his wife.

Billy was alone with Wee Mirren—Billy as quiet and pitiful as ever on his chair before the fire with a book, the baby sound asleep in the curtained bed.

The peace of the kitchen was lovely, but it frightened Danny for its contrast with the storminess of the passion that surrounded it. He suddenly saw his little children as helpless victims of an insensate misunderstanding. Billy the more pathetic than the baby for being so clever and quiet and patient. Billy so much deserved peace; he asked so little of others; and Danny's soul was racked to think of the baffled misery he must undergo when the inevitable storm should break. He ached to take him in his arms and tell him that, whatever might befall, he could be sure to the end of one man's unfaltering love and care. But the cruel blade was there in the quiet air, ready to fall. They could not, these two small ones, escape pain. And how they would fare in the days ahead their father could not bear to think.

Quietly and gently he got them settled down for the night. It was his own plan to be in bed before Agnes came home, and he was determined at least to seem asleep so that their settlement of the differences between them could take place in the morning with the boy safe away to school. He was under the blankets before Peter and Rita came in, both of them a little the worse of drink and very talkative, but he pretended to be unconscious, and they passed into their own room. He listened for a long time to the giggling of his daughter-in-law and to the deep grumble of Peter's voice. He started to hear Rita utter one delighted, animal scream. But he waited in vain for the familiar step on the stairs outside and the turning of the lock.

He admitted to himself after the University clock had struck twelve that she was not coming home at all.

The certainty had been lying at the back of his mind, but it was terrible to have to face the naked fact. His mind became a welter of emotions. At one moment he could see only the enormity of the thing, and in the next comforted himself with the reflection that it had to be and was all the better for coming quickly. He was haunted by the outrage on his deep-seated sense of the decencies, and was then exalted by the glorious prospect of being a free man once again. He thought hotly of lying down beside Jess in her kindly bed. He worked out bitter, final things to say to Jim and Lizzie. He wondered if the Boss would be interested. He wanted very much to tell the Boss all about it.

Sleep came to him, but fitfully. Dreams tormented him, and while they lasted he still knew that they were only dreams. By five in the morning he was completely awake again, his head heavy but his mind working with a strange clarity. He was up at six and, moving cautiously, raked out and relaid the fire. In the kitchen cupboard he discovered what Agnes had got in for breakfast. (He was planning to do it all very orderly.) Wee Mirren was awake and talkative in her baby way before, at seven, he roused Billy to wash himself at the sink.

"Where's my mother?" the boy asked suddenly.

"Staying with your Aunt Lizzie," answered Danny, slicing away at a loaf. "I'm getting you out to school for a change. Get on with it."

They had a cheery breakfast together, Billy delighted to find his father in high fettle and a holiday atmosphere about everything. The baby was as good as gold, taking it as a game that her father should change and feed her. It was great fun for Billy that his mother should be away for the night and his father doing his clumsy best with the household chores.

"When is she coming back?" he asked.

"Oh," said Danny, demurring largely, "before you're back from school, I expect."

When the boy had gone with his leather satchel on his back, Danny knocked at the door of the room his son shared with Rita.

"Peter!" he called guardedly. "Peter!"

"Hullo!" came the grumbling response at length.

"Peter, your mother hasn't come back, and I've got to go to my work."

"Oh!" said Peter.

"D'ye think Rita could look after Wee Mirren till I come back?" Danny urged.

There was a rumble of private conference in the room. "Whazzat?" he heard the girl demand of her husband. Then her voice came clear and reassuring.

"Okay, pop! Leave the kid with me."

"That's good of you, Rita," Danny was moved to thank her.

"Attaboy!" answered the easy voice. "Now scram, and let a girlie sleep."

A right tear was Rita, when you came to think of it. Danny chuckled all the way down the stairs.

The sharpness of the early winter morning braced him—frost on the grass and a quiet amber sky, barred with motionless strata of cloud. To hell with Agnes! was the expression of his mood. Not missed just as much as she thought. They might all very well be a dashed sight happier if she stayed away.

But the possibility lay heavy on him as he chopped firewood in an outlying cellar of Leslie Pagan's house. It was not, when he came near to it, a thing for humour or defiance. It was big with import, and his heart rose to his throat at the thought of its dreadful finality. The world he knew was crumbling. If she really did not come back—by God! it would be a lousy business.

He had been used to get his midday meal at the big house, but on this occasion he excused himself elaborately to the cook and hurried home. There he found Rita alone. Rita in a chair before the fire, smoking calmly, her slipperless feet on the hob. The bed was empty.

"Has she been?" he cried to his son's wife.

"I'll tell the world," said Rita lazily. "She's been, and nobs on."

"Is she away?" he fired at her.

"Search me," said the aggravating girl. "*And* the baby. All away up a 'ky. Some girl, the mother-in-law."

"But for Christ's sake, Rita—" he appealed to her, urgent.

"She's been and gone. I've told you. And one bloody row before she went, I'm telling you."

Rita went the length of taking her feet off the hob.

"I've been called some names before, but I learned a lot of new ones this day. Oh, we had it out all right. I gave her as good as I got. But if it wasn't me, it was you. You're fine and popular there—I don't think. She's away all right, and says she's never coming back, and—oh, right upstage! We'll do fine without her for a while, if you ask me. She'll come back: just you wait and see."

"Do you think so, Rita?" asked Danny desperately.

CHAPTER TEN

EMPTY DAYS

FROM THE ground-floor window of the library of the house in Kelvinside, Leslie Pagan looked mournfully down the length of the garden to where, in a far corner behind a shrivelled forest of cabbage-stalks, Danny Shields had built and was feeding a bonfire of vegetable refuse.

The wintry tang of the smoke brought its own suggestion of waste and decay and conclusion, and the mnemonic worked powerfully on a mind that had already made to itself certain sombre admissions. It was four o'clock of a November afternoon, the stormy darkness closing over Glasgow. He had come home from the Yard for lunch; he had decided that it was just a waste of time, a futility, to go back again. He had slept a little in his chair before the fire, and a cup of tea had given him no sense of refreshment when he had wakened. The world was bleak and empty. There was nothing for him to do, nothing that by dint of the mightiest personal effort he could do, save loaf about in a big, useless and expensive house and, his hands in his pockets, stare through the cold twilight over a wintry garden at another man pretending to be busy so that he might fairly enough earn his dole of charity.

The strict rights of the affair were with Blanche. He was wasting his time and substance when, like a wise man, he might be with his own wife and his only son in a more congenial place, interested at the least in the small crises of family life. This lingering on the scene of defeat was mockery.

He opened the french windows and, his hands in his pockets, strolled towards the dull flame and wreathing smoke of Danny's bonfire. The latter looked up with a grin, touched his cap, and bent again to shovel a pile of sodden, brown leaves on the blaze.

"Hullo, Dan!" Leslie greeted him. "Always busy."

"Just that, sir," Danny replied. "There's aye something to do. If it's not the one thing it's the other."

194

"That's right," Leslie agreed. He found himself without anything worth saying to the man and went on to a conventional question. "All well at home?"

"All well, sir," came the reply, but very curtly, if Leslie had been in the mood to notice such things. Danny had told him not a word of his trouble with Agnes. He envied his servant the simplicity of his affairs.

"That's good," he said mechanically.

"You'll have good news of the mistress and Maister John?" Danny hazarded politely.

"They're very well, thanks, Dan."

"Aye, but you'll miss them," said Danny sententiously, pressing his foot on the fire. "A man needs to have his bairn beside him. It's the wee ones you miss."

The wound made by that small truth smarted as Leslie strolled back aimlessly towards the house. It was indeed John he missed, for John something in him hungered endlessly. It was, he argued with himself, no infidelity to Blanche. But John was young and helpless. John had great need of his father, whether the child knew it or not. There was between them a bond, a dear and precious understanding it was a crime ever to strain, and he suddenly saw himself guilty of a breach of faith in thus deliberately separating himself from his boy.

Danny was right. Over that meeting of theirs by the odorous bonfire there had brooded the spirit of fatality. Aimless, to all seeming, it had been deeply significant. Not for the first time there had arisen between him and Danny Shields an issue touching the fundamentals. Queer how it worked between two men ostensibly so ill-assorted! Dear, dear John. . . . His mood swiftly lightening, as if to a burst of sunlight, he closed the french windows behind him and put through a long-distance call to Surrey.

Blanche's voice came to him, clear as a bell, and the overtones of happy excitement in it were stimulants to his tired mind. It seemed that she could give him no time to answer her eager questions and girlish exclamations.

"Oh, is it you, Lal? How lovely! No trouble is there? Oh, but that's sweet of you. It's *lovely* to hear you. Oh, perfectly marvellous, both of us, It's wonderful to hear you. We both miss you awfully. But they're looking after you properly? I've been so anxious.... Oh, good! You really can manage down soon. Do try, dear. It would be lovely. John would be so happy. What? I didn't get that, dear. Oh, yes, he's here. I'll get him. Wait a minute, Lal, he'll love to speak to you. ... John! John!"

He heard her clear voice echoing down that panelled hall four hundred miles away, and it might have been next door. His heart bounded. His dear ones so near at hand, eager to speak to him! "John! John! Come and speak to Daddy!"

Then "Hullo!" came the grave childish voice.

"Hullo, Johnnie!" he cried. "This is Daddy. How are you?"

"Very well, thank you," the small voice answered politely.

"Being a good boy?"

"Yes, thank you."

"I'd love to see you soon."

"We'd love to see you, Daddy. Please bring me a 3A Meccano set from the Clyde Model Dockyard."

"All right, old boy," Leslie laughed happily. "I'll bring one in the Night Scot tonight. Really I will. Tell Mummy to speak. Bye-bye!"

"Bye-bye. Thank you," said John gravely.

He heard them talk at the other end of the wire, then caught the gasp of Blanche's whirlwind return to the instrument.

"Lal!" she called. "You weren't teasing John, were you? Are you really coming tonight?"

"I'd love to, dear," he answered, enthusiastic. The voice of the child had touched him to desperation.

"But can you, will you? (Yes, another three minutes, you fool!) Oh, it would be lovely! I'll go up to Town to meet you. You will come?"

"Of course I'll come. Make a day of it. Meet you at the Piccadilly end of the Burlington Arcade at eleven tomorrow. Buy you some pretties. Cocktails, lunch for two in the Berkeley. Tea with John at Cuckton. How will that do?"

"Darling ... how glorious!"

Tomorrow—really with Blanche in London in the morning, with John in the peace of his Surrey nursery in the evening, the bare boughs of the old apple tree almost tapping at the window, the sparse lights of the Weald spread far below in the easy security of

England! He rang a bell.

"He's off again," said the housemaid morosely to the cook a little later. "His cases to be ready for seven. She's been at him, I'll bet you."

"Aye, and she'll keep him," said cook, thickly buttering another pancake of her own baking. "Nice look-out for the likes of us!"

Leslie was like a boy released from school for the holidays. He was impatient waiting for the girl to have his traps ready, then still more impatient for the taxi to come, pacing the hall in his big travelling coat. More than three hours before the train was due to leave, but he had to get out of that imprisoning house. For once in a while the Club seemed alluring, an anteroom to freedom. He would have a jolly little dinner alone at a small table with a gleaming surface of polished mahogany, smoked salmon, a wood-cock, and a whang of creamy Blue Cheshire, with a half-bottle of the vivacious Beaujolais of '23. He might find some old pal to play a hundred up before the train went. Or he would just sink into a deep leather chair and drowse the intervening hour away.

So it transpired, sheer happiness saucing the luxury of that last evening alone. The familiar attendant was there on the station platform to greet him with salute and smile.

"Number twelve again, Mr. Pagan. Your usual call in the morning, I suppose, sir."

By the time the mighty train rolled silkily out of the Central he was in bed, the light out, and did not care whether he slept or not, so many pleasant things had he to think of if he must be awake.

2

It was a happier house to live in with Agnes gone, and Danny did not deceive himself as to that. The admitted failure of their marriage had wounded him deeply. He missed Wee Mirren, and it hurt him to think of Billy without a mother's care. But if all that was of her deliberate choosing, then the consequences had to be traced; and when it came down to brass tacks they were all a sight cheerier and happier without an ill-tempered woman barking and snapping and looking for trouble every hour of the day.

Danny kept the large significance of Agnes's desertion out of his mind as much as he could. There were many moments when its finality appalled him. He experienced deep and angry urges to go and demand to know what right she had to take the baby from him. In moods of jealousy and bitter suspicion he determined to discover in just what doubtful conditions she was living; for the sinister figure of Alf would not go out of his mind. All he had to go on was Peter's careless testimony, garnered he knew not where, that she was living with Jim and Lizzie in their villa out Langside way.

But the urge to act in accordance with his passions was never strong enough during these early weeks of their separation. His own emotional world was full enough with the affair of Jess and the satisfaction of a job at the Boss's house. Even when he realised that the emotional factors on both sides cancelled each other out, some dim sense of pride told him that Agnes was best left alone to work out her own salvation. Never once was he tempted to exclude the possibility of her return and of his own patient welcome.

For the rest, they got on well enough—Peter and Rita and Billy and himself. The girl kept house in a sketchy, easy-osy fashion, and it would have been gloriously dirty and untidy except that Danny and Billy would occasionally set to and do a bit of scrubbing, of making beds and washing pots and dishes. There was just no use fretting if a meal were late; Rita would ultimately produce something at least edible in her own good time. As to the expenses of running the place she was a queen of practical communism. Danny was the last man to forget to give her his share of the expenses at the week's end, but if he did forget, or if he was pressed for the rent or something of the sort, she would say never a word but keep on producing the service of that strange household. And if Peter occasionally grumbled as to his responsibility in relation to the baby about to arrive, her large, soft indifference to detail of the sort would make him look foolish in the long run. Peter's small asperities were as nothing against that spacious tolerance.

Relieved in this way from the anxieties of housekeeping, a happy enough camper-out at the end of one of life's alleyways, Danny could go on pretending to himself that in his job up at the big house in Kelvinside he was really doing something. He planned mighty rearrangements of the garden against the summer to come. He dreamed of pleasing the Boss with an elaborate series of small repairs his tradesman's eye saw desirable, if not quite necessary, to the externals of house and outbuildings. The cook had complained of this and that, and he was bent on proving even to her his indispensability about the place. He had noticed in the course of one of his occasional excursions through the big rooms that the wireless set served one apartment only, and it became a dream of his to achieve a masterpiece of wiring and have the receiver serving the Boss's library, the nursery and the kitchen simultaneously. Such matters were challenges to his artisan's sense of propriety, and in contemplating them he recovered his pride.

It was a shock to him when, full one morning of a scheme affecting the layout of the kitchen garden, he asked the cook when she expected the master home again and learned that he had left in haste for London two nights before.

A little dazed, as he walked back to his vegetable beds, Danny cast his mind back and recalled that afternoon of the bonfire. There had been something queer about the Boss then, now he came to think of it: terrible quiet and unhandy somehow. There had been that smell of burning leaves and the wet menace of a West Scottish winter in the air.

"He'll be busy," Danny had said hopefully to the cook.

"Aye," replied the cook sardonically, "busy making up to the mistress again."

That sort of challenge Danny found it easy to dismiss. His faith in the Boss could not be shaken by any woman's cattiness. It would be business that had taken him to London: perhaps the chance of a big order for the Yard. Or young Master John had not been so well again and he had hurried away to his bedside as a good father should. Anyhow, it would be something so obvious and rational that Danny did not trouble to indulge in speculations but went on cheerfully with the replanning of the kitchen garden, a fine surprise for the Boss whenever he came back.

On the Saturday, however, there was something to cut into that fine confidence. It had been the custom that Danny's pay, in an envelope, was left in the kitchen with the cook, and it had been his habit to collect it before he got down to the forenoon's work. On this particular morning his mind had been much on that gratifying packet, for he had planned to see the great match of the Old Firm at Parkhead, had allowed himself in advance a glass and a pint after the game, and did not intend to be kept waiting when the time came to knock off at noon. But when he went to the kitchen window and cracked the usual joke with the girls at the breakfast table inside, the cook looked suddenly blank.

"Your pay's not here, Dan," she said, looking hopelessly at the mantelpiece where the envelope usually lay beside the blue alarm clock.

"But are you sure?" Danny challenged her blankly.

"There's nothing here, I'm telling you," the cook retorted in defence, "and nobody said nothing to me."

Danny got to the match, Rita obliging with what she called "the len' of three bob, and see you an' pay up or I'll put the polis on ye," and on that and the coppers left to him he contrived also the refreshment. But when he was home again and alone with Billy in the evening—at an hour, when in the old days, a chap would have been out on the ran-dan—a real fear came upon him. Bad enough that he would have to go on for a day or two with next to nothing in his pocket, but the possibility that the Boss had really forgotten after all was an almost intolerable thought. Loyally he wrestled against it, and in the long run the victory was with faith. The Boss's business in the South had been of a uniquely pressing nature. He would remember over the week-end, and the cash would roll up in a day or two.

Too sensitive on the subject to ask her outright, he made it his care every morning of the following week to get into personal touch with the cook, but she said nothing about the missing pay, and he knew that she would not be careless in a matter affecting her own fiercely-defended probity and diligence. He looked eagerly for the post every time he got home, but there was never for him a comforting oblong of white with an English postmark.

It was all very queer indeed. He had wild thoughts of writing to the Boss, but was dissuaded from them by his sense of his proper place and by doubts as to his handiness with pen and words. Best wait till the second Saturday and see for certain, he decided. It was all a misunderstanding. There would be two weeks' pay in the poke before the weekend came.

It was the cook who ultimately put a desperate notion into his head. She was waiting for him on the second Saturday morning, the look of alarm on her face.

"There's nothing come for you, Dan," she hurried to clear herself, implying that it was a mad and cruel world. "There must be a mistake. I'd go down to the Yard and see, if I was you."

In another mood he might have seen the notion of laying his appeal before the grim rearguard of officials in the shipyard office to be at once pretentious and futile, but in his horror of disappointment and fear for his position at home the suggestion seemed a brilliant line of escape. In that moment he could see no difficulties ahead. Probably he had always been paid from the office. The sergeant at the gate might know all about it. He had even the right as an old and trusted servant of Pagan's to ask to see Mr. Dakers himself. Why had he never thought of it before, for that matter?

He had not taken off his jacket, and without another thought to house or garden, simply afraid that he had been completely forgotten and was penniless, Danny turned away and set out, since there was hardly a copper in his pocket, to walk the miles to the shipyard gates.

Sergeant Macewan received him ironically. His uniform jacket open at the neck, his cap off, and his feet against the fireplace of his box, he turned a spectacled face from the *Noon Record* and "Meridian's" optimistic tips and indulged himself in heavy humour.

"It's no good coming till Monday, Dan," he observed. "We're not laying the keel of Number 534's sister ship till then. But I expect they'll be wanting you as yard manager now that Williamson's away to Hong-Kong."

"I'm not looking for a job," said Danny flatly. "I'm in a hell of a hole, Sergeant, and I was wondering if you can help me. It's like this—"

The sergeant heard him out gravely.

"That's too bad, Dan," he observed at length, speaking as if the honour of Pagan's rested largely with himself. "There's been a mistake somewhere."

He rose from his chair, buckled his collar, and put on his uniform cap.

"I'll have a word with Mr. Dakers. Wait you here," said the sergeant.

Changed days, that the small complaint of an unemployed riveter could give the sergeant at the gate of Pagan's an excuse for seeming important! Danny was aware of the irony, but his passion for his rights had grown so warm that he did not let it affect his sense of importance. When the sergeant returned to announce with seriousness that Mr. Dakers would see him, Danny marched to the interview with his shoulders back and chin high.

The secretary was at once brusque and tolerant.

"What's all this, Shields?" he began.

And when Danny, twisting his cap in his hands, began to expound his case with a vast elaboration of reason and regard for circumstantial detail, Dakers quickly interrupted him.

"I know all that. But you've had no pay these two weeks?"

"Nothing, sir. It's this way, you see, Mr. Dakers. On the Tuesday—"

"I don't want to hear it," said Dakers, "It's been an oversight." The word seemed to please him. "It's merely an oversight. I'll put it square with Mr. Leslie. In fact, I'm writing him today. I've no right to do it, mind you; it isn't office business; but I'll advance you two pounds. That keep you going?"

"That would be fine, sir."

"Right! No more than two pounds, mind you," he warned, pressing a bell on his desk. "And I'll take a receipt from you. Wait a minute."

It was much for a man to be going home along the Dumbarton Road with two pounds in his pocket. It was an assurance of personal security and, at the same time, an admission from on high that he, Danny Shields, was still the authentic employee of Leslie Pagan, the Boss. There had been a misunderstanding, an oversight. Now that had been put right, and existence could proceed on a solid basis once more.

He did not go back to work at the house that morning. He felt that the obligation balanced nicely against the discomfort he had innocently suffered. A belch of sour smell from a swinging doorway agreeably reminded him that on Saturdays, in the Glasgow area, the public houses open at ten and close at noon, and the fact fitted beautifully with his mood: just the time and the circumstance for a refreshment.

Choosing a nice looking place he had never entered before, Danny ordered a glass of whisky and a chaser in the shape of a pint of beer. The shop was not busy and the barman was chatty as to the football prospects of the afternoon, so that a second pint came to seem reasonable. When the bar filled at length with carters and railwaymen rushing to gulp their morning drinks against the clock and he lost the barman's attention to his thesis that Motherwell were a snip for the Scottish Cup, Danny was content to call it a morning well spent and, in fine fettle, marched eastwards to settle his account with Rita.

The transaction left him with twelve shillings in his pocket, and the knowledge that there was more to come gave him the feeling of wealth. The blind desire to spend filled his mind. In an access of private benevolence not unmixed with self-flattery, he thought of giving Billy a treat, take him to the pictures or an afternoon recital in the City Hall. But it was perhaps the drink he had taken that inclined him to think mainly of his own pleasure, and it was easy enough for him to adjust his mind to the categorical imperative of seeing a football match that afternoon. There were the Hearts and Third Lanark at Cathkin, St. Mirren and the Thistle at Firhill: a delicious choice.

By giving Billy threepence to spend as he pleased and deciding to go to Firhill—with the possibility of being able to take the boy somewhere in the evening—Danny ridded himself finally of all his besetting problems.

It was a grand game. Not religiously concerned with the fate of either team, as he would have been had the Rangers been engaged, he could enjoy the skill of the players impartially and rank on the section of terracing he favoured with something of the distinction of an arbiter. As it happened, most of those about him were on the side of the Thistle, so that when that team took the lead at half-time he inclined in sheer reaction to side with a solitary man from Paisley who believed in the St. Mirren through thick and thin. Loyal to his splendid neutrality, Danny gave it out as his opinion that the Saints on play—"as play, mind ye"—were at the very least worth a draw.

This brought him into disfavour with the majority about him. Some laughed sardonically at his pretence to expertise; others made before him the first coarse-worded approaches to a fight. It earned him, however, the warm estimation of the man from Paisley who produced from his hip-pocket a half-bottle of tepid whisky and invited his ally to have a swig.

St. Mirren equalising early in the second half, the bottle came out again, and when the visitors snapped a winning goal five minutes from time, they finished it between them, gulping the raw spirit as if it were water. Danny felt very pleased with himself, firm again on the top of his little world. Fired by the whisky, he taunted the Thistle supporters and would assuredly have been in trouble had not the man from Paisley dragged him away, muttering anxious counsel.

"Shut yer stupid mouth!" hissed his new friend. "These blocks'll kill ye. Come on and we'll find a pub."

That was easily done on those northern heights of the city, and, snug together at a little table by the fire in a crowded bar, the pair proceeded to enjoy a long and conspiratorial exchange of views on football form, the practice of betting, the trials of the unemployed, the prospects of shipbuilding, and even the economic policy of the United States, about which the man from Paisley had decided views.

"Ah've studied the question," he cried, "and ah've come to the conclusion that the Yanks is a set of dirty twisters. . . ."

The drank both copiously and variously, while they talked, and the more they drank, the clearer it became to each that the other was altogether too fixed in his opinions and too copious in illustrative anecdote.

The first asperity showed itself over the question of the big Cunarder on the stocks at Clydebank: Danny claiming the authority of the practical shipbuilder, his friend voicing the claims of serious and dispassionate study of this particular vessel, reinforced by close observation of her over a period of Sundays from the Water Neb at Renfrew.

A sudden emerging ground of agreement made them bosom pals once more, and they were almost in each other's arms for a space, scaling great heights of nobility and altruism; but anon they parted again on an issue affecting Earl Haig's conduct of operations towards the end of the war, and then, old soldiers both, their voices rose loud and angry.

"That's enough, you two!" another voice cut in on their quarrel suddenly. "Shut your faces or get to hell out of here."

"We're only having a bloomin' argument," Danny protested.

"Then keep quiet about it or get out."

"Away or I'll—"

Danny was now in the mood to fight for freedom of speech. It seemed to him perfectly clear that what the interfering barman wanted was a good clout on the jaw.

"I'll teach ye—" he threatened, rising from his seat.

Strong hands gripped him. He struggled, but in vain. The back of his head pushed open the swing-doors of the shop. He was on the pavement, picking himself up. It was dark and wet; His friend had disappeared. "Hey, Paisley!" he cried.

A small girl, a shawl about her pinched face and a shopping-bag of straw in her hand, paused to stare at him in the poor, green light of a gas-lamp.

"Ger-out with you!" he gestured away that disturbing, accusing face. Once again he cried: "Hey, Paisley!" But there was no answer.

On the kerb he stood swaying slightly. He knew himself to have taken too much drink. He knew that he ought to go home. But in the same moment the knowledge turned to an angry resentment of the imperative. The mere encounter with facts inflamed him with a determination to be bigger and grander and more powerful than they. He would show them! He was as good a man as any of them. He was damned if he was going to be held down any longer.

In that fantastic mood his mind seized on the rawest of his grievances, and he plunged into hot and angry thinking about the desertion of Agnes. That was a dirty business, if ever there was one. Agnes stolen from him! And Wee Mirren. . . . He suddenly saw Agnes as a victim, his poor deluded sweetheart. This was the doing of Jim and Lizzie with their money and their swank, ridding themselves of association with a common five-eighths of a riveter—and a damned sight better man than Jim would ever be.

This was the tangible issue his passion hungered to meet, and he set off downhill to the nearest tramlines. A car going towards the centre of the city picked him up at a corner, and he sat inside, muttering to the great alarm of the women with shopping-baskets who sat near at hand. Alighting at the Central Station, where Union Street was afire with the glow of neon lights, he blundered into another public house and ordered more whisky and more beer.

The fact at the drinks were served to him without question revived his confidence. He was not so drunk after all, but a man burning with a righteous indignation. He saw it as his duty to himself and to Agnes to have it out with Jim and Lizzie. Gloatingly he envisaged the encounter as a necessarily violent affair, in which there would be fighting and noise and the stretch of muscles contending.

A dim memory of previous visits guided him to a red tram going South. To avoid explanations with the conductor he uttered a reckless "All the way" and paid over his tuppence-ha'penny, to be rewarded in due course with the sight of landmarks subconsciously remembered. It came back to him that he should get off at a corner where stood a church of queer design—Byzantine if he had known it—and a natural, though confused, sense of distance and environment moved him to rise exactly in time to make an accurate landfall. Jim's house, he knew, was up the dark suburban road to the left. He recalled the words "Kia Ora" on a copper plaque on the gate.

There was nobody about in that street. Decent folks of the suburbs were indoors for the night and at their domestic ease behind the glowing windows. Trees swung and shivered over the footpath, throwing fantastic shadows. In his ever so slightly erratic passage Danny now and again brushed against cropped hedges of privet and escalonia overhanging the low walls that upheld the lawns of the small villas.

At last "Kia Ora"—there it was under a lone lamp. He crashed the iron gate behind him and advanced up the concreted path. Six steps, and his push on a white button kept a bell ringing within for at least twenty seconds.

Somebody was moving about the hall. The shadow hesitated. The door was opened. There stood Jim in an overcoat as if ready to go out.

206

A woman's voice, crying an anxious question, sounded from an inner room.

"Dan!" cried Jim.

"Aye, Dan," answered Danny grimly. "And I want to know where Agnes is."

"Now look here, Dan—"

"Shut your face! Is she here?" It was a roar of challenge.

"Never mind where she is—"

"I'll break your—"

The background suddenly filled up. The decent paraphernalia of grandfather clock, telephone on table, and brass ornaments in the hall were occluded from Danny's sight by the forms of women and one other man. He recognised Agnes, Lizzie, Alf.

"By Christ, you!" he cried and rushed.

The door swung in his face. He heard screams. He pushed against the door. Several shadows pushed against him. He was forced to let the door close, though he strained to keep it open. Then he started to kick at it and to beat his clenched fists on its lozenges of painted glass. Somewhere at the back of his mind he knew that the telephone within was working and that a woman's voice was calling "Police! Police!" The thing was to batter through that door and get at them.

The resistance of the wood to his boots and of the glass to the soft side of his fists infuriated him. He stepped back and ran at the glass with a foot upraised. It collapsed before him with a splendid crash. He hardly felt the icy slash of a razor-edge of glass across his calf or saw that his trouser-leg was torn. Back he went again to another charge at the door.

This time he was altogether too successful. His leg went through the pane up to the crook of the knee, and he slipped on his back, the lower part of the limb hanging over the ragged shards of glass left in the framework of wood. Then to the accompaniment of another outburst of screaming, his foot was gripped by two powerful hands. He kicked, then shrieked to feel the sawing of the broken glass into the tendons.

The hands released their grip. Very gingerly he withdrew his foot from the jagged orifice he had made with it. Sitting up, he had a glimpse of Jim's face peering out at him.

"Get out of here!" Jim cried rather feebly through the breach.

"Come out, you!" roared Danny.

He was scrambling to his feet when the door surprisingly opened and he saw before him, blocking the light from the hall, the tall figure of the man called Alf, Jim and Lizzie and Agnes forming an agonized frieze behind him. In a flash Danny recognised his essential enemy. This was what he had come for.

He put himself into the position of a boxer and, for all that blood was seeping into his boots, pranced on his toes like any favourite of the ring.

"Come on you!" he cried his challenge to Alf. "Put up your jukes and fight it out like a man. Come on and let's see if you're a man at all! Come on! Come on!"

Alf did not respond in the spirit of the challenge. His dignity remained with him.

"That's enough of that," he said. "You'll only get into trouble."

"Trouble!" roared Danny. "Trouble! That's what I'm here for, and you're the bloody mug I'm going to bash the face off. Come on, Sheeny! Come on!"

He started cavorting again, and he did not hear the tread of rubber-shod feet behind him. The fall of two pairs of hands on his arms was an outrageous surprise. The police—he knew it at once. This was how the dirty skunks got to work. He lashed out against the monstrous tyranny.

They dragged him down the steps. He kicked out at blue legs and had his own viciously swept from him in response. The two locks on his arms tightened remorselessly. A fist clipped him under the jaw. He tried to brake the progress towards the gate with his feet braced out before him, but they lifted him from the ground. He contrived to jerk one knee up to catch one of his tyrants in the pit of the stomach.

"Aiow, ye little bastard!" cried the policeman and wrenched his wrist.

That hurt damnably. The pain persisted and, superimposed on the ebbing of his strength, cut through anger to occupy the foreground of his mind, but there was no more passion in reserve to meet the humiliation. Every sense told him that he was beaten, and the battered ego could hold out no longer. He went suddenly limp in the great arms of the constables.

"It's all right," he said, almost sobbing. "You've got me beat."

They canted him on to his feet and marched him down the road.

3

No more than any other police court is that of the Southern Division of Glasgow designed to please the eye and raise the spirits of the law's suspects. At nine o'clock of that Monday morning when Danny Shields made his appearance in its dock, when the lamps were lit to mitigate a fog and officials coughed in their anxiety to get through the heavy weekend calendar of cases, it seemed to him the dreariest chamber he had ever entered.

He was miserable and ashamed. His wounds had been dressed, but they hurt him when he moved, and all his muscles were sore from their strain against the grimly applied might of the policemen. These pains had kept him wakeful through the first night in the cell, and on the second he hardly slept at all for the consciousness of shame and disgrace that burned in his mind.

He did not count himself a good man, but he cherished a firm ideal of decency, and he knew that he had in the folly of drink outraged it. The facts were all in his favour, no doubt. His grievance against Agnes, and against Jim and Lizzie and Alf as her abettors, was substantial and one he would continue to cherish. But to go and get drunk on a few much-needed shillings, to go out and create a disturbance, to get into the hands of the police and fight them, and to be thrown like any habitual waster into the cells! He must have been mad, and he was certainly a fool from beginning to end. Danny Shields in the nick for drunkenness, breach of the peace, and assault on the police in the execution of their duty! He was stunned by the enormity of it.

The officials of the court could make no sense of him. His head hanging, he insisted on pleading guilty to the charges gabbled from a blue sheet by the bar officer. When asked if he had anything to say in extenuation of his crimes he merely shook that lowered head. To get it over quick, to get out of the range of inquisitive, unfriendly eyes—that was all he wanted. Why must there be a long, whispered consultation between the magistrate and the Superintendent of

Police acting as prosecutor?

"This is a serious business, Shields," began his doomster pretentiously at length. "The prosecution tells me that you had provocation, and I doubt if you would have done this if you hadn't gone and got drunk. But you were drunk, and you did a lot of damage and made a nuisance of yourself, and you'll have to pay a fine of thirty shillings or go to prison for fifteen days. You've got the police to thank that it's not twice as much. Next case."

Dan had no grudge against the police at all. When he had sobered up on the Sunday they had been right decent chaps to him, patiently asking why he had been such a bloody fool and listening sympathetically to his hangdog tale. They had made it easy for him before the beak, as they had made it easy for Peter months before.

Nothing wrong with the police—but Peter! Why, they had sent from the office to tell the boy what had happened, and had he turned up even to repay what his father had done for him in that High Court? A poor, poor creature was Peter; and Danny was saddened by the proof of it. Thirty shillings . . . Peter could have managed that. But no sign of Peter in cell or court! By God, it made a man prefer fifteen days in Duke Street or Barlinnie, where at least he might reflect on the infidelity that had been superimposed on his remose.

He was surprised at Rita. Perhaps Peter had kept the truth from her, or she had not been able to take the facts seriously. He could not believe that she would have remained aloof had she known of his suffering. Jim, Lizzie, Agnes, it was perhaps too much to expect anything of them, even to save their faces, but the fact of their silence added to his burden of loneliness. No doubt they had been somewhere in court, ready to give evidence against him.

As for the Boss, he was far away, and he, Danny Shields, had decisively exiled himself from the scope of that sympathy. There were only Billy left now, poor wee Billy, and Jess. And when he thought of facing Jess again, and reflected on her overwhelming decency, he seemed to see that only from Billy now could he hope for love and the trust that makes a man a man.

The days in Barlinnie were very long and grey, though he became a favourite with the warders for his tidiness and his quiet anxiety to abide by the rules.

They let him out early on a morning of sparkling frost, so that he shivered to be expelled from the steam-heated atmosphere of the prison, was confused by the largeness and the noises of this outer existence, and was ashamed to emerge with a stain that must be palpable into such a bright, clean world.

An official of the Discharged Prisoners' Aid Society was on the spot to offer him a somewhat self-righteous comfort and a strictly reasonable need of help, but he presented to that intrusion a proud if grateful resistance. His leg had healed, his garments had been mended and cleaned, and the police had punctiliously kept for him the sum of two shillings and fourpence-halfpenny found in his pockets. He could very well make his own way and take what was coming to him; his anxiety was simply to get away in a tram out of the environment of the prison.

A red one took him down to Argyle Street past the Central Station, and it seemed years since, flown with beer and whisky, he had stumbled out of that pub in Union Street to embark on his mad adventure on the South Side. The early streams of suburban and rural dwellers filtering through the gateways of the terminus belonged to a better and safer world than his. They did not now what he knew of poverty and pain and insecurity. He was happier a little going westwards towards Partick, recognising something natural and humble in the very smell of the vehicles and in the drabness of the few people who moved about the streets. It's the poor that helps the poor, he reflected, and the poor that understands and does not condemn. The neighbours would have something to say to each other, he knew, but they would not make him out utterly a pariah. His apprehension, indeed, was that the women would make a hero of him, a martyr on account of that stuck-up besom, Agnes, whom they all disliked for her pretensions.

The little house on the second floor seemed deserted when, his heart pounding, he let himself into it at last. Two dirty dishes and a cup on the untidy table told him that Billy had had his breakfast and gone off early to school. Probably he had made it himself out of scraps in the cupboard. A pair of beige knickers hung over the grid above the hob, a characteristic symbol of Rita's proximity. There was in the sink an assortment of dirty pans and crockery. The disarray of the big box bed suggested that it had not been touched since last he quitted it unless Billy had left his pallet on the floor to use it. It would never have been made, all the same.

Danny looked with revulsion on the dead fire in the grate, oddments of silver paper, half-burnt cartons and wisps of female hair on the grey ashes.

Suddenly the characteristic untidiness of his son's wife seemed hateful and, seizing a poker from the rusting fender, he started to rattle it between the bars. He would have order in the house. He would have a blazing fire. He would re-establish what had been and would be again in spite of all that had happened.

The door of the other room opened behind him as he laboured.

"Oh, Christ!" he heard Rita's facetious voice. "Here's Charlie Peace back again."

He turned to her and grinned uneasily. She was very heavy with child, and the foetus, deep in her belly, made her ugly and absurd.

"They've let ye out, have they?" she persisted, half-mocking, half-challenging.

"Aye, they've let me out," he responded slowly. "It's a pity for you and Peter, I doubt."

"Aw, can it, for God's sake!" was her reply.

Then she shut the door on him. He could hear them talking together, but he was determined not to listen. All he wanted to care about was the lighting of that fire, the washing up of those dishes, and the making of that bed. There was plenty to do, and it gave them all a good twenty minutes to make up their minds what they would say.

Peter, fully dressed but with a lowering uneasiness on his sullen face, appeared at length.

"Hullo!" he said.

"Hullo, Peter!" responded Danny.

The boy, his hands in his pockets, stood rooted to a spot on the other side of the table. His lower lip hung loose and wet. Stupid, he let his father leap into command of the situation.

"Is that all you've got to say?" asked Danny.

"Not much to say, is there?" grumbled Peter.

"No, I suppose not."

Danny turned to give his waxing fire an intense moment of attention with the poker. Then he wheeled round on his son.

"Aye, ye can stand there," he said, his voice clamant. "But damn the bit of ye did I see the Sunday before last. Oh, no! The old man's in the nick, and the best place for him. Too proud, I suppose you were; or too bloody mean; or just wantin' the guts. You could greet plenty when you were in trouble yourself. Cried for yer old da then, ye did—blubberin' like a bairn. But let me get into a bit o' trouble, and you sit on your fat arse and let me go to hell for all you care. Too much trouble! An awful disgrace for you! Well, my lad, thank God I stopped at gettin' tight and kickin' up a row, and didn't get myself mixed up with a lot of scabby razor-slashers."

It was as if his words had beaten Peter to the ground. The boy stood motionless, his face flushed and down-cast.

"Ye've a hell of a lot to say for yourself," he rumbled.

"Aye, and a sight more if you want it," thrust Danny.

Rita appeared between them, her eyes bright.

"Will youse two shut yer faces!" she scolded bitterly. "What the hell's the good of it?" She turned on Danny. "You keep yer tongue to yerself. You don't need to worry about us. We're beating it."

"You're going?" he gaped at her.

"Aye, we're going. I'm going to have a wean, and I'm not going to have it here with you and Billy about the place. And if you think me and Peter's going to stand for this Means Test stuff, you can dam' well think again.

"Means Test?" The phrase had for Danny the significance at once of vague familiarity and ominous novelty. "I heard something. . . ."

"Oh, aye!" she mocked. "Ye'll hear about it all right. It takes a week or two for these things to get into that old nut of yours, doesn't it? But keep your hair on. We'll be out this afternoon, and you can see how you and Billy get on wi' your own tea. It'll be a change from Barlinnie, I'm sure."

Sick at heart, he walked the streets all day, seeking strange places and discovering queer, quiet streets on the suburban slopes above Partick—streets he never knew before existed, streets that told him a doleful story of the city's vastness and complexity and indifference. He saw it to be a city that had no more use for him.

At half-past three he went back to the house again. Rita had let the fire go out once more and was gone with her husband. There was nothing left in the room save untidiness and a stuffy, sweaty smell.

He relit the fire in the kitchen. He got the kettle going. There was the heel of a loaf in the cupboard and some margarine, and out of his few remaining pence he had bought some fancy biscuits as a treat for Billy. Sitting down with a slice of the bread on a toasting-fork, he listened for the sound of the child's footsteps on the stairs.

Billy came home, his demeanour uneasy but his eyes bright.

"Hullo, sonny boy!" cried Danny gladly.

"Hullo, Dada!" the child responded at once.

He went to his father, who put his disengaged arm round him and pressed him to his side.

"Lord, but I'm glad to see you, son!" whispered Danny. "It's you and me for it together now."

"I know," returned Billy calmly. "Rita told me."

"Are you frightened?"

"Not if you're staying."

"I'm staying, son, and don't you worry. Wait you till I get this toast done, and then we'll have a right feed and a talk."

CHAPTER ELEVEN

MERCHANTS OF FIREWOOD

"EVERYTHING READY for the school, then, son?"

"It's all in my bag, Dada."

"All your books and your exercises? And you've got the tuppence for the wreath to wee Jimmy Macfarlane?"

"It's in my pocket."

"Good for you, Billy. Ye'd best get off now. That was the quarter striking. I'll have something nice and tasty for your dinner. So long, lad."

"So long, Dada."

Thus it was, for Danny and the boy left to him, after breakfast, on most mornings of the week.

They got on splendidly. After the bad tempers of Agnes and the irresponsibilities of Rita, it was fine to live in a calm and orderly atmosphere once again.

Father and son were of a sort: neat, simple and grave. Each could exist in a world of his own. If Billy missed his mother and was worried by the empty quiet of the house, he showed no sign. What came to him he encountered without fuss. He asked no questions; it was as if, preternaturally wise, he understood everything.

He went to school and did well there, by all accounts. (Danny had to drag from him the admission that he was usually top of his class.) He came home at the back of twelve for his midday meal, and at the end of it helped his father to wash up the dishes. He was away again till four, and without a word he took upon himself then the regular burden of laying the table for tea, toasting the bread, and boiling the kettle. There were lessons that kept him absorbed till seven. Then he was prepared to meet Danny at halma or, if Danny felt like going out, to sit and read before the fire until it was time to go to bed. It was the man's only complaint against the boy that an absorbing book could always keep him from his right place between the sheets.

Danny was happy while he and Billy lived alone together. For one thing, the small cares of the house kept him occupied. Not for nothing had he been for three years batman to the Boss. It was easy enough to improve on the housewifery of Rita, but it became a delight to be more orderly than even Agnes had been. When Billy had gone, he would wash and dust and polish in the strictness of ritual the Army had imposed upon him. It greatly entertained him to go shopping, and he came to take seriously the business of chaffering with tradesmen and of comparing prices. He recovered the joys of cookery, proudly producing delight out of the short commons on which they had to live. He became expert in the economy of coal, even on the darning of stockings and socks and underwear. One whole afternoon he spent on a patch on the seat of Billy's trousers and found it a job well worth a man's interest and pride.

Danny Shields, in short, had a job again, and that was nearly everything for a man of his sort. And if in his heart he knew it to be a makeshift, a function unworthy of one who had walloped rivets into the steel sides of great ships, he was sustained in it by the discovery of the love a man may bear for his son.

Often now he found himself unable to look at Billy without feeling the tears at his eyes. It was a glow that hurt and stung and satisfied, a possessiveness that could be at once a pain and a benediction. It was not that Billy was all life had left to him. It was the sweet, budding, innocent essence of Billy, blossom of his seed, that ravished him with delight. He was proud of the quietness and cleverness in the boy. He wondered that such a frail, pure thing should be given him to cherish and care for. When he saw the child naked—long legs and slender flanks, head deliciously poised on a thin and graceful neck—he was heartbroken with pity and fear and love.

There went with that agonised joy, however, the cold bite of his concern for their future. It was the bite of two sharp teeth: one which urged that Billy should be safe whatever happened, the other nagging that never, never, never should they be separated. And what was that future? Agnes gone with Wee Mirren, Peter and Rita gone, Leslie Pagan gone, and not a penny of money coming into the house. He had been forced to face the facts. From Barlinnie he had come home with just a shilling or two in his pocket, and how he stood with the Boss and how with the Buroo he had no notion at all. Considerations of the kind irked his pugnacious independence. He would rather not have given them any thought at all. But there was no escape from the terrors on his path. Every time he looked at the unconscious Billy the need to face them fell like a hammer on his mind.

So, uneasily, he went up one morning to see how matters stood at the house in Kelvinside. Of his status there he was dubious, and his diffidence was duly encountered by the hostile manner of the cook, whom he asked to see. She came to the back door, a challenge on her face, ready for battle. It was as if she sniffed at something unclean. To his excessively polite enquiries she gave warlike answers.

"Oh, aye!" she said. "So they've let you out, have they? That was a fine carry-on you had out on the South Side."

Danny felt like a schoolboy before a sarcastic teacher, flushed and ashamed. But to think that his escapade had reached the ears of even an old bitch like this! Alarm seized him. Perhaps the news had come to her direct from the Boss and she was the appointed instrument of his disapproval.

"There'll be nothing for me, then?" he suggested tentatively.

"Oh, there's something for you, all right," the cook admitted. "More than you deserve, mebbe. It's fine to be a favourite, I'm sure."

He knew then that her grievance was not against him and in the same moment understood that something threatened the whole establishment.

"Has there been trouble, Mrs. Scroggie?" he asked earnestly.

"Oh, no trouble at all!" she replied sardonically. "Only that me and the girls has got our month's notice. Nice for us, I'm sure—and fine for her wi' her fancy ways in London. Closing the house: that's what she says. No trouble at all! That's all. . . . And that's what you get from a stuck-up English bitch."

"That's a pity, Mrs. Scroggie." Danny was diplomatically sympathetic. "Man, I'm right sorry to hear that." (He was actually in a state of cold alarm.) "So they're shutting up the house? Dear me, that's a pity."

"Oh, I suppose you'll be all right," said the cook, still hostile.

"I don't know about that. But mebbe there's a wee bit note in . . . in what you've got for me."

He was careful not to open the envelope in her presence, especially when he saw the eager curiosity in her eyes, but on the way down the road he paused under an over-hanging bush of laurel and tore it open. So many notes and so much silver and copper—and nothing else save an account written and ciphered in an inhumanly clerkly hand, showing three weeks' wages due to him, less the two pounds advanced by Mr. Dakers.

It had come from the Yard. From Leslie Pagan himself, from the only Boss he acknowledged, there was no word at all.

Danny accepted it as final. His heart was very heavy, and he was assailed by alarm for the future, but he had no sense of grievance at all. The Boss had treated him as a toff and gentleman would, and now that he had for his own good reasons decided to close down the house in Kelvinside, the contract fell through in the most natural way. That silly old sow of a cook had to make a grievance of it. Could she not see that they were all in the same boat? Perhaps she felt herself peculiarly virtuous. He, Danny Shields, had no illusions about himself in that respect. He counted himself lucky to have three weeks' screw for less than a week's work done. The Boss could always be trusted to treat a fellow decent.

On the cash thus put into his hands he felt for the best part of a week confident enough about the future of Billy and himself. It was his way to live at short range, as it were, and to be content so long as he had coins in his pocket. What he came slowly and sombrely to realise, however, was that Agnes, with all her faults, had been a competent manager of his domestic affairs, and that Rita must have been more accommodating than he had known. It gradually began to appal him to see how the simple wants of Billy and himself in the way of bread and margarine and jam and eggs and sausages, with a bit of steak thrown in for a treat now and again, could eat into money. Then he realised one night that the roof under which they sheltered had to be paid for with inexorable regularity. And the gas was always burning these winter nights, and they had to have coal—a continual process of consumption to which there would be no end if he and Billy must live.

So Danny encountered the fact of bankruptcy and for the most part of one dreadful night lay numb with fear. At last he was reduced to knowing his own insignificance and futility against the vast indifference of the world. The props and sanctions had been swept away; and with all friendship gone, save that of a ten-year-old boy, he was lost utterly. There was no escape. The high, smooth wall of Fact stared in his face across the path, menacing. He was as helpless as a child lost in the jungle.

Queerly, his mind would not even then entertain the notion that he had any claim on Public Assistance. Because he hated the dependence it implied, he was quick enough to believe that he had somehow cut himself away from the scope of official charity. Nor did it please him to think that he might at least enquire as to his position in that respect. Dour and headstrong, he could only see it as his own affair to meet for Billy's sake what might be coming. Even in the last issue a chap had to stand on his own feet, and no nonsense about it. Theft, a personal appeal to Leslie Pagan—such extremities he could contemplate, though nervously. The falling back on charity, even from the State, was what he could not bear to think of again.

The filtered sunlight of a fine winter morning heartened him a little when he wakened from the sleep he had fallen into about four. He remembered his alarm and distress; indeed, they hung heavy on his mind as will horrible experiences survived; but now in the brightness of day the difficulties of his situation did not seem to hem him in so completely. It was a big world, after all, with places in it for the willing man. Even on his own he could surely discover some way of turning over the few shillings they needed now. What was in hand would last them at least a week, and that seemed a long time. In a spirit of optimism as blind as his despair of the dark hours he instructed Billy as they sat together at table, eating a breakfast of tea and rolls warmed in the oven.

"I'll be out all day, son," he explained, "so ye'll take the key and let yourself in at one. I'll leave a bite of dinner out for you, and you can fill yourself a glass of milk from the jug. There's a wee bit of a job along the road I'm going to look at."

"Where's the job, Dada?" asked the boy eagerly.

"Oh, a chap I know was telling me. I'll let ye know," explained Danny largely.

The boy gone, he tidied the house rapidly and reached for his overcoat. It was lamentably worn and shabby, he perceived with a shock. Only then he realised that he was down to his last suit, though it was in the mercy of God a good one. But clothes were dear, costing very big money in the scale in which he must now think.

He thought with a spasm of pain of the thin raincoat that was Billy's only outer protection against the cold, and of the darned grey jersey below. His own boots were wearing, with the layers of leather showing at the toes, and it must be wet feet for him when the rains came. A nice thought when he had just been boasting and lying to Billy about a job in prospect!

Once in the street he realised the enormity of his optimism, for his first few steps along the Dumbarton Road brought him face to face with the stigmata of the blight that had fallen on Clydeside. He could not escape the significance of so many empty shops "To Let"—newsagents, cash butchers, wireless dealers, and small tobacconists: small people driven out by the sheer lack of custom. He saw the hordes of the new salesmen, seedy men in bowler hats, and even Hindus, carrying their satchels of cheap gewgaws from one poor door to another. The workless faced him at every second step: men unmistakably and irretrievably stamped with hopelessness and under-feeding, men without coats or collars, their pinched faces grey-green with cold, their hands deep in the jacket pockets, their shoulders hunched in the stoop of the damned. Again about the busy window of a Jewish cobbler he came on a dozen of them, gathered just to watch, with dull eyes and in silence, other men at work.

Yet the terrible stringency thus manifested braced Danny to a keenness of observation quite unusual in him. With anxious eyes he regarded every aspect of the streetscape, straining his mind to think what in the way of profitable activity it might suggest. He was not looking for a job, for he knew that only a divine accident could bring one his way. He was contemplating in extremity and after long years of submission to the industrial scheme how his own enterprise could find some small opening in this complex world and develop it into a means of livelihood. He saw men selling apples from barrows, men oscillating between mendicancy and commerce with boxes of Russian matches on the pavements' edges, men selling briquettes from hired floats, and men imitating Charlie Chaplin to the music of piano-accordions.

The possibilities of all such ways of coaxing pennies from the public were duly reviewed and assessed in his mind, and he lingered with delicious alarm over the notion that he might join a band of street musicians. He used to be able to sing a song with the best in the Corporals' Mess, and Billy had a boy's sweet treble. An idea there; they might compose a turn at once unique and appealing! But he came to reflect on the legality of using the child in such a way, and he saw it was the betrayal of his dear son into the shame of beggary, and, the impulse weakening, he remembered that every back-court in Glasgow resounded daily to music of professional standard, and that even to the rich passing along Sauchiehall Street there played fiddlers of the first class, sacked from their picture-house jobs with the coming of the talkies.

It seemed that men longer tried by distress than he had already explored every niche that observation and ingenuity could suggest. He half-realised that he was just a riveter, a specialist in a job outmoded, and too old to learn a new one worth having. The Dumbarton Road, merging into Argyle Street, seemed endless and hopeless, a turnpike leading both ways to misery and bafflement, and that sense of having a high, smooth wall frowning over him oppressed him once again. Clouds were gathering in the east to blot out the thin sunshine, and in the valley of the Kelvin there was actually a gathering of fog. He could see the idle men walking slowly along the terraces of the Park.

The sheer need for company and confidence turned his footsteps at length into the pend where Jess lived. Her he had seen only twice since the dreadful affair of his imprisonment, but he had been particular to call on her as soon as he was free. It was for him a spiritual necessity to know that she had not turned against him, and miraculously she had proved to be her old gentle self, quick to see him a man outraged, indeed excessive in her sympathy with his lot and in her bitterness against Agnes. But now they could no longer go to the pictures together. There was no money left for that and, Agnes gone, that stubborn firmness of Jess's was against their meeting except in the most open way. What had somehow been sanctioned in her simple mind when Dan had Agnes to return to in the evening now took on the nature of the furtive and indecent.

There could be no wrong, however, in turning in to see her in broad daylight, and indeed she waved him a greeting from the high porch where she had come out to beat carpets against the white-washed wall.

"Hullo, Dan!" she called to him cheerily. "What's brought you here at this time of day?"

"Och, the usual," he responded, "on the prowl for a job. You haven't seen one knocking about?"

"Indeed I have not," she answered gravely. "Things just seem to go from bad to worse."

"You're about right there."

He climbed to where she stood at the top of the wooden steps, and they gossiped for a while like old neighbours of the little things of mutual interest: of the children and their boots and clothes, of foodstuffs and the price of them, of the goodness of the old days and the badness of the new times. She did not ask him indoors for the cup of tea he would have enjoyed, and he did not suggest that they should resume the intimacy of those brave nights when they were able to go to the pictures together. Even on the simplest of human actions the depression had laid a chilling hand.

They were speaking of Billy and the fate of a motherless boy when a ramshackle door, opening out of a wooden shed on the yard below, swung outwards, and a fat, small man in little less apparently than singlet, trousers and carpet slippers appeared, straining under the load of two large sacks. With a gasp of relief he dumped them on the ground. His sweaty face turned up to grin at Jess.

"There's a pickle mair firewood for you, Mrs. Stirling," he wheezed. "Help yersel'."

He disappeared into his shed, the shaky door closed behind him, and Jess explained the comic apparition to Dan.

"That's Mr. Allison, the cabinetmaker. Such a right decent man! We're never wanting for firewood. 'Deed, we could keep the fire going all day with what he throws out. I doubt the most of it just goes to waste."

It was then that the idea came to Danny in all its beauty.

"Throws it out, does he?" he ruminated. "I wonder now. . . . Here, let's have a look at that stuff."

He rattled down the steps and opened one of the sacks. Glowing, his eyes fed on the fragrant treasure inside it. He picked a piece from the top, and his craftsman's fingers went lovingly over the resinous, smooth surface of the queerly-shaped fragment.

"That's lovely stuff," he breathed reverently. "Oak, the very best. And there's a bit of white pine. That'll be birch, likely. . . . Man, but it's bonny wood. And you tell me he throws it out?" He turned to his friend with a slow smile. "I'm beginning to see a job for me at last, Jess."

She was slow to take the point, and he explained to her urgently. If it could be contrived with the cabinetmaker, he would set up in business as a merchant of firewood. Folks in the big houses always wanted kindling: nothing better for them than the promise of a regular supply. He would pay this fat man Allison a fair price and see to it that Jess had always first pick of what was thrown out. Perhaps Allison, being in a small way of business, could not provide all the wood he might want, but it would be easy to organise supplies from a score of sources he could think of out of hand. It would be a right business chopping up the stuff and stringing it in bundles, but a real job for a man. (He gloated on the ideal of neatness he would establish.) And Billy could give him a hand in the evenings with the selling of the stuff. Nice light stuff, firewood, for a wee boy to handle.

Jess was convinced. She was hesitant at first, seeing absurd difficulties and fearing imponderable risks, but he won her over to enthusiasm.

"Oh my, Dan! Isn't that an idea! Come on and we'll see Mr. Allison. He's a right good friend of mines."

The fat man's temperament was according to tradition. He wheezed over his bench and was off-handedly expansive.

"Right you are, son, right you are!" he assured Danny. "I'm aye glad to see a chap making the best of a bad job. . . . Get out of there, you black bitch, or you'll get your rump shaved," and he knocked a purring cat away from the allure of his humming saw. "That's all right, son. As long as Mrs. Stirling here gets what she needs. You can take the rest and welcome. I'll keep what I can for you. Glad to see a chap fightin' for himself. Pay—your Auntie Kate! . . . There's that silly bitch of a cat again."

There was kindness in the world after all.

2

It was a glorious excitement to be occupied once more, and Danny went about his preparations for a business career with a trembling gravity. A faintly portentous manner grew upon him; with Billy or Jess or Mr. Allison he would anxiously discuss his small problems of organisation and attack, as if they were matters of international import; high resolutions of probity informed his every step, and he was so grave and earnest in his dealings with a bag-merchant that the man laughed in his face, threw him half-a-dozen old sacks, and told him to go away and play himself—as if it was one of the best jokes he had encountered in a month of Sundays.

No joke at all for Danny, this eager invasion of the fat fields of commerce. All sorts of things for him to think out lovingly and delicately decide. He came first of all to the large conclusion that he would operate from the yard at the end of the pend off Argyle Street. This was his source of supply and lay in tactical proximity to his likeliest market, the big houses and well-to-do flats about the Park. He ascertained that there would be no objecion to his working in Allison's yard, and it was much for him to feel that he was near Jess once more and that she had a fond interest in his enterprise. He would spend the day splitting the wood and making it up in two sorts of bundles to sell at threepence and sixpence each. In the evenings after tea he and Billy would come along and, agreeably loaded, set out on their rounds. But all that just for a beginning, of course. He could not count on the fat man keeping him in a sufficiency of wood, and he envisaged a series of depots up and down the line of the Dumbarton Road wherever it was bordered on its northern side by the villas and flats of the middle class. He saw himself ultimately employing Jess's children, all of them in a sodality of common interest and decent, hard-working comfort.

And so, three days after his original decision, in the dusk of a sharp winter evening, he and Billy set out hopefully on the

224

adventure. Danny had modestly planned to try their luck at first along the western extensions of Sauchiehall Street, and he was happy to think that the lour of a sombre sunset over the Kilpatrick Hills and the nip in the still air suggested the comfort of fires and warm domestic interiors. He was soon to learn, to be sure, that he had unwisely chosen his ground for his first experiment. He found that the terraces of his choice were largely defended by the pre-occupied receptionists of doctors and dentists, by suspicious and efficient mistresses of boarding-houses, and by the frankly hostile clubmasters of political and regimental associations.

"I doubt we'll have to try somewhere else, son," he, defiantly cheerful, said to Billy when they had explored both sides of four hundred yards of street in vain.

He was dashed, but by no means downed. Even to his sanguine heart he had had to admit that it could not be easy to begin with. And of this busy Sauchichall Street, clangorous with trams and motor-horns and with all sorts of supplies within hail, he had never entertained high hopes. His mind had not worked without shrewd-ness, and confidently enough he fell back on the second line of defence his cogitations had prepared. A sure instinct took him up Kelvingrove Street to where the grave Victorian terraces lined the southern edge of the Park and all was very quiet and solid.

At their third call they made their first deal. One ring at a main flat bell had brought a pert maid who simply shut the door in their faces. Another—first floor—earned Danny a lecture on the sin of bringing small boys out at that time of night; the child should be in bed. Then they encountered fortune, for to the great door of the top flat, a door composed largely of broad panes of glass frosted with floral designs in the Victorian taste, there came a fair youngish woman in tweed skirt and jumper. The cries of small boys at play within sounded a pleasing note of domesticity in Danny's ear, and his heart leaped to recognise that here at last was a brisk housewife prepared to deal with him on a businesslike footing.

"Let me see your sticks," the little matron demanded.

Danny was eager to thrust forward the choice bundle he had ready to hand. She took it and turned it over under a critical eye. Keenly he watched her face, marvelling at the same time at the aura of light the amber globe in the hall conjured out of her fair head.

"That's very nice stuff," she said, pronouncing judgment. "I'll take sixpence-worth now. And if you can keep up that quality I'll take the same twice a week, Tuesdays and Fridays. Wait till I get my purse."

She came back with the sixpence—and a penny for Billy.

"Has that boy got enough clothes on?" she demanded severely, cataloguing Billy with the quick eye of an experienced mother of young children. "Well, you can come on Friday again. But I'll want the same quality, or you can take it back."

"You'll get the very best, mum," Danny assured her fervently. And it was as if that practical, tart little lady had changed their luck. Their very next call brought to the door a soft old creature, all a-flutter with eleemosynary concern, who bought a second sixpence-worth and seemed to indicate that she was good for another sixpence-worth whenever they cared to appear and rounded off her tremulous generosity with a shilling slipped into Billy's hand.

"That's for yourself, sonny, all for yourself," she teetered pathetically. "You keep it and spend it on a nice present for Christmas. Now, I hope you're nice and warm and that you don't stay up too late, and you're clever with your lessons, and that you take a good breakfast before you go out these cold mornings. . . ."

Danny found himself very sorry for the old lady, so kind, so stupid, so sorely troubled with her swollen, fat feet.

But the luck continued to hold. There were repulses again from the wives and maids of doctors and one passionate scene with a bachelor gentleman, apparently, who called Dan a lazy tout and told him that his kind ought to be bloody well conscripted and made to work: capping it all with a recommendation to take his bloody wood to blazes and himself with it. Only the presence of Billy prevented Danny from offering this purist a stand-up fight to see who was the better man. And there was his new business in the neighbourhood to think of.

Yet he found the ruck of these well-to-do people very decent on the whole, and a dashed sight better than their maids. Some shook kindly heads and closed their doors gently, but there were others who betrayed surprise at this new enterprise and were delighted by the promise of wood so good and neatly bundled and were glad to say, however tentatively, that they would buy again. At half past eight in the evening Danny decided that he and Billy had done a fair day's work. He had taken in cash the sum of five shillings and threepence. Billy had been dowered with one shilling, three separate pennies, and two rosy apples. There were definite repeat orders from three households, and four others could be considered certainties.

Thus the firm of Shields, merchants of firewood, was auspiciously launched. There were ups and downs, to be sure. A household that had been friendly on the opening night would suddenly turn surly, and a tentative ring at a doubtful bell would bring an unexpected and cheerful bit of business. Danny quickly learned that it was all very much a matter of the moods of women, but with his regulars, as he came to call them, it soon began to look as if he had found security at last.

The takings fluctuated wildly. One week there would be only fourteen shillings to his credit; the next there would be a sudden and incalculable rise to thirty-seven. On such occasions he could afford to take Jess to the pictures, and taking it by and large, he and Billy found their feet. A nice wee house of one apartment for the two of them, and they would be laughing.

The development of the little business was aided in all sorts of odd ways. One night he had to leave Billy at home with an alarming cough, and when he came to the door of his first customer of all, the competent, fair young woman on the second floor, he caught a shrewd, appraising look about her eyes and felt the impact of a quick question. "Where's the little boy?"

"I had to leave him at home, mum," Danny explained anxiously. "He's got a cough, a nasty cold on the chest altogether. I'm on my own the night."

"I see," said the young woman slowly.

He took the point at once. She had been moved to suspect that he had hired Billy as a decoy in the first place, and he saw that the appeal of the child's innocence and slender fairness went far with these housewives. It became his technique thereafter to remain out of sight while his son delivered or offered the bundles. Likewise he discovered from various encounters that, even in the matter of how wood should be cut for kindling to give good value, the tastes of women vary.

So the job settled down into the nearest approach to regularity that he could expect. Indeed, six weeks of experience showed him that it could not occupy all his time, and that most of his customers could be satisfied on the Tuesdays and Fridays of each week. Dreams of expansion came to challenge his native caution. If he could tap another district, perhaps he could establish a Monday and Thursday trade; and not all his reserves and innocence of the ways of the prosperous world could suggest good reasons against the calculation.

One day in a bold mood he set out for the unknown regions along the northern edge of the Park, found at length a jobbing joiner near the Arlington Baths very glad to receive a small offer of cash for his spare wood, and arranged to have the use of a backyard for his operations as he used the pend off Argyle Street. That was the day when, passing a humble shop, he was seized with the idea of offering his wares in attractive form and bought from a slightly surprised old man with thick glasses half a dozen trig, clean spale baskets of the sort gardeners use.

It was his plan to tackle now that group of huge and superannuated mansions, which crowns one of Glasgow's characteristic clay drumlins and gives it much the appearance of an enormous battleship bearing across the Park upon the University. Big folks up there, he knew, the survivors of Clydeside's Golden Age hanging on against the encroaching tide of hostels and hotels and nursing homes; and there would be any amount of smart stuff from maids and housekeepers. But Danny believed now that he knew his trade. He had faith in the excellence of his goods and the appeal of Billy. One soft night of drizzle and mist in the Kelvin Valley they set out across Woodlands Road on the assault of that fortalice of the rich and established.

They had a poor enough evening of it. Those mansions were so large and so austerely run as to have lost the quality of domesticity. Hereabouts no fair young women came to their doors, only starched girls and grumbling caretakers. From the doors, even the side doors of nursing homes and hostels they were driven with hostile words. Their first sale was to an elderly, enfeebled couple from the basement of an otherwise empty house, to whom Danny was constrained by pity of their pity of him and the boy to hand a sixpenny basket for threepence. A manservant surprisingly answered another imposing door and still more surprisingly directed them courteously down the basement steps, where an ample cook seemed delighted to see them, declared to God that firewood was just what she was needing, took a shilling's worth, and told them to be sure to come again.

That was all. They carried heavy loads through the quiet ovals and terraces of Woodside towards their depot. But Danny was not in the least disheartened. He knew his difficulties now and had conquered the greatest of them by making a beginning, however small. Seeing the strained look on young Billy's face, he laughed to cheer that anxious boy.

"Well, that's that, son," he said largely. "Not what you'd call a rush of business, but we've got started, and better than I expected. There'll be a tidy wee job for us up here before the month's out."

They were coming down through the Circus into Lynedoch Street and towards the bright lights of the main tram-route, and it startled them to see two young men with sinister faces under tweed caps rushing out from behind a corner to bar their way. They were tough customers of the unmistakable hooligan sort, white mufflers of artifical silk crossed under their chins, the trousers of their cheap serge suits flaring out to bell-mouths, their rubber-soled shoes finely pointed.

"Here you!" snarled one at Danny. "What the hell's your game up here?"

"Selling firewood, son," said Danny promptly and cheerfully. "What's it got to do with you?"

He was ready to drop his bags and fight. The two men closed in upon him, their faces dark and cruel.

"Well, you can bloody well cut it out," said their spokesman, his little eyes vicious. "This is our pitch, see? We're not standing for no bloody competition, see? You cut it out or you'll get what's coming to you. See?"

Out of the corner of his eye Danny could indeed see that two half-empty sacks lay against the railings. It was at least not a hold-up of the authentic sort. But he was anxious for Billy and was at the same time in no mood to surrender.

"We'll see about that," he said. "It's a free country."

"Aye, and if you want to bloody well keep on living in it you bloody well cut it out. See?"

"I heard you the first time," Danny retorted. "Come on, Billy, and we'll get home."

All the way, and for the boy's sake, he made light of that encounter, but the memory of it disturbed him. He knew not to underrate the black menace of Glasgow's violent, desperate unemployed youth of a given type. He was not by any means going to surrender at the bidding of two louts, but he knew that they could make trouble, and his concern was always for Billy. Yet to leave Billy at home while he went on these forays up the hill would be to confess the danger of them.

It was an anxious dilemma, and he escaped from it uneasily as they set out on their second journey into that strange territory.

"Remember those blocks that stopped us the other night, Billy?" he began with a great display of the casual. "Well, I don't think they'll try it on again, but if they do and start any funny stuff, don't you mind me—I'll be all right—but run for your life for the nearest policeman. That'll sort them. Understand?"

As it turned out, they were not molested that evening and they were lucky enough to do more than double the amount of trade they had done on the first night of all. At every turn, however, Danny had the queer feeling of being watched and followed. More than once he clearly saw two figures skulking in the swinging shadows set up by the street lamps. Indeed his enemies were about, watchful like jealous animals of his movements. But would they really dare to attack?

On his own part he grew nervous on account of Billy as the night wore on, and his heart rose to his mouth when, waiting on a stairway while the boy offered their wares on the top floor, he saw through the barred window of a landing that they were evidently following him deliberately and were passing the mouth of the close with their pallid faces turned to watch the entrance. He was afraid to move. Billy came down, another sixpenny bundle sold, but he kept the child by his side and watched the length of the lighted pavement below. The men came back, moving quickly now, but again their eyes were fixed on the doorway. Danny pondered anxiously. Must he risk it? . . . Then there came, stately along his beat, a policeman. "Come on, now," father commanded son in a rapid whisper.

Keeping station behind his moving mass, they followed the policeman by devious ways and down steps and slopes to the lights and safety of Charing Cross.

The episode alarmed him. It was a cruel business for poor little Billy to be mixed up with. But the more he thought of it, the more angrily was Danny determined to go on with the exploitation of his new district. It was, by God, a free country after all. He was offering fair competition, and let the best man win. The business promised well, and he was damned if he was going to be frightened out of it by a couple of dirty keelies from the Cowcaddens. Let them try it on, and they would see what the police had to say about it. Only for Billy was he afraid, and Billy knew what to do at the first sign of trouble.

There was clear moonlight on the night of their third excursion, and the quiet terraces on the hill had lost their shadowed mystery. He could see to the far end of every one of them, and only an ambush could have surprised him. So he went carefully around every corner and into every close, his hand on a length of lead piping he had picked up from among a pile of rubbish outside Mr. Allison's door. They would get what was coming to them, these two bits of dirt, if they tried on any funny stuff, and though he joyfully intended to hit first, it would be in self-defence. He almost came to hope that they would appear, so that the issue might be settled for good and all.

But of his rivals he saw that night nothing on the crown of the hill; and, as it turned out, business was good, remarkably so. By eight o'clock they had taken six shillings and acquired two new promises of regular custom. Their sacks were nearly empty.

"That'll do us the night, Billy," announced Danny at length. "We're laughing, son. All the same," he added circumspectly, "I don't think we'll go back to Woodlands Road, for all we have to carry. We'll just slip through the Park and get down to Argyle Street."

He was dissembling his lingering apprehension and could only hope that the boy was deceived. The moonlight was on his side; even the paths of the Park, lined with sparse lamps and shadowed

231

by great growths of laurel, rhododendron and willow, could not conceal the enemy. And it was a night for lovers. There would be an interlocked couple, even two, on every seat and others in all those corners where bad men might choose to hide. He was not unduly nervous when they passed by Lord Roberts, looking from his bronze charger along the unfamiliar terrain of the Kilpatrick Hills, and started down a path towards the broad walks by the Kelvin. He carried the length of lead piping in his right hand and recovered the thrill of trench raids in days long past.

Even so, the suddenness of the attack left him helpless. They sprang on him from a bench he had imagined to support a couple lost in the lusts of the flesh. One had his right arm in a painful grip before he could raise it. The other spat bitterness into his face.

"By Christ, you're for it now," the man hissed.

Even then he thought swiftly how they must have followed him after all and made a quick detour to catch him.

"That'll learn ye, ye bastard!"

Something caught him heavily on the side of the neck, a sickening blow that stung as well. His knees gave under him. He felt the warm flush of blood over his shoulder. His stomach rose, and black blinds closed over his eyes. He was on the ground. The blinds lifted momentarily.

He saw the face of Billy, white and helpless in the moonlight. The boy's hands were stretched out towards him in a searing gesture of appeal.

"Run, son, run!" he contrived to gasp. "Get the polis. Quick!"

Then he was all alone again, a worn stone in the moon-flooded pathway filling his eyes with the finest details of its shape. But it was too tiring to stare at a thing so unresponsive. The black blinds fell once more.

3

Through the chill antiseptic air of the ward the doctor, in his long white coat, clove a purposeful way to the side of the bed where Danny lay.

"Hullo, old soldier," he asked cheerfully. "How's that tough neck of yours?"

"Fine," said Danny, grinning.

"Let's see, then," said the doctor.

Danny loathed what was about to happen, but he did not wince. The doctor was one of the best: exactly like that Australian chap the old mob had had out on the Sinai Desert, so cheery and decent that the boys would just not go on sick parade for fear of troubling him.

"Steady, old son," warned the doctor, flicking aside the first turns of the long bandage. "I'll go gently."

Danny knew that. Though it could hurt, he admired to the point of love the light, strong ruthlessness with which the last circles of the bandage were torn from over the sodden dressing on his wound. No bloody nonsense about this M.O., and Danny could give his heart to any man who knew his job.

The raw wound tingled to the cold air.

"There you are!" cried the doctor triumphantly. "Not too bad, was it? My God, they did give you a good dose of the old bottle trick! Dirty swine, these Glasgow hooligans. Look at it, sister. Another thirty-second of an inch and it would have been into the jugular." He turned on Danny with a bitter-sweet smile. "And that would have been your number up, old soldier. The dirty swine. . . . Steady till I give it a wipe. . . . I know it hurts like hell, son. I won't be long. . . . The gauze, sister. . . . Thanks. . . . Anyhow, they're jolly well jugged, your two beauties. Sheriff Court yesterday. Nine months for the bottle expert and three months for his friend. You see, the police were watching *them*. . . . Dammit, man, I'm going as gently as I can. . . . The silk, sister. No, woman, the *silk*. . . . Lord, Shields, I'd have taken you for a clumsy suicide. . . . Now, that should be better. Come on, you old stiff, give's a grin. If that wound's not healed by tomorrow it's M. and D. for you. *And* a Number Nine."

Danny grinned dutifully, though it hurt damnably to do so. He was a right tear, the doctor, and a gentleman. A toff and a gentleman: one of the very best. The military joke between them had endured ever since Danny, a tangle of torn flesh and blood-soaked clothes, had been carried into the Western Infirmary and dumped into the casualty ward and, smelling the anciently familiar smells of iodine and anaesthetics, had thought himself back in the

C.C.S and burbled of the crumps smashing on the Line. Then the doctor had swum into his ken, brusque and reassuring.

"Hullo, son," he had said, and his eyes were near at hand and blue in a fresh, shrewd face. "What's your crush?"

"Lowland Division," Danny had muttered.

"Mine's the Highland 51st. . . . He's going again, sister. Quick—!"

"Good old 51st," Danny had whispered generously.

It was a bond. Old soldiers understood each other.

The doctor had stood by, solicitous of pain, deft with his cool fingers, off-handedly cheerful always. It was a great joke between them, this old bit of chaff about M. and D. and Number Nines. The bloke knew his stuff all right, too—could tell a chap stories of Beaumont Hamel and that day behind Kemmel when they turned their machine-guns on the Pork and Beans in precipitate retreat. Delighted to hear a good yarn about the Palestine show, too—like that one about Poof Wilson and the General's A.D.C., or what Willie Macfarlane wrote home to the wife from Nazareth. And he had met Leslie Pagan, the Boss. Not that he was standing for any nonsense, the doctor. When he came on parade, you knew about it. In fact, a real gentleman, a topper. Danny was happy to be in such care.

Of the Infirmary as a going concern he approved thoroughly. It was a long time since he had enjoyed cleanliness and the sweet rhythm of order in which he took so much delight. There were no frills: that was the point. They had you wakened and washed remorselessly in the early morning. It was just no use trying to put any soft stuff across the nurses; they could be cold and cutting if need be. When the doctor came, he expected everything to be just so and thought nothing of ticking off the whole ward if it were not. But the machine worked. Not since he had been with an Army in the field had Danny seen anything which worked so well, and his soul rejoiced.

He had sunk back out of life without regrets. Very seldom did he worry about this brutal interruption of the promising little business he had been making for himself. What had happened had happened, and if he must he would start again. He did not doubt that his old customers would rally more strongly round him on hearing his story.

But the talk of the doctor had really worked the biggest change in his outlook. The doctor had taken an almost violent interest in his misfortune, and allowed Danny to recline on the belief that, in some vague official way, he would not be allowed to suffer. There was some sketchy talk of a course of treatment for the injured muscles of his neck—a longish job, the doctor seemed to hint—and he was allowed to assume that, by his rights as a citizen, he would be supported out of the public funds. Always respectful of authority and as human as any other man, Danny was happy to leave his immediate fate to the doctor and to fall back into the refuge always open to the acknowledged convalescent.

Yes: things had worked themselves out happily. Jess had taken Billy into her home—and what more natural in all the world? Jess had seen to the closing and displenishment of the old house in Kingarth Street, realising a decent little sum by the sale of its furniture and fittings. . . .

A queer thought that for Danny through the grey period of the afternoon rest! The past utterly and finally wiped out by a blow on the neck with the jagged end of a broken bottle. Agnes gone. Wee Mirren gone, Peter and Rita gone. Only the thought of Wee Mirren could cut to his heart now. He wondered long and fondly if he could get her back. But perhaps she was part of the price he had to pay for the new freedom and ease.

There was always Jess. Every visiting day, as regular as the clock, she was by his bedside, usually with Billy, sometimes alone. (Nor could he prevail on her not to bring him little gifts of flowers or fruit, and he stopped trying when he realised that it was a pleasure necessary to her kind and simple heart.) Their intimacy grew sweetly and naturally at these meetings. Now the admission that they belonged to each other seemed to be made beyond any withdrawal whatsoever. He would take her hand in his on the coverlet, and one evening he asked her for a kiss in the way of goodbye, and she bent down and kissed him, blushing like a girl, and never afterwards did she leave him, even when Billy was there, without kissing him.

So the day came when he was fit to leave the Infirmary. For more than a week he had been padding about the wards in his soft slippers, here giving the nurses a hand with some job or other, there pausing to talk to a man still in bed: it might even be a chap hurt in one of the yards that were still going on the strength of repair work. His legs grew steady under him, and he had been warned that he was about due for discharge, and he was prepared.

Not altogether happy about it, was Danny, nevertheless; he would fain have clung to this secure bough above the world's strife and he looked unhappy when the doctor came round on what, the night sister had warned him, was almost certainly his last visit. His friend grinned.

"Come on, old soldier! No more scrimshanking. I think it should be M. and D. for you now. Let's see that neck of yours."

Now the doctor could run the tips of those strong-soft fingers of his over the jagged scar.

"Yes, yes. . . ." he perpended. "Not bad when you come to look at it. But I don't like the way that mastoid is shaping. Look, sister. See how it's pulling down his head. There's an incipient something there. Yes, there's an incipient something there. Look here, Shields. . . ."

"Sir!" answered Danny promptly.

"I want to see you tonight in my house. I'm going to discharge you, but that neck of yours wants looking at. Look here—I'll send my car for you at five tonight if sister can keep you till then. That all right, sister? Good! Give him plenty of work to do. He's only an old sweat, and there's nothing wrong with him. But have him down at Church Street at five. So long, soldier."

He patted Danny's shoulder and swept, the tails of his white coat flying, to the next bed.

In the evening the doctor's car hurried Danny through Hillhead to a lighted doorway in one of the terraces of the Woodside he well remembered visiting last with a sack of firewood over his shoulder. A trig maid showed him into a brown dining-room where, on the far side from the gas fire, he sat at an oak table and turned the leaves of a periodical called *Punch* that seemed to him only remotely diverting—the sort of stuff the toffs liked, he supposed. Then the girl came back, pert as you please, and led him through the hall to a small room where, entrenched amid enamelled basins and various formidable sorts of apparatus, the doctor sat at a desk.

There was a reassuring grin for Danny.

"Hullo, Shields! How does it feel to be out of jug? Sit down there." And Danny relapsed into a great leather chair. "Have a cigarette. I want to talk to you. You're a funny old case, you know."

The doctor passed his packet of Prize Crop and snapped a lighter from his waistcoat pocket.

"That old neck of yours. . . ." began the doctor. "It's really a bit of a teaser. You see, soldier, it wasn't just a cut that could be healed and then finish. That dirty dog of a hooligan got at certain nerves—you wouldn't understand—and the fact of the matter is: if you don't get the right sort of treatment now, you're going about for the rest of your natural with your left ear somewhere near your left shoulder. That's what I wanted to see you about."

"Will it be an expensive job, sir?" Danny asked sombrely.

The doctor laughed and even Danny saw that it was with relief.

"It's not going to cost you or me anything, soldier. Look here—" The doctor flicked his ash into the gas fire. "That's just the point. You're a proud old devil, Shields, and what I want to get in to that head of yours is that you are a pensioner. No, no! There's no use trying that independent stuff on with me. I'm telling you as a medical man that you're going easy for the next six months at least. Shut up, will you? Now, it's all arranged. What you've got to get is a spot of massage and electric treatment, and what you've got to do is to turn up at the clinic in Borgue Street tomorrow and get your orders. Dr. Bulloch, a nice woman, will see you. *Then,* you've got to keep your silly old mind easy and go to the P.A. twice a week with this line. Shut up, Shields! It's all arranged. Just you do what you're told. . . . Golly, that's my next patient. You'd better beat it, soldier. And I'll want to hear from you every fortnight at least."

Dazed, Danny suffered the doctor to push him through the hall to the front door.

"The car's still there," said the doctor. "Swan will run you home. Tell him where you want to go. And don't forget what I told you."

"Sir—" Danny began, blundering, "you've been a toff—"

"Oh, don't try it, man," the doctor said, squeezing his arm

237

above the elbow. "Just take it that it's between two old soldiers. You understand."

"Old soldiers, sir!" Danny cried happily, then gulped.

As if it were second nature, he drew his heels together with a click and brought his hand up to the peak of his tweed cap and back to his thigh with the swagger of a Guardsman on parade.

"Goodnight. . . ."

Through tears he made his way down the steps to the pavement and at the open door of the car realised that he had no home to go to after all.

4

The warmth of his greeting to the house in the pend off Argyle Street overwhelmed him.

Jess was out at the top of the steps to welcome him in, Jess fresh and neat and warm in a new blouse and a clean apron. Against the glare of the big fire within he saw the bobbing heads of excited children. They all swarmed round him, Jess's face very close to his own and kindly with blushes, the infants pressing against his legs. Eager questions assailed him, and he felt lightheaded in the confusion. Then there was Billy, silent but quivering with joy, to offer himself for a hug.

He was dragged indoors. They had a big chair ready for him before the fire, and he was pushed into it. The boys wished to see the scar below the bandage that still surrounded his neck. The girls sat on the mat at his feet gazing up into his face as into that of a beloved hero. They gave him no peace at all with their chatter, and Danny felt like a king returned from exile to his proper domain. Over the young heads he exchanged sweet glances of understanding with Jess.

It was she who dispersed the rabble with great good humour.

"Come on the lot of you," she cried. "The kettle's on the boil, and the man's got to get his tea. See that your hands are clean. Out the road you, Isa, till I get the pot het up. The toast's in the oven, Billy. Come on, come on, the lot of you!"

It was great fun for everybody. The children rose, screaming to get to the table, and Danny felt as if he had stumbled into a

Hallowe'en party at its height. Their gaiety infected him, so that he smacked their little bottoms with glee and made funny faces to draw their laughter. This was a homecoming indeed, and Jess had done him proud. When he saw the table set for the feast—a white cloth, and plates of cold ham for everybody, and biscuits and cakes in astonishing array—he knew that she had planned greatly for this day and for a moment felt the salty bite of tears at his eyelids.

The fun they had! The children guzzled and champed unblushingly but were ready to laugh at anything. If he was not gazing with wonder and surmise at their bright and eager eyes, or pondering their queer moments of gravity, he was making funny faces and thinking out comic things to say, so that he was sore and tired before the meal was finished. There came a tremendous moment when he rose and called Billy into a corner and handed him a coin and whispered a secret; and there was a taut, fierce strain of happiness in the air until Billy came back, bearing a box of crackers.

Then it seemed that the roof must come off. Jess sat with her hands to her ears in a horror of delight. Paper hats and whistles and mottoes, and trinkets emerged gloriously from the explosions. The yelping and chattering of the infants made a shimmering curtain of sound.

Jess tapped Danny on the arm, and her eyes were wet.

"You shouldn't have spent all that money, Danny," she reproved him.

"Ach, I like to see them happy," he chaffed her roughly.

It's our own wee family, isn't it?"

"Oh, Danny! . . ." Jess blushed again.

They had no peace at all until the plates were cleared away and the girls had helped their mother to wash and dry the dishes at the sink. Then the young folk fell into quietness about the fire, and Danny and Jess could talk more freely and directly: the small ears eager to catch the interesting things their elders were saying, and a yawn now and again betraying that the play was out of them and their day done. So they talked on of this and that until, about nine, Jess realised that little Isa was fast asleep on the hearthrug, her weary head in the crook of her arm.

"Bairns! Bairns!" she cried, rising to her feet. "What like a time is this to be out of your beds? Isa! Isa, it's time to get to your beddie-ba, hen. There's a good wee lassie. Oopsy, now, mama's wee girl, and toddle off to your blankets. None of your nonsense, you boys, or I'll warm your dowps for you. No, Billy, you can't get reading, so just you away and take your clothes off. Come on, now, the lot of you."

Comforted and content, Danny sat in his chair by the fire and watched Jess marshal the group to bed. It was their own family, hers and his; it was beautiful and wonderful and yet the most natural thing that they should all lie down together. He trembled a little to think of the ultimate implication of what he saw happening. He had seen that Jess was a woman excited and, in a queer way, desperate. But he was not aware of any quiver of embarrassment. They were, he and Jess, a decent man and woman of middle age, true friends bound in a sodality of misfortune. What might happen would happen in the most natural way imaginable, sanctified by the near presence of the sleeping children about them.

And when they were alone together before the fire at length, the children all asleep, an instinct, imperative and sure, urged him to woo her as he might a girl. Like a girl she fluttered under his caresses and buried her head against his shoulder, but she suffered herself to be drawn on to his knee and kissed and petted. Her arms were round his neck, and his hands explored her hair, the softness of her neck and the curves of her breasts. Soon she was lying quiet, his own to have and do with as he would.

The clangour of the University clock striking eleven clove through his obsession, and he whispered into her ear. Her answer was the slightest nod of the head buried in the crook of his arm.

"Jess!" he murmured.

She rose, blushing, and he watched her move between the beds where the children lay, peering into their sleeping faces and tidying the sheets. Then she looked at him and made a silent little gesture of invitation and slipped behind the screen at the far end of the big room. After a decent interval he rose in his turn and joined her there.

240

CHAPTER TWELVE

DISSOLUTION OF PARTNERSHIP

SPRING WAS coming to London, and Leslie Pagan could smell it in the morning air that streamed through the windows overlooking Hyde Park. From the road that hissed and drummed with traffic there rose the unmistakable smell of the West End—that heady blend of petrol fumes and face powder and the smoke of Virginia cigarettes. But there came with it this gentle morning a subtle overtone, a hint of something sweet and rare and virginal: as if lilac were in bloom not far away or the bright lime green of the budding trees of the Park had faintly scented the air. There were riders, smart men and bright women and children, in the Row across the way. Faintly, on an air from the south-east, there drifted to him from where they were changing the Guard at Buckingham Palace the confident, cheering noises of brass and drum.

He was stirred. A vague urge to be out and doing something fretted behind the screen of preoccupation with the mere spectacle. It troubled him the more since his conscious mind was filled with the senses of idleness and frustration. On the day before, the dazed and worried victim of pressures he vaguely resented and could do nothing to resist, he had put pen to a fatal paper in an office in Lincoln's Inn. Now he was fixed beyond appeal in his status of rich man, but a rich man without a job. There was nothing to do.

Blanche was happy, to be sure—incalculable, shrewd, and yet primitive Blanche, who had discerned in a flash the interest and flutter and publicity of the wonderful life which, as a very young publisher not long down from the University, her young cousin, David Primm, had indicated was led by the literary population of London: a dazzling amalgam, it seemed, of Bohemia and Mayfair, of authentic great men and eager female novelists, of sharp literary agents and useful men from Fleet Street, of arty aristocracy and deliberately realistic novelists out of the lower middle-classes of the North. And how astutely she had cultivated young David! A few discreet and ever-so-anxiously-managed parties, and they had found themselves on the fringes of that highly vocal and competitive world of ideas and books. It was all very bright. The ideas seemed valid and constructive when you heard them. But the secret man that was Leslie Pagan, uneasy by a Knightsbridge window on a morning of spring, resented it all from beginning to end.

There had been the Tremmer party the night before—little Tremmer the publisher, the acute and humorous and intellectual and faintly shabby Jew, spending hundreds in Claridge's to entertain a horde of writers, reviewers, politicians on the make, politicians of the past, retailers of gossip, other publishers, other publishers' pet novelists, the half-witted debris of poets' liaisons, and the rest. He remembered how he had stood alone and lonely by the buffet, calculating what it was costing little Tremmer—whom he strangely liked. Five hundred at the least, And because Tremmer loved them all and merely wished to see people happy?

That was a little too much to believe. Bitterly there came back to him what he had thought of there at the corner of the buffet—jostled by apologetic waiters in red coats and black silken breeches, Blanche lost in the female flurry about the latest success. . . . Of how the cost of the party would keep a workless man of Clydeside, his wife and family of three, for the best part of five years.

It had been a contrast sharp, fantastic and obscene. He had thought then of the shabby, soft, idle men in their thousands at the street-corners of Glasgow. He had seen in painful recollection the rooks and starlings nesting in the gantries of the Yard by the Clyde, bleak and silent under the wet skies. He had heard the voice of Danny Shields eagerly proposing the culture of brussels sprouts behind the big house in Kelvinside. And then there had flooded upon him a sour and intolerable sense of guilt—as if he had discovered himself in an act of betrayal, naked to judgment.

It was all very queer, to say the least of it, all very confusing and indecisive. . . .

Into the melancholy calm of his brown study at the window Blanche came charging freshly. Slimming now, she had taken her unsweetened tea and finger of dry toast in bed. She had bathed ritualistically. She had manicured and powdered and dressed herself to a state of perfection exactly fitting the condition into which it had pleased God to call her. She was ready for her world;

and now, at the back of ten o'clock, she entered it with the easy confidence of one who knows that everything is going as it should.

This morning, however, there was about her an air more urgent than she usually brought to this, their first serious meeting of the day. The cook and the maids Leslie knew, would be faithfully and efficiently dealt with in due course, but he saw with faintly amused pleasure that something had this day occurred to flurry her out of her wonted forceful calm. She offered him a sheet of notepaper.

"A letter from Parker's about that place in Hampshire we thought of," she explained. "It seems more perfectly adorable than ever. We really must go and look at it."

Leslie took the sheet and read the staid communication through.

"Why not run down today?" he suggested at length. "I've nothing else to do."

She glanced at him quickly, her eyes at once glad and wary. "Will you really, Lal?" she cried. "Let me see. . . . Oh, I can put off the Glen-Purvis girls, and we'll be back in time for the Shotter party. Will you order the car—half-past eleven?"

While doing so, Leslie told their man, Watkins, that he could have the day off, and when Blanche came down to join him, brisk in tweeds, he was at the wheel.

"Hullo, driving yourself?" she exclaimed. "Good! We'll have a picnic."

He liked driving through London. Its exquisite exigencies filled the mind and challenged a man's fitness. Idle minds were so apt to become haunted and idle faculties so slack. Almost fondly he took the great car along through Kensington in the fuss of west-bound traffic, rejoicing grimly in a quick acceleration that overtook a bus, in a deft and noiseless change-down of gears, or in a sure, slight turn of the wheel that cleared the mudguard by inches from those of a squat taxi.

Putney Bridge and the Hill began to promise the open country, and he exulted in risks amid the eddying streams. Across the Common and by Richmond Park he gave the engine throttle till even Blanche laid her hand on his knee and smiled a caution. Riverside towns reproduced in miniature the crises of Kensington High Street, and he had the feeling of fighting through them to freedom. Esher behind, the car climbed and ran among the bijou pines and the worn heaths of Southern England. Still the road rose, and they were circling the green pit of the Devils' Punch-bowl. (Leslie thought of another, greater pit where the hills make the inferno of the Devil's Beeftub above Moffat.) Hindhead, pretty compromise between the suburban and the rural, was a quick shot in a moving picture. Then they followed at speed the white ribbon that drives over the bald but shapely downs on its urgent way to Portsmouth.

At Petersfield they lunched, heavily and comfortably fed by the true England. Leslie knew himself to be in foreign parts. These were not his own folk who served him austerely with ill-cooked food, filling and expensive, these not the good stone houses of his northern land. He had the feeling that it all dripped, as it were, of complaisance and wealth and good nature, and he suffered a stound of nostalgia. But while he drank outrageous coffee in the lounge and smoked a morose pipe, Blanche had been busy at the office, had brightly discovered exactly how they must go to their destination, and hailed him off to the wheel once more.

By quiet side-roads, white with the detritus of chalk, they went in search of Butler's Cottage by Dreffield where, with one described as old Jim Iden, lay the keys of Dreffield Manor. The hamlet of Dreffield itself was a sleeping clot—a triangular green, an inn called the Red Lion, a church with a belfry, a shop or two behind small windows, and a sprinkling of dogs sleeping on the road in the thin spring sunlight.

"How adorably peaceful!" sighed Blanche.

Leslie hailed a hobbledehoy working in a field beyond the village and was slowly and vaguely directed up a lane. "Old Jim's like to be wi's bees," hazarded the youth. "He be mighty proud o's bees."

This was England indeed! A Scot would have gone into the most exact detail of the route and have left old Jim to reveal himself. Strange, thought Leslie as the big car hummed between the hedges, the unkept tendrils of bramble striking on mudguard and running-board—strange that a man of grey, urgent, materialistic Clydeside should be seeking along these sleepy by-ways a footing and a share in the old certainty of England! Surrender, desertion, and betrayal: a seduction from a worthy loyalty? But a man had to look for peace for his soul, for a fortalice for his kith and kin.

Old Jim revealed himself as a crabbed ancient with a pink, shaven face framed by an unbroken fringe of white whiskers. He wore a floppy hat, corduroy trousers, and a sleeved waistcoat. Yes, he admitted grimly, he had had the letter from the agents in London, and, as instructed had lifted the keys from the bank in Petersfield. Mr. and Mrs. Pagan were indeed expected, and from a decorous seat in the back of the car he would guide them to the Manor. A very fat old lady kept curtseying to Blanche from the porch of the creeper-hung cottage. As they went on through gates past an empty lodge and down an aisle of elms, it was intimated to them that there could never again be a squire so manly and perfect as the General whose death, six months before, had left Dreffield Manor empty and its bondsmen disconsolate.

"Quaint old darling!" whispered Blanche.

So they came at length to a grey Georgian house, of which the comely bows faced a little west of north towards the Downs. They saw it at once to be adorable, the perfect expression of an endlessly experienced manner of living. There was a weathered terrace before it, and under the terrace lay an oblong of lawn on which, however, the moles had been busy. The scarp of the lawn fell again to a stretch of rougher grass studded with ornamental small trees until, at a high and orderly fence, the demesne gave place to pasture on which, at the moment of their first vision of it, a herd of shorthorn heifers grazed with a clumsily gracious deliberation.

For four miles, until it encountered the low chalk-hills, this stretch of grazing country ran flat and peaceful, broken only by the line of a hedge here and there or by the smoky domes of elms. Against the purple-brown of an occasional coppice there gleamed faintly the white patch of a cottage wall. Above a clump of trees in the middle-distance, the familiar rooks soaring and crying above them, rose the belfry of Dreffield's church—exactly, thought Leslie, as if from the very point at which he stood Thomas Gray had first contemplated his Elegy. The tinny bell of its clock struck three as he looked with wonder and surmise on the English scene.

"Come on, old boy, and don't dream," Blanche awakened him. "Let's see what the house is like."

It charmed them. On the ground floor the great rooms, panelled or painted white and every one with its suave parquet floor, suggested light and life. Only an Englishman of means could have devised such easy comfort and contrived such a lovely compromise between the old and the new: electric light shining on floors once paced by men in stocks and ribbed waistcoats and tight trousers, if not wigs; a discreet lift where a butler had once wrestled with dishes carried from below by ruddy, sweating girls. But the small devices of the new age had not been suffered to affect the atmosphere of the old. The house was a monument to the continuity of tradition, to the easy, conservative adaptability of a race. Even when, as in the fitness of silken bell-cords beside an Adam fireplace, beauty had been preferred to the sharp efficiency of a twentieth-century button, no squire of Dreffield had been guilty of aesthetic error.

Happy and exclamatory, Blanche pattered from room to room, and Leslie rejoiced quietly to see the woman's mind at work, urgent in its business of home-making and home-keeping. In broad lines she sketched great plans—mahogany for the dining-room and maple for the light, white drawing-room. (Not a word now of the chromium that had served dark mechanical Glasgow.) They would have such-and-such a cretonne for the chairs in the hall, and she envisaged coverings in dove-grey for the library. As for the long corridors of the upper floor, she placed the household with precision in the various bedrooms: John's nurseries here and Nannie there, a boudoir for herself, four rooms for guests, and for themselves the great chamber with its dressing-room next the westernmost gable of the main building.

The windows of that room overlooked even more effectively the expanse of pasture and trees that had fascinated him when he first beheld it from the terrace, and there he stood while Blanche trotted about on hard, high heels to decide just how she would arrange beds and dressing-table and chairs. The pressure of her arm slipping under his woke him from a dream.

"Isn't it enchanting?" she whispered.

"That's the word. Perhaps too much so," he suggested wryly.

She turned her head quickly to challenge his cryptic word, but he avoided that glance and made for the door.

"I suppose you'll want to have a look at the kitchen and so forth," he said. "I'll take a stroll round the garden."

But he did not move far from the terrace and its command of the wealden flats and the ramparts of the Downs beyond. For he knew himself to be in the very hour and article of decision, and beyond the elms that dreamed in the haze he saw too clearly the stark gantries above the steely, thick waters of a northern river.

They were far away. In but a few months they had lost in imperative significance. But ghosts they were and ghosts they must remain, haunting the easy life he might be choosing. For the tinny clang from the belfry of Dreffield Church the deep and inexorable note from the University tower; for old Jim Iden in his cottage a man called McDougall, once a plater, standing fat and greasy and slack and hopeless at Govan Cross in a canyon of grey tenements; for the peach trees on the walled garden of Dreffield Manor the brussels sprouts in the damp loan behind the glorified villa in Kelvinside. He thought of the Highland hills as you see them from about Dumbarton—a glorious frieze against the western sky and finer, bolder far than these pimples the English called the Downs. He thought of John and his inheritance. He thought—the last, most moving symbol of the old life—of Danny Shields, faithful to a dim ideal in war and prosperity and depression. And where was Danny now?

But as soon as the problem with its raw edges, like a strand of broken glass, had wounded his mind, even so soon was it resolved. The thing stood out in the most elegant simplicity. Obviously, Danny would come south out of the grey desolation of the North and be happy in that empty lodge behind the wood. It was the easiest thing in the world to see Danny happy there: Danny very busy and professional about the whimsies of the lighting plant, Danny checking with grave deliberation and a pugnacious fervour all sorts of supplies for the establishment, Danny envisaging for the garden glories far beyond the dreams of Kelvinside. From that point Leslie's mind leaped. The land appertaining to Dreffield Manor was considerable. A man with vigour and vision could bring out of doomed Clydeside a colony of good men, workers all, to till the land and live in happy productiveness.

Blanche's voice tinkled from behind him.

"Lally! Lal-ly!" it called girlishly. "Time to go home."

"Yes," he said, turning from the comfortable line of the Downs.

She was beside him. The warmth of her affected his skin; he felt in his nostrils the tang of her tweeds. Playfully she kissed him under the angle of the jaw and announced her roguish challenge.

"Well?"

"Well yourself?" he replied lamely.

She laughed. "My dearest Lal!" she protested. "You've just got to make up that funny old mind of yours." She cuddled closer to his side. "I think it's adorable. We could be terribly happy here."

"And we're going to be," he said.

2

The Night Scot roared across the Border, the smoke from its mighty engine all aflame in the morning sunlight. Brown flats of Westmorland gave place to green rolling pasture of Dumfries, red tiles to blue slates on the roofs of whitewashed cottages, brick to the Old Red Sandstone in the townlets flashing past.

Queer, thought Leslie Pagan, staring at the kaleidoscope from his berth, how definitely the fact of nationality asserts itself even in the matters of landscape and domestic architecture. It was Scotland that streamed past before his eyes; no other country could present that particular aspect. Even in the figure of a girl, out with an early pail at the back of a steading on a knoll and pausing to see the great train pass northwards out of the unknown towards another mystery, he believed himself to recognise a woman inveterately of his own race.

The sense of return to a natural element grew upon him as the train entered the narrow valley of the Annan and climbed towards the watershed by Beattock. Now the hillsides closed in upon his window, and the bronze-green of them, stained with fans of fallen stones from occasional torrents and marked by a rare, wind-blown thorn, was as recognisably Scottish as a Glasgow street. The austerity of these uplands moved him strongly. He thought of black-faced sheep wandering far on the chill fells, of shepherds with only the skyline to mark the frontiers of their remote bailiwicks, and of the innocence of these aboriginal Scottish people, related to the world only by wireless sets mouthing jazz from the night-clubs of London—comparison at once absurd and intolerable! Tremmer's party and the hard, poor life of a cottage set in a moorland where no trees could grow and the nearest farmhouse was itself an outpost, five miles away at the head of a glen!

It was indeed outrageous in its vehemence, this contrast between the lights flickering ruddy and nervous about Piccadilly Circus and the wicks gleaming dim and soft through village windows that would be wholly dark at ten of the evening. But it struck him as even more fantastic that he should be on the point of deserting this land that was so inveterately his own for that shallow, foreign vale of Hampshire, with its fat kine, its enormous trees, and the clock tinkling out the quiet hours from the belfry of Dreffield Church. Here he belonged, there he could never be else but a colonist, uneasy and without foundations.

Desertion, betrayal, surrender—the old problem swooped upon him once more. But he averted its pressure on his unquiet mind. The conductor came in with a cup of tea; and Leslie set himself to think of all the things he had to do in Glasgow—the lawyers to see, and then the bank, and the agents about the villa in Kelvinside, and Dakers at the Yard. It was an awkward thought, that question of the Yard and the end of a century of shipbuilding; with an array of engagements in prospect he contrived to push back the subtle thrusts of conscience and see himself as a man about to be very busy with important affairs for the next day or two.

Back again in the central streets of Glasgow, however, he could not escape their challenge to his smouldering sense of apostasy. They were as familiar as the back of his hand—Gordon Street, Renfield Street, St. Vincent Street, Buchanan Street, all on the short way from station to Club; but now he had to see them with the detachment imposed by only a few months of exile in the South. He saw the greyness put upon this sprawling city of the North by climate and her queer industrial history. He marked the dominance of clumsy trams and the surprising preponderance of shops devoted to the sale of smart wear for men. There were so many horse-drawn lorries about, and even on the pavements of the richest streets of all, so many shabby men in tweed caps. He saw it to be a fact that the business man of Glasgow inclines to a bowler hat in the curious shape of a crucible and to square-toed, solid shoes, and that, though the spring morning was warm and sunny, the smartest girl in that city of rain would not venture forth without her fur-collared coat, no matter how light and pretty the dress beneath it. There was a pang for him in the sight of the shivering trace-horses and the cheeky characterful boys who look after them at the foot of steep and cobbled West Nile Street.

It was his own city, for better or for worse. Never could he escape it. By no adjustment of the selfish mind; by no prepared indictment of its social deficiencies, its ugliness, its smugness, its sentimentality, its brutality, its dirtiness, its wetness, its greyness, grimness—by no elaboration of personal criticism could he escape its grip on him or his awareness of responsibility to it. A city that had had its day; a city built on exhausted coal-beds and empty shipyards; a city now of middle-men and Jews and pimps, eternally bemoaning over the coffee-cups what they called "the drift South," rationalising their own inertia; a city living on a sordid past and selling its war-gotten War Loan to buy pesky and expensive motor cars. . . . Very well! But a city that was still Glasgow, peopled by such as Danny Shields, the salt of the earth.

His heart was at his throat as he turned the corner towards the door of the Club. He knew himself to be running away from the industrial mess out of which his people had made wealth for him. It would be Eton and Sandhurst and the service of the British Empire for John and God alone knew what for young Billy Shields. And he knew that he should keep himself and his wealth and his will for Scotland. He thought in almost tearful bemusement of Blanche and of the big house overlooking the Hampshire vale and of the dearness of John and of the tinny clang of the church bell, vibrating among the elms from Dreffield.

The quiet service of the Club advanced to distract him. He could certainly have Number 4 and a bath at once. He would have breakfast no doubt. Ah, yes, sir, the usual—bacon and eggs and strong tea. The big cases would come in the evening? Very well, sir. . . . All very beautiful and easy, if you could afford to pay for it. . . . But the melting warmth of a bath had the power to make a man at ease with himself. Changed from the skin outwards, glowing with comfort, Leslie Pagan at length went downstairs again, thinking only of the sweet goodness of the bacon he could smell cooking for himself alone.

Then the day started, and the illusion of big affairs in hand fell between the imminent significance of Glasgow and his sensitive mind. He had an hour of it with old Mr. Clerk in his writing chambers in West George Street—an absorbing, aggravating hour of detail and lawyer's unending reservations and safety-first cautions. Mr. Macdonald in the bank was more cheerful, though plainly apprehensive that the main account was to be taken to London; and then, realising that the bulk of the Pagan funds and all the family securities were to be left with him, proposed lunch and hinted at what a glorious feast it might be.

There was a dispiriting quarter of an hour with house agents in Bath Street, people who might very well have been letting his Sauchiehall Street house to Pritchard the Poisoner. They had no hope of letting the house in Kelvinside, and only a little more of selling it—as a nursing home or something of the sort. "They're just a drag on the market, Mr. Pagan, these big West End houses. I'm afraid we can't hold out much hope. You know what things are in Glasgow? Not like the old days at all, at all." And Leslie could not bring himself to go and see those silent rooms with the dust-covers over the furniture and at every turn some sharp reminder of a way of life, cosy and happy and hopeful enough, now abandoned.

The Yard he had to face. He had to walk from gatehouse to office and see how shabby the buildings had become, how poles and gantries had tilted and rusted, and how grass grew where the shadows of great ships and the boots of hundreds of men had darkened the ground. It was high tide in the leaden River, the moment for a launching, but there would be no more ships with the name of Pagan on the brass plate under the bridge. Somewhere off the Brazils the *Estramadura* showed to an alien and incurious world the symbol of end, Yard Number 611.

From the walls of the empty, musty Board Room, the story was shouted at him—such, in one view, a quaint collection of pictures and models and plans of ships long superannuated, and in another so pathetic. He had been appalled by the silence of the office when he passed through the spring-doors—not the ripple of a telephone bell nor the whisle of a boy nor the clatter of even one typewriter. Dakers might have been lying dead in his chair. On the way to his own room he encountered no living person. The Board Room had nothing to say to him beyond the chorus of reproach from the walls. There was dust on his desk, and the apparatus of ancient activity, neatly set out had not been touched in months.

His irruption into Dakers' room surprised that drab spirit into a display of wonder and delight, but it relieved Leslie to discover, as he did very shortly, that the man's true concern was not with the dramatic significance of their meeting so much as with the vast importance and interest of the business details they had to discuss. It was for Dakers a field-day. Extremely accurate, elaborately casual, he ranged the field of debate from the disposition of the money to come from the Sale to the question of whether or not a watchman should be appointed and whether that would not be an economical and entirely just way of dealing with the problem of Sergeant Macewan. There would be equipment, of course. Dakers had already instructed the auctioneers and looked to a satisfactory result. On the whole, he thought, they would come out of it very well. Perhaps Mr. Pagan could give him some sort of power of attorney and not be troubled unduly by the irritating smallness of these last rites.

Of course, they were both coming out of it very well and could afford to discuss in a strictly businesslike way the winding-up of the concern. Dakers, a saving man, had his share of the fantastic profits made during the war, the assurance of a large sum for services rendered and his pension. He, Leslie Pagan, had the tens of thousands made out of the Yard by three generations of canny, hard-working men. As a mere matter of personal security they could let it go with a laugh and fall back on the cultivation of their gardens. But Danny Shields and hundreds of his kind were out of work for ever. The long tale of ships, beautiful and fit and efficient, was at an end, petering out in squalor.

He took his last look at the Yard from the office door. It was as if in selfishness he said farewell to an honest mistress. The place had all the look of something deserted by fallible man. So many rich interests, so many hundreds of human lives had centred about it; so many men had, honestly and with love of craft, done so much fine work where now grass and docken and dandelion had the field to themselves, growing in idleness undisciplined. And as he stared towards the enigmatic ribbon of the ship-channel there passed up to the Broomielaw a Belfast steamer built by Pagan's in the hideous boom year of 1919.

"Central Station," he snapped, turning on the driver of his waiting taxi.

He just caught, and no more, the hopeful salute of Sergeant Macewan as the car swung for the last time through the gates into the Dumbarton Road.

3

He could have gone back to London then. That was his intention, indeed. But in the Club, his things packed and the steward looming helpfully at every turn, he found that he could not leave Glasgow so, slipping down to the Night Scot and into a sleeper and away with a casual "Goodbye to all that." It haunted him that there should be ceremony about his going—even a last, authentic, fatal drink, with a friend. But he could not think of a friend to ring up and invite to the feast. A man who had fought in the War seemed in the last issue to have no friends.

It seemed at the same time that ghosts were about to remind a fellow that no man could pursue a clean-cut way through life. One thing shaded ever so finely into another, and there was neither act nor experience but had its consequences. A far cry from Kelvinside to Hampshire it was indeed, but there was still a balance of responsibility to be carried over; there was a cord that could not be cut, least of all by the will of one man alone.

Suddenly he recalled the vision that had come to him on the terrace of Dreffield Manor, and as suddenly, as if in response to the thought, there returned to him the name and address of the secretary of his regimental association. He rang for the telephone book and in a minute or two was speaking eagerly into a mouthpiece in a box, asking questions.

"But, my dear man," returned the patient voice over the wire, "if you would only take the trouble to look at the circulars I send you, you wouldn't be asking silly questions."

"I didn't see any circulars," Leslie protested. "Of course, I've been moving about a lot these last few months. I suppose you sent them to the Yard with a ha'penny stamp. . . . What's this you're talking about?"

So he heard that a reunion supper and smoker of the survivors of the old days would be held in the upstairs room of Matthew Dron's pub at St. George's Cross at seven on the following evening.

"O my God, Sinclair! I mustn't miss that," he cried. "Put me down for a certainty. And, I say, Sinclair," he added, "do you happen to know if my old batman, Danny Shields, is coming?"

"I don't know," replied the voice. "Don't think so. But I'll check up and see. I can very easily rout him out for you in any case."

"I wish you would," Leslie said. "I most particularly want to see him. In fact, if you could get him to meet me at six o'clock—say, at Simpson's Corner—I'll be tremendously grateful."

"That's all right," answered the cool voice. "I know a man who's in regular touch with him. He's had rather a bad time lately, I believe."

4

A wild storm of rain was sweeping down Sauchiehall Street as Leslie jumped from a tram, and, hunched behind an umbrella held low, dodged across the street to the corner upon which a mere music-shop had conferred a name.

There was wind behind the rain. It was as if a half-gale from the sou'-west had scooped the surface off the Firth of Clyde and was throwing it at the city. Groups of people sheltered in shop doors from its vehemence. Those who dared it sailed along like vessels running to port under a threatening sky, overcoats and water-proofs and skirts pressed against soaking ankles. As a tram appeared there at once ensued a contest of ruthless shoulders and umbrellas that swayed and glistened and interlocked. No night, thought Leslie remorsefully, for a workless man in thin and scanty clothes to be out waiting for him. He should have convened the meeting for a cosier place.

His first sight of Danny reassured him, however. There stood the little man in a doorway, his hands in the pockets of a decent overcoat, a woollen muffler round his neck.

"Hullo, Danny!" he cried eagerly.

"Sir!"

The short, stocky figure sprang to attention and fingers went up in a proud curve to the peak of the tweed cap. They shook hands.

"You're not soaked, are you?" Leslie asked.

"Not I, sir!" protested Danny. "I got a blue car to the door here, and I haven't been standing two minutes."

"Good! Where will we go for a drink and a yarn? There's Lauders' over there. Come on, Dan."

They scurried across the street and into the crowded heat of the great tavern with its innumerable bars, its atmosphere burdened with the smells of tobacco and sawdust and beer, and its air of a place sacred to the sleek gentlemen of the entertainment trades. Through the throng, simultaneously consuming yards of cigarettes, quarts of whisky and gallons of beer in the eternal quest for escape, they made their way to the relative peace of an alcove where a Special Bar offered a degree of seclusion at special prices.

"And now, Danny," said Pagan. "I want to have a talk with you before we go to the show along the road. There's an idea I want to put to you. But tell me all about yourself. . . . I'm afraid the two of us got wandered these last few months. . . . Tell me what has happened and how you are placed and let's see if we can't straighten things out a bit."

He watched how Danny's fingers, rather fine and pale now, nervously turned the stem of the glass on the counter.

"Och, things are not so bad, sir!" the little man protested. "I'm doing pretty well one way and another. There's hundreds worse nor me."

"I know all about that," said Leslie impatiently; then, deliberately assuming his old authority: "But I want you to tell me exactly. This is a pretty important thing we've got to discuss, a job, in fact."

"In the Yard?" cried Danny, his face lighting up.

"No, not in the Yard exactly, but a job, and a good job for a man with some guts. You're still out of a job, aren't you?"

"That's right, sir. That cut in the neck I got . . ."

"What cut in the neck?"

Out of Danny he had to prise the information, as it were. The reluctance he understood perfectly. It spelt pride, in the first place, and an unwillingness to burden another with his troubles. There were moments when Leslie felt himself to be bullying and prying unforgivably. However, firm in his faith that there was something he could do for this man, and making every allowance for the need to assuage his own conscience, he did not hesitate to play the Major to his former batman.

"And now," he could insist, "tell me exactly how you stand with the wife and how the children are placed."

So at length he got the whole story, and it appalled him. He realised the magnitude of his responsibility even to this single man among all the men who had worked for him, but especially to this Danny Shields he had made symbolic of the lot, whom he respected endlessly, nay, whom he loved with all his heart—his brother in war and peer in craftsmanship. Yet even this individual he had deserted in his extremity, leaving him to flounder through poverty and suffering and struggle.

"I see," he said thoughtfully. "I see how it is. Your luck has been hellish, Danny."

"Och!" cried the little man, inveterately valiant. "Mine's no worse nor most, and a dashed sight better. I can look after myself. As soon's this neck's better I'll get back on the job wi' the woodselling. No' a bad wee job thon at all, sir. And when you get the Yard going again, you'll see me at the gate wi' the rest o' the boys, and as fit as a fiddle."

"The Yard will never be open again, Danny," said Leslie Pagan. "Oh, my God!"

It came upon them as suddenly as that—question and answer, revelation and realisation. Now Pagan saw how circumstance had trapped him and Danny too. The Yard was closed, but on terms the little man could never understand. In the midst of such as Danny Shields you kept a business going or you closed it down, and while that might be your own business, it was yet an offence against the faith. Not for such a simple understanding was the complex of international economics that had reduced the world's carrying trade to a dribble and the tonnage output of the Clyde to a fraction of what it had been. The working man knew better than most that there were times when trade was bad, but it had always been so for him; and now the older men were waiting in patience for the wheel to turn again. What they did not know, what they could never know, was that in any calculation of which the human brain was capable, at least one half of Scotland's shipbuilders were out of work for ever.

He looked at Danny and saw his troubled eyes on the liquid in the glass before him, and he felt the tingle of tears at his eyes, seeing the pathetic gallantry of the stocky frame within which faith had still a habitation.

"You've got to understand this, Danny," he started to explain quietly. "Shipbuilding isn't what it was and is never going to be again. I know it's damnable to think of, and it's all far too complicated to explain. But there it is, old man, whether you like it or not. I've sold the Yard. They made me sell it. There was just nothing else to do—except lose everything. And get it into your head, Danny, that the people who bought it aren't going to build ships there. They bought it just to stop anybody building ships there! Don't you see. . . ?"

The drinks they had shared seemed to have brought them together in close and warm confidence. It was man to man now. He grasped Danny's forearm.

"You've got to get this straight, Dan," he pleaded. "I've got to talk plainly to you. But it's no good, the shipbuilding or the riveting or any other bloody thing. It's just no good. And for a man of your age, with all this electric welding they're using nowadays. . . . Look here—"

Eagerly he plunged into the exposition of his plan. It had become dear to him. Leslie Pagan believed in it and could have upheld its wisdom in high argument, and he hammered away at Danny Shields, determined to break down into a smile that averted, resistant, set look on the man's face.

"There it is anyhow," he perorated at length. "You don't need to worry one scrap about your private affairs. I've got nothing to do with that. You can bring whom you like with you. All I'm saying is that there's a cottage for you and a bit of land and good, clean work for a willing man—and a damned sight better chance for the kids than there is in this lousy hole. . . . What about it, Danny?"

"I'm not right sure, sir," said Shields.

The words expressed at once resistance, doubt, wonder, excitement and fear; and it was of the strength of the dour Scot's resistance that Leslie was most sensitively aware.

"Leave it just now, then," he urged. "We'd better be getting along to the Smoker. Think it over, Danny. I'd like to catch the London train tonight and we could have a word after the show. Or if you want to talk it over with—with somebody else, I'll wait till the one-thirty tomorrow."

"I'm not right sure, sir," said Danny again. At length he raised his eyes from his glass and looked straight into those of the Boss. He was smiling apologetically. "You're a right toff, sir," he added, "but I doubt I'll be wanting to stick to my trade."

5

The big upper room of Matthew Dron's esteemed establishment at St. George's Cross had the look of having been furnished by a mariner of a singularly roving and acquisitive disposition. While the furniture, the panelled walls, and some good pieces of shining pewter bespoke a decent taste in the Georgian, the note was so confused by large and ugly shells, peacocks' feathers, the carved green eggs of emus, model catamarans, Japanese fans, strange Malayan weapons, tortuously-carved ebony, boomerangs, stuffed rainbow trout and such that the place had much the air of a communal museum.

So was the company assembled for the regimental reunion fantastically mixed as to type, disposition, and social standing— ex-Colonels of the Public School sort, big figures on the Royal Exchange, hobnobbing with tramway drivers, clerks and commercial travellers fighting their battles over again, shipowners rubbing shoulders with newspaper compositors, and lawyers recalling the vicissitudes of Sinai to the dulled memories of the unemployed. Yet it was through such strange aggregations that battles had been won for the British Empire; and, as he entered the crowded, noisy room and was immediately involved in warm encounters and struggles to remember names and follow a whole complex of reminiscence, Leslie Pagan, his heart in his mouth with emotion but his mind still working in detachment, marvelled that such a sodality should survive on the strength of an old and bitter experience commonly shared.

The King, the Country, the Regiment. . . . None of these symbols furnished an explanation. Few men ever fought for an idea. Old Colonel Gall over there, rolling in the fat, false profits of stockbroking, would be absurdly generous to any individual case that might appeal to him and could yet classify the unemployed as "shirkers" and work and vote against them. Tall Fred Tierney, to whom he was speaking, professed Revolutionary Socialism and would, according to his public utterances, hang all stockbrokers from the lamp-posts. Yet here they were, and scores of pairs like them, melted into a harmony by a sentiment. But of what? Of hard experience shared, of common congratulation on escape, of esteem for fundamental worth? There was no answer. Significant, perhaps, that they all talked, and loudly, of "the old Mob." There was the symbol, possibly. Strange, however, that the spirit did not prevail into the conduct of their lives and affairs in an industrial civilisation! Could it be that the warmth of the reunion was an illusion? Perhaps it was the expression of a fundamental reality. Perhaps it was just nothing at all.

Leslie found himself prominent at the top table, and down on the list for a speech and he felt that it was all rather empty and pretentious—rich men feigning to be delighted with a high tea of bacon and eggs and pastries unlimited, poor men deluding themselves that it was at once an honour and their right to have "the officers" sitting down with them to a real good feed at not less than three bob a skull. To the mind detached, the speeches also rang a little false. The King, The Regiment, the Battalion, Our Fallen Comrades: endless minutes of luxuriant claptrap! Not in all that lay the reality!

But when the table was cleared, and the drinks began to circulate, and songs were sung and stories told, it seemed that all these men sloughed the skin of formality and emerged honest and lovable. It was lovely, the comradeship revealed in the singing of old familiar choruses and in worn but ever-glowing domestic reminiscence of training in Fifeshire, of Egypt and Gallipoli, Sinai and Palestine, France and the Occupation. It was an escape to honesty through confession of the common humanity. For the brief hour they were men naked to each other, hopeful, sentimental, scabrous, noisy and crude.

259

Escaping from every bond of Presbyterian reticence or social awareness, they rioted in primitive emotions. Even the old Colonel bellowed that violent opening chorus of the "Thistletops" which tells how they got drunk at Gibraltar and even nearer to nature at Malta. Corporal Shanks told the cloacal tale of Bull Gibb and the General's A.D.C. when they met at the incinerator behind Pink Farm, only to be capped by Lance-Sergeant Macfie with the one about the Bible that was stolen from the Padre's tent to serve a sanitary purpose in the latrines at El Arish. Tall Major Power sang the song of "Oh, lucky Jim!" as lugubriously and successfully as ever he had done since, a trembling subaltern, he had first sung it in the big marquee at the Barry Camp of 1908. Band-Sergeant Whyte had specially composed verses and patter of extreme intimacy for the occasion and had a success any vaudeville artist might envy. A hush fell when Danny Shields got up to sing, with tremendous gravity, "Bonnie Wee Thing, Canny Wee Thing," and as they all joined in the lugubrious chorus it was as if all the nostalgic sentiment of Scotland were concentrated in that one room above a Glasgow pub, and as if the ultimate loveliness had been suddenly revealed to this unique body of hard-bitten men.

As the night wore on they became more maudlin, more quarrelsome, more natural. Save those few who were teetotallers and those whose guard upon themselves and their attitude to the world could not be surprised, every man revealed himself for what he was.

There were men truculent, men lachrymose, men surly, men friendly, men indecent, men jolly, and men witty. Band-Sergeant Whyte, for instance, flown with beer and the success of his act, got up to shout at the Colonel that he might think himself a fine bloody toff but that the war was won by the non-coms—the poor bloody old non-coms, the finest bloody men. . . . He was thrown out by a party led by Danny Shields and was heard to knock over a tray of glasses in the passage outside. . . . One tearful man, whom Leslie vaguely recognised as an orderly-room clerk in the old days, laid an affectionate arm about his shoulders, breathed whisky into his face, and told him what an honour it was to see him again and how his wife and children would be informed of the encounter and duly impressed. "We're only poor people, Major, but there is not a finer

260

woman in the whole of Glasgow than my wee wife," he asserted.

"I'm sure there isn't," Leslie agreed heartily. It was a nuisance not to be able to remember the man's name.

After all, it was turning out to be an escape with the aid of alcohol. There could be no reunion without those pints of beer and glasses of whisky. But did the drink produce false illusions of grandeur, or did it merely stir the things, fine and foolish, that lay dormant in every man? This might be the ultimate reality, this free and bawdy comradeship. Or it might be the last foolish illusion.

Knowing himself to have drunk more than was usual with him, Leslie was still the master of his own private situation. In that last hectic half-hour of the Smoker he was seeing the assembly and its implications with a clarity quite unusual. His mind was driving towards an understanding of it all. His lips and tongue were trembling to frame a sentence that would embody the quiddity of the spectacle. It seemed that he would understand all life if he could only do that. At the same time a censor, watching from the heart of his consciousness, told him that he could never understand and need not try to do so.

He took pains to regard Danny Shields and was touched to see that the little man went slow, sucking wisely at a pint pot of beer and with easy jest turning away the offers of drink—"Just a wee half to go with your beer, Danny"—that were thrust upon him. Danny was thinking. Danny had not abandoned himself to the madness of the evening. Leslie knew that his friend was seeking to solve for himself that problem which was but a representative part of the larger problem of all existence. He was sorry to have spoiled Danny's night for him, but the thing mattered tremendously. There were so very few choices before a man in this life. He could go on, trimming eternally for his own safety. He could, like the desperate clansmen, cry "Furth Fortune and fill the fetter?" Or he could, as so many men found it easily possible to do, adopt and abide by a system of loyalties.

Peering through the haze of smoke, Leslie wondered what this small man, Danny Shields, so dear and representative, would do. And as he brooded on the problem a chord on the piano brought him to his feet like the rest to join hands and sing "Auld Lang Syne," murdering in their conventional sentiment the words as they were written by Robert Burns.

It was the song of parting, the song that marked an end. The Battalion would reunite next year and be happy in its way, but it would be a reunion different from this, for the minds and souls and circumstances of men must change in the course of twelve months. Some would be dead before the date came round again, some would be so bruised by events that they would forget the ancient loyalty and the warmth that comes of foregathering. He might himself, reflected Leslie, be so wrapped in the life of England that the secretary's circular would appear a negligible bidding to a scanty feast in a remote and unfriendly country. As for Danny Shields. . . . He wrenched himself free from the tangle of introspection and, looking about the room, caught a gaze hopefully directed upon himself; and an exchange of signs fixed it that they should meet at the door below. Then the swirling of the throng separated them.

It was difficult to get away. Old soldiers, benevolent with drink, pressed round him to renew acquaintance and recall events in which they had all been dramatically involved. The Colonel suggested the Conservative Club and a chat over the cigars. Somebody proposed the Piccadilly, dancing partners of singular enchantment, and a night of romance. But Leslie was laughingly polite and firm at once, fought a relentless way to the cloakroom, and hurried downstairs to find Danny Shields dutifully waiting for him. A taxi, which he had ordered through a waiter, throbbed by the kerb.

"Hop in, Danny," he commanded. "There's not too much time if I'm going to catch that train."

They settled themselves in the back seat.

"And now, Danny," Leslie began firmly, "am I going to catch that train or have I got to wait?"

"I'd catch my train if I was you, sir," said Danny.

His tone was respectful but strangely distant.

"You've made up your mind?"

"Yes, sir. I think I'll stick to my own trade. With all respect to you, sir. . . ."

"Don't be too sure about that," Leslie said bitterly, for now he saw his last bid for the retention of self-respect fade and recede.

"It's not a thing you can decide in an hour or two. I can quite easily wait another day or so."

"No, sir. I'd catch my train if I was you."

They said no more while the taxi rushed through the empty streets. At the Central, the business of instructing a porter, getting luggage out of bond and finding the sleeper in the great shuttered train stood between them and the immediacies. But they had to face each other on the platform at length. The clock above the bookstall pointed to 11.40.

"Five minutes to go, Dan," observed Leslie. "Let's walk up to the front."

The lights high up in the spans of the station's roof shed but a dismal radiance on the scene. The surface of the platform was damp, the air chill, and all the depressing features of a trunk train's departure conditioned their uneasy ceremony. They saw women dabbing at their eyes with white handkerchiefs. They saw drunken soldiers and sailors, hirelings of Empire, sway and stagger on their way to the camps and dockyards of England. They saw the industrialists of the new Scotland proceed, lordly, to conference with their masters in the City of London. They saw a happy bride and bridegroom ecstatically impelled with rice and confetti towards their strange epithalamium.

At the top of the platform the big engine hissed its restlessness, but up there they were in isolation from their kind. The sheets of rain, storming across the arch of the station in the glare of an arc-lamp, made a curtain to mask the frontier at which they were parting.

"Well, Dan?" said Leslie, wheeling to face his friend. "There's only a minute or two to go."

"I think I'll just stick to my trade, sir," came the answer, respectful but dour.

"Good God, man! Have you the slightest idea what you're talking about?"

"I heard tell that Brown's is starting work again on the big Cunarder soon. And I'm pretty well in with one of the foremen riveters down there."

"Oh, I suppose they'll finish the beast some day," cried Leslie, the bitterness returning.

The man would not, could not, understand that the game was up. If it were only a few shipyards closed down! But even in the time that he had been idle the monster men called Progress had overtaken such as Danny Shields and left them behind, rejects, on the deserts of industrialism. Now in the place of the riveter was the welder, joining the plates of ships with a melting jet of white flame; and no riveter of the old school could hope to graduate in the fierce new art. Now one man and a boy, working a machine, could do in the way of making hatches what it used to take fourteen craftsmen to do. Now boys manned piano punching machines, each halflin with his engine displacing twelve helpers. Another dozen helpers were out of work because a hydraulic machine, operated by a man and a boy, could bend ships' frames. One man, commanding a single-drill punch, displaced six of his kind. So the number of men employed in the yards fell by one half in the ten years from 1920— and would go on falling.

If there was only time to drive these facts into the thick head of Danny Shields! If only the man could see what was happening about him and could realise that in the good earth, English or otherwise, lay his only hope! But it was too late. The minute-hand of the clock shivered on the edge of the quarter.

"Don't be a damned proud fool, Danny," cried Leslie, almost desperately. "It's just no use. . . ."

"I'm going to stick it. With all respect to you, sir. . . . You've always been a right toff."

A whistle shrilled down the gaunt arcades of the station and automatically—so little is there in the fatal decision of men—Leslie Pagan ran for the nearest door of the long train.

"Let me know, Danny," he gasped as he ran. "If you want to come. . . . I wish to God you would come. . . . Anything I can ever do for you. . . ."

He was safe in the corridor of the train. As it began to move he leaned out of the window.

"Old soldiers, Danny," he appealed to his friend.

Danny Shields stood for a moment at the salute, the arm trembling at an angle to the tweed cap. Then the arm smacked back to his side, and Leslie Pagan saw him turn and walk away towards the barrier and those dim loyalties by which he was so fondly determined to abide. When Danny looked back it was to see the red lights of the Night Scot hurry away across the bridge towards the South.